BLADES OF WINTER

"... SF, set in a ... story, starring a snarky, hormonal ... Scarlet, who will capture your heart ... on. First-rate."

—... VAN LUSTBADER,
bestselling author of *The Bourne Legacy* and *Father Night*

"Smart, sassy, and seriously appealing. *Blades of Winter* is a fully realized alternate history with extraordinary detailing and pace, high-velocity writing, and—top of the list—a heroine finding herself via weapons of mass destruction, bionic strength, and the heartbeat of a whole new generation. *Seventeen* magazine mainlines *Terminator* in this stunning debut."

—JEFF LONG,
New York Times bestselling author of *The Descent*

"A fun, fast-moving alt-history romp!"
—S. M. STIRLING, author of *The Council of Shadows*

"G. T. Almasi's *Blades of Winter* is a smart, punchy deluge of radical thought packed into a febrific alternate-history thrill ride. Almasi is an author finding his stride, mind ablaze with kaleidoscopic insight, creativity, and action. And did I mention humor? Because there's a lot of that, too."

—JAMES WAUGH,
senior story developer, Blizzard Entertainment

"Almasi has created a vivid and entirely believable alternate history that is steeped in historical fact, future science, and international intrigue. *Blades of Winter* has all the action and excitement of today's hottest video games and an absolutely unrelenting pace that will keep your heart pounding. The pages practically turn themselves."

—JAMES A. BROWN, lead level designer, Epic Games

"*Blades of Winter* starts with a freeze-frame bullet to the face and only takes off from there. Vicious action sequences and brilliant SF tech make for some of the best pacing I've consumed in a really long time."

—SAM STRACHMAN, writer, IP developer, Ubisoft

By G. T. Almasi

Blades of Winter
Hammer of Angels

HAMMER OF ANGELS

A NOVEL OF THE SHADOWSTORM

G. T. ALMASI

DEL REY • NEW YORK

A Del Rey Mass Market Original

Published in the United States by Del Rey, an imprint of Random House, a division of Random House LLC, a Penguin Random House Company, New York.

DEL REY and the HOUSE colophon are registered trademarks of Random House LLC.

RANDOM HOUSE WORLDS and HOUSE colophon are trademarks of Random House, Inc.

ISBN 978-0-440-42356-0
eBook ISBN 978-0-440-42357-7

Printed in the United States of America.

www.delreybooks.com

9 8 7 6 5 4 3 2 1

Del Rey mass market edition: March 2014

To Anne, Margot,
and all the children destroyed by war

HAMMER OF ANGELS

01

Insanity isn't nearly as crazy as people make it out to be. After a while even delusions begin to follow a pattern, and because of all the practice I've had, my little trips to la-la land have gotten much less disorienting. For example, the black-haired girl sitting over there is a product of my subconscious, and I *don't* have to pull out my pistol and kill her right here on the Metro platform. I've hallucinated this same cookie before, and one positive aspect of this illusion's repetitiveness is that she hasn't morphed into something else, like a fire-breathing dragon or the Creature from the Black Lagoon.

As usual, this chick is 5'4", the same as me, and has the same small-framed gymnast's build that I do. We both have fair skin, but her eyes are burned brown, not green like mine, and of course I have my mom's auburn hair, not the shiny black ponytail this bird sports.

A new detail is how she's dressed for the weather. Unlike my ultrastylish maroon leather jacket, my imaginary nemesis wears a thick black peacoat to ward off the January chill. When someone walks past, she moves her foot out of the way. Dream Girl's black Keds are tied really tight, as though someone might steal them right off her feet.

My hallucination's deluxe resolution and situational responsiveness mean I'm either healthier or nuttier than when I got home from Riyadh last October. Dream Girl was already seated on a bench here in the White Flint Metro station as I came down the escalator. Her ominous presence set me on edge, but it's not like she's actually there. Still, for a make-believe person, she works awfully hard to avoid looking at me.

I mentally instruct my implanted Nerve Jet neuro-injector to give me a quick dose of Kalmers. The drugs flow into my bloodstream, and within seconds my relative lack of sanity stops bothering me.

It's been a couple of weeks since one of my spells, which has made both me and Dr. Herodotus happy. I'm trying to decide whether to tell him about this one when a southbound train finally arrives. I enter the car and take a seat. Dreamy gets on and sits a few rows away, facing me. At this hour, only a handful of other passengers travel with us.

We ride like a pair of grim statues into Grosvenor-Strathmore. Past the girl are ads for crappy action movies and lame-ass technology schools. We're so close, I can smell her—an appetizing blend of Noxzema and cheeseburgers—but our eyes don't meet until our train leaves the station. Then she makes her move.

The girl slips her hand into her coat and—it's such a cliché—pulls out a pistol. My illusions never pull out flowers or tickets to a Redskins game. It's always a fucking gun.

Big dark lenses slide down from Dream Girl's brow and cover her peepers like sunglasses. She points her little dream weapon at me. I stick my tongue out at her. *Nyah-nyah!* I've had this delusion so many—

BANG!

Well, *that's* unusual. Dreamy normally vanishes before she takes a shot at me. The make-believe bang gives me an involuntary surge of adrenaline, which prompts my neuroinjector to release a dose of Madrenaline. Swell. Now it'll seem like all day before that phantom bullet goes away.

The nonexistent chunk of lead spirals toward my face. Imaginary scuffs have been scraped into the bullet by the illusory rifling in the barrel of my friend's phony sidearm. I shift out of its way just to humor her. The slug passes by and smashes the window behind me. Such realism!

Wait. Why has everyone freaked out? The other passengers all run away or dive under their seats as Dreamy fires another shot. Finally it occurs to me.

Phantasms don't need Noxzema.

She's real.

The black-haired skeezer's second bullet hurtles toward my stomach. I grab the ape-hanger bar on the ceiling and crank myself up and over the incoming projectile. The slug cracks through the back of my seat and leaves a jagged hole.

I reach for Li'l Bertha, the pistol I inherited from my father. She practically jumps out of her leather holster. The WeaponSynch pad embossed on her grip snaps into the matching recess in my palm. Li'l Bertha's targeting software jacks into my Eyes-Up display and flashes "Target One" over Dream Girl's head.

I swing my gun hand out in front of me, and Li'l Bertha's gyroscopic aiming system does the rest. Her status changes to "Target Acquired," and I let 'er rip. A swarm of .45-caliber bullets smashes into Dreamy's face, neck, and chest. The girl's mortal remains splatter all over the windows, walls, and seats. It's like someone sneezed out a gallon of spaghetti sauce.

The civilian passengers lose their minds and scream like teenagers at a Beatles concert. I dash to the end of the car, yank the emergency brake, and hang on tight while the train comes to a shuddering, shrieking halt. I kick open the exit door, leap down to the tracks, and sprint up the tunnel.

My staccato footsteps and heavy breathing are chased by an older woman's voice crying out to Sweet Merciful Jesus.

I lean forward so the driver can hear me over the salsa music that roars out of his cab's radio. "Right up there, next to the Metro stop."

I pay the cabbie, climb out of the taxi, and swing into Mario's, a little Italian restaurant on the corner. Mario shoves pizzas in and out of his ovens and asks what I'd like without turning around. He nods at my order for three slices.

While Mario finishes his game of pizza checkers, I stare out at the street. The window's monochromatic reflection shows my hair as slate gray instead of its actual red. I notice a dark smudge on my chin and forehead. I go to the ladies' room and look in the mirror.

Oh, for heaven's sake, Alix. There's dried blood splattered all over my face. It's a good thing I took a cab.

Sometimes a gunshot wound makes a neat little hole and almost nothing leaks out. Other times it's like smashing open a blood piñata. I wash my face and go back out front, where my slices are waiting for me, wrapped and ready. On the walk home, I use my Eyes-Up display to review my retinal cameras' recording of what happened tonight and some of the events that led to it.

I've made great progress with my self-assigned mission to collar Jakob Fredericks, the nutso American intelligence officer who betrayed my father to the Germans. I knew it wouldn't be easy, but damn, just finding Fredericks's house has been a bitch! Nearly all the data in his official records is missing, and what *is* there is mostly wrong. His listed home address turned out to be Griffith Stadium, where the Washington Senators used to play.

Fortunately, I've had some free time to overcome this annoying obstacle. The latest diplomatic disaster with Germany has all the Beltway brainiacs working day and night to maintain the North Atlantic Alliance and prevent World War III. The D.C. mind-meld includes the smarty-geeks at Extreme Operations Division, where I work as a covert field agent. All of ExOps's Job Numbers are on hold until a course of action is hammered out, which has left field personnel like me with idle hands.

I took a week off to help my mother settle us into our new house. My boss let me borrow a company car, supposedly for trips to the hardware store. In fact, I used it to follow Fredericks and find out where the prick really lives.

Fredericks runs the Strategic Services Council on K Street at 15th. As he left work one evening, I tailed him to the Whitehurst Freeway. He lost me in the daily Key Bridge traffic pit, where half the assholes in D.C. try to cross the Potomac River at the same time. The next couple of days found me stage trailing him north of the city. Yesterday he led me to a small neighborhood past Wildwood Shopping Center in North Bethesda. The loaner car had to go back this morning, so tonight I took the Metro instead.

I rode to White Flint, walked past the shopping center, and waited at a bus stop. Fredericks's Saab came along, punctual as ever, and turned onto Tilden Lane before taking the first right. I hustled through a few backyards and poked my head out from a clump of hedges at the end of the block. The Saab coasted into the attached garage of a capacious house.

Gotcha, fucko!

I spent two hours carefully skulking around his neighborhood, casing different approaches. Behind his house is a small unlit park. It'll be a great way to sneak in. My plan is to scam some surveillance toys out of the Technical Department and plant them in Fredericks's house.

I arrive home. Mom and I have only lived here in Arlington for a couple of weeks. We bought this house to replace our Crystal City house that the Blades of Persia blew up last year. It's a medium-size gray wooden Garrison in a neighborhood full of medium-size brick Colonials. Mom's little Chevy is parked in the driveway, and the light is on in her room.

It's late, but I'm twenty years old and way past having a curfew, so I simply walk in the front door instead of sneaking through my bedroom window like I used to. I put my pizza on the kitchen table and go upstairs. My mother is in bed, reading one of her eighteenth-century novels.

"Hi, Mom."

Cleo puts her book down. "Hi, angel." She smiles at me. "How was your day?"

"Fine." I sit on the foot of her bed and lean forward to stretch my back. "Brando and I did research."

"Have you eaten?"

"We went out after work, plus I stopped at Mario's."

"You two didn't go to that dump Cyrus likes, did you?" Cyrus, who's both Mom's old friend and my boss, is a regular at the Foggy Bottom Grill.

"Guh." I snort. "That shithole? No way. Too many career bachelors turning into bar stools."

Mom laughs and then inclines her head. "You look tired, Alix."

Right on cue, I let out a yawn. "Spending all day in the ExOps archives is even more tiring than karate class."

"Don't you have a DCT later this week?"

"Yeah, Wednesday afternoon, but I'm ready." Mom is an associate supervisor in ExOps's administration department, so she knows all about Development Cycle Tests.

"Want me to pick you up after?" she asks.

"Sure. Around six?"

"All right. I was thinking we could catch a movie."

I squint at my mother suspiciously. "Which movie?"

"Well, it *is* your turn to pick, but not another one of those horrible slasher flicks, please."

"Oh, come on, Cleo. You had fun last time!"

"I certainly did *not*!"

"Of course you did. There was blood everywhere!" My hands wave in a circle to illustrate fountains of gory delight.

Cleo sighs heavily and props her novel in front of her face. From behind the book, she intones, "Good night, Alixandra."

I traipse out of her room. "G'night, Mom."

03

I swig coffee from my jumbo plastic travel mug and wipe my mouth with the back of my hand as I saunter into ExOps. A graveyard chill follows the coffee down my throat when I spot my field partner, Brando. He sprawls in one of the lobby's monumental leather chairs as he whips through the *Washington Post*'s crossword puzzle.

I activate my infrared vision. He becomes a warm orange blob on a cold blue chair, so yes, he's there. I switch to normal vision.

He catches sight of me, neatly folds his newspaper, and stands up.

Blood streams out of his pant legs—

Brando's clunky black Doc Martens ferry him across the polished floor.

—and leaves crimson streaks across the lobby—

Our paths meet at the stainless-steel elevators.

—nobody notices them—

"Morning, Alix."

—but me.

I squeeze my eyes shut. When I open them, my partner is quietly watching me.

"Hi, Brando." I try to keep my voice steady. "What's cookin'?"

His name is Patrick, but I don't call him that. He's the spitting image of my late partner, so greeting him by the same name is more than I can bear. His middle name is Brandon and his favorite movie is *The Godfather*, so I call him Brando, or sometimes El Brando when we're joking around. He seems to appreciate his nickname, like he's been accepted into an Indian tribe or something.

But my tribe isn't all jokes and nicknames. People die young here, although they hang around even after they're dead. For example, my old partner Trick still visits me despite getting killed three months ago. We talk and catch up, but I have to be careful. One time I forgot other people were around, and the stares they gave me could have turned sunflowers into dog shit.

This is why I check Brando with my vision Mods. If he shows in infrared, he's Brando. If not, he's Trick. Either way, my gut clenches and my palms sweat. It occurs to me I should've used my infrared on the subway slag last night. Next time for sure.

Brando jabs the elevator's up button. He pushes a curled lock of brown hair off his high forehead and says, "The Front Desk wants to see us. I thought we'd catch a minute beforehand."

All ExOps Levels and Info Operators, like me and Brando, have commphones implanted in our heads so we can talk during missions without making any sound. They're also handy for private conversations at work.

Brando comms, "Are you feeling all right? You look pale."

"I'm fine."

He silently stares at me.

I narrow my eyes. "I'm *fine*! What does Cyrus want to see us about?"

"This." He presents his newspaper. The front page features a large picture under the headline "Metro Shoot-out Leaves One Dead." The image looks like someone sloshed a modern art masterpiece all over the inside of a subway car.

The elevator arrives. Since it's midmorning, all the nine-to-fivers are safely ensconced in meetings, which leaves us to ride up alone. I read the article and *hmph* at the part about me vanishing into thin air. If only. There's no point trying to fool Brando, or anyone else at ExOps for that matter. They always know when it was me, so I've learned to ignore the wrist slaps and bask in the attention.

I give him his paper. "At least they got my gender right this time."

He takes his glasses off, wipes the lenses on his shirt, and addresses me by my field handle. "Scarlet, I wish you'd brought me in on this. I could've helped you maintain a lower profile."

"I know, but it was late. I didn't wanna roust you outta your test tube."

"Jesus, Scarlet," my partner barks, "I don't sleep in a tube!"

He's right, of course, but sometimes I can't resist teasing him about being a clone.

Brando has the same handsome features as my first partner, Trick. But he isn't quite as impervious to my cruel jibes as Trick was, especially about being a clone. El Brando is sensitive about that.

Patrick Brandon Owens is a product of the Reproduction Using Asexual Cloning Heuristics program. RUACH replaced America's original cloning program, the Asexual Reproduction Initiative, because the blockheads running ARI were spectacularly irresponsible about how they acquired cell samples from their Originals. All the ARI cell samples were destroyed, but the Patrick clones had already been incubated, so they were transferred to RUACH. Destroying incubated embryos was not an option. RUACH's charter grants lab specimens the same rights as naturally conceived citizens. Basically, clones are people, too.

This is all fine and dandy if you don't fall in love with someone, witness their corporal dismemberment, and then meet their carbon copy. Every morning it's like a kick in the stomach when I see him. The gruesome hallucinations don't help, either. I try to play it cool, but I still get uptight and say stupid shit I don't mean.

Whenever I aggravated Trick, holding his hand was

usually enough to cool him down. The first time I tried holding hands with Brando, he stared at me like I had two heads. It wasn't that he minded, but he didn't know it's my way of saying "Hey, I'm sorry for whatever stupid dumb-ass thing I said or did."

Brando has received the same Mods as Trick, and he knows about all my missions. When he volunteered to be my new partner, the Med-Techs infused Brando with Trick's archived memories of all the Job Numbers we'd pulled together.

The hypnotic transfer process isn't supposed to include nonwork experiences. This is part of ExOps's privacy policy. The Meddies discard their subjects' personal memories. Except Trick and I were much more than field partners, which means Brando "remembers" sleeping with me as vividly as I remember sleeping with someone who looks *exactly* like him.

This is why I almost had a heart attack when he picked me up at the airport last November.

The Front Desk—my boss, Cyrus—had planned to meet my flight personally so he could soften my introduction to Brando, but the White House called just as he was leaving. Cyrus had his secretary say he was unavailable, then continued down to the ExOps garage with Brando.

They'd barely buckled their seat belts when a hulking black van blocked their exit. A gang of Secret Service agents escorted Cyrus out of his car and into their vehicle. President Jackson wasn't taking no for an answer. Brando knew my flight was arriving soon, so he drove Cyrus's car to fetch me by himself.

Earlier, while Brando was remotely guiding me through our mission in Riyadh, I noticed his comm-voice sounded like Trick's. That was our first time working together, and I only knew him by his field name, Darwin. I thought that maybe all Info Operators picked up the same accent from their training or that it was just my head fucking with me. It never occurred to me my new partner comms like Trick because he basically *is* Trick.

While Brando drove me to ExOps headquarters, I shakily asked him who he was. He told me the CIA transferred him from the U.S. embassy in Berlin to ExOps's German Section to replace Trick.

"No, that's where you *came from*," I said. "Trick, er, I mean Solomon, didn't have any family. Who the hell *are* you?"

"I'm his brother," Brando answered. "Sort of."

"Sort of?"

He hesitated. "I'm sorry, Alix. Cyrus wanted to tell you all this. Solomon and I were incubated from the same genetic material."

"*What?*"

"His full name was Patrick Allan Owens. He was selected to be your partner at ExOps. I went to Berlin as a diplomatic liaison. My other brother—Patrick Charles—works in Japan as a strategic analyst."

"There are *three* of you?"

"Yes . . . well, no." He took a long, shaky breath. "There's only me and Charles now." We rode in silence while my brain staged a no-holds-barred neurological demolition derby. I stampeded through anger, skipped to confusion, made a quick stop at grief, and then charged through anger again.

Trick was a clone.

I grasped my armrest so hard that I ripped it off the door.

All that time together and he never told me. Cyrus must have known, and he never told me either.

I turned to this new Patrick. "We're gonna be partners?"

"Yes."

"Well, *partner*," I snarled. "Don't you *ever* fucking lie to me! You tell me everything, no matter what fucking Cyrus says." I jabbed him with the dismembered armrest. "Got it?"

"Got it."

"Where did you and your . . . brothers come from?"

My new partner's answer was a mind-blower. The short version is the three clones produced by the American cloning program in 1960 grew up and became the three Patricks.

The original Patrick was born to Marty and Nancy Owens, a married couple from Lawrence, Kansas. Original Patrick inherited his braininess from his parents, both of whom taught graduate-level science classes at Kansas University.

They were invited to be potential cell donors for ARI, the fledgling American cloning program. Original Patrick, who was fourteen at the time, watched fascinated as the medical personnel took cell samples from his parents. He begged his parents to let him donate his DNA, too. The ARI technicians humored the boy and took his samples after promising his parents they wouldn't include their underage son's cells in the selection process.

A few years later, ARI knocked the world on its butt when they produced a trio of cloned human embryos. ARI then set the Olympic speed record for spectacular collapses when they inadvertently revealed that their clones were grown not from any of their legitimate donors but from cells of the distinctly off-limits Patrick Owens.

When this story broke, ARI went from "Top of the World, Ma" to "Public Enemy Number One" in nothing flat. Religious leaders decried their God playing, and human rights activists protested their theft of genetic material. Even their fellow scientists had to admit ARI had fucked up royally, although they didn't quite say it that way. Congress shut ARI down, formed RUACH to manage ARI's assets, and left the remaining decisions about clones to future generations of Capitol Hill whoremongers.

The three embryonic clones were given their Original's first and last names with unique middle names to tell them apart. Original Patrick's parents couldn't bring themselves to raise three copies of the son they already had, so RUACH quietly found a foster family. RUACH's psychologists, fearing the boys would be social outcasts if their unique origin was known, created a cover story and issued each of them a revised birth certificate. The boys were fostered as orphaned triplets by a childless couple from the Treasury Department.

The adoptive parents, working closely with RUACH, eventually told the boys their true origin. As planned, when the brothers reached high school, Patrick Allan, Patrick Brandon, and Patrick Charles were presented with opportunities to work in the prestigious American intelligence community. But there was a catch: they couldn't work at the same agency.

Hiding their unnatural births from regular civilians was one thing, but keeping it from a building full of spies was another. If triplets of the correct age walked into the same agency together, everybody would figure out who they were and the boys' mental well-being could be jeopardized. So Charles took their Original's brains to the CIA's Tokyo office, Brandon took his interpersonal skills to the American embassy in Berlin, and Allan, my Trick, brought his sense of humor to Extreme Operations. All three of their files were altered to state they had no siblings. Contact between the brothers was permitted, but it had to be done secretly.

If my experience so far is any indicator, clones don't come out to be exact duplicates of each other. Brando is more serious than Trick, which I'd say is a result of their work environments. Embassy employees live in a delicate world of well-mannered diplomacy unknown to us Wild West covert operatives. There's also a certain swagger that comes from being biotically enhanced, and Brando is still acclimating to his Info Operator Mods. But it's mostly because—unlike Trick—Brando is grieving for his dead brother.

This earned me a scolding the night Brando met me at

the airport. As soon as he finished the story about him and his brothers, I blew my stack and mounted an epic bitchfest. When it became clear I wasn't going to pipe down, Brando finally let me have it.

"Godammit Alix, *enough*! I know this is a shock and that you've lost your partner. But I lost my fucking brother! So cool it, all right?"

I folded my arms across my chest and spent the rest of our drive silently trapped in a bog of resentment, sadness, and guilt. The next day we began working together, which has gone perfectly well since we already know so much about each other. It hasn't been easy for either of us, though. I have my spells, and if someone mentions a job I pulled with Trick, Brando gets testy and bites his fingernails.

When we aren't wigging each other out, I'm teaching him the in-jokes I had with Trick. Brando "remembers" some of them but not all. It was surreal to explain Freaking Unstoppable Cranium Krusher to the person who invented F.U.C.K. in the first place.

The elevator doors open. We step out and walk across the German Section's busy office. Phones ring, computer terminals beep and blink. It's a modern beehive of earnest activity. Across the floor, in the Front Desk's office, Cyrus broods in his chair and glowers at the world outside his window. His brows are jammed tightly together. He's pissed. Again.

I breeze past Cyrus's secretary and enter his office. Brando follows and shuts the door behind us. We stand at attention.

"Sir," I blurt, "I know we're supposed to minimize our actions in front of civilians, but quickly eliminating that female competitor last night was the best way to avoid collateral damage."

My heart pounds. Cyrus silently regards me, then Brando, then me again. He rises from his chair. "Agreed. Zero civilian casualties, apart from emotional stress, is acceptable given where you are in your Development Cycle."

I exhale twelve pounds of anxiety.

"Now, Scarlet." Cyrus plants his fists on his desk. "Why the hell are you following Jakob Fredericks?"

CORE (CATALOGUE OF RECORDS: ExOps)
PER-A59-1460

From the desk of Dr. Thomas Herodotus, ExOps Medical Director

Cyrus,

Scarlet has made steady, if painful, progress with her recovery from the trauma endured while investigating Winter's Blades of Persia and their Darius Covenant. Her fiercely self-motivated personality, inherited no doubt from her father, has helped her greatly during this process.

She has found a measure of support from our grief therapy group, although her first partner's violent death still haunts her terribly. Scarlet continues to suffer debilitating nightmares and hallucinations, especially when unoccupied with work.

To answer your original question, yes, your star Level will be ready for ANGEL, but please include me on Scarlet's reports so I can track her status.

Respectfully yours,
Tom

04

Cyrus repeats, "Scarlet, why are you following Fredericks?"

How does Cyrus always know? "Ahh . . . uhh." I grope for words, freshly reminded of how smart my boss is. "Sir, may I sit?"

Cyrus leans back in his chair and steeples his hands in front of his face. He takes a long time before answering. "Yes, sit. You, too, Darwin."

We flop into Cyrus's guest chairs. "Sir, I'm following Director Fredericks to practice tailing an experienced target." I gesture to my partner. "Darwin doesn't know about it."

Cyrus shuts his eyes and rubs his temples. "I should've known you weren't going to any damned hardware store." He inhales slowly and deeply. "Scarlet, Extreme Operations Division prohibits freelancing."

"Yes, sir."

"*I* prohibit freelancing."

"Yes, sir," I repeat.

"Do you know why?"

No fucking idea, boss. "Uh, do you mean yourself, sir, or Extreme Operations?"

"Either one is fine."

"Umm . . ."

Finally, he just tells me. "Freelancing is prohibited by Extreme Operations because the brass hats upstairs think that agent is probably moonlighting for a competitor. Freelancing is prohibited by *me* because sooner or later the brass hats order me to interrogate—and often eliminate—that agent."

Jesus H. Christ. Those twelve pounds of anxiety rush back into me.

"Imagine my thrill, Scarlet," Cyrus rumbles, "when the phone rang at four o'clock this morning to inform me one of my people had pulled a mission I knew nothing about. My first thought was of you." He catches me smiling. "That was *not* a compliment! Wipe that smirk off your face!"

I squeeze my lips into a flat line.

He continues, "I traced your No-Jack data and saw that the first thing you did with that agency car was drive it to Fredericks's office. Then you spent the better part of a week using it to track him to his house in North Bethesda, *where he's lived for five years*!"

Like a complete doofus, I ask, "You know his real address?"

Cyrus uncoils to his full height of 6'2" and booms, "Alixandra, I'm Front Desk of the German Section at Extreme Operations—"

Uh oh . . .

"—I've known the man for almost twenty years—"

. . . this is gonna be a loud one.

"—he's brilliant, he's dangerous—"

Here it comes!

"—and he tries to KILL my agents! OF COURSE I know where the FUCKER lives!"

The chatter and clatter outside Cyrus's office stops. His eyes bore into me like drill bits. "Now, why are you following him? And cut the 'practice' bullshit or I'll stick you behind a desk in Dubuque!"

"Sir," Brando pipes up, "if I may interject."

The eyebrows swing toward my partner. "What is it, Darwin?"

"Well, sir, it doesn't strike me as reasonable to expect a fully trained Level to wait for someone else to go after the person who betrayed her own father."

"It doesn't strike you," Cyrus says very quietly, "as reasonable?"

Ohhh, boy.

"Darwin, when I want to know what strikes you as reasonable—"

Here we go again!

"—I'LL BLOODY WELL ASK YOU!" Cyrus stands and pounds his desk. "We are NOT cowboys!" He's so steamed that he paces back and forth a few times. "Alix, I don't know who would kick my ass harder if . . ." He stops, frowns at his reflection in the window, and says, "Never mind. You stay away from Fredericks. Justice has warned me he's untouchable, at least until we sort out this thing with Germany."

This "thing" with Germany is America's worst international crisis in three decades. It turns out the German public has little tolerance for crashed cars, shot-up college campuses, trashed public facilities, and bullet-riddled city streets. My sheboomigans in German territory last year featured all this and more, but our ambassador in Berlin kept it quiet by distracting the local politicos and mediarazzi with buffets of all-you-can-hump professional virgins. However, nothing could suppress the story of fifty kids in a German Youth troop being blown up by a U.S. Navy cruise missile.

That cruise missile eliminated the global threat posed by the Darius Covenant and the Blades of Persia. It was also supposed to kill the Blades's leader, a man known as Winter. In fact, I snuck in with the ill-fated German Youth troop and snatched Winter only moments before blam time. We coordinated all this to give the kids plenty of time to make it out of there.

But they didn't.

The German press went wild. When the forensics came back "Made in U.S.A.," everyone from Herr Chancellor to Herr Six-Pack called for American heads to roll. This really screwed the pooch.

To protect our corruption case against Jakob Fredericks, Winter's existence has to stay completely under wraps. He's the one person who can prove Fredericks purposely sent my father into a trap. But our star fink is as good as dead if ol' Jakob finds out about him.

ExOps's big cheese, Director Eduardo Chanez, told Cyrus to keep my mission strictly in-house. This meant no paperwork, no CORE entries, and no official meetings. He didn't even tell the White House. Only a couple of his close contacts at the Department of Justice know we're harboring a witness who can stick Fredericks in front of a firing squad.

This is why President Jackson was totally blindsided when German Chancellor Honecker blusteringly declared that he wants Greater Germany to dump the U.S. and join the Pan-Asian Pact. Now America is facing the recurring Shadowstorm nightmare where three major powers team up and gang rape the fourth one.

The U.S. *must* have an ally, and it won't be Russia or China. Those creeps are still pissed about our presence in Japan and Korea. Our relationship with Greater Germany is crucial, and the effort to rescue it is being directed by Washington's top strategist: SSC Director Jakob Fredericks. The fucker is considered so indispensable right now that we can't even bust the bastard for treason. So "until we sort out this thing with Germany," we've stashed Winter in a safe house out in the boonies. Hopefully, given some time, nobody will ask how in hell we got our hands on such a hot potato.

Meanwhile, I'm still in the shit shack. Cyrus's burning glower could melt bronze.

Brando hesitantly says, "Sir, Scarlet and I may have uncovered something else."

Cyrus sighs, "Let's hear it."

My partner takes a deep breath. "Director Fredericks's career has a unique pattern. He's made great contributions but has not been commensurately rewarded."

Our boss, still scowling, says, "Go on."

"He's intelligent and experienced enough to direct a

substantially larger office than the Strategic Services Council. Something like CIA, NSA, perhaps even the State Department." Brando clears his throat. "However, he's been kept from higher posts by his . . . uhh . . . lack of social skills."

Cyrus snorts but says nothing.

"Also," Brando continues, "his resentment toward his superiors is well known."

"Him and half of Washington."

"Yes, sir, but consider the way Director Fredericks handled the ExOps security breach eight years ago. He knew there were three competitive agents inside ExOps—Virgo, Libra, and Scorpio—who—"

"Yes, Darwin. I remember," Cyrus says irritably. "I lost a lot of good friends from the Russian Section, and Langley nearly shut us down. Make your point."

"Sorry, sir." Patrick clears his throat again. "Virgo and Libra were captured quickly, which halted the leaks from the Russian Section, and then Fredericks broke off the investigation."

Cyrus's glare broils us. "And?"

"Sir," Brando says quickly, "we think Jakob Fredericks is Scorpio."

A pregnant pause while Cyrus clasps his hands behind him. "You believe Scorpio was our most senior Front Desk at the time."

Brando and I both nod our heads.

"I suppose this is why you've spent so much time in the library lately."

We nod our heads again. According to what we found in CORE, Virgo and Libra exposed all of our agents and informers in the USSR, many of whom were executed or remain in prison. The third mole—Scorpio—continued to pursue a separate agenda after the two Russian agents were packed off to Leavenworth.

The Office of Security interviewed everyone at ExOps and discovered dozens of staffers who had briefly misplaced their IDs sometime in the previous year. The investigators determined that all of those IDs had been used to access classified data about the Asexual Reproduction Initiative before magically reappearing someplace like the cafeteria, a restroom, or out in the parking lot.

Cyrus rubs his jaw. "I assume the Scorpio reports you read were sanitized."

"Yes, sir. No names."

"Well, let me tell you, then, since I was here when all that happened. After security started monitoring the traffic into CORE, they only tracked one query for ARI-related materials. By the time they traced it, the trespasser was already gone. That was the last we ever heard of Scorpio."

Brando asks, "Whose ID had he used?"

Our boss fixes a stare at us to say, *Guess who.*

I grumble, "Fredericks." My partner and I check each other to see if we've grown big cartoon donkey heads.

Cyrus returns to his desk chair. "And before you ask, he was at Camp David with President Nixon. He didn't realize his ID was missing until he tried to return to his office later that night."

My boss stretches his arms toward the ceiling. "So I'm afraid Fredericks is not a likely Scorpio suspect." A couple of his joints crack as he extends his hands over his head. His armpits are dark with perspiration. "I've always thought it was Russia or China trying to jump-start their cloning program by stealing it from us."

"The same way we stole ours from Germany?" I butt in.

Cyrus scrutinizes me for a moment. "You *have* been doing your homework. Yes, exactly." He opens one of his desk drawers. "Fredericks has more than enough clearance to access ARI, but he wouldn't waste his time. He knows as well as I do that we're a long way from getting involved with cloning again." Our boss nods toward Brando. "Despite the positive results achieved."

Brando lowers his eyes to his lap. "Thank you, sir."

"Your efforts are commendable—" Cyrus pulls a pair of file folders out of his desk drawer. "—but Scorpio is a mystery for another day." The drawer shuts. "There are more pressing matters to attend to." He passes the files to us. "Scarlet, this should keep you out of trouble for a while."

My partner and I each grab a folder. The cover reads "Top Secret: Operation ANGEL."

Cyrus rises from his chair and paces across his office. "This is the largest covert action I've ever seen. Every section's Front Desk will contribute all available resources. That's Russian, Chinese, American, and, of course, our German Section."

Brando peeks inside his mission brief.

"Scarlet, you and Darwin will travel to York in northeast England. There you will establish contact with an underground resistance group called the Circle of Zion. This is a great opportunity for you two, but make no mistake. The country's fate hangs in the balance. Our cousins in Berlin *must* be diverted from joining the Pan-Asian Pact, and the appeal of such an alliance to Moscow and Beijing must be undermined. We can't fabricate the proper situation from outside Germany's borders, but we *can* induce it within them."

Meanwhile, Brando's eyes have almost bugged out of his head.

Cyrus stops pacing. Then he knocks our socks off. "ExOps has been ordered to incite a slave revolt inside the Reich. And you're going to start it."

Oh, my God!

It's the job of a lifetime! I turn, dumbfounded, to my partner. His mouth has flopped open, and I think he's stopped breathing.

CORE   MIS-ANGEL-006

DATE: 20 January 1981
TO: All Directors and Operations Coordinators
FROM: Office of the Executive Intelligence Chairman
SUBJECT: **Operation ANGEL**

FOR YOUR EYES ONLY

Mission Parameters

The goal of Operation ANGEL (Affected Naturaliza-
tion of Germany's Enslaved Labor) is to preserve America's alliance with Greater Germany. It will temporarily
destabilize the Reich by instigating a revolt among
the slave population in Europe, beginning in England.
This rebellion will be supported by America's clandestine community until our embassy in Berlin persuades
Germany to rejoin the North Atlantic Alliance. At that
point, our prorebellion support will cease.

Long-term success of the insurgency is undesirable, but
to achieve this diplomatic goal, our deployed field agents
must develop a convincingly chaotic situation. You will
withhold our true purpose from your operatives and direct
them as though this uprising is to actually succeed.

Background

This situation has been brewing for months. On 3 October of last year, agents of Extreme Operations Division severely damaged a Carbon installation in Zurich.
News of this event was not happily received by our opposite numbers in the Reich, but they suppressed the
story to maintain Carbon's minimized media presence.

Three weeks later, a thermobaric cruise missile fired
from a U.S. Navy ship annihilated a terrorist base mas-
querading as a research facility outside of Riyadh. All
the lab personnel were killed, along with fifty members
of a visiting German Youth troop. This story was carried by every news outlet in Greater Germany.

Four days later, Chancellor Erich Honecker declared he would sever Greater Germany's alliance with the United States.

That same day China loudly renewed her demand for the United States to transfer control of Korea and Japan to the Nationalist Republic of China.

These events occurred during an election year and severely damaged President Reagan's approval ratings. Democratic challenger Henry M. "Scoop" Jackson made significant gains. Two weeks later Mr. Jackson was elected president.

Upon taking office last week, President Jackson immediately initiated his combination of liberal domestic programs and aggressive foreign policy. In his first presidential press conference he condemned Greater Germany's plan to "betray" the North Atlantic Alliance and threatened dire consequences should they follow it through.

ANGEL is a harbinger of those dire consequences.

05

"Scarlet, ten left," Brando's comm-voice says, "and stay down."

I dog it ten yards up Main Street, crouched so low that I'm almost doubled over. Then I hit the deck. My heavy breathing blows little puffs of dust off the floor. Dirt sticks to my sweat-soaked face. I blink the salty grime out of my eyes.

A turret pops out from a plastic bush on the left and noisily expels a stream of rubber ordnance. I drop to the ground. Li'l Bertha locks on to the bullet-bot, and I pull the trigger. Her lightweight practice slugs ping off the turret's metal shell, which signals the Training Control Center, *Ya got me, pardner.*

Brando comms, "Next station, sixty right, fly-by."

"Fly-by" is IO slang for "don't stop moving," so this next part will be something extra hairy. I spring to my feet and pump my legs for sixty feet. A bright light flashes from a little house on the right side of Main Street. As I swivel to fire on this target, the floor plunges out from under me. I have just enough momentum to grab the far edge of this insta-pit before my body smacks into the chasm's wall and knocks the wind out of me.

Oof!

My partner comms, "C'mon, Scarlet! We've only got thirty seconds for the last station."

That's easy for you to say, Darwin. I pull myself out of the pit and wheeze on down the road.

"Okay, last one. Three hundred straight ahead, top speed."

I ignore my burning lungs and jet to twenty-something

miles per hour. My limbs swing faster and faster, and my hair flutters in the wind. I can hit high thirties with Madrenaline in my blood, but we're required to complete this training unit without my Enhances. Each run-through is different, and I've blown it three times already. This is the closest we've come to beating this sequence.

Brando comms, "Twenty seconds!"

Ahead of me is a clear path to the finish line. All I need to do is jog to it and—

Wrong.

Three bullet-bots drop from the roof in front of me. They bounce on long rubber bungee cables. Each bot emits a thin red laser beam. All three beams point at my chest, and the bots fire a volley of rubber bullets.

Li'l Bertha tries to find the bots while I leap away from their bullets and laser beams, but her target indicator is blank.

"Darwin, what's happened? Why can't I lock on?"

"They're jammers. You'll have to—"

I charge the leftmost bot.

"—find a way around them."

The left bot locks on to me as it swings to the bottom of its arc. I throw myself at it and grab the bungee cable above its body. The bot hoists me toward the roof. I swing like Tarzan and wrap my bot's cable around the other two bungees before I let go at the bottom of the next bounce.

The bots are still live, but now they can only point in a fixed direction. I avoid the static laser beams and dive across the finish line with less than a second to go.

"*Yes!*" Brando shouts. "Made it!"

I flop onto the ground. My view from Gaspville Junction shows a very high curved roof supported by metal trusses, like an airplane hangar.

"Terrific," my partner comms. "Now for the driving test."

Sure. Whatever. "Gimme a minute." It takes a minute anyway, since he has to bring the car around.

A vehicle coasts up next to me and stops. I peel myself off the ground. Man, I miss my Madrenaline. Brando switches to the passenger seat, and I pour myself behind the wheel. Something must have happened to our previous training vehicle, which was a beat-to-shit black-and-white Dodge sedan, probably a former police cruiser. This new car, a white BMW two-seater convertible, is quite a hot little number. The relatively few dents and scrapes tell me this sexy momma hasn't seen much track time here yet. While we coast to the start line, I take in the gorgeous tan interior.

My partner sees how impressed I am with our new wheels. "Drug bust," he says.

Ah, of course. Sometimes when ExOps helps local cops, they let us keep the perpetrator's ride. If the D.C. SWAT team can't take care of a situation or if the FBI is in over their head, Director Chanez will send one of his Levels out with them. It never takes long after that. Regular crooks can't compete with a million-dollar murder machine designed to help topple whole governments.

"Think there's any cocaine left in this baby?"

Brando turns up the heater. "Nah, the mechanics probably found it all."

I position the Cokemobile on the start line. In front of us, a pair of titanic hangar doors grind open. My partner riffles through his instructions and nods to me when he's ready.

I comm, "TCC, Scarlet and Darwin in position."

The Training Control Center comms, "Roger that, Scarlet. Arming the tree. Go on green."

The tree is a tall pole supporting a vertical series of lights; red on top, yellow in the middle, and green at the bottom. Right now the top lights glow crimson, holding us in place. I press the clutch down and shift into first gear. My right foot floors the gas and holds it there.

Reds, yellows, *green!*

I slip my left foot off the clutch pedal. A white cloud of tire smoke billows behind us as we screech off the line. The tachometer redlines, I shift into second, and we bound out of the hangar. The sun smacks me in the face, and my vision Mods adjust their gamma to compensate.

I holler, *"Yeee-hahhhh!!!"*

As we tear-ass up the first straightaway, Brando feeds me his pace notes. "Turn One. Left, one-zero-five in, long sweep, nine-five out." This means we should enter this long sweeping left turn at 105 miles per hour and exit it at 95.

The Cokemobile rockets to a buck ten before I tap the brakes to initiate a spectacular power slide around Turn One. I countersteer and wallop the gas before we've even passed the corner's apex. Cokey leans into this scandalous driving like a drunken businessman doing the motorboat between a hooker's tits.

Oh, I am totally getting one of these honeys.

We thunder out of the curve. My partner yells, "Turn Two. Right, six-zero in, opens, eight-zero out." When Brando says "opens," he means the turn gets broader as we go around.

I twist the wheel ninety feet away from the corner and downshift from fifth to third to transfer the car's weight forward. Overloading the front tires like this makes Cokey plow into the curve. When we're almost at the pavement's outer edge, I stomp the gas and pull the car's center of gravity onto her rear wheels. The unloaded front tires suddenly grip tighter than a Scotsman's wallet and whip us through Turn Two.

"Turn Three. Right, seven-zero in, opens, seven-five out. Jump at apex."

I hook us into Turn Three with my right toes on the gas and my right heel on the brakes. My left foot peppers the clutch as needed to keep our revs up. I'm doing great until we pass the turn's midpoint, where a nasty bump kicks Cokey into the air and ruins my driving line. The car flies sideways and lands inches from the outside edge. I overcorrect, and the Bimmer tilts onto her two left wheels. Brando and I both lean the other way. I jiggle the wheel left to put us on all fours, but now we're headed off the track.

I haul up the emergency brake, crank the steering wheel right and then left, then shove the e-brake down again. This throws us sideways. I look over my left shoulder to see where we're going.

God almighty, we'll be lucky if there's any rubber at all on the tires after this one. My training has ingrained into me—when dealing with an all-out mental-patient driving disaster like this—do *not* slow down. If I even breathe on the brakes right now, we'll spin out of control. I bury the gas pedal and hold my breath. Brando clings to his door handle for dear life.

We exit Turn Three at seventy-nine miles per hour in a massive cloud of scorched rubber.

"Hah!" I wipe sweat off my forehead. "What's next?"

We're doing so well that I only need to drive like Maniac Junior for the rest of the lap. We come off Turn Eight and enter the main straightaway, ready for Lap Two.

We receive a comm from the Training Control Center. "Scarlet and Darwin, switch seats. Lap Two will be a target lap."

Brando calls out, "Fire drill!" and grabs the steering wheel. I scrunch up my legs and crouch on the seat. Then I drag my partner bodily across the center console. He keeps his eyes forward as his legs unfold onto the pedals. Meanwhile I transfer myself to the passenger seat.

I pluck Li'l Bertha out of her holster and click her into my left palm. Her status cluster—bullet caliber, elemental effects, and ammo remaining—overlays the lower left corner of my vision. I look around to see what my field of view is like. With the convertible top down, there are clear firing lanes in practically every direction.

Brando prudently brakes into Turn One, neatly clips

the corner, and smoothly accelerates out. The tires barely chirp.

"You call that driving?" I tease.

"Look, Miss Hot-Rodder, I clocked the same time as you did without scrubbing a year off the tires."

"But you'll never make the highlight reel!"

He smiles, then sets his jaw while he concentrates on Turn Two. As he brakes into the corner, he comms, "Target! Right side, yellow on red."

I pivot and aim Li'l Bertha. A red sign with a large yellow dot has jumped out of the ground twenty-five yards away. I hit it with a short burst, and the target falls back where it came from.

Brando races the Cokemobile around the course and calls out each target. There's barely time for me to aim and fire before the next one appears.

We exit Turn Eight and return to the main straight-away. I relax, smugly thinking we're done, when Brando glances in his side-view mirror. He yells, "Target far left, yellow on black." I swing my head around. A yellow-and-black sign is already behind us, plus it's very low to the ground.

While Brando says, "Crap, we were almost perfect, too," I stand on my seat and climb onto the car's trunk. Biting wind hits me like a refrigerated hurricane, but it's a much better angle up here. I hook my foot into the roll-over bar and sight on our shrinking target. I unload Li'l Bertha at full auto until she clicks empty. The target tips over.

"Got it!"

"Scarlet, sit down! We've gotta get inside to finish."

Brando presses the brakes and turns toward the hangar. The change of direction starts pushing me off the car. I wrap my arms over my head and dive into the passenger-side foot well. The top half of me ends up smooshed under the dashboard. The engine is much louder down here, and hot air blows into my ear. The car swerves right, accelerates, then comes to a stop. All

I can see are my legs and feet, and past them the hangar's metal roof.

Brando's grinning face appears from the driver's side. "You all right, Hot-Rod?"

"Did you know there are tiny men down here who make the heater work?"

"How do they do that?"

"They eat bowls of hot peppers and fart into the duct-work."

He laughs and tries to extract me, but I'm jammed in here so awkwardly that rescuing me requires him and one of the ExOps training administrators to haul me out by my knees.

"Hey," I say to the admin as I dust myself off. "What's with that last target? It didn't activate until we were past it!"

The admin gently shrugs. "Yeah, well . . . it wasn't actually a firing target."

Brando swacks car-floor crumbs off my jacket. He asks, "So we weren't supposed to shoot it?"

"You were barely supposed to *see* it. We use it to record how you'd react to having missed one."

"Has anybody ever shot it before?"

The admin slowly shakes his head. I hold my hand out behind me, and Brando slaps me a low-five.

06

"Mom!" I holler. "Where's my pants?"

"Which ones?" she yells from the laundry room downstairs.

I straighten up from my duffel bag so I can shout better. "The black ones with all the pockets!"

"Hang on; they're coming out of the dryer!"

Dammit, I'm gonna miss my flight.

I shovel two fistfuls of socks and underwear out of my dresser and cram them into my bag. I use my Eyes-Up display to reread the packing checklist Brando commed me last night. Let's see: waterproof outerwear, thermal shirts and pants, commando makeup, repair kit for my Mods, three dozen vials of neuroinjector drugs, Li'l Bertha, ammo, and—oh, right!

Almost forgot my mission briefing. ExOps requires its agents to keep track of their classified materials, naturally. Cyrus has to check them in or he can't clear me to leave the country.

I bounce across the bed and snag the mission brief from the floor next to my nightstand. I peek under the bed to see if I've forgotten anything else. It's still pretty tidy down there. Mom and I only moved into this house a little while ago, so there hasn't been time to subject my new bedroom to my usual Bad Housekeeping routine.

Cleo hustles in with my black pants draped over her arm and a small red felt pouch in her hand. "Here you go, honey. Do you need anything else?"

"Thanks. No, I think that's everything." I stuff the warm pants in my duffel.

"Okay, well . . . here." Mom hands me the red felt pouch. "I got you something for your trip to wherever Cyrus is sending you." Cleo could find out where I'm going, but she takes mission security as seriously as everyone else at ExOps, so she hasn't looked. From all the cold weather gear I've packed and the ongoing political shitstorm with Germany, I'm sure she knows it's Western Europe somewhere.

I open the little pouch. Inside is something metallic and cool . . . jewelry? No.

It's my dad's watch.

"Oh, Mom," I whisper as tears spring into my eyes.

Cleo smiles and reaches out to stroke my cheek. "I gave it to your father when we got married. It's durable and easy to read, so I knew he'd like it. He used to tinker with it in his shop, and he wore it during some of his missions." She takes a deep breath. "I want you to have it."

I can't think of what to say, so I put it on. It's a man's Bulova with a black face and white numbers and arms. It dwarfs my skinny wrist. There's no way this will fit me. I hold my arm down, ready for the watch to fall off, but it bumps into my hand and stays there. I turn my wrist over and inspect the strap.

Mom says, "I had a smaller strap put on and new batteries installed."

"How long have you been planning this?"

"It was with some of your father's things at the house in Crystal City, and I brought it to a jeweler to have it sized for you. I'd actually forgotten. They called a few days ago to remind me."

I study the watch and imagine Dad wearing it on his jobs. The dial says "Waterproof," and I decide to never take it off, even in the shower. I wrap my arms around Cleo and kiss her cheek. "Thanks, Mom. I love it!"

"You're welcome, sweetheart. Oh! There's your taxi."

Beep! Beep!

My cab has arrived, ready to take me to HQ and then the airport. I open my bedroom window and holler, "Be right down!" The streetlight illuminates the driver in front and Brando in back.

Cleo tries to lift my bag for me. She grunts and oofs at its weight. She can barely even drag it.

"Mom, how about I take it and you hold the door for me?"

She lets go and brushes a stray hair off her face. "Ha-hm, yes, how about we do that."

I squat down, wrap the bag's carrying strap over my shoulder, and heave. The bulging bag swings into my legs as I schlep it downstairs and out to the street. Mom waits with me while the cab driver dumps my duffel in the trunk.

Brando rolls down his window. "Good morning, Mrs. Nico."

"Hello, Patrick. Are you all ready?"

"Yes, ma'am. How do you like your new house?"

"We're still settling in, but I think we'll be happy here."

The cabbie slams the trunk shut while I scoot in with Brando.

Mom leans down. "You two be careful." Her voice is calm, but her eyes reveal how anxious she feels. "Come back safe."

Brando and I both say, "We will."

The taxi drives us away. Cleo hugs her arms to herself and goes inside. I check my dad's Bulova.

My partner says, "Hey, nice watch."

"Thanks. My mom gave it to me."

He says with a wry grin, "I didn't know they made brass knuckles that tell time."

"Yes, it's huge, wise guy. You'd better hope I don't

brass knuckle *you* with it. You'll thank me when we're in—" I glance at the driver. "—uh, where we're headed, and we can tell time in the dark."

"I thought your Eyes-Up display had a clock in it."

I face Brando and shoot daggers from my eyes. It's too dim for him to see them, so I say, "It's my *father's* watch, dummy! Plus, I can't hit smart-asses like you with my Eyes-Up display." I whack him on his arm with my chunky Bulova.

"Ow!" He winces and rubs his arm. "Fine! I agree. An old mechanical wristwatch is a perfect addition to our state-of-the-art collection of digital covert activities equipment."

I swing at him again, but he blocks my strike with his carryall bag. The bag—his constant companion—is a forest green military-style tactical pack he bought in Berlin. The outer surface is an orgy of buckles, zippers, and straps. The flexible design allows it to hang over one shoulder, strap on like a backpack, or sling across the chest, which is how my partner tends to wear it. Like my late partner's bag of tricks, Brando's tactical bag holds way more stuff than I'd think possible. A big X of black tape on the front flap covers the hole I made when I thought he said it was bulletproof, which is why we call it the X-bag.

He opens his X-taped carryall and rummages around inside. Then he hands me an update to our mission brief. I try to read the paper in the passing streetlights. I can't catch any of it. My night vision is good for unlit spaces, but it isn't so great for reading. Then an old memory surfaces.

Some evenings my father would pass out on the couch in his shop from either too much work or too much drink. In the morning, if I found him down there, I'd snuggle against him. No lights, though. I'd already learned my lesson about waking him with bright lights when he'd had some drinks. If Dad wasn't totally conked out, he'd put one of his arms around me, mumble, "Hi, Hot-Shot," and gently run his fingers through my hair. One morning I was fiddling around with his watch and found a tiny button that made the whole face light up. I flashed myself all the Morse code messages Dad had taught me.

My attention returns to the taxi I'm riding in with Brando. I put the sheet of paper on my lap and hold my dad's Bulova over it. When I press the light button, the watch face casts a bright glow onto the brief. It's our mission communication codes. My partner nods appreciatively. I stick my tongue out at him, then memorize the comm-codes we'll use once we've been inserted into England.

CORE   PUB-GG-2399

BusinessWeek, September 12, 1978

> Greater Germany's fiscal dominance
> fueled by their "peculiar institution"

Joseph Florein of Goldman Sachs built his career as an investment banker with carefully thought-out strategies and a down-to-earth communication style. His direct and honest personality has led to his second occupation as a financial news commentator for *60 Minutes*. He's a voice of calm reason in good times and in bad, but there is one thing that makes the normally imperturbable financier raise his voice.

"Year after year, financial analysts prattle on about the strength of Greater Germany's economy," Mr. Florein said last week. "Yes. Their economy is strong because it's based on slavery!"

Mr. Florein spoke at a fund-raiser for Free for All, a charitable organization he founded to abolish slavery in Greater Germany. Mr. Florein feels that Free for All should appeal to every American citizen, whether they are Jewish or not. "Our country suffered through slavery's shame," he said. "When we abolished it in 1863, we were the last industrialized nation to do so. How can any American sleep at night knowing that across the Atlantic, our *ally* holds millions of her citizens in bondage?"

07

The English night has fallen in on us like a moldy ceiling. I check Dad's watch. It's barely past five o'clock.

I comm, "I still can't believe how early it gets dark here."

"Yeah, I know," Brando comms. "We're a lot farther north than places we've been before."

Zurich—
DISMEMBERED
—covered in blood.
BURNED
I shut my partner's eyes and—
GLISTENING
—scream my heart out.

I inhale deeply through my nose, then exhale slowly through my mouth. Dr. Herodotus has me do this when I have these death flashes, or "intrusive thoughts." Dr. H. said they would go away after a while, but it's been five months, and I swear they're worse.

Brando knows he hasn't actually been in those places with me, but his hypnotically implanted memories are so vivid that he can't help saying "we" instead of "you and my dead brother." When this happens, my mind flashes through a gruesome picture gallery of Trick's mangled corpse.

I observe Brando and continue my slow breathing. It helps me to see him all in one piece and not a smoking, mutilated mess. Naturally I think he's attractive—he's Trick's twin—but I can't fall for Patrick again. It's weird enough already. He *is* handsome, though, especially with longer hair.

I've discovered the Patricks are blessed with great wavy hair. Brando has grown out his government-short hair so he'll have an easier time passing for a civilian. It's so long that he has to push his bangs out of his face as we stare across a dusky field at a German passenger train chugging toward the little English town of Haxby.

My partner follows the train with a pair of high-powered starlight binoculars. "The five-sixteen, right on time," he comms. Brando hands his binoculars to the Circle of Zion's local leader, a no-bullshit fifty-something woman named Miriam.

She says, "Let's hope *die Teutsch* are always so predictable." Miriam speaks in the German-British accent found over here, although now and then she sprinkles in some Yiddish.

Die Teutsch is fifteenth-century German that simply means "the Germans." Using such old-fashioned language represents the Circle's abolitionist position that slavery is archaic. Symbolic or not, Miriam infuses the words with enough blazing hatred to set fire to a bucket of water.

Brando and I have spent a week with these people—most of whom are runaway Jewish slaves—to establish contacts and open routes for smuggling in food, supplies, and of course guns 'n ammo. I've received a crash course in Jewish history, or as I call it, Our Intergalactic Space Dude Fell Asleep at the Wheel and All We Got Was This Shitty Existence. The first interstellar colonists will probably be Jewish astronauts looking to bid shalom to this round hell.

For now, we're here to make Earth a little less crappy for the Space Dude's Chosen. The United States has agents all over Britain, waiting to begin the festivities. Party time will begin in London when the Germans' central communications facility inexplicably explodes. This will be closely followed by a series of electric power grid disasters. That's when smaller groups like us will go to work.

Our job tonight is simple. We need to blow a chunk out of the rail line to York while the nightly trash train passes over it. Destroying container cars full of relatively indestructible garbage will be appropriately disruptive without garnering the extremely negative public reaction we'd incur by derailing a trainload of killable passengers.

The commuter train's rhythmic passing fades as it enters town. A minute later, the area's lights all blink out.

The rebellion has begun.

Miriam rises and leads us across the field. Our muscles and joints protest vehemently. We're all stiff from lying in a February ditch for ten hours. Days like this are why Brando and I brought the high-tech long underwear we're wearing beneath our plain brown pants and coats. We also wear those funny Scally caps, like kids who deliver newspapers in old movies. Miriam wears very worn-out boots, torn pants, and an ancient coat topped off by a brand-new, very official-looking policeman's hat. It's the closest we could get to a railway inspector's uniform. Miriam will supervise us while we "repair" the rail.

As we cross the field, Brando asks Miriam how she escaped to the Circle.

"I was at a fish cannery in Hull when the Rabbi made contact. I told him about the factory's routine, and he conceived a plan to help us escape. That night, our overseer—a real *farbrekher* with a thing for raping young females—came to the women's shack. We knocked him to the ground, then the others pinned him while I slashed his neck open with a can lid." Miriam's stories always get right to the point. "We carried his body to our master's front porch, set fire to our shack, and hid in the warehouse. When *die Teutsch* came pouring out of their big house, the Rabbi snuck in and stole their rifles. He brought them to us, and we shot all the Germans." Miriam indicates a rut in the ground. "Watch your step."

While Brando watches his step, I ask Miriam, "What happened next?"

"The Rabbi led us deep into the forests. *Die Teutsch* can't see into caves or through thick tree canopy. They rely too much on their toys. We always hear their vehicles coming and make it dangerous for them."

"So you win those fights?"

"No." Miriam shrugs. "But neither do they."

We arrive at the tracks. My partner and I crouch over the rail while Miriam stands behind us. She smacks her hands together to resemble an indolent train company *Unterführer* trying to stay warm.

Brando reaches into his portable warehouse and produces a six-volt battery, a coil of unshielded copper wire, and a block of C-4. I help him wire the tracks so the passing train's wheels will complete an electrical circuit and set off our bomb. We'll damage the track and derail the train simultaneously.

We return to our ditch away from home and lie down again. It's important to make sure our bomb actually goes off. If it doesn't, we can't leave it there to be discovered later. That would muster extra German security without the benefit of "creating a chaotic and hazardous situation," per our orders.

While it was light, we kept our hands over our mouths, partly to warm them but mostly to hide the little puffs of steam our breath makes in the winter air. Small details like that can make or break an operation. It's dark now, so we can breathe normally. We can also talk a little more.

Brando goes first. "Miriam, who is the Rabbi? We've heard about him, but not from anyone who's actually met him."

Miriam contemplates the stars. "The Rabbi is our

heart and soul. He led us out of bondage, taught us to hide, to fight, and—most important—to survive."

She tells us the Rabbi was born into slavery and had lived his whole life on a farm in Holland. The farm's owner fell ill and remained sick long enough that when he passed away, it wasn't exactly a surprise. However, the dearly departed's will granted his slaves unconditional freedom, which *was* a surprise.

This rarely happens, and when it does, it's quite awkward because there's no place in Greater German society for Jewish people. The Reich's normal protocol is to quickly and quietly deport the noncitizens out of the country.

The Rabbi, however, disappeared underground and founded the first cell of an abolitionist network for escaped slaves. This network now spans all of Greater Germany. The escapees can leave Europe or stay and help fight slavery. Many opt to stay.

Miriam stops talking and cocks her head to one side, her eyes pointed slightly upward. For a moment, this gesture makes her look like a Hollywood glamour girl from the 1920s. But that moment passes quickly—I don't imagine Hollywood starlets having a Star of David tattooed around their left eye. Nor do I imagine them speaking Yiddish.

"Ach!" she says. "Here comes the *verkachta* train. It's showtime, my little *meshugenuhs*."

We wriggle to the top of the ditch. Brando lets Miriam use his starlight binoculars, and I tell him what I see with my night vision.

"There it is, coming out of Strensall." The train chugs toward Haxby. When the engine passes over our little present, a flash of light is closely followed by a muffled bang.

A derailing train is a stunning sensory experience. The ground quakes and the air shimmies from the clamor of a dozen hundred-ton frying pans clanging together. Metallic groans and shrieks echo across the field as the train cars crumple into their earthy resting places.

Mission accomplished. Miriam cackles as we exit stage left.

08

Don't forget to look up.

One of my professors at Camp A-Go-Go gave an entire lecture on the human tendency to watch for danger by scanning left and right. What I remember from his explanation is that this two-dimensionality has something to do with our prehistoric lives on the flat savannas of Africa. His class was called Hiding in Plain Sight. The professor's next lecture was about exploiting our lateral tendency. We explored all sorts of ways to sneak around security systems based on this one idea.

The maneuver I'm doing right now, the Spider, was developed during these sessions as we practiced adhering ourselves to an interior's high points. Hiding on a ceiling affords an unobstructed view of the room and allows an agent to attack her target from a completely unexpected direction. The trick, however, is the stick. Not all spaces lend themselves to this move. Luckily, York's venerable town hall has lots of fancy woodwork and decorative flourishes I can use as climbing handles and perches.

I feel like a gargoyle. My feet are jammed into a corner molding while my hands press against the ostentatiously decorated ceiling. Brando has crawled under the mammoth couch in front of the mayor's heavy wooden desk. It'll take him a few moments to get out of there, but he doesn't need to make a sensational entrance like I do.

Getting in here was a breeze. We jimmied open a second-story window that overlooks the back alley, then followed a CIA schematic of the building, sprinkled with notes from one of the janitors, straight to the mayor's office. Brando picked the lock, and we got ourselves into position.

05:30. It's been a hell of a couple days. As we expected, the Fritzes responded to our opening salvo with an all-Britain crackdown. Our rail bombing spurred the mass arrests of suspected dissidents all over Yorkshire. The mayor of York is in charge of these roundups, which is why we've made ourselves an early appointment with Herr Bürgermeister to dissuade him from killing the people caught in the raids.

Once we pull this operation, everyone who works in this building will be prime suspects, whether they're antislavery or not. Miriam has already evacuated the Circle sympathizers to the Rabbi's camp.

05:35. My drugs keep going out of balance. Right now my skin is vibrating from an excessive amount of Madrenaline. My mind is hyperaware but can't focus. I take a few deep breaths and try to calm down. This doesn't work, so I have my neuroinjector dose some Kalmers—a little—to try and find equilibrium.

As usual there's a lot riding on our mission, but this one feels more personal. We've spent time with these people. We know their names, and we've seen their scars. Slaves always get the badoingers beaten out of them, and Europe's Jews are no exception.

Miriam told us one story I'll never forget. Her first master, a fat German factory owner named Günther, housed his slaves in an old shipping container behind his factory down in Hull. Günther's facility was right on the harbor, so it was simple to ship raw materials in and slave-produced items out.

One night, old Günther was reviewing his accounts. His business insurance had skyrocketed because the local Circle of Zion cells were sabotaging so much of the region's industry. Earlier that month a nearby clothing company had been attacked. Circle activists dumped a shipping container of raw cloth into the harbor and then spirited the factory's slave labor force away in boats. Günther bitterly saw he was now required to carry so much additional coverage for his slaves that should they accidentally die, the insurance payout would be higher than the cost of replacing them.

Which gave him an idea.

As Miriam tells it, one night she and her fellow laborers were in their unlit, rust-covered container. They were woken by a heavy tractor growling to life outside. A loud clang at one end of their metal living quarters rousted the few slaves who'd managed to remain asleep. The rumbling shipping container screeched over concrete as the roaring tractor shoved them past the loading bays. Chips of paint and flakes of old metal rained down on the people trapped inside.

Miriam pounded on the door until her whole world tipped over. Screams pealed through the darkness, followed by silence. They weren't being pushed anymore, but they weren't sitting still, either. One voice guessed that perhaps their masters had simply relocated them. Then another voice said he felt like they were floating. Finally, a third voice, farthest from the door, confirmed what Günther had done.

"Water! There's water coming in!"

Miriam was crushed against the front door as everyone pressed forward, bellowing in terror. The sea flooded in through the rusty, hole-pocked floor. The container's front edge caught on an old dock piling, and their floating coffin tipped onto its back end. Miriam grasped the door handle as her fellows slid and sank to what was fast becoming the bottom of their tomb. A ferocious battle erupted, hands and feet slashing out in the blackness to stay on top and gain a few extra seconds of life.

The cries and thrashes became weaker and fewer until they finally stopped. Miriam hung from the steel box's top, in water up to her chest. She prayed and prepared to die. She took a breath, then another, and another. The water had stopped rising. The container had come to rest on the harbor's floor, standing on its end with the top still exposed. Although the door was locked, there were enough holes and cracks that air still flowed inside. Miriam floated among the corpses until morning, when Günther had his crane operators retrieve the container.

When they found Miriam still alive, Günther transferred her to his cousin's cannery outside of Driffield so he could write off his slaves as a total loss to his insurers. He also didn't want Miriam contradicting the details of his story about being raided by the Circle of Zion. Günther's cousin in Driffield, by the way, is the lummox whose neck was sliced open with a can lid. Miriam had clearly had enough of slave life.

05:50. I shift my weight a little and try to stretch my legs. The drugs have finally balanced out, so my skin has stopped trying to move to another ZIP Code. I mentally review this assignment for the umpteenth time. It's a classic snatch job, featuring the extra thrill of being deep in enemy territory and surrounded by bad guys. I'd check in with Brando, but we're on comm-silence. He's probably busy proving some obscure mathematical problem like $E = mc$ to the square root of pluribus unum.

Footsteps echo in the hallway. A key clicks in the office's lock. I note the time on my father's watch.

06:00. The door opens beneath me. A plump little man waddles in, shuts the door, and crosses the dimly lit office to the desk. He switches on a small lamp, and a pool of light pours onto his face. The man wears a suit and tie, and his hair is neatly trimmed. I compare this man's face with the picture in my mission briefing. It's him. I give myself a dose of Madrenaline and vault across the room. My hair brushes the ceiling for a second until I begin my descent.

The pudgy Bürgermeister has just settled in his chair when I cannonball into his lap. The impact reduces his wooden chair to its component boards and fasteners. He crashes to the floor while I roll to my feet. I body-slam him and fire my knee into his groin, which elicits a loud cry. I stifle his blabber-box with my hand, muffling his shouts while Brando pulls himself out from under the couch. My partner rushes over to us, digs into his X-bag, and plucks out his egg-shaped drug-injector gadget. Its name is Drug Optimization System: Epidermal, or DOSE for short. We used to stab people with plain old hypodermics before we got these high-tech jobbies.

My partner holds the DOSE against Chubbo's leg and triggers the injector. The effect is almost instantaneous. Our target goes limp. In fact, he stops moving altogether.

"Jeez, Darwin. Did you kill him?"

"Of course not; he's only unconscious."

"For how long?" I climb off the mayor's squishy body.

"Honestly, I'm not sure. This stuff is new and hasn't exactly been tested." Brando begins searching the mayor's desk. "It won't kill him. They assured me of that."

Let's hope so. I bend down and grab Chubbo's hands. Then I hoist him onto my back and start to lug him out of the office. We're halfway across the room when the door opens. A young woman enters. She wears a tarty little black dress over black stockings and strappy high heels. Seems the Bürgermeister likes a hot breakfast.

I jettison the mayor and pounce the chick like a gorilla attacking a banana salesman. I clamp my hand across her yapper and pin her against the wall. I whip out my pistol and hiss, "*Stille!*" *Be still!*

The tart whimpers, then shuts up when I press Li'l Bertha's barrel against her cheek. Hot breath from her nostrils rushes over my fingers, and her legs tremble against mine.

Brando says, "Scarlet, don't kill that woman!"

"Darwin, I don't see a lot of options here."

"Hang on; I'll take care of her." Brando comes over and administers a DOSE of Snooze-Fast into Tarty's arm. She's transformed from a stiff statue of terror to a flaccid leaf of boiled spinach in nothing flat. The woman droops forward and slumps to the floor.

"Swell. Now what?" I gripe. "I can't carry them both!"

"You bring the target, and I'll take the woman. She's small."

"Darwin, who's going to check our flanks? Let's leave her."

Brando hikes Sleepy Tart over his shoulders. "No, I think she'll help us make the mayor an offer he can't refuse." My partner heads for the door. "C'mon, let's get outta here."

Fine. I pick up Herr Bürgermeister again and follow Brando down the corridor. The town hall is still silent except for our captives' shoes scraping the floor as we drag them toward the window we snuck in an hour ago.

I open the window and drape my burden across the sill. Then I jump to the alley and get ready. Brando tips Herr Bürgermeister outside and over two hundred pounds of sausage-fed blobbiness whops into my arms and damn near dislocates my shoulders. Hot, stinging pain lances through my Modded elbows and knees.

"You all right?" Brando comms, "That looked like it hurt."

"Yeah, no shit; he's a fuckin' blimp." I lay Bürgerpüdge on the ground, then hold my arms out and waggle my fingers. "C'mon, gimme the fraulein."

Tarty weighs less than I do, and catching her is much easier. My partner drops down to join me and our floppy hostages.

Ground floor: tools, guns, kidnapped Krauts.

I run out front to the street. Our getaway driver waits in his truck, parked a block away. I point my father's watch in his direction and flash the light twice fast, then twice slow. The truck engine starts. I hoof it to the building's rear, passing my partner as he lugs the Bürgertart toward our pickup point. I boost the mayor off the ground and haul him after Brando.

The truck parks next to the town hall, and the driver gets out. He's an antislavery activist named Arvid who delivers milk to supermarkets by day and fugitive slaves to the Circle by night. He also takes advantage of his circuitous delivery routes around Yorkshire to gather intel on German police activity.

Arvid helps us dump our guests into the rear of his truck. We climb in after them, and our driver shuts the doors behind us. Moments later, Arvid reappears in his seat up front and accelerates away from the town hall. As Brando secures Mister and Mistress Mayor, I check my watch.

06:04. Not bad. We'd hoped to make our exit in less than three minutes, but four minutes is acceptable considering what a giant improv we had to pull when that woman snuck in.

Brando tapes balls of cloth into our captives' mouths, then we go sit with Arvid. The truck's cabin is warm and smells like hot coffee. Arvid lifts a plastic mug out of a cup holder and gives it to me. I open the top and take a swig. The coffee burns my throat a little, but the heat feels good. I hand the cup to my partner, who holds it under his nose to let the warmth wash over his face.

We jounce along one of York's insanely narrow streets from Ye Olde Days, our tires brumbling over well-worn cobblestones. Timber-framed houses pass so close on either side that I feel like we're being squeezed out of a tube of toothpaste. The truck zigzags through the old part of town and coasts onto a modern two-lane highway.

Arvid says in German, "You two had better sit on the floor. I've seen lots of police this morning. Best if you're less visible."

We smush ourselves onto the cab floor. We'll have to ignore my whole not-too-intimate-with-each-other thing. I park myself between Brando's legs and lean into his chest while he wraps one arm around my waist to keep me from sliding around. Now all I can see are Arvid's feet on the truck's pedals, the man's hands on the wheel, and part of his face.

"So, Arvid," I ask, "what brings you to this kind of thing?"

He says, "My mother was in television before the war.

When the Nazis came to power, all of her Jewish colleagues were fired. After Hitler was assassinated and the Social Democrats were reelected, she assumed her Jewish friends' jobs and civil rights would be reinstated. When they were not, my mother began working to help the Jews escape from Europe. She was caught in 1946, but by then she had helped many people run away."

Arvid holds his hand up, palm facing out. "Shh," he whispers. We hear a line of heavy vehicles motoring the other way, toward York. Arvid's eyes flit between the road ahead and the passing convoy.

"Ten trucks full of soldiers, plus two trucks towing artillery pieces," he says, mostly to himself.

I whisper to Brando, "Artillery? Who's that for?"

He pauses, then quietly says, "Us."

Shit. My upgrades won't help me steer clear of fucking artillery shells. We're agents, not soldiers. I try to distract myself by asking our driver, "What happened to your mother?"

Arvid's face darkens. "*Die Teutsch* took her to Berlin and chopped her head off."

CORE   HIS-NAZI-021

Legacy of the Nazi Party

The Nazi Party had hordes of members installed as civil servants, policemen, and military commanders when it was effectively dissolved by Hitler's assassination in 1942. Although they removed their swastikas, many of these men and women retained the twisted worldview of their deceased Führer. Several Nazi agencies live on, albeit with modified charters and leadership.

Abwehr

Although not a Nazi agency, the Abwehr (German for "Defense") was heavily engaged by Hitler's command to collect and interpret intelligence. The Abwehr's performance was at times inconsistent.

In June 1940, two glaring Abwehr breakdowns occurred within hours of each other. First the agency filed an analysis that wildly overestimated the USSR's preparedness to withstand a German invasion. Their next report to Hitler is so inaccurate, it appears to be a complete fabrication of Great Britain's supposedly advanced progress toward developing an atomic weapon.

Spurious or not, the historical impact of these reports was significant. Hitler was shocked that "the gangster" Churchill might soon have the Bomb, and he dedicated all of Germany's resources to the successful invasion of England the following year.

To this end the Abwehr provided sterling assistance. The agency's director, Admiral Wilhelm Canaris, personally convinced Spain's President Franco to grant German troops access to Spanish facilities for their attack on the British naval base at Gibraltar. Thus began the Axis's eventual domination of the Mediterranean theater, a critical step on Hitler's path to London.

Today, the Abwehr continues to provide top-tier information and analysis.

SZ

Today's SZ is a direct descendant of the sociopathic SS. After Hitler's death, the SS were given a choice: manage Greater Germany's new institutionalized slavery system or be disbanded for "reckless depreciation of the principles of the Fatherland." The SS generals accepted their reassignment and rebranded their army as the Staatszeiger, or "State's Hand." This new name did little to curb their behavior, and their human rights record is nearly as stained as the original SS.

Purity League

Antidiscrimination activists have been alarmed by the recent resurgence of the Purity League. Members of this civilian group spout racist propaganda and dress in brown uniforms as an homage to Nazism's early days. Violence seems to follow wherever they go, and they are notorious for bringing their children to their demonstrations.

Gestapo

The most feared organization in Europe is the Geheime Staatspolizei, which has survived the passing decades almost unchanged. The Gestapo maintains an iron grip on German society through a combination of disinformation and terror. Even Reich officials are afraid of them and their hoarded secrets. It is said every shadow in Germany hides a Gestapo man.

09

SAME MORNING, 9:15 A.M. GMT
CIRCLE OF ZION CAMP, YORKSHIRE,
PROVINCE OF GREAT BRITAIN, GG

I'll give the Bürgermeister one thing—he doesn't faze easily. Despite being snatched from his office, drugged, hog-tied, tossed in a truck, and delivered to a hostile camp full of rebel slaves, he wakes with stoic dignity. The first thing he said when Brando's knockout formula wore off was, "*Gute Morgen*, could I trouble you for some water, please?"

His girlfriend is another story. Even though she got the same dose of sleepy-time as Karl, Tarty has taken longer to come around. When she does, she totally freaks. Her eyes bulge out of her head, and she hides behind her boyfriend, shouts curses, and sobs into the mayor's shoulder.

"Darwin," I comm. "They're awake."

"Be right there."

While we waited for our guests to rise and shine, Brando took their IDs and sent a report to ExOps in Washington. This took him a few minutes. He has to prerecord his reports, encrypt them, and then compress the living shit out of them so his transmissions are as brief as possible. This minimizes the Germans' chances of finding his long-range comm-signal with their radio trackers.

Fraulein Tart is still carrying on when Brando and Miriam walk into the tent. My partner brings his X-bag and a folding chair. He unfolds the chair in front of our two captives.

Miriam sits down, glares at the mayor's girlfriend, and barks, "Isabel, enough! Stop crying or we'll give you another shot. Stay calm like Karl here." Being addressed by her name helps Tartface—I mean Isabel—regain some composure. She pipes down and huddles next to Mayor Karl.

Miriam says, "Herr Bürgermeister, you see that you and your . . . secretary are unharmed?"

Mayor Karl calmly answers, "I see you are runaways, and you shall be dealt with accordingly."

"We have no desire to hurt you, *mein Herr*," Miriam says. "We only want you to help us restore Germany's honor."

"And how," he replies, "would you have me do that?"

If the mayor had flatly refused, we would have switched to plan B, where we try to ransom him for the Circle members caught in last night's roundup. But he has not refused, not yet, anyway. Miriam proceeds with our original plan to turn Mayor Karl to an agent in place, working for us from inside the German bureaucracy.

Miriam holds her hand out to Brando, who gives her a sheet of paper. "Release the people on this list for lack of evidence."

Karl takes the list from Miriam and reads through it. After a minute he says, "What about Isabel?"

"She will be returned to you tomorrow morning, after our friends have returned to us."

"I cannot vouch for the physical condition of your comrades," Karl says. "The Gestapo has had them for hours."

"All the more reason for a prompt decision on your part, *mein Herr*."

"I want your word you will not harm Isabel."

Miriam's face flushes. "You won't get my word on ANYTHING, *Teutsch*!" She seethes. "I want my people back without a battalion of troops following them. Your cooperation will be rewarded by Isabel's safe return."

"Releasing these prisoners is one thing, but I have no authority over the army." Karl spreads his hands. "And how would that appear? I am a civilian. I cannot directly meddle in military affairs if you expect me to be useful to you."

Miriam warily regards the mayor's face. "Are you saying you will join us?"

Karl the Bürgermeister rubs his nose and glances at me. "Let's say I hope to avoid further encounters like this one."

CORE   MIS-ANGEL-128

DATE: January 4, 1981
TO: Director Chanez, Extreme Operations Division
FROM: Task Force Zion
SUBJECT: Bürgermeister Karl Brun, Classification Level 14.

Dear Sir,

Attached please find my file on Herr Karl Brun, mayor of York. I will summarize their contents for your convenience.

No one in Brun's immediate or extended family has ever owned slaves, nor do they socialize with slave-owning families. The man is quite discreet about his views on this topic, unlike his fellow officials, who openly vocalize their support for slavery. When pressed for his thoughts on the matter, the mayor becomes evasive and changes the subject.

I believe Herr Brun is secretly sympathetic to the German abolitionist cause and is worth pursuing as a potential asset for Operation ANGEL.

Sincerely,
Special Agent Barney Frank, CIA

10

Next morning, Wednesday, February 4,
1:30 a.m. GMT
Circle of Zion camp, Yorkshire,
Province of Great Britain, GG

Alix!

I startle awake to a thumping heart and a sweaty sleeping bag. I wipe perspiration off my forehead, activate my night vision, and inspect the tent I share with Brando.

He's asleep next to me. I almost made a boneheaded move last week when we pitched camp here. I was about to zip our sleeping bags together when I remembered this Patrick and I aren't all snuggly. It's like that the first time we do most anything. I'm so used to doing it all with Trick.

It's worse now that we're in the field together. When we're awake, there are clues to help me remember he's Brando and not Trick, like how we aren't physically affectionate or how he forgets to let me win at cribbage. He also wears more black clothing than Trick used to. But when Brando is asleep, those hints go away. He even sleeps with his mouth half open exactly like Trick did. Every night I have to resist the urge to caress his cheek.

Our tent is waterproof and insulated, but we still need to sleep in our long underwear, socks, and oversized sweatshirts. I wriggle out of my sleeping bag, then crawl outside under our camouflage netting and carefully arranged tree branches. A lungful of frosty night air helps clear my head. It's pitch black, of course. Even if the rebels had electricity, they'd stay dark at night to make themselves harder to find.

The Circle's members avoid detection by being thoroughly decentralized. This policy even manifests itself in how they organize a camp. Rather than clump together, they spread out all over the woods. My built-in heat sensors show nothing but silent trees and frozen sky, yet there are three hundred sleeping people hidden within a quarter mile of where I'm standing. All of them have been granted shelter by the Rabbi.

As leaders go, the Rabbi doesn't cut a particularly heroic figure. A charitable description would be "undertall and overwide," although he can shake a leg when there's a job to be done. No matter how dangerous or gruesome, he's the first one in and the last one out.

The man says he's on a diet, but when someone brings a deer into camp, he helps himself to seconds until there's nothing left. He punctuates his stories with his deep, expansive laugh, and everyone here clearly adores him.

Part of our mission is to assess what the Rabbi can accomplish. His cell is effective, but their influence is limited to Yorkshire. A full-scale uprising will need a leader with an abundantly broader reach.

One such hombre is former Wehrmacht colonel Victor Eisenberg, known as the Hammer, who seems to operate all over the Reich. According to the Rabbi, only Eisenberg has the military training, practical experience, and underground connections to lead a real rebellion against Germany's slavery system.

Another person of interest is Johannes Kruppe, a despicable former Staatszeiger colonel. Kruppe is retired now, but his repression of Europe's Jews continues through his membership in the Purity League. The Rabbi told us Kruppe is one nasty mofo. When I replied that Kruppe ain't met nasty until he's met me, the Rabbi cautioned us not to take him lightly.

The Kruppe family is old and wealthy and has extensive influence with the government, including the Gestapo. The Rabbi heard that Johannes had himself surgically upgraded with Mods like the ones Levels have—extremely rare for a civilian—and that the man retains a team of Protectors as bodyguards.

Our mission directives include hoovering up any information we find about either of these men. My partner commed the intel about Kruppe to HQ the moment he heard it. Brando's Info Coordinator, Bill Harbaugh, laconically responded: "Data received, nice work." But from Harbaugh that's like a flying end-zone chest bump.

I'm about to go inside when my heat sensors spot something warm. The heat source is too far away to make out a distinct shape, but since I don't hear an engine, it's safe to assume it's a deer. I shift my focus, then snap my eyes back. Still there. Must be a deer.

Or . . . is that a person?

I scamper into the tent and poke Brando awake. "Darwin, wake up. I think someone's coming into camp." His eyes open, and he shimmies out of his sleeping bag. I strap on my holster and stuff Li'l Bertha inside. We pull on our outer layers and whip outside. The heat source is closer, nine hundred yards or so. I indicate the approaching figure's direction while Brando puts on his vision-enhancement goggles. The person-shaped heat silhouette continues surging straight at us.

"What do you think?" I comm.

"The timing is right for it to be someone from York."

I crank up my hearing and detect the *whup-whup* of an approaching helicopter. The chopped-air sound grows louder. And louder.

Make that a bunch of helicopters.

11

"Rabbi, this is Scarlet. Come in." Among the equipment we've smuggled in and distributed are walkie-talkies with built-in hand-cranked chargers. We gave some to the Rabbi and showed him how to tune them to our comm-frequency. They're only effective at short range, but they're perfect for this type of situation.

The heat blob is four hundred yards away, but it's so dark that he or she can't see us. I take a few steps away from Brando and aim my father's watch toward our guest. I flash the watch face's light twice slow, then twice fast. The blob picks up speed.

My commphone activates. "This is Rabbi. Go ahead, Scarlet."

"Sir, I have eyes on an unknown person inbound, and I hear helicopters."

"Can you tell if they're coming here?"

"Affirmative."

He broadcasts to the other walkie-talkies. "Attention, fellow mice. The cat is returning in force. Disperse and we will regroup via our usual channels."

Time to vamoose. Brando kicks the shrubbery away from our tent while I toss our bedrolls and backpacks out. I roll up the sleeping bags as my partner collapses the tent and folds it down. Our ExOps trainers insisted we be able to bug out of a bivouac in less than one minute. To accomplish this we keep our backpacks ready to go at all times. Anything we take out of the pack goes right back in when we're done with it. All we have to do is strike the tent, bundle the sleeping bags, and disappear.

While my partner finishes getting us ready to leave, I run toward the incoming person. My vision Mods indicate something metallic, but it doesn't fit the profile of a weapon. Then I realize—it's a bicycle. The helicopters' racket is so loud that I can safely yell, "Hey, over here!"

The cyclist calls out, "Rabbi?"

"No, he's busy." I pull out Li'l Bertha and aim at the stranger. "Who goes there?"

The figure pedals toward me and stops. My night vision reveals the perspiring face of a young blond-haired woman. "You are the American?" She speaks with the same German-British accent as Miriam.

"Yeah, that's me."

She breathlessly asks, "I must be sure. How many home runs did Babe Ruth win?"

"How the fuck should I know?"

"Well, okay," she pants. "I suppose only an American would answer in that manner." She shakes her hair off her face. "I am Greta, a friend of Arvid's. I live not far from here. The Gestapo down in York forced Mayor Brun to help them discover his abductors' location."

Damn.

"Did Arvid say how many troops are coming?"

"He said five helicopters from York took off in this direction." Greta leans over her handlebars, huffing and puffing. "He was not able to see what the helicopters carry."

"Darwin, Rabbi," I comm. "Five birds incoming, contents unknown."

Brando comms, "Roger that." The Rabbi doesn't answer. Hopefully he's already gone.

I say, "Thanks, Greta. You'd better clear out."

Without another word, Greta spins her bike around and pedals away.

I hustle to my partner. "Darwin, how we doin'?"

"The Rabbi's people are mostly away. We're packed, but we have the element of surprise and I have an idea."

"Surprise? The Krauts found *us*, remember?"

"Not exactly," he says. "The Germans think they've found a camp of lightly armed escapees."

"Right, 'cause that's what they *have* found."

"They don't know about you."

Goose bumps dance onto my arms. "You want me to F.U.C.K. 'em up?"

Brando recites a line from our orders. " 'You shall create a chaotic and confused situation at every opportunity.' "

Story of my life.

"Wait a second," I say. "This is gonna have 'Level' written all over it. Won't that blow our cover?"

"I'll ask ExOps to fake some comms implicating the Russkies."

Ahh, Mother Russia. Is there anything we can't blame on you?

"Okay, then." I rub my hands together. "Let's do this."

The choppers swoop over our heads. Those helicopters are our main target. Our challenge will be to wreck the machines and harm as few of the Wehrmacht troops as we can. The German press and public will eventually forgive antislavery fighters—Russian or otherwise—for destroying some pieces of war equipment. But if we kill any of these regular army dudes, it'll be a very different story.

Spotlit trees writhe in the thrumming air as the pilots hunt for a place to set down. They find a clearing about a hundred yards north of our position. I dose a tall drink of Madrenaline and speed toward their intended landing zone.

The first chopper and I arrive at the same time. Airmobile troops pour from the aircraft and make for the tree line. A second helicopter floats down next to the first. More troops spill out, some before the skids even touch the ground. Officers bellow commands to their men and lead them to cover.

I sneak behind the first helicopter, taking care to avoid

the tail rotor. The second aircraft is off to the left, so I run to this chopper's right-side pilot's door, rip it open, and punch the pilot square in his jabber hole. Then I open his safety harness and drag him out by his head. Li'l Bertha precedes me into the helicopter and riddles the control board with .30-caliber Explosives. This bird ain't goin' nowhere.

I jab my pistol at the remaining pilot and blare, *"Raus! Schnell, mutterfinken!" Get out, motherfucker!*

Pilot Schmidt—his name is printed on his coveralls—frantically unbuckles his harness. The man throws himself out the door and runs for it.

I chase him across the small clearing. Schmidt makes it to the second chopper. The pilots gun the engine as I hurl myself into the big side opening. The craft's floor slaps my chest and the ground drops away beneath us. After a few seconds my dangling feet find the landing skid. I push off and crawl inside.

Herr Schmidt has seen more than enough of me and cowers in terror by the other main door. Up front, the pilot on the right draws his sidearm. Li'l Bertha sights in. One of her .45-caliber slugs carries away Pilot Right's pistol, pieces of his hand, and all of his moxie. The schmuck howls while his injured arm squirts blood all over the control panel and windscreen.

I leap forward, clench another knuckle sandwich together, and smash it into Pilot Left's face. While he drifts off to lagerland, I sit on his lap and take the controls. I'm no expert at flying helicopters, but I've been taught the basics. My right hand clutches the cyclic stick, and my left hand twists the throttle to zero and rams the collective controller down.

Oh, jeez, that may have been a little heavy-handed.

The ground rushes up and smashes into the aircraft. Our thunderous impact sets off a chorus of warning lights, wailing sirens, and the screeching drumbeat of metal grinding itself into scrap. The main rotor blades snap off, and without their wind resistance the engine spins like a Tasmanian dreidel.

Schmidt bails out again and staggers toward the woods. I unbuckle the pilots and shove them out their doors. Then I jump out.

"Darwin, we good?"

"Fantastic. The clearing can't hold more than two choppers at once, so the other three can't land to help."

I have Li'l Bertha unload a volley of Incendiaries into the two disabled aircraft. Flames gush from their interiors. I haul ass back to Brando and our stuff. He straps on his gear, I shoulder my bag, and we melt into the shadowy woods. When we're a safe distance away, we stop to watch my handiwork. Two fiery blasts sharply silhouette the German troops as their rides explode in their faces.

If I'd been a Girl Scout, their slogan would have been: "Take only pictures, leave only blazing helicopters."

CORE   MIS-ANGEL-212

TO: Office of the President of the United States
FROM: Office of the Executive Intelligence Chairman
SUBJECT: **Popular opinion of the Gestapo within GG**

Dear Mr. President,

As requested, we discreetly polled a representative selection of Greater German citizens about their notorious secret police. In brief, it is the most loathed organization in Europe.

One of the few Nazi holdovers, the Geheime Staatspolizei has maintained Nazism's dark traditions of bigotry and terror-mongering. Citizens labeled as dissidents are abducted by Gestapo officers to "protect the Reich from social weakness." Most Germans are appalled, frightened, and frustrated that ". . . our advanced society acts this way." It can be fairly said no German in their right mind welcomes a visit from the paranoid and violently unpredictable Gestapo.

We conclude that officers of the Geheime Staatspolizei should be considered "fair game" during Operation ANGEL. Germany's current antislavery sentiment will be immune to the fate of these sadists. No one will miss them but their mothers.

Yours,
George H. W. Bush, XIC

12

We lurk in the shadows like a pack of coyotes, eyes beaming, and peer up the street at Gestapo headquarters. Our hiding place—a dank unlit alley—is just a couple blocks from the town hall, where Brando and I snatched Mayor Brun two days ago. Now we're here to liberate the forty or fifty victims of last night's roundups. Ironically, one of the victims is Mayor Brun.

York is small. It occupies less ground than Washington's National Mall. The ancient city center is a charmingly disorganized heap of old houses and cobblestones dominated by a towering cathedral called the Minster. Despite its diminutive scale, York is still the biggest pile of bricks this far north of London. This is why the Germans, like the English before them, use it as a base for controlling upper England and Scotland.

Before the war, the town hall was one of the few official buildings here. Then the Reich converted what seems like half of York into government offices. Those Teutons love their bureaucracies.

The Gestapo moved into a long, low rectangle of stone that used to be a fine arts academy. The first two floors are original and fit in with the street's Olde England vibe. The top three floors were obviously added much more recently by some blind, piss-drunk bureaucrat with absolutely no sense of style.

Gestapo HQ is the most feared building in the region. Streetlights strike the facade at odd angles and obscure its shape instead of revealing it. A razor-wire-topped fence circles the property, but its purpose is to keep prisoners from getting out. Nobody tries to break *into* this place.

Our mission brief practically begged us to use "unlimited force" against the Gestapo officers inside. Apparently the secret police are so reviled—even by Greater German citizens—that the suit-and-ties back home aren't worried about us turning popular opinion against the Rising by liquidating as many Gestapo creeps as we can.

A puff of wind shoves tiny icicles into my eyes. Behind me, a voice whispers, "Shit, I'm fucking freezing." It's Jade, the other Level on this job. She presses against her Info Operator, a quiet, thin, brown-haired twenty-two-year-old named Pericles.

Even though Jade is a bit older than me, I'm senior to her since I graduated from Camp A-Go-Go before she did. At Level 5, she's also four Levels junior to me, but that doesn't matter too much tonight as our assignments are so different. Jade and Pericles's job is to conduct good guys to safety, while Brando and I are here to ferry bad guys to the Great Beyond. Jade's an Interceptor like me, but her Skill Ratings lean toward sneakier missions, more like an Infiltrator. This contrasts with my Skill Ratings, which skew toward the bada-boom things a Vindicator does.

Brando and I met Jade and Pericles earlier this afternoon. My partner and I spent the day in Arvid's dairy truck, riding along as he did his deliveries. He returned to Milk Central at lunchtime to retrieve the second Interceptor-IO team. I have no idea how they were transported to Yorkshire, and if I asked them, they wouldn't tell me. We compartmentalize our contacts and sources in case any of us are captured by the Fritzes. The rest of our information, however, is all shareable. Brando and Pericles spent the ride to York syncing their intel. They looked so serious that I suggested they do a Vulcan mind-meld. Jade laughed, held her fingers in a V shape, and said, "Live long in jodhpurs."

While the boys transferred their mungobytes of data, Jade and I compared our gear. Her sidearm is the reliable .30-caliber Lion Ballistics LB-502. We've got a lot of the same Mods and Enhances, except for our defensive setups. I'm protected by my reinforced skeleton, and I use Madrenaline to help me evade enemy gunfire.

Jade doesn't need any of that. She's equipped with an amazing radar system called Vapor. The Vapor Mod senses incoming objects and zaps instructions to her muscles to slip her body out of harm's way. Vapor makes Jade almost impossible to hit, which plays into her stealthier mission style.

At 5'8" Jade is four inches taller than me, so she's a faster runner, and her hand-to-hand skill rating is better than mine. My acrobatics rating blows hers away, but to be fair, it blows everyone's away; I was on the Olympic gymnastics team when ExOps recruited me.

There's no Skill Rating for looks, but the girl is gorgeous. She has lush hair, porcelain skin, and ice-blue irises set in almond-shaped eyes with very long lashes. And that's only from the neck up. The rest of her is equally hubba-hubba.

This isn't a beauty contest, though, so the fact that she's better-looking than me is irrelevant. Not that I'm *bad*-looking. Honestly, a man who's shorter or younger than Jade might ask me out first. Especially a man who's both. Like my partner, y'know, just for example, could choose to walk right around her and grab little ol' me.

Hypothetically speaking, of course.

Some ultra-attractive women don't bother with personalities, but Jade is an exception. She has a good sense of humor and is *très* cool even though she wigged out when I showed her Li'l Bertha.

"HOLY SHIT! What are you doing with a 505?"

I shrugged, like, *aw shucks*, but she pressed me on how I'd acquired such an advanced weapon. By then, Arvid had delivered us to our sparsely furnished safe house in Haxby. I looked around the room conspiratorially. Brando and Pericles were engrossed in a game of chess on Pericles's magnetic travel set.

I leaned in close to her. "Can you keep a secret?"

Jade slyly peeked over both shoulders and nodded her head.

"She used to be my Dad's."

"You have Big Bertha's pistol?"

"Wait," I said. "How do you know about him?"

"Scarlet, every kid at camp knew about your father."

"You went to the one in Maryland?" I asked.

Jade looked at me like she thought I was kidding, then saw I was serious. "Scarlet, I was there with you," she said. "We used to call you A-J, remember?"

Wow. I'd forgotten some of the kids at AGOGE used to call me that. One of our teachers was a stuffy and proper old gentledoof who called attendance with his students' full names. He'd bellow, "Miss Alixandra Janina Nico!" and I'd raise my hand. To spite him we used really short nicknames with each other, like A-J.

I couldn't remember being in class with Jade, but she didn't seem put off by my absentmindedness. She was a little starstruck by my reputation and dazzled by my amazing gun. I resisted telling her how Dad woke up his pistol's AI and turned Li'l Bertha into the world's first sentient firearm. I'm not supposed to have this insane weapon in the first place and don't need Jade bugging Cyrus about why her sidearm isn't a smart gun, too.

Then it was my turn to gush. I'd been instantly envious of Jade's Vapor Mod. The Med-Techs began offering it right after ExOps had my skeleton plated, and Cyrus refused to let me undo the plating so I could have the radar grid installed instead. They can't be combined because the Vapor system requires the user to be as lightweight as possible. He also pointed out it wouldn't protect me from explosions or long falls like my standard defensive Mods can.

But I was still fascinated by Vapor, and I got Jade to let me check it out. I stood directly in front of the girl and tried to smack her, anywhere. Nothing. Not one hit. She dodged everything I threw at her. I even bull-rushed her, but Jade easily sidestepped me, and I bashed into a rickety old table full of expensive spy crap.

All this commotion finally distracted the boys from their chess match. We huddled together on the floor and wolfed down dinners from unheated ration tins and went over our options. I forget who mentioned it first, but from this conversation came the fabulous idea of pulling a daring rescue mission at Gestapo headquarters.

CORE   MIS-ANGEL-1030

TO: Office of the President of the United States
FROM: Office of the Front Desk, German Section
SUBJECT: **Gestapo and SZ atrocities**

Mr. President,

As you know, my agency has requested your authorization to employ unlimited force against the Geheime Staatspolizei and the Staatszeiger. Director Chanez has asked me to supplement our request with anecdotal evidence to aid you in your decision.

The following events all happened in the last twelve months.

• In Amsterdam a young couple was discovered harboring escaped Jewish slaves. Gestapo agents entered their house and removed the runaways. The secret policemen then nailed the young couple to their kitchen floor and burned their house down around them.

• A group of partisans was captured after bombing an SZ general's motorcade in Paris. The Staatszeiger rounded up each prisoner's family and forced them to watch as a firing squad systematically machine-gunned every partisan into a mass grave.

• An Italian family of seven was arrested by the Gestapo when they were betrayed by a neighbor for smuggling food to Jewish slaves in hiding. The entire family was liquidated, and the gold fillings in their teeth were used to plate the local Gestapo chief's office doorknob.

• In Derby, Ireland, a family of Jews living as Christians was betrayed to the Gestapo. The children were removed and sold in London. The parents' limbs were tied to the bumpers of two trucks, and when the trucks drove off in opposite directions, their bodies were torn to pieces.

As you have no doubt read in other reports, a large proportion of the Reich's population is aghast at such incidents. Please feel free to contact me if you require further details or clarification.

Cyrus El-Sarim
Front Desk, German Section

13

Six young men play basketball on the frigid cobblestones. One team of three has blond ponytails, while the other team has short buzz cuts. A ponytail sinks a bank shot for two points. The ball leaves a red smear on the backboard. The buzzes inbound, but one of them misses the pass, and the ball rolls toward me and stops at my feet.

It's a human head.

The head winks and whispers—

"Scarlet!"

The gruesome basketball game fades into foggy wisps that float away down the murky street.

"Scarlet, what's wrong?" Brando asks. His brow is knitted in concern.

I rub my forehead to clear my vision. "Nothing; I'm fine." I shiver, but not because of the cold.

My partner's mouth pulls to one side. *Bullshit.* He stares at me evenly.

"Okay, okay," I say. "Yes, it was another spell. But I'm fine!"

"Hmm . . . well, get ready." To Jade and Pericles he whispers, "Here they come." Brando has been keeping watch with his millimeter-wave radar scanner in one hand and his starlight scope in the other.

We're across the street from a hardware store, which is next to Gestapo headquarters. Jade closes her eyes. Her expression reveals intense concentration. Her nostrils flare as she psyches herself up. She opens her eyes.

I comm, "Ready, Jadey?"

"Ready, A-J."

Jade and I attach silencers to our pistols. A convoy of black cars and paddy wagons drives past our alley. Their tires rumble over the cobblestones before they fade into Yorkshire's black fog. As senior Level, my place is on point, so I move out first. My partner is in my hip pocket as we scuttle across the street. Pericles is behind him with Jade holding the rear. Our little murder club skitters behind the hardware store and approaches the Gestapo building's ominous, somber exterior.

My partner and I both spot them. Two guards on the roof, surveying the street.

Brando comms, "Two targets, straight ahead, high."

"Sneaky or shooty?" I ask.

"If they see us, our mission's difficulty will go up to insane."

Shooty, then.

I comm to Jade, "You take the one on the right."

She nods and readies her LB-502. I set Li'l Bertha to match Jade's .30-caliber ordnance and take aim.

"Now."

Our slugs spit into the night and drill through the guards' heads. The wind swallows the thuds of their toppling bodies. We wait a few seconds, then advance to the ten-foot-high chain-link fence surrounding our objective. Razor wire coils nastily all along the top. A metal sign on the fence shows a flailing person getting fried by a flock of lightning bolts.

We scan the area beyond the fence with night vision, infrared, and radar. All clear. The only remaining guards are at the front entrance. Here in the back it's five grim tiers of bricked-up windows complemented by a lonely fenced-off slab of cracked concrete.

Jade and Pericles are going in first. Part of their assignment is to knock out the generator that electrifies this perimeter, which means they've gotta bounce over it. Their ingenious execution of this move impresses the hell out of me.

First, Jade faces the fence and gets down on one knee. Next, Pericles grabs her hands and climbs onto her shoulders. The two of them squat, so they're like a little stack of coiled springs. They simultaneously thrust their legs and Pericles catapults over the fence. Finally, Jade scrunches down and hurls herself over to join him.

The way I've always done this stunt is to grab my partner and jump us over together. It's absolute hell on my knees.

I lean toward Brando and raise my eyebrows. "Yoink."

"Definite yoink," he replies, equally inspired.

Jade and her partner cross the barren yard to a padlocked bulkhead. According to our hand-drawn map, that hatchway leads to the basement where prisoners are kept. The map is from one of our Circle of Zion contacts. He worked here as a clerk before being dismissed for "unpatriotic tendencies." This could mean he did anything from pissing off a panzer general to picking his nose in public. Not a lot of wiggle room in the Reich.

"We're in," Pericles comms. I check my watch. Less than a minute. He's quick with a pick.

Brando reaches into his X-bag and pulls out a compact set of bolt cutters. He extends the folding handles and locks them in place.

Jade comms, "Here we go." The floodlights blink off, replaced moments later by dim battery-powered emergency lamps. The men out front call to each other, basically saying, "What the fuck?"

Brando chomps his bolt cutters through the fence's links. He makes a tall slash that we pull open and pass through. I keep Li'l Bertha ready to repel inquisitive guards, but so far we still haven't been detected.

A creak emanates from the shadows. Li'l Bertha swings over. The bulkhead door has flopped open. Pericles pops out and leads a long line of people to Brando's hole in the fence. One noticeably rotund figure is Karl Brun, former mayor of York. Finally the last person exits, closely followed by Jade.

She comms, "All captives away." Jade tips her head toward the darkened building. "We took out the guards downstairs. You wouldn't believe what they did to some of these people." She follows the escaping prisoners. "The ground floor is empty, but we saw a lot of heat sigs on the upper floors."

"You mean a lot of dead men."

Jade winks. "Fuck 'em up, A-J." Then she wheels away and disappears through the fence.

I face the bulkhead. My mind flashes with gruesome images of Gestapo atrocities while Brando tucks in behind me and gives my shoulder a squeeze. I grit my teeth.

It's magic time.

CORE   MIS-ANGEL-1388

TO: Office of the Executive Intelligence Chairman
FROM: Office of the Ambassador, London, England, Greater Germany
SUBJECT: Operation ANGEL progress report

Dear Chairman Bush,

I am pleased to report our agents are generating considerable discord for the Greater German authorities. I think it's only a matter of time until the Reich asks for our assistance with the Jewish slave uprising, but we may find our plan to help extinguish this rebellion has a problem.

As expected, there has been a marked increase in official acts of retaliation. One event from Wales deserves particular mention:

Last week a German Army platoon raided a rebel camp in the forest outside Moulton, near Cardiff. It was a disaster for the German attackers thanks to the extra firepower provided by one of our Vindicator Levels. No rebels were captured while four German vehicles were destroyed and a dozen Wehrmacht soldiers injured.

Next morning, the regional Staatszeiger commander sent a battalion of his men to Moulton with orders to sweep the town clean. Any resistance was met with immediate incarceration.

An elderly woman who loudly voiced her disapproval was beaten by SZ troops. Townsmen who tried to intervene were shot. Women and children who ran to their aid or fled for their lives were also shot. The youngest victim was only four years old. Amateur photographs of this tragic event were anonymously sent to our embassy and are included for your reference. These images were also sent to every news outlet in Britain. They were strictly repressed, naturally, but the Circle of Zion published the pictures in their underground newspaper.

I fear reprisals such as these will make it impossible for us to reverse public support for the rebellion. I'm beginning to doubt we can stop what we have started.

Your humble servant,
John J. Louis, Jr., American Consulate, London

14

Gestapo headquarters used to be the Yorkshire School of Fine Arts. The place has been converted from a stately, spacious temple of creativity to a twisted warren of tomblike offices and interrogation chambers. Airy studios are now dark, sterile hollows reeking of cigarettes, stale sweat, and chronic paranoia. The backup lighting provides such dim illumination that I need my infrared to distinguish what's alive in this place from what isn't.

The hallways are lined with dozens of padlocked black filing cabinets. Reich officials are notorious for being fastidious about their records. It's as though they don't want to forget any of the bullshit they've pulled. Gaps in the otherwise solid wall of drawers indicate where we'll find office doors.

Li'l Bertha is clicked into my left hand, and my partner wears his optic-effects goggles. We sneak down the main hall, scanning for heat signatures. Jade was right. There are shimmering orange blobs upstairs, but the first floor is clear. This must be where all the younger field agents are stationed when they aren't out on raids.

The building has two stairways, one at each end of this corridor. Brando opens his X-bag and grabs what appears to be a pudgy tea saucer. It's a proximity mine, one of two we have with us. We sneak forward and soft-shoe up the stairs to the first landing. I lay the mine down and push the red button on the top. The mine's motion sensor will wait until I move away before it arms itself. Brando carries a remote control that'll disarm the mine if we need to move it. He calls it his Mine-O-Matic.

"Okay," I comm. "Now what? Should we do the guards out front or go up the back stairs?"

"Back stairs." He pauses. "We have help out front."

"Is Jade done already?"

"No, she's headed north. This is a late addition . . . and he brought his Bitchgun."

"Raj is here?"

"Yeah." Brando has a glint in his eyes. "Let's secure the rear exit, and he'll nail anyone who comes out the front."

Raj is an ExOps Level 9 Vindicator, and the Bitchgun is his gigantic 50-mm grenade launcher. Last summer he directed the recovery mission to rescue my mother. Then, in October, when I snatched Winter, Raj helped me escape from Riyadh. Being in action together gave us a chance to adapt what had been a nasty, juvenile rivalry into a mutual appreciation society based on our shared enthusiasm for ass kicking.

Brando and I run to the rear stairway and up to the second floor. I register three heat signatures in the first office on the right.

Finally!

I signal to Brando: *We got three.* He nods. I increase my neuroinjector's Madrenaline flow until my scalp twitches. Then I approach the office of warm figures, take a deep breath, and kick in the door with a splintering crash.

The first Gestapo officer is directly in front of me, faintly lit by the red emergency lights. He's yelling into his desktop phone to find out why the power is out. I'm so zooted that I have time to watch his face shift from angered annoyance to confused perplexity. The second expression is what he'll wear into Kraut heaven since it's the last thing he ever does. Li'l Bertha's .30-caliber rounds tear through his chest and neck, knock him out of his chair, and ram him into the wall.

The remaining two agents stand on the other side of the room, their arms crossed, waiting to find out when the electricity will be back on. They gape at the sudden demise of their officemate. I nail extra eyeholes into each of their foreheads. Blood schpritzes across the room and splashes my cheek.

"Scarlet," Brando comms, "there's a guy in the hall-way."

I scoot into the corridor. The dunderhead coming out of his office spots me and screeches something like: *Holy sausages, who's that crazy chick with blood all over her face?* Li'l Bertha spits out a pair of slugs that rip the top of Screechy's head off. It already looks like Dante's Inferno in here, and we've barely begun.

More doors open, toward the front. Four men behold the gore-streaked hallway and realize this power outage is no accident. Three of the bruisers retreat into their offices. One makes a break for it and pitches over as my next shot smashes into his neck.

Now I have three competitors to clear out, each in his own office, two left and one right. Li'l Bertha's infrared sensor labels them as Targets One, Two, and Three. I dive into the first left-side office. Target One is in here, desperately trying to open his gun locker. Instead of greasing him outright, I have Li'l Bertha ding a bullet into his spine. I catch him and hold him in front of me as I return to the hallway.

We approach the second office on the left. My human shield screams in agony and leaves a trail of piss behind us. Inside, Target Two has armed himself and certainly hears us coming, but when his colleague comes through the door first, he holds his fire. Target Two's hesitation earns him a complimentary .30-caliber face-lift.

Brando comms, "Scarlet, that last enemy is coming your way."

I whirl and face the door, my right arm still clutching Target One. Target Three barges in already firing his pistol. I drop to the floor. Target One takes a round in his chest and collapses onto me. I press my feet against a desk and thrust myself out from under his body. I cannon into Target Three's legs and knock him into the hallway. My pistol finishes off my stunned competitor with a blast through his heart.

"Nice call-out, Darwin; thanks." My thumb ejects Li'l Bertha's depleted ammo pack. I pocket the empty, slap in a full pack, and rejoin Brando at the rear stairway. As we begin to move upstairs, a loud *whump* resounds from outside. The steps pulse under our feet, and flakes of plaster drift from the ceiling.

"Raj, you all right out there?" My partner uses our team channel so I can hear it, too.

"All clear, Darwin. The guards at the front entrance heard the commotion and tried to escape. I took them out, but now all of Yorkshire knows something is going on. Hurry up."

"Roger that. Floors one and two are clear. We're moving to three." We resume our ascent, then Brando comms again, "Actually, scratch that, Raj. Since you've engaged anyway, we'll move straight to five. Brace for our competition on the lower floors to be flushed to your position out front. We'll mine the back stairs."

"Roger that, Darwin." Even though Raj and I are both Level 9s, he's senior to me because he entered the field first. But this is *my* mission, so he's expected to follow reasonable direction.

Brando comms just to me, "Raj is right. We don't have much time. You go to the top floor, and I'll set our mines here."

"What about the one we used out front?"

He's already bounding down the steps. "I'll go retrieve it and reset it."

Damn. It feels wrong to separate like this, plus I don't like my partner being so involved with the combat. I curse under my breath and run up the stairs.

Our presence has clearly been noted. My infrared shows me the fifth-floor hall is filled with pistol-packing competitors edging toward the front and rear stairways.

I hear them mumbling into the little commphones plugged into their ears.

The Germans invented commphones almost thirty years ago, so they've had time to develop a lot of different models. Most police forces use the earplug model, like these clowns are using. Military personnel use a helmet-mounted system that's essentially a ruggedized version of what telephone operators wear. High-end field agents like me receive the super-deluxe surgically implanted model.

I wait a few paces below the fifth floor and press myself against the wall. When the closest toughie approaches the corner, I surge upstairs, karate-chop his gun out of his hand, whack Li'l Bertha against his temple, grab his throat, and spin him around so we both face the same direction. Li'l Bertha prods into his ribs. Herr Toughie is a lot taller than me, so I have to stand on tiptoe to see over his shoulder.

I propel my strangling bullet sponge into the hall. There are eleven schmoes in here, all of whom pivot and point their pistols at me.

Toughie croaks, *"Nein! Nicht scheissen!"* *Don't shoot!* His buddies hold their fire and take cover behind filing cabinets and doorways. Gunfire chatters from outside, punctuated by several larger booms that jiggle the floor like Magic Fingers. More plaster falls from the ceiling. Cracks appear in the walls. Raj must be fighting the pinheads trying to escape from floors three and four. I hope Brando is okay.

I snarl in Toughie's ear, "Tell 'em to drop their guns. They won't get hurt." He does what I say. At first nothing happens, so I tighten my grip on his throat and growl, *"Wieder!"* *Again!* An explosion echoes from the back stairway. Brando must have reset his mines. It feels like an entire platoon is attacking instead of just the three of us.

My prisoner repeats himself, but the racket from downstairs is so loud that even I can't hear him. Then one of the younger Gestapo agents takes a shot at me. *So much for prisoners.* I stay behind Herr Toughie while Li'l Bertha blind-fires a long burst of medium-caliber Incendiaries into the crowded corridor.

The hall resonates with the cries of combusting dickazoids and the snarling snaps of disintegrating architecture. The world suddenly tips over a few degrees. I lose my balance and stumble sideways. Herr Toughie sinks to the wobbling floor.

"Darwin, I think this place is coming down. Get up here and grab your intel."

Brando streaks past me and charges into the commandant's office.

I run after him. "Raj! What's going on out there?"

"Scarlet, Darwin, be advised we've inflicted structural damage on the facility."

My partner runs to a blocky steel safe in the corner.

"Hey," I comm, "whaddaya mean *we*, Rah-Rah?"

"Well," Raj answers, "maybe I meant *I*, but either way it's—"

The shaking floor plunges a foot, dropping right out from under us. Everything in the office—including me and my partner—hangs suspended in midair for a split second. Then the office furniture pummels the deck like a metal monsoon. The desks and cabinets gouge the linoleum tile and the safe craters itself into the ground.

Brando squats in front of the half-buried steel box and resumes manipulating the combination dial.

I shout, "Darwin, forget it. Let's get the fuck out of here!"

"Hang on," he yells, "I've almost got it."

Li'l Bertha vibrates in my hand. I glance at her targeting panel in my Eyes-Up display.

Someone's behind me!

I lash out with a reverse roundhouse kick that smacks a Gestapo agent in his stomach. He grunts and falls away. Li'l Bertha perforates the sneaky sucker's knee, thigh, hip, and chest. He corkscrews into the dust-filled hallway. I jump on top of him and crush his larynx with my mechanized right hand. I push off from my dying victim and swing my sidearm around to see who else feels like a hero.

It's a disaster area. Gestapo agents sprawl with multiple injuries from gunshots, burning chemicals, flying debris, a thirteen-foot length of collapsed wall, or in some cases all of the above. The choking air reeks of burned flesh and roasted building. The corridor isn't even square anymore. The ceiling has separated from the wall, and the floor is tipping over on itself.

"DARWIN! Let's go!"

"I'm inside. Gimme a sec!"

I don't think we have a sec.

But he wasn't kidding. It really is only a second later when he zings out of the office, his arms full of file folders and data pods, and hightails it for the front stairs. He disappears into the dust cloud. I take off after him.

The building swings and bounces us from one wall to the other as we sprint down four flights of stairs. We rush outside into the street, closely followed by a hot cloud of smoke as Gestapo HQ collapses into a crumbling heap.

My partner comms, "Raj, hold your fire! We just came out the front."

Raj answers, "Don't worry. I'm engaged up the street. That Gestapo raiding party is trying to return to their headquarters."

"Do you need help?"

"Not if you can exit the area right now."

Brando replies, "We're out and away. Break off now."

"Roger that."

I call over the pandemonium, "Darwin, you go ahead! I have one last thing to do."

"No way! We've—"

"It'll be quick. I'll catch up!"

I run into the dust cloud churning around the ruined headquarters. My infrared leads me to the still-warm bodies of Raj's victims. I yank my F-S fighting knife out of its holster, push one of the dead agents onto his back, and aim my blade at his face.

Something to remember me by.

CORE   MIS-ANGEL-1393

Cyrus,

I snared this signal as it was sent from London to Berlin:

"Gestapo York liquidated. Yorkshire has gone dark. Situation in England degrading rapidly. Send reinforcements and instructions."

I think I can guess which Interceptor you sent there.

Yours,
Grey, Infiltrator

15

Normally, after such an overtly destructive operation, we would spirit ourselves out-country as fast as frickin' possible. But our complete annihilation of York's Gestapo has put the entire territory on full-time lockdown. No movement is allowed anywhere, anytime. Our Circle pals anticipated this and set us up with a terrific hiding place. Terrific so long as we don't move too much, breathe too much, or think too much.

We're hidden in a spacious, well-kept crypt in the Haxby graveyard. Carved letters over the entrance identify this as the Harrington family necrominium. The earliest tenants are from the days when having a horseless carriage meant you could only travel downhill and a common cause of death was receiving medical care from your barber. The clan's matriarch—a staunch abolitionist—relocated the remains of her older, bonier ancestors so their five-star hole in the ground can serve as a honeycomb hideout for us.

Honeycomb is a good word for it, too. We're in the deepest chamber, ensconced in heavy stone caskets. I tried convincing my partner that we could just unroll our sleeping bags on the ground, but he shot me down. Brando admitted the authorities are unlikely to open every grave in England, but he said they might investigate a large burial vault like this one. So here we are, Brando, Raj, and I, buried alive in Yorkshire while the German Army scours the country for us.

Hiding Raj was a challenge. These old body boxes are built to last until Judgment Day, but they're small. People were a lot shorter two or three centuries ago. Raj is

6'5" and weighs over three hundred pounds. We solved this issue by breaking the bottom out of the largest sarcophagus. Then the three of us dug out a space for Raj to lie in and dragged his box over him. Brando and I then got into our own coffins and prepared our stasis feeds.

It's the same kind of stasis feed I was on last year when they packed me into a pine box with Trick's body to ship us out of Zurich. It's a semistasis that drastically slows the subject's heartbeat, breathing, and digestion without stopping them entirely. This state is intravenously induced with a chemical cocktail developed by ExOps's Med-Techs. What little air we need comes from a can of compressed oxygen connected to a face mask.

We'll be here for a week. When we wake up, we'll receive instructions for our next Job Number. Until then our bodies can rest and heal. I came through our mission without a scratch, but both Brando and Raj were wounded during last night's adventure.

Raj was hit by flying stonework from the building. He has nasty bruises on his shoulder and both legs, but he'll be all right. Brando, however, nearly got blown up by one of his mines. He was resetting it when a few baddies charged down to make their escape.

Info Operators don't deploy with a sidearm, so he had to use his Mine-O-Matic to detonate the mine as the Gestapo goons ran over it. The blast took a bite out of everybody, crippling the competitors' legs and lacerating my partner's face.

Brando says his wounds sting like hell, but they aren't too deep, and they should heal just fine. What's not fine is that he'll attract all the wrong kind of attention if he goes out in public with bandages and cuts on his face. Hopefully, he'll mend well enough while we're here that his injuries won't be so noticeable.

I strap on my breathing mask and set sail for the world of pure imagination.

CORE   MIS-ANGEL-1477

DATE: February 4, 1981
TO: The Office of the Front Desk
FROM: Darwin-5055 (IO), Scarlet-A59 (L9 Interceptor),
Raj-A10 (L9 Vindicator)
SUBJECT: Operation ANGEL/Job Number G86

Sir,

We are pleased to report the Gestapo HQ in York has
been destroyed. All captives were retrieved, including the
mayor of York, Herr Brun. I'm sure you will receive an
after-action report from Pericles and Jade, but let me state
here that they executed their assignments with speed and
precision. They were highly competent, and it was a pleasure to work with them.

Per our orders, the devastation wrought upon the German secret police was comprehensive. Scarlet and Raj
together accounted for forty-one Gestapo officers killed.
Raj also inflicted significant structural damage to the facility itself. Scarlet took your "unlimited force" directive to
heart and made a special point of leaving some of our victims in especially grim condition. The details of her actions are difficult to adequately describe in writing and
may need to wait until you debrief us in person. Be assured
the story of this attack will have every German official in
England jumping at shadows for months.

We will check in for new orders when we come out of
hiding.

Obediently yours,
Darwin-5055

16

I'm in the mountain temple, sitting in lotus position and breathing chilled mist deep into my lungs. My blood heats the mist, and when I breathe out again, it floats around me like a warm cocoon, protecting me from the frigid winter night.

The monk in the saffron robe strolls in and lifts me by my hair. It feels strange, but it doesn't hurt. It's like I'm a doll that's been molded into this pose. He carries me outside and casts me off a cliff. I try to maintain my posture, but as my body bounces down the mountainside, I come undone, smash into the river below, and die.

My father appears. He asks if we're in heaven or hell, then hands me a rifle. He walks downrange and stands in front of the target. I fire at him, but he catches the bullets with his fingers and puts them in his pocket. Dad catches the last one in his teeth, spreads his arms, and says, "Tah-dahh!"

I put down the rifle and join a procession of monks climbing a steep mountain path in their bare feet. I'm wearing a saffron robe. When we reach the path's peak, the monks in front walk off the precipice into thin air. They do not fall. I try to hold back because I have not mastered this yet, but the monks behind me press forward and I fall over the edge.

Finally, I realize this is a dream. I stick out my arms like wings and ride the air currents, swooping in wide circles. I coast past the floating monks. When they see what I'm doing, they glance at each other, then at me.

They hold their arms out to fly and plummet to their deaths.

I flap my arms and ascend to the temple. I land on the terrace and walk inside to the main room. The monk in the saffron robe sits in lotus position. He smiles at me. Without parting his lips, he says, "The egg opens, the body dies, but the spirit soars and lives forever."

17

Nine days later, Saturday, February 14,
12:55 p.m. GMT
245 Westbourne Grove, Notting Hill, London,
Province of Great Britain, GG

London is like a ghost town. Martial law has the civilians locked inside their houses, while most of the cops and troops have been sent out to deal with all the chaos we've stirred up. Our Yorkshire insanity bomb is being matched by similar unrest in Wales, Ireland, and especially Scotland. The Scots aren't a surprise. Those maniacs would rebel against gravity if they could find a way to keep their whiskey from floating away.

As the Rising has gained momentum, our job has been made both harder and easier. The crackdown makes it more difficult to move around, but we have many more places to hide. There are a lot of Greater German citizens opposed to slavery, many of whom are willing to help us stamp it out by lending us their homes as safe houses. We even get fed, although I think the three of us are gonna turn into roly-poly sausages. When I asked if these people ever eat vegetables, Raj said that's what all the beer is for.

Even though London's citizens can't go out unless they have a pass, they've had it easy compared to the rest of Britain. During our week in Cryptville, the Circle extricated thousands of Jewish slaves and burned down hundreds of the buildings they worked in. The slave-based industries began grinding to a halt, along with the related businesses that supply the farms and factories, transport their output, and distribute it to markets and stores.

London is mostly offices and shops, so there aren't nearly as many slaves here. The raids, firefights, and bombings sweeping the rest of the country haven't affected the capital too severely.

Until now, that is. It's not like we're here to sell insurance.

Our next Job Number is a good old-fashioned jail break. It's based on intel acquired from our new CIA stringer, Karl Brun. After we spirited Brun away from the Gestapo, he revealed that the Germans had captured one of our persons of interest, Victor Eisenberg.

Herr Eisenberg is the forty-something former Wehrmacht colonel who led a famous raid on the Bergen-Belsen slave labor camp outside Hanover. Eisenberg's commando squad, recruited from his former troops, freed the enslaved workers and torched the facility. This action was the genesis of his reputation as a fearless guerrilla leader, which he cemented by fighting his way south through the heart of Germany and into the Alps. He was dubbed the Hammer of Iron for his hard-hitting tactics and because Eisenberg means "Iron Mountain" in German. The man possesses the military training, leadership skills, and aristocratic family connections that have made him a VIP in what became the Circle of Zion.

Before this, Eisenberg was a decorated Wehrmacht officer with a sterling record built by defending the Fatherland's eastern border from the Great Red Threat. These tours of duty brought him into regular contact with forced labor camps. The inherent cruelty of the Reich's slavery system sickened him, and he silently vowed to eradicate it.

After Eisenberg did his twenty years in the army, he retired and began to write passionate articles about the moral corruption of slavery. Through this he became the de facto spokesman for the fledgling abolitionist movement. Eisenberg's portrait in our job folder shows a handsome face with eyes sparkling with intelligence and determination. His blond swept-back hair has a touch of gray at the temples. The file says he's 5'10", not short but not quite the typical *Übermensch* height of six-foot-whatever.

When the Rising broke out here in Britain, Eisenberg traveled across the English Channel to assist and rally the rebels. Despite Eisenberg's experience as an underground fighter, he was captured by the German police as he crossed over from Holland. The Fritzes planned to ship him to a Berlin prison where he'd have time to reconsider his loyalties.

Then we pulled our Gestapo extermination mission in York, and everything changed. The German government decided to make an example of him and scheduled his execution for March 1, fifteen days from now. This will be soon enough to drive the lesson home while giving the authorities time to assemble a large turnout as a show of force. They also moved Eisenberg from his cozy Kensington jail cell to the Tower of London and surrounded him with SZ troopers.

Our job is to bust him out. It's two weeks until his execution, but we can't risk staying in one place that long. Cyrus's mission brief gives us three days. We can use whatever in-place assets we see fit, and we are again authorized to use unlimited force.

However, today's task requires brains, not brawn. We need to plan how we're gonna break into the Tower, learn where the prisoners are kept, and find out what kind of resistance we can expect. To do that, we need more intel about the ancient fort than we have right now. This is why I'm finally meeting Grey today.

Grey is one of those mysterious Infiltrators we have at ExOps. We've never met even though I've had two adventures because of him. The first was when I swiped his Creep 'n Peep and had to fight my way out of the dictionary's entry for *clusterfuck*. The second was when Trick and I fried a captured competitor to death while Grey broke into the Manhattan offices of the CIA.

We've been told not to bother trying to contact him. Grey will find us. So here we wait, rambunctiously play-

ing cribbage on a coffee table in our Notting Hill safe
house. Brando and I are sharing a bedroom while Raj
goes stag next door. It's been a little awkward rooming
with someone I'm not involved with, but that's the field
protocol for Levels and IOs.

When Raj isn't reading or sleeping, he hangs out with
us. The three of us talk shop, maintain our gear, or play
cards. Moving by night and hiding by day has left us
some time to kill. Raj saw us playing cribbage one afternoon and joined in.

Card games are way more exciting with Raj playing
because he either wins big or goes bust. There's no in
between. After years of playing with Patrick the human
calculator, it's refreshing to play against someone I can
genuinely beat sometimes. During a hand, Rah-Rah
rubs a religious necklace his mother gave him for luck.
When I asked him who the patron saint of card players
is, he said, "Are you kidding? Kenny Rogers!"

There's a rap at the door. Raj lumbers over and peeks
through the peephole while I take Li'l Bertha out of her
holster.

Raj comms, "It's Mr. Christie."

I hold my pistol below the coffee table's edge. Raj
opens the door to reveal the building's ancient yet tireless caretaker. Mr. Christie wheels in a service cart
draped by a white and red striped cloth, loaded with
covered dishes, glasses, and bottles of sparkling water.
We ask for the fizzy stuff so we can have belching con-
tests. Mr. Christie guides the cart inside, and we distribute the goodies all over the table. The old man swivels
his cart around, accepts a tip from Raj, and trundles
away.

I return my sidearm to her holster and tuck into my
chow. Then a dude I've never seen before walks out of
our bathroom. He has dark gray hair and a thin 5'6"
frame. Li'l Bertha leaps into my hand again and aims
at—nothing. A trickle of dust drifts down through her
sights. I look up. The little fucker is stuck to the ceiling

like an insect. The dust has been displaced by his fingers, which have clawed right into the plaster. I shift my aim upward, and—I swear to God—he vanishes.

Don't tell me I'm having a spell, not in front of Raj.

I say, "Raj, do you see this?"

"Affirmative." He draws his sidearm, an LB-503, and swivels his head all over the room.

"Darwin, what the hell is happening?" My partner doesn't answer me. He's still sitting on the couch. Actually it's more like he's rolling on the couch, laughing his ass off. "Relax, guys, it's okay," he comms.

At this point both Raj and I have full doses of Madrenaline pumping through us, so relaxation is out of the question. The gray-haired man appears on the couch right next to Brando. The prowler grabs my sandwich, takes a bite, puts it back, and disappears again.

Now I'm really pissed off. Nobody fucks with me when I'm eating. I override my neuroinjector's normal doses and flood my bloodstream with Madrenaline. My skin feels like it wants to crawl out the window, but I'm as fast as I can be. Time slows down so much that it might as well be standing still. Brando is frozen in the middle of wiping a tear from his eye while he exhales a laugh. Raj isn't completely motionless. He's on Madrenaline, too, so his head gently turns from side to side as he searches for the intruder.

A shadow moves in front of the windows. I spin around and glimpse—barely—the gray-haired man running on the walls with a shit-eating grin on his face. Jesus, this son of a bitch can practically fly! He "disappears" by moving so fast that you can't track him. I anticipate where I think he'll be in a few microseconds and throw myself into Mr. Invisible's path. He bashes into me and wipes us both out. We skid across the floor and knock over a side table. A heavy lamp and a heap of empty beer bottles crash all over us. My G.I. Joe kung-fu grip grabs Mr. Invisible's ankle so hard that I almost rip his foot off. I climb his body until he's pinned to the floor.

"Got . . . you . . . FUCKER!" I bark in his face. My captive doesn't respond because now he's laughing, too. I dose some Kalmers to bring time to normal speed.

Brando stops cackling long enough to say out loud, "Good to meet you, sir. That's Scarlet on top of you, and the big fella over there is Raj." He pauses, then says, "Guys, meet Grey."

CORE   PER-S33-034

Grey
Position: Level 13 Infiltrator
Full Name: Terrence H. Steadman III
Summary: Grey's family has been part of America's clandestine community for three generations. His father and grandfather both graduated from Yale University and worked at the CIA as strategic analysts. Grey followed his seniors to Yale but decided to pursue a more physically active role in America's intelligence apparatus. Rather than apply for a desk job at Central Intelligence, he joined the upstart Extreme Operations Division as a field operative.

Grey's exceptional agility, intelligence, and interpersonal skills make him a perfect Infiltrator. Grey has achieved a Level promotion for every year he has worked at ExOps, a rare feat. Many Levels consider themselves to be doing well if they earn a promotion every twenty to thirty months.

Most of Grey's missions are carried off with little to no violence at all. The quieter his Job Number goes, the more successful he considers himself. He is, of course, still a Level and is entirely capable of executing rapid and lethal attacks as needed.

18

Raj and I dawdle on the little porch outside our room and wait for our doses of Madrenaline to dissipate. Brando kicked us out here when he heard all the colorfully gory threats we blustered at Grey.

I take in a lungful of keen English air. "Fucking douche bag."

Raj grunts, "Yeah. That was a stupid stunt. I'm tempted to report him."

For once I'm glad my bulky teammate is such a stickler for process and procedure. "Why wouldn't you?"

"Grey outranks me," Raj says.

"So what?"

"So we're not allowed to file disciplinary reports on our superiors."

"What?" My voice rises. "Why not?"

"Think about it, Scarlet." My blank expression prompts him to continue. "We could try to accelerate our promotions by clearing senior Levels out of our way." He lets that sink in and then says, "Besides, Grey is one of the best Infiltrators we have." Raj's dark eyes take in the compact streets and leafless trees of Powis Square. "Maybe I'll informally mention it to the Front Desk."

My partner comms, "Scarlet, Raj, if your systems have recovered, why don't you come in so we can review what Grey has for us."

We walk inside. Brando and Grey sit next to each other on the couch. I get a better look at Grey now that he isn't moving so fast. He's older than the rest of us, I'd say around thirty. Part of his speed is an illusion created by the active camouflage system all Infiltrators have. It reflects what's around them and renders them nearly invisible. Grey is also exceptionally lightweight and acrobatic, so his running-on-the-walls trick was real. It just wasn't the only reason we couldn't see him.

Grey says, "Hey, you two, I apologize. I was only spoofing you." He speaks with a fancy-sounding accent, like a combination of Cary Grant and Bobby Kennedy.

"Sir." Raj's tone is tightly clipped. "With all due respect, that stunt didn't reflect well on your rank or your reputation."

I jab my thumb toward Raj. "Yeah, what he said. What were you thinking, playing slap and tickle with Interceptors and Vindicators? You're lucky we didn't tear the entire fucking house apart to nail you."

Brando holds his hands up. "Okay, okay, enough! This is my fault. Grey commed me to say he wanted to make a memorable entrance. We've been under a lot of strain, and I thought it would be funny for him to ride in on Mr. Christie's cart and try to hide in the bathroom. Next time, I'll remember how focused you are on food." This is a knock that two Levels like Raj and me were taken by surprise. Maybe it's a good idea Raj isn't filing a report about this. None of us seem very smart right now.

Raj sits in a chair. "Fine. Point taken."

I grab my defiled sandwich and—senior to me or not—plop it in front of Grey. Then I reach for a fresh one. Our gray-haired guest shrugs as if to say, "It is right and just that I've been stuck with this sullied grub."

We dig into lunch again. Grey talks while we eat. Once he starts rattling off the torrent of information he's collected from all around England, we forget about his stupid entrance.

"The Krauts have been taken entirely by surprise in the north. The smoking crater you left in their intelligence apparatus will require months to fill in with new assets and case officers." He takes a big bite of sandwich and continues as he chews. "That's if they can even acquire new people to work there. I've heard rational men spreading rumors of a Jewish ghost returned from the dead to slake its thirst for German blood. That's probably a result of your knife work, Scarlet. Carving Stars of David into those imbeciles was a nice touch."

Raj raises his brows. He never entered the Gestapo HQ, so he didn't know about that part.

Grey continues. "The unrest in Yorkshire is absorbing a massive number of German troops and police, most of them from London. This has created an interesting opportunity for us." Grey comms us a set of files. I open mine in my Eyes-Up display. A map of London superimposes itself over my view of the room. The map has three bright markers on it. "The blue mark is where we are now. The green mark will be your drop-off and pickup point under Tower Bridge in the Thames River. The red mark is where Victor Eisenberg is being held, in the Tower of London. I've made contact with the Tower's Ravenmaster, and we've worked out a plan."

I say, "Ravenmaster. Cool handle."

Brando smiles. "It's a real job. There's a legend about the Tower ravens. When the Germans took over, they let the birds stay as part of their attempt to win over their new British subjects."

Grey says, "The Ravenmaster is an English historian and ardent bird enthusiast. Not exactly covert field material, but his knowledge of the Tower guard is invaluable."

I ask, "Do we have a way inside?"

"We have a *great* way inside." Our new confederate crumples his empty sandwich wrapper into a ball, then flashes a flat metal case from his shirt pocket. As if by magic, a cigarette appears in his mouth. He flicks a Zippo in and out of his pocket, which somehow lights his cigarette without seeming to come anywhere near it. Grey inhales and then releases a mouthful of smoke toward the ceiling.

He grins at Brando and me. "When was the last time you two went scuba diving?"

19

On the surface, the Thames is a charming ribbon of liquid commerce, wending its way through Olde London Towne. Beneath that watery veneer, however, are two thousand years of human waste and industrial slag. It's not even a sewer, because sewers typically aren't clogged with car tires, wrecked boat hulls, unexploded bombs, human body parts, and cattle skeletons.

Brando and I swim downriver toward the Tower of London. My partner pulls along a waterproof dive bag stuffed with our bare tactical necessities. The thing seems to be a magnet for clingy blobs of yuck, and he has to keep brushing them off.

I comm, "This must be the most disgusting place in the world!"

Brando replies, "I've heard the Ganges is mostly manure and the Tiber is crammed with corpses. But yeah, this is fucking gross."

We began this repulsive excursion by jumping off a fishing boat. The boat's captain, a fellow abolitionist, will wait for us under Tower Bridge. If anyone gets nosy, he'll pretend he's having mechanical problems.

It's a short swim to our objective, but we stay submerged the whole way to avoid searchlights. The Tower's external security measures don't present much of an obstacle for us, but the guards inside might. This is why Raj and Grey are positioned on the far side of Tower Hill, ready to provide a patented ExOps-style diversion.

We pass under the stone arch that serves as the Tower's main gateway for watercraft. Our finned feet propel us to the citadel's infamous point of entry for conspirators, spies, and seditionists, known as Traitors' Gate. The gate itself is made of heavy timber slabs, painted black. Right now it's submerged beneath high tide. Traitors' Gate has an array of electronic sensors to prevent exactly this sort of sneaky ingress, but tonight they're out of order thanks to our accomplice, the Ravenmaster.

I swim ahead and start digging a hole that'll allow us to pass under the gate without disturbing it. My excavation fills the water with even more gunk than before, and our visibility plunges to zero. I dig faster, and as soon as the hole is wide enough, I pull myself in, kick my legs, and zip under the gate. Brando swims right behind me, following by touch.

We gently surface like a pair of alligators, our eyes barely above the water. We float in front of a steep flight of stairs that lead to the Tower's interior. I activate my infrared and amplify my hearing.

There's nobody in the immediate area. Almost all the structures in the Tower are made of rocks, which effectively blocks heat signatures, so I switch to radar and night vision to make sure. Still clear. According to the Ravenmaster, most of the London garrison was sent to Yorkshire, Scotland, Wales, and Ireland to contain the massive shitstorm us ExOps Levels are whipping up.

We climb a few steps and shrug ourselves out of our scuba tanks, masks, and fins. Brando unpacks our dive bag. He hands me my F-S fighting knife, Li'l Bertha, her holster, and a few Multi Caliber ammo packs. He extracts his X-bag, then pins our scuba gear under the air tanks, below the water's surface.

My partner hoists his spy-stuff depot. His teeth shine in the gloom as he asks, "Ready?"

Part of our prep for this job included smearing each other's faces with camouflage makeup. Now, moisture from his hair beads up as it flows across his obscured features. I feel the same thing happening on my forehead, nose, and cheeks.

"Ready," I say.

We trail a stream of brown sludge up the stairway to what my Eyes-Up display informs me is Water Lane. In front of us is the thirty-foot-high inner wall, topped with square crenellations like castles in fairy tales.

Now for some old-school cloak-and-dagger stuff. The Ravenmaster has marked a hidden trapdoor in Water Lane that will get us past the inner wall and into the main courtyard. He said it was built ages ago as a secret emergency exit for some royal somebody or other. It sounds like the Tower is riddled with these sort of things. Our man wasn't sure what he'd be able to use as a marker, so we'll have to search carefully. He won't have used a piece of white chalk to draw a big arrow or anything. It'll be something that won't seem out of place.

We know it's right near Traitors' Gate, so we scout around near the wall. I look left while my partner moves right. Our head-to-toe black scuba suits and darkened faces transform us into a pair of shadows. After a minute Brando curses under his breath.

"What's the matter?" I comm.

"I just stepped on a wad of bubble gum!" he gripes.

"Could that be our marker?"

He scrapes his foot on the pavement. "I'm sure it is, but now my damn boot sticks to everything." Brando is as fastidious as Trick was. A blob of goo stuck to one of his extremities is definitely *not* his idea of a good time. I try to keep a straight face as I walk over and examine the walkway near what's left of the marker.

The ground is paved with cobblestones, but tucked between two of the stones is a small, smooth gray disk. I press it. Nothing happens. I bunch my fingers together and press hard on the disk. The round button clicks down, and a manhole-size slab of cobblestones pops up an inch.

"Hey-y, not bad," Brando comms. We lift the secret hatch out of its mount and peer inside. "I'd better go first so you can put the cover back." He sits at the opening's edge, drapes his legs in, and drops down. He lands with a gentle thud.

"All clear," he comms. "It's even dry."

I swing my feet in, grab the lid, and shimmy into the hole. Brando holds me up by my legs so I can reseat the cover. The hatch clicks into place, and my partner lowers me to the ground.

The tunnel is jet black. Even my night vision can't see anything. Starlight technology works by enhancing available low light, but in here there's nothing to amplify. I click on my watch's light, and Brando takes a small flashlight from his X-bag. He leads us through the tunnel and, presumably, under the inner wall. After only sixty feet the tunnel ends. We shine our lights at the ceiling, revealing another trapdoor.

I boost Brando onto my shoulders. He waves his flashlight around until he finds a small gray button. This one presses in easily since it hasn't been exposed to God knows how many years of weather and bubble gum.

The round cover clicks open. Brando slowly shoves it off to the side. Taking a cue from Jade and Pericles, I bend my knees, then lunge straight up and bounce my partner through the opening like a Brando-in-a-box. Then I squat down again and boing myself out of the tunnel.

My feet land on either side of the hatchway. I reseat the lid and look around. Shelves of canned food, boxes of cereal, and bags of flour. The tunnel has led us into someone's pantry. I exit through the adjoining kitchen and enter a living room.

We're in a traditionally decked-out British row house. A quick infrared scan shows me nobody's home. This cozy parlor is appointed with overstuffed furniture, patterned drapes, and a rocking chair set in front of a small fireplace. On the mantelpiece are some heavy brass keys and a shiny brass lamp. Brando surveys the Tower's inner courtyard through a lace-curtained window. I ex-

pect a Hobbit to walk in and offer us tea and crumpets.
What I don't expect is . . .

Alix!

I freeze. My left cheek twitches. Was that Brando? No,
he'd say "Scarlet."

Alix, sweetheart, is it really you?

Spiders of ice burrow out of my scalp and skitter
down my neck. No, this cannot happen. Not in the
middle of a mission! Of all the times I could pick to lose
my mind, it can't be now.

Please, Hot-Shot. I need your help.

Brando walks to the door and puts his hand on the
knob. When he checks to make sure I'm ready, his eyes
open wide. "Scarlet, what's wrong? You're white as a
sheet."

There's no time for beating around the bush. "Darwin, you know my father was kidnapped by the Germans and that he eventually turned up in their Carbon
Program."

My partner slowly says, "Yeah-h-h?"

"When we—when Solomon and I—were in Zurich
last year to investigate Carbon, I heard my father's voice
speak to me."

To his credit, Brando absorbs this crazy-ass shit very
quickly. "Why are you telling me this now?"

"I just heard it again."

He takes off his glasses and gives me a look.

"I know, I know. It sounds like one of my spells. But I
swear, it came through my commphone."

He polishes his lenses on his shirt. "Scarlet . . ."

I stamp my foot. "No, Darwin! I heard it!"

He jams his glasses on and scowls at me. "All right.
Comm me into your Day Loop."

I grant him access to my twenty-four-hour audio/
video log and rewind it a couple of minutes. We listen to
our footsteps in the tunnel, the quiet rumpus of me
boosting us up here. Then:

Alix!

Brando jumps in surprise at the unexpected voice. A sheen of perspiration forms on his brow as he listens to the rest of the transmission. He whispers, "Ho-o-oly crap."

"The only time I heard it like this was in Zurich, at the Carbon lab. Maybe there's a Carbon facility near here. We have to check it out."

Brando indicates our surroundings. "Scarlet, we're in the middle of an assignment. Whatever that's about has to wait until—"

"It *can't* fuckin' wait! If my dad can comm to me, it might mean he's nearby. Call your boss and find out if the Krauts have a piece of Carbon in the area."

"Scarlet, that transmission could have been from anyone!"

I cross my arms and lean against a side table covered with porcelain figurines from the Bible. Brando sees my utterly implacable expression and clenches his teeth.

"Okay, *fine*." He comms his Info Coordinator, rams the request through, and grumpily waits for an answer. Then his face goes blank.

"Jesus," he says. "Carbon *does* have a facility in London. It's right here, in the White Tower."

I haul Li'l Bertha out of her holster. She's already switched herself on. Her system connects to my Eyes-Up display, but her target indicator is blank. Dammit! Where is he?

I place my pistol—my father's pistol—next to my head and comm, "Daddy? Can you hear me?"

We stand as still as blocks of granite.

Yes.

It works! My eyes brim with tears, and my breath catches in my throat.

Brando is so astounded you could play marbles with his eyeballs. "He can *hear* you?"

"Yes!"

My partner gapes at Li'l Bertha. "How is he doing that?"

"He must be here in London."

No.

"No? Where? Dad, where are you?"

It's . . . not a . . . large city.

"Daddy, how are you doing this?"

Carbon has its own comm-net. I . . . honey, I have to stop. This takes . . . Keep searching, baby.

"Dad?"

Nothing.

"DADDY? Uh, Philip? Big Bertha? Hello?"

Still nothing. I pull my hair and shriek, "FUCK!"

Brando holds my arms. "Alix, what'd he say?"

"He said Carbon has its own communication network." I feel light-headed from breathing too fast. "He must have hacked in through his commmphone somehow."

"But how did your father know you were . . . that you'd be able to . . ."

"Maybe it's something he did to his pistol."

Brando looks utterly bewildered, as though I've gone nuts so convincingly that he's been dragged along for the ride. Talking to my sidearm wouldn't be the craziest thing he's ever seen me do. Levels aren't always the most stable people, and some Levels have cracked during missions. Meanwhile, I get even dizzier and my peripheral vision begins glowing red.

"Scarlet," he says gently, "how about we ask Cyrus to send us back after we finish this assignment?"

I smack his arm with my heavy watch. "Fuck that, Darwin! After this snatch job we'll *never* get back in here. It's now or never, and you know it."

My partner glares at me and rubs his arm. Then his hand stops moving, and his gaze moves to some indeterminate point on the ceiling. I can tell he's forming an idea, so I refrain from whacking him again. Instead I totter to the window and examine the White Tower. It's not exactly white, but it's certainly a lighter color than the rest of the architectural heap that constitutes the Tower of London.

There aren't any windows or doors near the ground. The heavy stonework has long vertical ribs accenting its height and small windows emphasizing its weight. It's like it was carved into a living slab of protruding bedrock.

"Scarlet, c'mon," Brando comms. "Let's go snatch Victor Eisenberg."

I whirl at him. "What about my father?"

"Eisenberg can help us find your dad."

I throw my arms around his neck and hold him while the room reels around us. Then I press Li'l Bertha against my cheek. "Dad? We're gonna find you."

There's no answer, but if it's possible to comm a nod and a smile . . .

Brando leads me out to the main courtyard. I'm still trembling as I follow, but the fresh air alleviates my vertigo and my vision returns to normal.

The courtyard is even gloomier than it was outside the main walls. We dart across a lawn and past a stone path. We're halfway across another small lawn when my partner signals me to stop. We crouch down to scan the area. Forcing myself to focus on the moment, I crank up my hearing and switch on my infrared.

The cold masonry becomes a black backdrop for the little row of gently glowing orange houses across the courtyard. Ten red man-blobs patrol the walls and towers.

I comm, "Not too many guards."

"Yeah. The Ravenmaster was right about them stripping the garrison."

"Which building are we headed for?"

Brando holds up his index finger. "Hang on. I'm asking Grey and Raj to begin their diversion."

The boys must have been champing at the bit for this request. Brando has barely finished comming to me when a bright flash illuminates the sky at the Tower's north side. A loud boom and rumble indicates that Raj has opened fire on one of the outer guard posts, as removed from our path as he can make it.

My partner remains crouched. "We're headed for the Waterloo Block, that building against the west wall. We need to wait until the guards in front are drawn away."

Raj and Grey have sucked the guards into a noisy exchange of small-arms fire that rings piercingly off the walls. I scope out the front entrance of the Waterloo Block. The two troopers posted there vacillate between staring at each other and gawking toward the firefight.

Meanwhile, it's even chillier. "I'm freezing! Did the temperature drop all of a sudden?"

"It might be the ghosts," Brando comms back. "We're on top of the old scaffold site."

"I didn't think that many people were executed in here."

"Oh, *lots* of people died here, but only a handful of them were famous."

An explosion outside hurls a fireball into the sky, and the two bozos bolt for the walls. *Finally!*

This ungodly racket will lure cops like a multistory neon doughnut sign, so we hot-foot it across the courtyard. Brando pulls one of the Waterloo's front doors open. I brace Li'l Bertha in front of me and rush through the entrance. My partner waits a few seconds, then slips in behind me.

We're in a large, unoccupied, dimly lit hall. The floor, walls, and twelve-foot ceiling are all made of wide oak planks. The furniture consists of a bunch of small tables with metal folding chairs around them. An incongruously colorful jukebox roosts in the corner, blasting American rock songs so loudly that I can't hear the shooting outside.

"Where are we going?" I call over my shoulder.

"Eisenberg is on the third floor with the other politicals."

"How many guards are left in here?"

Brando pauses. He must be comming with Grey or Raj while he's talking to me. Then he says, "The Ravenmaster wasn't sure, so we need to watch out."

The rules of engagement for this Job Number include lethal force, but only for SZ troops or if we're under extreme duress. Otherwise I need to attempt nonlethal takedowns. That's why we've been a pair of Sneaky McSneakersons and why we have the boys doing all this diversionary nonsense instead of simply killing our way in here like we normally would.

We find an ancient stairway beside the main hall. Heavy stone blocks rise from the treads and form a shallow arch over our heads as we trot up the bleak spiral. The jukebox is gradually drowned out by a radio broadcast from upstairs. We pass the shadowed second story and ascend toward the third. We enter a wide, open area.

This chamber may have once been part of the king's quarters, but now it's a hodgepodge of cages bolted to the floor. Two uniformed palookas sit at a table. One thug reads a newspaper while the other jamoke leans toward a small radio and listens to a very loud German news program.

Radio Guy slowly rotates his head as we come out of the stairway. Whatever he was expecting, it obviously wasn't a pair of scuba divers. He blinks hard, confirms that yes, it *is* two face-painted scuba kids, and draws in breath to call a warning to Newspaper Guy. Before he can form any words I'm already right on top of him. He's so shocked by how fast I move that he tips over backward in his chair to get away from me.

Since Radio Guy is already on the floor, I shift my trajectory to lance myself feet-first into Newspaper Guy's chest. He exhales a loud whoosh as a cubic meter of beer breath gusts out of his lungs. I spin to Radio Guy, who's regained his feet and drawn his sidearm. I lunge forward and swipe his pistol right out of his hand. Then

I punch him so hard that he flips over, lands on his head, and sploogles onto the floor.

I lean over Radio Guy and stick my finger in his face. "Stay!"

His flabby chin waggles. "*Jah!* Okay! *Jah!*"

I yank a pair of handcuffs off his belt and slap them on his wrists.

Meanwhile Newspaper Guy crawls around on all fours. There's a puddle of puke under his wheezing clam catcher. Blood drips out of his nose into the vomit. That may have been my best flying kick ever! I'll have to tell Raj about it. Of course, if Raj had done it, this goombah's bones would have exploded out of his skin like calcium rats leaving a sinking meat ship.

Our dramatic entrance has the prisoners on their feet. I load Grey's image of Eisenberg onto my Eyes-Up display and jog along the rows of cages until I find a matching face.

"Victor Eisenberg?" I say to the thin, fierce-eyed prisoner behind the bars. One gander at him and I can see why he's called the Hammer. The man bears his lean, muscled body like a ramrod, his chin could chop down trees, and his burning stare threatens to cook the inside of my skull.

Eisenberg's file says he's in his forties, but he looks early fifties. Not regular fifties, mind you. More like that super-rugged, frontiersman fifties where he still drinks the young cowpunks under the table and then chucks their boozed-up asses over a barn.

"American," he says. It's not a question. He examines all sixty-four inches of my scuba-clad body, nods appreciatively, and states, "It's about time."

I'm not sure if he means it's about time Americans got involved in the abolitionist movement or if it's about time an American chick in skintight clothes busted him out of jail. Brando grabs a ring of keys from Radio Guy and opens the door to Eisenberg's cell. Victor walks out, stretches his arms over his head, then takes Brando's keys and tosses them to the prisoner in the next cell. The other prisoner opens his own door, then dashes around unlocking all the other cells. My partner and I each drag one of the guards into separate cells and lock them in.

The freed prisoners gather in front of Eisenberg.

"Men," he says, "introductions will have to wait, but I think you all know me. We arrived separately, yet we will escape together. To do so, we will harness our energy as a group and overwhelm our opponents. Are you ready?"

The man next to Eisenberg responds, "Yes, sir!" This is followed by a ragged but lusty chorus of "Yes, sirs."

Eisenberg turns to us. "Okay, little Americans, what's the plan? Victor Eisenberg and these men are at your service."

Brando comms his boss to report we've acquired a squad of pissed-off guerrillas, and can we grab him anything as we torch our way out of here?

CORE   PER-BB-342

6/21/1971

To Captain Bourbon,

Hey, Cyrus, I finished the upgrades on your LB-505 and put it in your locker. You'll find a new fire mode called "Auto-Pilot." This enables your pistol to shoot at a locked target with no trigger pull required. As long as your palm is in contact with your weapon's grip pad, it can fire itself. I also rewired the gyroscopes for extra spin so the targeting system can maintain a target lock even if you fall down a flight of stairs (ha-ha).

I tried to give your weapon a persistent personality like mine has, but I couldn't get it to work. To be honest, I'm not sure how I did it to mine in the first place. You should let me try again sometime. The way Li'l Bertha anticipates what I need from her is amazing.

Enjoy the upgrades and remember all us little people

when you make Director. If I ever get pulled out of the field, maybe you can give your old buddy a job in the Tech Department.

Sincerely,
Captain Vodka

PS: Don't forget, you're coming over for dinner on Sunday. Cleo will make pork chops and her homemade applesauce. Alix has volunteered to help peel apples, and she asks about her Uncle Cy all the time.

20

ExOps agents are trained to handle surprises, the expectation being that surprises are bad. But Victor's instant company of fighters is a pleasant exception. Their current lack of weaponry limits our tactical options, but we're about to rectify that shortcoming.

I've snuck up to the outer wall's parapet. In front of me, twelve regular German Army guards exchange small-arms fire with Grey and Raj. Behind me, half of Victor's men slink through the darkness like a long, angry shadow.

I set Li'l Bertha on "incapacitate" and direct her attention to the nearest guard's backside. She sets the other eleven posteriors as Butts Two through Twelve and jiggles her gyroscopes to signal me she's ready. I mash down on her trigger. She shoots Butt One, shoves my hand a little to the side, bangs a shot into Butt Two, and spins on to Butt Three. Moments later, she's unloaded a dozen assfuls of liberty.

Victor's boys rush past me, swarm the wounded guards, and stomp their heads until the Fritzes lay silent. The ex-prisoners load up on German weapons, and we all scurry down to the main courtyard, where the rest of our group waits for us. Victor distributes the captured rifles to the guys with the most military experience.

Brando comms, "Grey and Raj, hold your fire. The wall guards have been neutralized."

The racketing gunfire stops, only to be replaced by police sirens.

Raj comms, "Darwin, we have competitors crossing

the Tower Bridge. Grey and I can slow them down, but let's move it along in there. We're behind schedule."

"Roger that," Brando comms. "We're dealing with significant scope creep. Do you need help holding the bridge?"

Raj answers, "Affirmative, if help is available." He pauses, then shifts to a more conversational tone. "What'd you do, recruit Mary Poppins?"

I comm, "More like Peter Pan."

Brando confers briefly with Victor, who dispatches ten of the gun-toting members of his company to fight their way outside and help Raj fend off *die Kops*. This leaves us with Victor and eight of his men to bust into Carbon.

The outer Tower guards have been disabled with bullet wounds to their asses and blunt-force trauma to their heads, so they're out of the game. It's a quick run from the Waterloo Block to the White Tower's base. Up close, the old keep is as imposing as it must have been the day they built it. I circle the building to find an entrance. The only doorway is twelve feet off the ground. My partner catches up to me, followed by Eisenberg and our new comrades.

Brando says, "This can't be how they enter and exit this building every day. There must be another way in."

"Well," I say, "we don't have time to search for it. Darwin, let's use Jade and Pericles's cheerleader routine. I'll bounce you up to that doorway."

"The Krauts may have drained their garrison," Brando says, "but this is still Carbon we're breaking into. We'll need more than two of us."

We turn to Victor. He's not too heavy-looking. I can get him up there. Victor looks at me quizzically—he's not sure what we're talking about.

I say to Brando, "Sure, but let's boost you first so we don't have to explain it."

I position myself beneath the high doorway. My partner climbs onto my shoulders, and we crouch like springs.

"Ready?" I ask.

"Ready."

We flex our legs, and Brando flies up to the small landing in front of the high doorway. Muffled exclamations come from the men.

I point at Eisenberg. He directs his men to form a perimeter around the building. Then he walks in front of me and says, "Okay, red hair."

Victor's not as graceful as Brando, but he makes it to the landing on his elbows and stomach. His legs dangle over the edge until Brando grabs his arm and helps him up. I bend down, suck in a long, cold breath, and fire myself into the air. Brando and Eisenberg reach out to help, and I make a nice two-point landing. *Presto!*

Now for the door. I activate my sidearm. The door is heavy oak, but we only care about the hinges. I set Li'l Bertha to .50-caliber Explosives and fire seven times. Stone shards and wooden splinters crease the air and ricochet into the courtyard. We shove the door open and squeeze inside.

The moment I'm in, Li'l Bertha frantically spins her gyros. I switch to night vision and spot a charging figure with something metal in his hand. *Boom! Pow!* My assailant absorbs two .50-caliber Explosive bullets and flies away in a shower of liquefied idiot that schpritzes all over the ancient entryway. The man's weapon— a semiautomatic pistol—smashes into the wall and clatters to the floor.

I switch Li'l Bertha to less dramatic ammunition as Brando and Eisenberg follow me inside. The gore-streaked walls loom sixteen feet to a heavy wooden ceiling. We take in what happened to Herr Splat while Eisenberg retrieves the dead man's sidearm. He tries the weapon's slide. It doesn't move. A closer inspection reveals that the ejection port has been crushed by a direct hit. Eisenberg throws the ruined pistol away and passes his eyes across one of those old crossed-sword and shield combos hung on the wall. He pulls a sword from the display and takes it with him as we move into a large central room.

The Germans are using this area as an office, with rows of desks, filing cabinets, and computer servers. Thick electrical cables spill from the servers, snake up the walls, and vanish into the ceiling. In the back is a kitchen and meeting area. A large conference table in the far corner has sprouted three quivering pairs of hands.

We ease into the room's center. There's a lot of furniture and gear in here, plenty of places for troublemakers to pounce from. "Darwin," I comm, "go corral those three people and find out if we're in the right place."

My partner calls out, in German, "Stand up!" When the three pairs of hands don't move, he blares, *"Schnell!"* Six hands rise to reveal six arms, three frightened mugs, and three bodies wearing white dress shirts and neckties.

Eisenberg doesn't look at the men. He studies the rest of the room, in particular a large flight of stone stairs that leads to the next floor.

Brando corrals the three necktie schnooks and fires questions at them in rapid German. They answer in even faster German.

My partner comms, "They say there's a lab on the top floors for cloning humans." He pauses while the neckties tell him something else. "The guards are one floor up." Another pause. "It seems like these three are computer programmers. They write the software for Carbon."

"Ask them who attacked us when we came through the front door."

My partner barks his question at the programmers, listens to their answer, and comms to me, "That was an SZ sergeant assigned to watch them."

The Staatszeiger. "All right, then," I comm. "Let's crack some skulls."

Eisenberg asks, "What about these three?"

Brando says, "I've told them to hide down here.

They'll be perfectly happy to see us eliminate the guards."

Eisenberg glowers at the neckties and brandishes his sword. The programmers blanch and retreat behind the conference table. Brando, Victor, and I gather at the bottom of the stone staircase. An autocratic, commanding voice rings from above, then: *"Jah, Hauptmann."* Yes, Captain.

A pair of SZ troopers clomp down the stairs and almost run into us. I hook the first soldier's arm into my elbow, jam my hip into his, and flip him over me, slamming his body to the floor. I whip out my knife and bury it in my opponent's chest as the sword-wielding Eisenberg runs the second man through. Victor neatly pivots on his heel so his victim can fall past him.

Eisenberg and I yank our blades out of the dead troopers, then exchange short, appreciative nods.

I say to him, "You're pretty good with that pig poker, bud."

"Danke," he says.

I reholster my knife and ask Brando, "What floor is Carbon on?"

"The third and fourth."

I fix my partner with a steady look and raise one eyebrow. "So the second floor is fair game?"

He grins, gently rolls his eyes, and recites, "She will lay great vengeance upon them, and they will know her name is Scarletzerker."

I bang a bunch of Madrenaline and charge up the stairs. My body wings past the top step—and a half dozen black-shirted SZ men—then sails halfway down a door-lined hallway.

One of the soldiers I blew by fires his MP-50 submachine gun at me. I drill a few slugs into him and twirl through a doorway to dodge his 9-mm salvo. A brutish SZ trooper chases me into the room and reaches out to grab me. I slap his meaty paws out of the way, leap in the air, and ram my foot into his face.

The brute staggers backward as blood spurts from his nose. I shove him out of the room. Private Brute pitches into the hallway, where a panicked burst of gunfire rips him apart. His death shriek is followed by shouts and barked orders.

A quick look-around shows me a simply equipped kitchen: white tiled floor, basic white appliances, and several open doorways into other rooms sparsely furnished with metal-framed beds, small desks, and weapon lockers.

I switch on my infrared and track the other SZ slimeballs as they fan out to attack me from multiple angles. One glowing figure remains at the top of the stairs, pointing and bellowing directions to the other men. He must be Yes Captain.

I swing out of the kitchen, tear-ass up the hall, and tackle the officer to the ground. I crack my right fist into his temple, and he instantly stops moving.

I haven't been resupplied since we came to England, and Li'l Bertha is running out of her special ammo, so I grab Yes Captain's MP-50. The big automatic weapon blankets my small frame as I sling his belt and ammo pouch over my shoulder.

I cut to my left and mow down two troopers as they return to find out what happened to their boss. My feet vault over their bodies and hustle toward the second floor's back rooms. I find a large area with a few sets of tables and chairs. Someone's unfinished snack rests on one of the tables. This must be the mess hall.

A hot-orange person is sneaking through the kitchen where I met Private Brute. Herr Sneaky moves into a small office on the other side of the mess hall. I hoist a chair and sling it through the wall near my stealthy competitor. When I fly through my jiffy door, the startled Staatszeiger man opens up on me.

I evade Sneaky's full-auto hailstorm by bouncing across the room like a red-haired jumping bean. Brando calls this move the Scarlet Two-Step. I somersault behind a desk, spin, and fire. My gun's last few bullets rip through Sneaky's guts, and he collapses in a slithering heap.

Marauding soldiers rush at me from the room next door. I retreat to the mess hall and slap in a fresh clip. I kneel down, aim at the doorway, and get ready to fill these dunderschmucks full of lead. They don't come in, though. A hand waves past the doorway, and something lands with a thunk.

Grenade!

My feet press into the floor to launch me into the main hallway. As I lift off, the grenade explodes and something whacks into my lower right leg. I spin into the wall and roll like a tumbleweed. My captured MP-50 skitters toward the stairs where Brando and Eisenberg lie in wait.

Three SZ soldiers run from the mess hall, raise their weapons, and suddenly collapse in a rattling storm of gunfire. Above me, Victor's angular features flicker demonically in my submachine gun's sharp claps of light. This baleful display is abruptly blocked by Brando's worried face.

"Scarlet, you're hit!"

"I'm fine," I croak. My throat feels like it's coated in sawdust. "This is from the bad guys."

"No, it isn't. Your leg's cut."

"Don't worry about it." I hold my hand out to him, but when he hauls me up, a searing bolt scorches across my calf. "OW, fuck!" I hop on one foot until Brando makes me sit down.

My neuroinjector pumps Overkaine into me, and the throbbing subsides to a buzzing tingle. I catch my breath while Eisenberg collects another MP-50 and more ammo from the dead SZ men. He hands me one of the submachine guns and cradles the other in his arms.

"Ahh," he beams. "That felt good."

I smile at him. This guy is my kinda people.

Meanwhile, Brando dives into his X-bag for his first-aid kit and quickly wraps my wound.

I peek at my dad's watch. Only four minutes have passed since we first entered the White Tower. Nothing like a crazed firefight to make you lose your sense of time.

"That'll do for now," Brando says. He packs away his first-aid kit and helps me up again.

"All right, gents." I nod toward the stairway. "Let's go."

A low thrumming sound, like a vast beehive, echoes from the floor above. As we climb, the stone walls begin to reflect an unnatural blue light. The thrumming sound is deeper now, a long, low *wOWww . . . wOWww . . .*

"Darwin, do you hear that?"

"Yeah. Sounds like a generator."

We enter another large chamber. The White Tower is simply a stack of these voluminous rooms with connecting stairs. Here the walls are lined with about thirty metal boxes, each seven feet tall and three feet square. They resemble coffins except they have thick bundles of cables and tubes blooming from their tops. The cables and tubes stripe the walls and penetrate the ceiling.

In the center of this room is a doughnut-shaped counter, like an information desk at a museum, except the top surface is one big computer screen. Two blond women in white lab coats stand behind the desk and stare at us. One of them wears glasses, and the other has short curly hair. Victor and I aim our weapons at them. Brando calls out to the women to put their hands up.

Four-Eyes grabs for something in her coat pocket. I squeeze off a few shots that pound into her chest and blow her backward over the desk. Curly screams and cringes as her coat and face are spattered with Four-Eyes's blood. My partner yells at Curly to stand still. The terrified woman is trembling so hard, I think she might faint. She cries and breathes in shallow gasps.

Brando walks through a small gap in the desk that

serves as the entrance. He takes Curly's hands and leads her toward the stairs, speaking softly. Brando gently rummages through Curly's pockets and removes a few pens, a small notebook, and a short silver cylinder. He dumps all this stuff on the floor and kicks it away.

I comm, "What's that silver thing? A cigar tube?"

He replies, "I think it's a suicide needle. If Carbon gets breached, this woman is supposed to kill herself to protect what she knows about this program."

"Ask her what's on the fourth floor."

Brando asks Curly a hushed question. She continues quivering as she answers him.

"She says the Originals are all kept upstairs. The specimens here are clones." He indicates the metal boxes along the walls.

The clone chambers all have clear panels on the front. I inspect the nearest techno-coffin. A young, fair-skinned blond woman is inside. She's strapped into place and wired up all to hell. Blondie has a tall forehead and a long straight nose with a strong jaw. Her fair skin is smooth as polished marble, and her light blue eyes are open—wide open—like she's startled. Blondie's frozen expression of terror makes the fine hair on my forearms stand up. I check the next box and do a double take. It's the same woman.

Duh, Scarlet. Clones.

This Blondie is all strapped and wired, too, but her eyes are shut. I circle the room. Each box contains the same woman in varying postures and restraint systems. Three of the chambers are filled with a light amber liquid, with the specimen inside hovering motionlessly. These floating clones don't wear any breathing apparatus.

"Hey," I say, "why haven't these three drowned?"

Curly answers in a mild German accent, "Perfluoro-carbons."

My perplexed expression telegraphs that I have no idea what she just said.

"Liquid breathing," she clarifies.

"Like deep-sea divers," Brando says, "or premature babies. It looks like the Carbon engineers are testing multiple approaches."

I back away from the jumbo-size box of scientific creepiness. Even though my partner is a clone, he seems much more natural than these poor creatures. Yes, he spent exactly zero time in a real mother's womb, but he and his brothers were raised from infancy as normal kids. Plus, there were only three of them, like triplets. There are thirty copies of this blond woman in here.

There's no way making so many of the same person can be a good idea. People aren't Ford Mustangs. You can't just crank out an endless number of them. The moment these women emerge from these tanks will be the moment they go completely bonkers.

Eisenberg has stopped pointing his gun directly at Curly but holds it ready in case she tries any funny stuff. Brando says to him, "Mr. Eisenberg, will you watch this woman while we go upstairs?"

The man's lean face creaks into a smile. "Anything for you, my friends. And please, call me Victor."

21

He's not here. He told me he wasn't, but there was still part of me that hoped my father was being kept at this Carbon installation.

This uppermost chamber is lined with computer cabinets, deep racks of pressurized tanks, and a swarm of thick tubes slinking through holes in the floor. In one corner is a raised platform holding three computer terminals. It's obviously the control center. Brando makes a beeline for one of the workstations.

Centered in the space is what appears to be a gigantic sarcophagus: twenty feet long, six feet wide, and five feet tall. It's like a shipping container for a limousine. This must be the Original.

On top of the container is a thick glass plate for viewing the interior. I stand on tiptoe and take a look. Inside is a silvery rectangular slab the size of a dining room table. A thick rod connects the slab's short edges to the walls of the sarcophagus so that the slab is mounted in there like a piece of food on a spit.

The slab moves, rotating along its long axis, and smoothly flips over. The other side reveals the Original, a woman, although I can't see much of her. A breathing tube is mounted over her mouth and nose, and her hair is covered by a chrome helmet with a zillion thin wires coming out of it, like a metal Afro.

From the neck down the woman is tucked into the hollow core of the slab, which is essentially an articulated, padded body envelope. The cloning process must take enough time that the subject's position has to be shifted periodically. The silvery manvelope has a few large hinges along its length, I think so the subject can be bent at the waist and knees. Maybe to help blood circulation? Jesus, how long do they keep her in there?

Only the top half of the Original's face is visible. She seems to be asleep or unconscious. There are dark circles under her eyes. The overhead lights glare off the viewing glass, and I move a bit to see inside better.

The Original's eyes spring open.

I *yowp* and recoil from the sarcophagus. "Darwin, she's awake!"

My partner sits at the control station and reads from the screen in front of him. "Yes. It says here the subject has been placed into a locked-in state with a steady dose of pancuronium bromide." He gnaws one of his thumbnails. "She's paralyzed but cognizant."

When I lean over the window again, the woman's terrified gaze tracks my eyes.

"Can this lady feel anything?"

"She can feel everything. The Carbon researchers don't want the subject's mental activity dulled with anesthetics."

The woman's head doesn't budge. She can blink, and her eyes can move. That's it. Small pearls of water course down the sides of her face.

"She's crying." I place my hand over the glass. "We've gotta get her out!"

"Oh, my God, Scarlet. No way!"

"She's in agony, Darwin. They have her on a breathing machine!"

"Yes, exactly. Her respiratory functions are paralyzed along with the rest of her. We don't have any of the drugs we'd need to—"

"We can't leave her there."

"We *have* to, Scarlet! If we pull her off that ventilator, she'll suffocate and die."

The mission that killed my first partner resulted in a heap of intel about Germany's cloning program, including Carbon's success at speed-growing clones to the physical equivalent of twenty years old in one-tenth the time it would take naturally. That phase was called Gen-2, and for a few precious moments it was the most mental thing I'd ever heard of.

Trick and I also recovered data about Carbon's current phase, Gen-3, which instantly replaced Gen-2 as the most mental thing I've ever heard of. Gen-3's objective is to map an Original's living consciousness into a clone. This would create an exact age-shifted duplicate with all the maturity, memories, and knowledge of the Original. The Frankenkrauts call it psychogenesis.

ExOps's Med-Techs call it the craziest, most overreaching ego trip since the Tower of Babel. They swear up and down that psychogenesis is absolutely impossible. Then they haltingly admit that they said the same thing about Gen-2's goal of accelerated growth.

My retinal cameras take a picture of the paralyzed woman trapped in the chamber. She stares at me, desperately pleading. I sadly shake my head. She presses her eyes shut and keeps crying. My feet slowly back away from the sarcophagus.

Brando returns to his torrential typing. I rotate in a circle and photograph the lab. Formations of stainless-steel cabinets, Goliath-sized generators, racks and racks of pressurized bottles, wires, tubes, and cables—there's stuff everywhere. Even with the industrial-strength air conditioners mounted on the ceiling, the profusion of biotech thingamajigs keeps the room toasty warm. But I still shiver when Trick comes up the stairs.

"Hiya, Hot Stuff," he says.

I'm all set to respond—dead partner, no biggie—when what's happening hits me. I press my palms over my eyes. *Jesus, Brando will think I'm nuts.* I pull my hands down and cross my arms in front of me instead.

Trick is gone. I choke down a deep breath and command my knees to stop swaying.

Only a ghost, Alix.

Trick's voice echoes from behind me. "Scarlet." No, it's not Trick. "Check out this file." Brando comms me a data file. I swallow my anxiety attack and open the file in my Eyes-Up display.

It's a map of Europe superimposed with a scattered constellation of green dots. "What're these dots?"

"That's where all the Carbon facilities are."

"Are you kidding? There must be fifty of them!"

"Sixty-five," he comms, "but most of them are only for research, like the labs we saw in Zurich. There are nine cloning facilities like this one."

"Which one is my father in?"

"I don't know." Brando rapidly works the computer's keyboard. "My Info Coordinator may be able to help us figure that out."

A muffled thud echoes from outside. Sounds like our boys are really putting it to the German police. Raj comms to both Brando and me. "Scarlet, Darwin, we're running low on ammo."

Brando replies, "Roger that. We're leaving now." He types a final flourish into the computer, heads for the stairway, and calls out, "Victor! Let's round up Goldilocks and her three bears."

I follow my partner but stop to take one more gander at the tomblike metal cloning chamber.

He's in one of those things, waiting for me.

I hold Li'l Bertha next to my head. "Dad?"

All I hear is whooshing air and humming generators. My skin crawls, and a cold tremor from the cut on my leg courses through my shoulders and down my arms.

Dear Lord, please grace my father with Your strength and curse his keepers with one of those fucked-up Old Testament plagues. Boils will do nicely. Amen.

Heavily encrypted intercept, source unknown:
START TRANSMISSION : SHE'S IN LONDON :
TRANSMISSION END

22

The red-tipped cigarette stays between my lips as I exhale through my nostrils. *Look, Ma, no hands.* I feel like a total rebel until a burning twister of hot vapor burrows into my eyes. I wince and snatch the butt away from my mouth. *So much for James Dean.*

It turns out Grey smokes not only for the pure tobacco flavor but because the old "Can I get a light?" routine is such a perfect icebreaker for Infiltrator work. When Brando, Victor, and I returned with Curly and the three neckties, we found Grey casually smoking on the safe house's front steps. On an impulse, I asked him if I could bum one. I'd barely finished the question when he held his cigarette case out toward me.

"Don't tell your mother." His lighter seemed to magically appear in his palm, already lit.

I puffed the cigarette into life. "Thanks, Grey."

Raj came out and escorted our Carbon pals inside. Meanwhile, from the corner of my eye, I saw Brando tilt his head and look at me.

"What?" I said. "My leg hurts."

He quietly watched me smoke. We both know I have Overkaine for things like leg wounds. He turned to Grey without taking his eyes off me. "Sir, will you help me question our pris—uh, I mean, our guests?"

Grey had been observing our mostly unspoken conversation with a tilted smile. "Sure thing, Darwin," he said, "but drop the 'sir.'"

That was a few hours ago. Since then I've changed into my street clothes, rebandaged the gash on my leg, and had a bite to eat. Then I equipped Victor with a comm-headset so he can talk to us, stowed the scuba gear in its ExOps duffel bag, and bummed another cigarette off Grey before he sent me and Rah-Rah up here to the roof to keep a lookout for *die Fritz*.

We alternate from the front of the building to the back every twenty minutes or so to help us stay alert. Neither of us speaks unless we see something. It's early Sunday morning, and this is a residential neighborhood, so we're pretty much silent.

Brando keeps me and Raj tuned into how things are going downstairs. I can't follow the technobabble, but I gather we're harvesting even more Carbon intel than my haul from Zurich. The scientists we brought here are fed up with how much the Reich has "perverted their talents." The woman, Curly, says she might as well give it to us so "somebody can do some good with it."

Raj and I exchange knowing glances when she says this. He sighs and returns to his post. Suddenly he cranes his neck to check out something in the street.

He comms to me, Grey, Victor, and Brando all at once. "Team, this is Raj. A large six-wheeled van has stopped a hundred feet from our front door."

I throw my cigarette down and stand on tiptoe for a better view of the house's rear approach. "Raj, it's clear back here. Do you need help?"

"No, Scarlet. Stay there. If this is a raid, they'll come from all directions at once."

"Maybe we should have had Victor bring his guys with him," I comm.

Raj hunches down so he can watch the van below without exposing himself more than he needs to. "No, it was better to get those men out of the city. We couldn't have armed or supplied them, anyway."

This is true. In fact, we can barely supply ourselves. Raj and I have our ExOps-issued weapons, of course, but we've been in-country so long that we're running out of ammo for our specialized people perforators. To supplement our draining ammunition supply, we each have a stolen MP-50 with as many clips as we can hump around. Curly brought us out of the Tower via a series of abandoned tunnels that used to be some kind of intracity mail delivery system. One corridor went by an underground armory, where we got ourselves all heated up with weapons, a crapload of bullets, and some of those Kraut grenades on a stick.

I scan the house's backyard. The whole neighborhood is lined with two-, three-, and four-story white stucco buildings like the one we're standing on. In the middle of the block is a red brick church Grey calls the Tabernacle. It's surrounded by narrow trees, lush hedges, and small plots of remarkably green grass. Even after decades of occupation, the Brits still can't be beat for their gardening skills.

Then I spot a problem in paradise: snakes.

"Gentlemen, this is Scarlet. Three armed soldiers are sneaking through the park to our rear."

Grey instantly comms, "Okay, team, we're bugging out. Darwin, join your partner upstairs. Victor, cover the front door. I'll take care of our guests."

"Roger that, Grey," Raj comms. "You'll find your own escape route, I assume, sir."

"Affirmative, Raj. You exit with Scarlet, Darwin, and Victor." Infiltrators are so good at hiding that they have their own response to this kind of situation. It's called Evade in Place, meaning he'll stay here and use his Mods to remain out of sight. When he finds out what the Germans' intentions are, he'll report to ExOps.

Brando emerges from downstairs. He zips across the roof and surveys the street out front. Then he runs to my post and leans out over the backyard. "Crap," he says.

Raj comms, "Grey, that van just unloaded a dozen SZ troops in full riot gear. Should I engage them?"

Grey responds, "Raj, you big animal mother, I'll consider it a personal favor if you light those foxtrots right the hell up. Scarlet and Victor, the same for you: any SZ or Gestapo targets you see, you kill. Try to abstain from cops and Wehrmacht."

I pour myself a bucket of Madrenaline. My pulse, breathing, and blood pressure all speed up. A serving of Kalmers swirls in to steady my hands. I lean out from the roof's edge to see if the competitors slinking into the backyard are regular assholes I need to merely cripple or if they're extra-strength assholes I can send to the great Oktoberfest in the sky.

My upgraded googlies telescope in for a closer look. Their collars all have the Staatszeiger's silver insignia: zigzag SZ runes on the right and an upraised hand with fingers made of lightning on the left.

"Raj," I comm, "I have confirmed SZ back here, too. Let me know when you're ready."

"Roger that," Raj answers. "Here we go." He opens up on the troops in the street with a long rattling overture of fully automatic fire from his MP-50.

I carefully aim a series of short bursts, one at each of the three intruders trespassing through my little green heaven. Intruder One is easy since he doesn't know I'm up here. Intruder Two tries to hide under a small bench, but my second bullet tempest takes him apart. Intruder Three has the most time and disappears into a hedge. I pepper the place where he vanished.

"Scarlet . . ." It's Brando. I can barely hear him over Raj's cacophonous firefight.

"Hang on, Darwin. I'm trying to nail this fucker." I fire into the hedge on either side of Intruder Three's hiding spot to—

"SCARLET! DOWN!" Brando shouts. My weapon's sights abruptly swing away from the ground. I plunge— no, I've been *pulled*—backward. My butt lands on something softer than roof as a loud crack splits the airspace formerly occupied by my head.

"Sniper!" Brando comms from underneath me. "Across the block, behind us! On that four-story building; he's behind the big water tank."

I roll off my partner as another shot rips through the air. Raj slumps to one knee with a loud grunt. As I get to my feet, a third shot rings out from the rear. This one hits me, but it only tugs a hole through my shirt, under my armpit.

That's enough of this bullshit. I ditch my MP-50 and activate Li'l Bertha. She vibrates like a puppy, eager to please.

"C'mon, baby. We've got a job only you can do." Li'l Bertha jacks in, analyzes the situation, and sets herself to .12-caliber pellets.

I zoot myself up, then bound across the rooftops, circling toward the sniper's hiding spot. Li'l Bertha is still low on ammo, so I refrain from laying down the hail of suppression fire my sidearm anticipated for me. *Crack!* The sniper tries to nail me. *Crack! Crack!* I bounce onto the building at the block's back corner and pivot straight for him, dodging shot after shot.

He's on a four-story building, same as the one I'm on. Between us is a two-story house. I take a running jump and—

Fuck!

I haven't suppressed my opponent, so he has all the time in the world to line me up while I float toward him like a goddamn balloon. My weapon switches to .50-caliber Explosives as her gyroscopes thrust my hand out in front of me. She fires at the same instant as my opponent. The two bullets roar past each other like jousting hot rods.

Li'l Bertha's shot penetrates my competitor's right eye and detonates inside his skull. His head breaks open and expels its contents like a blender with the lid left off.

The sniper's bullet streaks toward me. I scrunch up as tight as I can and press my eyes shut. The rifle slug breaks the skin over my pelvis's left side, clangs into my plated hip bone at an oblique angle, fires through a few inches of abdominal muscle, and then ricochets off the bottom of my polymetal-coated rib cage. I'm so hopped up that I can track the round drilling through my flesh like some kind of sizzling metal insect. The bullet rips an egg-sized hole out of my left side and splats against the inside of my SoftArmor vest.

I crash to the roof screaming and skid into the semi-headless SZ sniper.

"SCARLET!" Brando comms from across the block. "Oh, crap; are you hit?"

"AGH!" My left side is drenched with blood and getting more soaked every second. "RRRR!" The pain is incredible, like I've been crushed in the jaws of a dinosaur. "*Fuck!* Patrick, *get over here!*" I let go of Li'l Bertha and press one hand on the entry wound over my left hip. My other hand fumbles with my SoftArmor straps, but I can't open them to reach the exit wound.

I'm growing faint. My neuroinjector cranks a shitload of Kalmers, Overkaine, and CoAgs. I rest my head on the roof, squint at the sky, and try to slow my breathing.

My partner finally appears. He doesn't have as many Mods as me, so he's had to scramble across the rooftops like a believably acrobatic person. He unslings his X-bag and digs out his first-aid kit. This kit saves my life because ExOps first-aid packages are essentially a miniature field hospital complete with plasma, pressure bandages, antibiotics, a suction pack, tools for heavy stitching, sterilized superglue to hold wounds shut, and even a patch of freeze-dried Exoskin.

Brando unbuckles my SoftArmor, rips my shirt open, and quickly inspects the two wounds. His face is knotted with worry, but his voice remains steady. "Only one shot?"

"Only?"

His hands whip in and out of his first-aid kit. "Sorry," he says. "I mean, this is all we're dealing with, right?"

"Whaddaya want, *more?*"

"C'mon, Alix! Fuckin' work with me here, all right?"

I take a deep breath, which hurts like a bitch. My face is drenched in sweat, and my spit tastes like copper.

"Yes, he only hit me with one shot. I'm pretty sure I felt it exit."

Brando slaps a fat pressure bandage on the exit gaper, tapes it down, and then focuses on the entry wound over my left hip. He tilts me onto my right side and starts picking at the bullet hole.

"OW! Darwin—AGH!—what the fuck are you doing? That hurts!"

"Sorry, Scarlet, but the bullet carried a piece of cloth from your pants inside you. If we leave it there, it'll get infected and you'll die. Stop moving! It's slowing me down."

No fucking way do I go out like this.

I lie still and hiss through my clenched teeth as my partner carefully uses his forceps to pluck out the bits of clothing. My molars grind together as a streak of roasted electricity swirls around my hip. Tears drip off my nose onto the roof.

Brando applies a bandage to the entry wound. "Okay, that should do it." He rolls me onto my back. His face floats above me. A brown lock of hair hangs across his eyes. He's backlit by a beautiful blue sky, and whatever he's saying helps me calm down.

I reach my hand behind his head and pull his lips down on mine. When Patrick recovers from his surprise, I find out he kisses just as well as his late brother.

I let go of him and gulp for breath. Patrick regards me with his gray-blue eyes for a long moment. Then his attention is drawn back toward our not-so-safe house across the block. "Raj needs us."

Oh, right. I find Li'l Bertha and stuff her in her holster. When I try to sit up, my midsection roils in agony.

I gasp and collapse to the roof. "Fuck! It hurts everywhere!"

Brando says, "The bullet made a shock wave as it passed through you. Try getting onto all fours first."

This works better. I crawl onto my hands and knees and then wobble to my feet. A wave of dizziness swims through my head. Before I fall down again, my partner puts his arm around me.

"Darwin, grab that jerkoff's rifle and ammo."

Brando leans me against the water tank and bends down to retrieve my dead adversary's weapon.

"How's Rah-Rah?"

Brando slips his arm around my waist again. "He'll have a nasty bruise, but he's okay. The bullet struck him at an angle, and his SoftArmor wasn't pierced."

"How about Victor?"

"He's defending the safe house's front door until we're ready to go. Here." Brando hands me the rifle.

"Thanks." I take it by the barrel and lean on it like a cane. "So what's the plan?"

"Raj is coming to us. We'll go down to the street together."

"Lemme guess. Then we'll swipe a ride and drive off into the sunset."

"Steal a vehicle, yes, then we pick up Victor. It's a little early for the sunset part. Grey has some kind of distraction planned to help us get away."

"Well, button my shirt first. I don't need Raj to see what color bra I wear."

23

Raj leans out from the doorway, peeks up and down the street, then leans into the front hallway of our temporary hideout. He says, "The Staatszeiger truck is across the road. I only see one soldier. He must be the driver." Our big man sets his stolen MP-50 into his cavernous mitts and checks the safety. He rolls his shoulders and grimaces. Then he glances at me.

Brando holds me upright. My blood is smeared all over us, and I'm simply drenched from the waist down. Brando's hastily applied bandages aren't adhering very well since I'm still walking around, leaving sticky red footprints everywhere.

I shouldn't be moving, of course, but we have to get the fuck away from here. All three of us know the only thing that will kill me faster than moving is *not* moving. This fact is being clearly reinforced by the gunshots echoing around the neighborhood.

Raj comms on the team channel. "Victor, you there?"

"Affirmative." Victor's voice crackles through the firefight. "Go ahead, Raj."

"Our exit is imminent. Break off contact now and come to us through the back garden."

"Understood. On my way."

Raj gives me another once-over. "Scarlet, I still think you'd better sit up front with us."

"Forget it. I can't drive like this, and one of us has to ride in back to fend off pursuers."

Raj's eyes move to where Victor will come from, then to me.

I cut him off. "No way, Raj. Victor is good, but he's not enhanced."

"Okay, okay, you're right," he grumbles. "Let's do this, then." My fellow Level faces the street and charges outside. Brando and I lumber after him.

Rah-Rah isn't as fast as me, but he's no slouch, either. Our athletic Vindicator quickly covers the half block and body-slams the driver right out of his boots. The Staats-jerk drops like a load of turnips. Raj circles the transport to make sure he hasn't missed anybody while Brando hoists me onto the truck's rear gate. Victor sprints from the garden across the street.

"Victor," Raj shouts, "you ride shotgun."

"I ride *what*?" Victor asks.

Despite the pain I'm in, this gets a laugh out of me. Germans don't have that expression, I guess.

Brando pitches in. "He means ride up front with us."

I thump onto the deck and drag myself between a pair of long benches into the cargo area. I slump against the cab's rear wall, facing backward. Brando, Victor, and Raj crowd in up front. Raj fires up the diesel engine, and we rattle away from the O.K. Corral.

My partner comms, "Scarlet, how you doin' back there?"

"I'm fine, but make Raj stop if you see a McDonald's."

"Only if it has an eighty-mile-an-hour drive-through."

The wheels bounce through a pothole.

Brando again. "Scarlet, you sure you're all right?"

"Yeah, why?"

"You yelled. It sounded like it hurt."

Hmm. I hadn't realized I'd said anything. "Don't worry about it." I switch to Raj. "Hey, Mario Andretti, can you avoid those bumps?"

"Sorry, Shortcake. Will do."

After a few minutes we pull onto an expressway. *Ahh, smooth, smooth highway.* The tires' fluid rolling sounds like a distant waterfall. Cars drift past and swush into the background. My head droops forward, like when I used to nap in math class.

Madrenaline is off limits right now because it'll make me bleed out faster. I could really go for some coffee or another one of Grey's cigarettes. I'm daydreaming about cappuccino and Marlboros when I hear from up front, "Do you think he saw us?"

"Yeah, I think so."

"Scarlet, we've got company."

A military motorcycle bounces over the median strip and pulls into the fast lane behind us. It follows us for a mile or so, maintaining a distance of about sixty yards. The motorcyclist holds one hand over his headset's microphone to block the wind. He's radioing for backup.

Well, that won't do at all.

I pick up my rifle and look through the scope. The crosshairs jiggle all over the place. I bend my legs up in front of me, prop the rifle on my knees, and sight again. Better. I might not score a head shot, but I'll still get this Heinie hopping.

My first round smashes the bike's headlight. The next one nails the motorcyclist's arm. I miss with my third shot as the injured soldier swerves into the breakdown lane.

"Guys," I comm, "he's stopped."

"Nice work," Raj comms.

I tug out my rifle's magazine, stuff in a new one, and settle in for the ride. After five minutes or so, my eyes shut and my breathing grows steady and deep.

Mmm, mocha latte . . .

I'm jolted back to reality by Raj's comm. "There's a roadblock ahead, Scarlet. You'd better hang on to something."

The truck's engine roars louder and louder as Raj accelerates. I drape the rifle's strap around my shoulders and grab the benches. Victor's submachine gun hammers from up front.

Shouts from outside, then we hit with a resounding

clong! that lifts me off the floor and smacks my head against the wall. I see white static, then dark gray with red spots.

A flurry of gunfire and German curses from behind tells me we've bashed our way through. Several cars and a couple of motorcycles detach themselves from the mess and race after us.

I blink the spots out of my eyes, prop the sniper's rifle on my knees again, and open fire on our pursuers. Victor tries to engage them, too—his withering fire showers the cars in sparks—but his awkward position makes it tough for him to do more than suppress them. I shoot four troopers before I have to reload. The two motorcyclists see their opportunity and roar forward.

The first rider pulls up to the rear gate, chucks something inside, and veers away. I don't have to look to know it's a grenade, but it's at the deck's far end. I lunge forward and curse in pain as I roll off my butt and onto my knees. I grip my rifle in one hand and crawl toward the fizzing potato masher. I stretch out with my rifle's barrel and poke the grenade out of the truck. It bounces three feet off the pavement. I flop down and hide in the crook of my elbow.

Boom! My right shoulder is hit. The first two-wheeler skitters off the road. The motorcyclist grimaces, and his body leans awkwardly to one side.

The second motorcycle maniac closes in behind us with a grenade ready to throw.

"Raj! Hit the brakes!" I comm.

"What?"

"BRAKES! NOW!"

Raj stomps on the brakes. We lurch and suddenly slow down. I skid toward the front like a hockey puck. Our competitor crashes into the truck's rear end and smacks his handlebars with his face.

"Okay, now *floor it!*"

The truck surges ahead, away from the teetering motorcyclist. His grenade falls to the pavement and skips alongside his ride before it detonates and blows the bike's front wheel off. A moment later, the motorcycle's gas tank explodes and sprays a flaming pool of gasoline across all three lanes.

I'm crumpled under one of the benches, tangled in the rifle's strap. My face presses into the grubby deck, which is gradually being coated with liquid, wet and sticky. The road buzzes in my cheekbones. I close my eyes.

A bump makes me open them again. A girl perches on the other bench, reading a Spider-Man comic book. She's about my size, maybe a couple of years younger than me. She puts down the comic book and gawks at me. Two dark lenses descend over her eyes. I see myself reflected in the lenses. Left Me sips a coffee, and Right Me puffs a cigarette.

Her left arm turns into a long knife that she uses to slice her legs and right arm off. Then she chops off her own head, which bounces across the floor until it stops directly in front of me. Her lenses retract and reveal her wide-open eyes. She says, "Die, my dear? Why, that's the last thing I'll do!" Then the girl's head breaks into wild, hysterical laughter.

24

When I was young, bath time wasn't about cleanliness—
it was about adventure. On my eighth birthday, my dad
gave me a fleet of toy boats and a set of kids' books
about ships. For months, I read the books over and over.
During my nightly bath, I'd splash around with the little
plastic boats and reenact the Battle of Trafalgar where
Admiral Nelson defeated the Barbary pirates or when
the U.S.S. *Constitution* single-handedly sank all the
Spanish galleons.

Even though I jumbled up my stories a bit, they taught
me the English Channel is the final resting place of
something like half the sailors ever lost at sea. You'd
have to be fuckin' nuts to use a small, open powerboat
to ferry a gunshot victim cross-Channel in the middle of
February. Naturally, this is exactly what we're doing.

It's a good thing I haven't eaten much lately or this
dinghy would have a fresh coat of barf beige. I don't
even remember getting into this tub. Raj must have put
me here. The last thing I recall is passing out in the
truck. Then there was a long, commercial-free series of
nightmares. I woke once, here in the boat, when Brando
connected a can of blood plasma to my intravenous
port. When the plasma was empty, he switched me to a
can of antibiotics and saline solution. That can is tucked
into a pocket in my SoftArmor vest.

I'm snuggled into the craft's prow, wrapped in an
enormous wool blanket. Brando is tucked in behind me
to cushion my body from the boat's pitching as it battles
the waves. Despite the cold, I'm covered in sweat. My
Eyes-Up display unhappily traces my rapid heartbeat

and low blood pressure. I try to divert myself by watching our new buddy pilot the outboard motor.

Victor Eisenberg's face is slick with salt spray. The low winter sun throws his chiseled features into high relief as his blue eyes beam anxiously across the approaching sea. He's right to be on edge. If a whitecap hits this teeny boat the wrong way, we'll flip over and go down to Davy Jones's locker.

"How's that?" Victor comms on our team channel. He holds one hand over his comm-set's microphone because of the wind.

"A little more left," Brando answers. "There. Good."

Victor has his hands full just keeping us upright, so Brando takes care of me and tracks our position. Navigation is easy for my partner because of his built-in global positioning system. You never get lost with El Brando around.

Between the arctic wind, the buffeting swells, and the blaring engine, it's too loud for regular talking. I comm, "Ahoy there, Cap'n Vicberg!"

Victor glances at me. His white teeth gleam when he smiles. "Darwin," he comms, "she's awake."

My partner shifts position so he can see me. "Hey! How do you feel?"

"Like shit."

"Can you give me some more detail?"

You asked for it. I bitch about my nausea, my dizziness, how cold I am, and that I'm as thirsty as a sailor on payday. I'm also in a lot of pain despite my Overkaine.

"Are you still bleeding?" he asks.

"Hang on." Beneath the blanket, I use my hand to examine my injuries. Then I wriggle my arm around until my fingers shake into view, revealing blue nails and moist, bloody tips.

"Affirmative," I comm.

"Damn. Our med-kit only has one can of plasma."

"How far do we have to go?"

Brando tucks me under the blanket. "We'll be in Calais

in fifteen minutes, but we still need to meet our contact. It's not like we were able to call ahead and make a reservation, so I have no idea if she's around."

I ask my partner, "Can I sleep some more?"

He thinks for a moment, then says, "I'm worried about you going into hypovolemic shock from losing so much blood . . . although you may have already. You were kind of raving earlier when Raj moved you from the truck to this boat."

"What did I talk about?"

"Your father, I think. You weren't speaking very clearly." Brando cranes over his shoulder to keep an eye on where we're going, then turns back to me. He rotates his seating position some more so we can see each other better. His face is drawn, and his hair has been blown into a blob of dark-brown whipped cream.

Mmm, whipped cream. Plump, squishy pillows made of—

"—Alix! C'mon, partner. Stay awake if you can," Brando comms. "Uhh . . ." He searches for something to talk about. "Victor and I were just discussing Johannes Kruppe."

"Who?" I comm.

"The guy from our person-of-interest list. Kruppe. Victor knows him from military school."

"Johannes is a complete asshole," Victor comms, "but very tough, too." He says to me, "You be careful fighting him, red hair."

I ask, "Since when am I gonna fight Kruppe?"

Victor tells me Kruppe is part of the Greater German slavery system. He acts as a liaison between the SZ, the Purity League, and even the Gestapo. He's a raging anti-Semite who makes it clear that he thinks "the Fatherland still needs to solve the Jewish problem once and for all."

"Ah, now I see. Yes, I am definitely gonna fight Kruppe."

I try to scrunch down to stay out of the wind and

elevate my legs a little more. The required effort is beyond me, however. After a minute I give up and pull the blanket over my head.

"Who's our contact?" I comm.

Victor answers, "A journalist. We met at a human rights conference in Hamburg. She was covering the event, and I'd been invited to speak about my experiences in the army."

Brando adds, "She's also a CIA stringer."

"What's her name?"

"The CIA calls her Garbo." My partner fusses with the blanket some more. "She supplies the boys in Langley with intel, and they help her transport escaped Jewish slaves out of Europe."

I'm very warm all of a sudden. "Garbo . . . Wasn't she . . . the eyes? No, that was Bette Davis. Which . . . one was . . . which . . ."

It's the house I lived in with my parents before it was blown up last May. I walk into the kitchen. Cleo sits at our table with a raven-haired woman I've never seen before. I keep my eye on this woman. She's going to have shiny bug lenses, and I'll have to strangle her right here, which Mom won't like very much.

The woman introduces herself to me, but the second she says her name, it flies right out of my head.

I'm in a bathtub. The raven-haired woman is in the bath with me. We're fully clothed, but we're both soaked from the frigid red water. She rises, splashing, and claps her hands together. For a split second I can see her skeleton, like I have X-ray vision. Then the woman steps out of the tub and sloshes a crimson trail of water out of the bathroom.

I follow her. The next room is a large barracks but kind of crappy, like in a POW camp. Crudely built bunks hold dozens of people. The woman stands in the room's center and draws a large shape in the dirt floor. It's a six-pointed star surrounded by a circle.

*The woman faces me, claps her hands once more, and
disappears.*

CORE   MIS-ANGEL-2799

Heavily encrypted intercept, source unknown:
START TRANSMISSION : SHE'S IN CALAIS :
TRANSMISSION END

25

I'm still wrapped in blankets, but the boat has turned into a bed and the English Channel has turned into a cozy little room. Someone putters around in the dim light. For a moment I think it's Cleo until the person says something. Mom's German is good, but she has a strong American accent. What I hear now is perfect German, although I'm not used to hearing it spoken so softly.

A woman's voice says, "Leave Scarlet alone, Moortje. She's sick. Off with you, now."

I tip onto my side and cry out as molten hell gushes through my abdomen. The woman rushes over to me. She's middle-aged, with thick black hair and dark eyes with green flecks in them. She studies my face.

"Not on side, please. You stay face-up," she says in German-accented English.

I grimace and return to my back. *"Jah, danke."*

"Ah, sprechen sie Deutsch?"

"Jah," I say, and continue, in German, "but not as nicely as you." This earns me a grin from her. She has a beautiful smile, and her face is very pretty. The woman holds her palm to my head to see if I'm feverish.

"You still need a lot of rest," she says.

"Garbo?"

She takes a moment to react. I don't think she's called that very often. "Yes, that's me. But you're in my house, so call me Marie."

"Okay. Marie what?"

"Van Daan. My husband's last name is Schultze-

Boysen, but professionally I'm still known as Marie Van Daan."

"Where's my partner?"

"Darwin is asleep in the next room. I finally talked him into resting after the doctor left and you were settled in."

"I'm in Calais?" I untangle my right arm from the blankets to check the time, but my father's watch isn't on my wrist.

"Yes, you've been here for a day and a half. It's just past eight in the evening. Here." She reaches over to a side table and gives me my watch. I strap it on and study the room to find the exits, not that I'd be able to do anything but crawl to them right now. There's no one else in the room.

"What floor of your house am I on?"

"We're on the third floor."

My head slowly unfogs. "Where's Victor?"

"Victor didn't stay. He helped carry you in, then went to dispose of the boat. He said he had to meet some people up north."

That's too bad. Even though Vicberg isn't enhanced like me, I feel safer when he's around. "Who's Moortje?"

"Oh, he's my kitty. His full name is Moortje Drei because he's my third black cat. The name is Dutch." I am then treated to a detailed description of the previous two Moortjes. Apparently, Marie had her first one when she was a girl growing up in Amsterdam before her family moved to Brussels. That's where she had black cat number two, but he didn't last long because he used to fight dogs. Marie and her husband have lived here in Calais since they got married twenty-five years ago. She's had other cats, but none of them were black. Blackie number three has been with Marie for about five years now.

I receive all this information as a nonstop run-on story. Marie is one chatty lady.

She says, "Little Moortje has been curled up next to

your feet since this morning, but then he started fussing for his supper. I didn't want him to wake you, but I was too late."

Supper. I haven't eaten in two days. Or is it three? "Marie, can I have something to eat?"

"You certainly can. How about a bowl of dumpling soup?"

This lady is adorable! "Yes, ma'am."

While I wait for Marie Van Daan to return, I examine my surroundings. I'm in a combination guest room and home office, tucked into a sofa bed with a bunch of orange pillows all over it. Two walls are covered by floor-to-ceiling bookcases. One case is crammed with books about history and mythology. The other is stuffed with paperbacks and shelf boxes of magazines. Marie is a reader with a capital R.

The wall opposite my bed has a small desk with a lamp, a telephone, and a little computer terminal on it. A wooden leaf extended from the desk's side holds a stack of notebooks. A swivel office chair is parked in front of the desk, and the fuzzy toy mouse on the rug must belong to Moortje. It's all very tidy.

I, on the other hand, am a wreck. My body's stabbing spasms compel me to move only when absolutely necessary. My right arm and leg have bandages stuck over numerous injuries from the grenades, my torso is wrapped in tape to press two large compresses onto my bullet wounds, and my head is swaddled in so much gauze that it hides my hair. I didn't know I'd taken a head wound. Must have been that last grenade in the back of the truck. All this is topped off with a liberal sprinkling of scrapes, bruises, and pulled muscles.

Put me in, Coach. I feel fuckin' great.

I'm also wearing someone else's pajamas—Marie's, I assume. They're striped, white and orange, like a Creamsicle. Next to my bed is a bulging green canvas backpack filled with a new pair of blue jeans, a few days' worth of new shirts and underwear, my SoftArmor vest, and my weapons. I fish Li'l Bertha out of the pack and stuff her under my pillow.

Marie walks in with a steaming bowl of soup. I'm so hungry, it'd be nothing for me to shotgun this whole serving in three seconds. I only avoid making a complete ass of myself because my mother's etiquette training obliges me to downshift from breakneck gobbling to hasty dining.

Between mouthfuls I ask, "Did the doctor say how long I'll be laid up?"

Marie pushes her desk chair next to my bed and sits down. "He said a normal person would need three months but someone like you may need only a couple of weeks. I'm not sure what he meant, but given the nature of our situation, perhaps my ignorance is for the best."

You don't have to be a doctor to spot a Level, especially one that's as loaded as I am. My synthetic right hand and artificial joints appear natural enough, but the WeaponSynch pad in my left palm and the array of data/IV ports in my hip are dead giveaways that I'm less than 100 percent natural. If this doctor has worked on other Levels, he'll have already seen how quickly we can recover our health.

The black cat saunters in. He stops to lick his paws while he decides which of us lowly humans is most deserving of his regal affections. Marie leans down and makes little kissing sounds at him until he hops into her lap. She strokes Moortje's head and says, "It's kind of a miracle you're here right now, Scarlet. You lost so much blood."

I say, "Sorry if I ruined a set of sheets."

"Pshh, don't worry." Marie waves her hand. "That washes out easily enough."

"Who fixed me up?"

"A colleague of my sister, Betti. She used to be a nurse and still has a lot of contacts from those days. Most of them are . . . sympathetic to the work Betti and I do, and they're willing to help without asking a lot of questions."

"Questions like 'How the hell did this chick get shot so many times in one day?'"

My hostess grins. "Yes, questions like that."

"So your sister is a nurse?"

"She was, but when our father retired, Betti took over running our family's company. It made sense. Betti's the oldest, and she's very smart in things like science and math. I've always been the more artistic sister."

"Ugh," I grunt. "Math."

Marie's expression sparkles as she leans forward with a conspiratorial smile. "Scarlet, my young friend, I never liked math either." She passes her palm across my head again. "You're still too warm. You'd better finish your soup and then sleep for a while."

"Okay." I've never been much of a cat person, but I add, "And Moortje can come up here if he wants."

CORE   PER-GARBO-001

Garbo
DATA STRINGER / DOB: 12 June 1929 / POB: Frankfurt
NAMES AND ALIASES: Marie Schultze-Boysen (married, 1955–present)
Marie Van Daan (legal, 1942–present)
Annelies Marie Frank (legal, 1929–1942)
RESIDENCE: Calais, Province of France, Greater Germany

This asset is a Calais-based journalist with access to a steady flow of inside cultural and political information. Garbo's sphere of operation falls within the Greater German provinces of France and Belgium. She began her covert career with a Belgian cell of the Circle of

Zion. Her concise, insightful reports caught the CIA's attention, who recruited her as a stringer.

Garbo's childhood was typical of Jewish experiences in Europe before and during the war. Driven from Germany by Hitler's anti-Jewish laws in 1933, her family emigrated from Frankfurt to Amsterdam. Germany invaded Holland in 1940 and began to persecute the Netherlands' Jews. Many Jewish families went into hiding.

Otto, Garbo's father, was preparing a hiding place in his office building when Hitler was assassinated in early 1942. The Nazi Party's tumultuous collapse and Berlin's chaotic power struggles allowed the Dutch Underground to operate openly for several months. Otto took this opportunity to have new identity documents forged for himself, his wife, Edith, and his two daughters. It was twelve-year-old Garbo who suggested calling themselves Van Daan because it "sounded like a good Dutch name." Otto had his company, Opekta, transfer him and his family to Belgium to open a new branch in Brussels.

They escaped the postwar roundups of Europe's Jews and quietly assimilated themselves into German society. The parents eventually retired and immigrated to Massachusetts, where Otto has family. Garbo's older sister, Betti, inherited control of the family business and is now president of Opekta, SA.

26

Tiptoe, tiptoe. Use bathroom. Don't flush. Tiptoe, tip-toe. Back to bed.

Marie and her husband are downstairs, entertaining some friends. They chat and clink silverware around a melodic Miles Davis song. These guests don't know that the Schultze-Boysens have two spies hidden on their silent third floor, and we need to keep it that way.

We're quiet as church mice, which is easy for us except I have to go to the bathroom so much from all the fluids I've been glugging. We don't want Marie's guests to hear water running through the pipes downstairs, so my partner and I leave our business in the toilet bowl until we can flush it later. I've never thought of myself as a prude, but this strikes me as especially gross.

This is our fourth day in Garbo's house, and each day the place gets a little smaller. The Schultze-Boysens are very nice and their doctor chum is clearly good at what he does, but I finished memorizing the ceiling after my first morning here. Except for the evening news, TV is a bust: soccer (*yawn*), soap operas (*snore*), and game shows (*zzz*). Brando and I tried using the Ping-Pong table Marie has in her basement, but my stitches are too fresh for my spastic playing style.

So I've been diverting myself with Marie's book collection. Her English-language shelf includes a bunch of novels by female authors like Emily Brontë and Jane Austen. I found the writing in *Pride and Prejudice* absolutely hilarious in places, although the story remained obstinately free of gunfire and explosions.

The music downstairs changes to James Brown. I

listen to Clyde Stubblefield pound through "Funky Drummer." It reminds me of Dad. He used to play this song on the stereo and dance around the living room. If he wasn't too drunk, Cleo would join him while I watched from the stairs in my jammies. I'll never forget the way their faces glowed whenever they danced together.

Patrick sneaks past my door on his way from the bathroom to the other guest room. I catch his eye and waggle my fingers at him.

"C'mere," I comm.

Patrick pads in, gently shuts the door, and sits at the foot of my bed.

"How are your injuries?" he asks.

"Better, but my sutures feel like they'll tear open unless I move slowly."

"Well, take it easy, then." He glances toward the stairs. "We wouldn't be able to get a doctor up here until these people go home." He studies my face. "You look much better."

When he tells me this, I do the last thing either of us would expect. I blush. Heat rises in my cheeks, and I stare down at my hands to hide the dopey grin on my face. We haven't had much time to talk this week. I've been really out of it until today, and one of the Schultze-Boysens is usually up here to make sure we're all right.

Neither of us has mentioned the kiss I gave him in London, but I've sure thought about it. Our mission began four weeks ago, but it feels like forty. All this crazy-ass time with Brando has diminished my heartache about Trick from a screeching, clawing eagle to a brooding, sullen crow that leaves me alone as long I don't poke at it.

I hold my hand out to Brando. He clasps his hand into mine. I search for something romantic and mysterious to say, but I can't think of anything.

Ahh, fuck it. He's cleaned bloody bits of my clothing out of a bullet hole, he's seen me basically naked, he already knows what a bitch I am before I have my morning coffee. Plus, we've had to use the same toilet without flushing. How much mystery is there going to be anyway?

Finally, I whisper, "So I liked that kiss."

He smiles and squeezes my hand. "Me, too."

"I've thought about it when I wasn't puking or bleeding."

"Same here, except for me it was when I wasn't worrying." He puts his other hand on top of mine. "Actually, I've done nothing but worry, so I guess I did both."

The corners of my eyes crinkle as I try not to laugh out loud. I coax Patrick up the bed until he's in range, then lean forward and plant one on him. He gently lays his hand on the side of my face and kisses me back.

I can't pull him into bed with me because of my stitches. Besides, it's not like I feel *that* good. My stomach is upset, and my abdomen still hurts. It's probably better for me to take this slow, anyway.

As I've become less frightened of losing my new partner, I've been able to appreciate how much I like him. He's really similar to Trick, of course, but he's not a duplicate. I know they had the same inception day, but he seems more grown-up. Sort of like Trick's older brother.

Okay, enough about Trick.

All this smooching makes me lose my breath. I lean on my pillows and admire Patrick for a moment. Past his head, the stars shine through a window overlooking the roof of a small second-floor porch.

I comm, "Let's go out on the roof."

"Are you nuts? It's February."

I ease out of bed. "Don't worry. I'll bring a blanket—"

"Well . . ."

"—for *you*, wussy-pants."

Patrick's eyes and mouth open into three perfectly round circles. He's about to slap my leg when he remembers I'm wounded. His hand wiggles back and forth, unable to find a safe place to spank, so he settles for sticking his tongue out at me.

I drag my bedspread across the room. Patrick follows me, quietly opens the window, and crawls through first. I hand the blanket to him and gingerly climb outside. We huddle next to each other, and Patrick wraps the cover around us like a fluffy igloo. Biting air stings my cheeks, and I blink past a couple of tears.

It's beautiful. The sky is clear and moonless, so the Milky Way is like a frozen fireworks display. I snuggle against Patrick. After a minute my attention shifts to the street in front of Garbo's house.

There are two unfamiliar cars parked out front. One must belong to Marie's guests, and the other belongs to . . . who? I switch to infrared, and a spike of acid burns across my midsection.

In the second car is a man watching the house.

CORE   MIS-ANGEL-3108

DATE: 19 February 1981
TO: The Office of the Front Desk
FROM: Darwin-5055 (IO), Scarlet-A59 (L9 Interceptor)
SUBJECT: Operation ANGEL/Situation Report

Sir,

On 14 February in London we snatched Victor Eisenberg, acquired significant intel about Carbon, established a link to Big Bertha's whereabouts, and escaped an SZ raid. Scarlet and I fled across the Channel to Calais, where we made contact with a CIA stringer named Garbo who graciously took us into her house.

Scarlet was badly wounded in London, but she has received first-rate medical care and is recovering well. As of five days ago, Raj and Grey were both still in England.

Please forgive the brevity of this report. As you can imagine, this past week has been rather exhausting.

Obediently yours,
Darwin-5055

It's finally morning. A chilled gray light seeps through the windows and bleaches away last night's starry bubble of interdepartmental romance.

Marie comes upstairs. I tell her what we saw from the roof.

She stops midstride and frowns. "A man?"

"His car is gone now. We spotted him at about six o'clock last night. He stayed out there until ten-fifteen."

She asks, "Did he see you?"

"Probably, yeah."

Patrick sleepily shuffles into the room, sits on the corner of my bed, and finishes my answer. "We didn't want to tangle with him while you had guests."

Marie resumes walking toward her desk. Her brow remains furrowed. "Ten-fifteen. That was only a few minutes before the Müllers left."

My partner yawns. "Maybe he was a friend of your guests."

"I doubt it." Marie settles into her office chair. "A friend would ring the bell."

Patrick's early-morning German is missing some subtlety, so I say, "I think my partner meant to ask if the man might have been following Herr or Frau Müller with some ill intent."

"That's not very likely, given how dull they are." She laughs and says, "All right, little birds, we will solve the riddle of this mystery man, but empty stomachs make for empty heads. What do you say to some *Frühstück*?"

Twenty-five minutes later, Marie lugs in a heavy tray

crammed with breakfast food for all of us. Patrick and I picnic on my bed while Marie sets a place for herself at her desk.

Marie's husband calls up the stairs on his way out. "*Auf weidersehn, schatzi.*"

She replies with the German equivalent of "Bye, sweetheart."

My partner and I eat quickly, as usual. Marie has barely gotten her toast covered with butter and jam by the time I'm done with my sausage. I wolf my soft-boiled egg and wash it down with a big glorch of coffee. Patrick chats with Marie while I go to use the bathroom. On my way back, I peek through a window at the street.

The man is out there again, watching the house from his car. Marie's desk phone blares like hell's bells and scares me half to death.

Our hostess answers the phone. "Allo, Marie Van Daan." She listens for a few moments, then says to the caller, "How long has it been there?" She covers the mouthpiece and says to us, "It's my sister, Betti. There's a strange car outside her house."

Not good.

I sign to Brando that he should come look out the window. He zips over to me and peers outside. "Damn, it's that same guy again."

Marie says into the phone, "Hang on, Betti." She crosses to the window and glares down at the street, eyes narrowing. She returns to her chair and picks up the phone. "There's a car here, too. No, it's not a police car here, either. I think it's the Purity League again. Yes . . . okay, I'll call you in an hour."

She hangs up, takes a long sip of coffee, and quietly regards us over the top of her cup as we return to the sofa bed. We both stare our questions at her.

"Scarlet, Darwin," she finally says, "I need your help."

Marie tells us about the work she and her sister do for the Circle. We already knew some of it, but Marie gives us a much more complete picture. The Van Daan sisters and their husbands are part of the Floating Railroad. This is an underground network that smuggles Jewish slaves from Europe to America. The Floating Railroad has a measure of popular support because there are a lot of Germans who don't agree with slavery.

Then there's the Purity League, which crawled out of Nazism's cadaver and has proved impossible to exterminate. You can tell how the economy is doing by the reactions they get. During boom times, their vitriolic hatred primarily attracts derision. When a slump hits, more people pay attention to the anti-Semitic diatribes in *Der Pure*, their self-published newsletter.

Many Purity League members also belong to the Staatszeiger, so the league has some muscle to go with its lack of brains. Both of these groups are notoriously anti-Semitic, but the SZ is ostensibly limited to enforcing order in the slave camps and catching runaways. The Purity League has no oversight, and since it's listed as a social club, they avoid the scrutiny an official political party would be subjected to.

Their charter states that the Purity League is dedicated to preserving pure German culture from subversive influences. Everyone in Europe knows that in neo-Nazi-speak, "pure" means Aryan and "subversive" means Jewish. Their racist agenda attracts extremists from all over Greater Germany. A typical to-do list might read:

1. Strut around like a jackass.

2. Intimidate and attack minorities and members of the liberal left, especially abolitionists.

3. Talk too loud, drink too much, and be too stupid.

I say to Brando, "Well, I've heard enough. When do we stomp these pricks?"

Marie answers, "You can start tomorrow night. We're going to a party."

Operation DATA-DAVID

Now in its tenth year, DATA-DAVID continues to deliver quality intelligence about Greater Germany at a bargain-basement price. Our contacts from the Circle of Zion maintain a steady flow of information in exchange for our assistance with their clandestine missions to extract escaped Jewish slaves from Europe. The most ambitious of these undertakings is a lengthy network of safe houses, secret routes, and black-market shipping known as the Floating Railroad.

DATA-DAVID routinely violates German sovereignty and so runs counter to official U.S. policy. In the event of exposure, the diplomatic damage with Germany would be significant but not irreconcilable. Domestically, the widely held belief in slavery's unethical nature ensures our agents will be shielded from all but token legal repercussions.

Activists within the Reich, however, will be on their own.

28

"How's your champagne?" Brando asks me.

I tilt my glass of Veuve Clicquot up at the frescoed ceiling, pour its contents down my throat, and hold the empty out to my partner.

"More," I say.

He studies my face for a moment, then takes my wineglass and mingles his way across the crowded ballroom toward the bar, weaving through the schmoozing horde of Greater German glitterati and their attendant flacks and sycophants. My partner looks quite dashing in the charcoal two-piece suit Garbo picked up for him downtown.

As he waits at the bar, Brando catches Garbo's eye across the room. She's smoothly inserted herself into the cozy flock of females surrounding a tall and very handsome patrician gentleman. The man is entirely composed and charming, but something about the perfection of his teeth reminds me of a shark among goldfish. Maybe it's the way his smile's stunning whiteness is echoed by his lush and equally white hair. Anybody that attractive at his age must be up to something really evil.

My partner returns with a fresh drink for me. He's got a funny expression on his face. He hands me the glass while his eyes drift down to my shoes.

Despite a litany of curse-filled predictions from yours truly, my normally booted or sneakered feet did not rebel against slipping into a pair of black stockings and high heels. My sinewy legs curve like wings of nylon-covered marble from my ankles to the hem of my sleeveless dress. It's a little black number Garbo lent me. The dress hugs my waist and presents my meager cleavage to heaven's cruel scrutiny. I feel naked, and not only from the dearth of material covering me. This outfit is so tight that I can't wear my sidearm or even my fighting knife. Plus, I'm freezing, my bandages itch like crazy, and—

"You look fantastic, Alix," Patrick comms.

My lips curl into a smile, and a crest of warmth ripples down my thighs. I lower my eyelids and comm, "Thanks, Brando." I move my wineglass to the side and briefly pose like a fashion model. Patrick catches himself staring, clears his throat, and forces his eyes to the boozy roomful of elegantly attired power brokers.

I swig my drink and nearly cough it right up. "Bleah! This champagne is awful!"

"It's ginger ale."

I scowl at my partner, who has resumed studying the room. He says, "We're on a job, Scarlet. We can't have you all . . . tipsy."

"Tipsy? Little old ladies get tipsy. Real women get tanked!"

"Fine, whatever," Brando replies. "Just stay focused. I think Garbo has found our target."

Part of Marie's work is knowing who's who and where's where. When she heard about our person-of-interest list, including our orders to "investigate Herr Johannes Kruppe," she volunteered to bring us to this glitzy fund-raiser.

Marie insisted that we tart up. "Scarlet, you cannot go to Chateau de Cocove dressed like a farmhand. Try this on." She pulled a wisp of fabric out of her closet and handed it to me. "I'm too old for this dress, and you have a very nice figure."

Most of the classes at Camp A-Go-Go were gender-neutral, but some were for girls only. One of those classes taught us how to work jobs in a skirt and high heels. I thought it'd be a total fluff class, but wearing heels while running, jumping, and especially brawling is *way* harder than it looks.

My partner and I discreetly watch Garbo ply her feminine and journalistic wiles. She wheedles her way deeper into the gaggle of groupies that no doubt forms around this handsome devil wherever he goes. The man says something to Garbo, and she holds her glass like a microphone and pretends to interview him. Then she tilts it toward him for a response.

That's the signal. It's Kruppe.

A waiter eases through the group around Herr Handsome and whispers in his ear. Kruppe nods and apologizes to the ladies while he extricates himself from their fawning affection. He walks out of the ballroom and into the kitchen.

Brando takes my glass. "Follow him."

My heels speed-stroll through the crowd. I enter the kitchen and catch a glimpse of Kruppe's white hair as he passes through a doorway across the room. I follow him through the door and down a wooden staircase to a dimly lit but impeccably maintained stone cellar.

Tall wine racks line a corridor that stretches back under the ballroom. The long formation of dark glass is interrupted only by entrances to small side chambers, which are also lined with neatly arranged wine bottles. Kruppe continues walking down the passageway. I slip into the first side room—out of sight from the main corridor—and amp up my hearing. The door above opens. Another man's footsteps come down the stairs.

I press myself against a tall stack of wooden wine crates and hold my breath. The steps crunch past my alcove to where Kruppe stands waiting.

"What news?" I recognize Kruppe's voice from upstairs.

"Madness," says the newcomer. "The Gestapo in England is in tatters, and the SZ here is overwhelmed by rebel slaves and the damned abolitionists."

"My organization is ready to join yours to save the Fatherland," Kruppe says.

"Save? From who?"

"The Jew-loving traitors, of course."

The second man sighs, then says, "Johannes, those 'traitors' have nearly as many well-placed associates as you do."

"My Purity League can take care of them."

"We shall see, Herr Kruppe." The second man rustles something. A piece of paper? "Meet my courier at this time and place. He will give you a mission. If you succeed, I will decide what other Gestapo duties your league of brutes can perform."

After a moment, Kruppe says, "Very well."

One of the men passes through the corridor and returns upstairs. I hear the remaining person breathing. After a minute he begins to walk toward the stairs.

Then he stops right outside my hiding place. Savory-smelling aftershave drifts into my nostrils. His feet step toward the alcove. If I were an Infiltrator, I might be able to hide in place with a cloaking Mod, but all I've got to disappear into is my skimpy dress. The man takes another step and leans his head into my gloomy side chamber.

It's Kruppe. His silvery head turns my way. I zing my hand into one of the racks and whip out a bottle. Before Kruppe fully faces me, I bash his head. *Thonk!* He exhales sharply and collapses like a rag doll.

I rub my fingerprints off the bottle and put it back. My toes flip my unconscious victim over, and my hands find the piece of notepaper his contact gave him. It reads:

7 March, 1800. Thiepval, 11A.

I return the note to Kruppe's pocket and skedaddle upstairs. My heels click through the kitchen and clack across the ballroom.

"Darwin, time to go."

"Roger that," he comms. "I'll get Garbo and meet you out front. Everything okay?"

"Yes, fine." I march into the front foyer. "Hurry up."

I fetch my coat and walk outside to the mansion's

limo-lined driveway. My breath steams past my teeth into the night's wintry air. My legs are still exposed, but for some reason I'm not nearly as cold as I was a little while ago.

CORE   MIS-ANGEL-3277

Darwin,

Your report of 21 February was reviewed with great interest. Johannes Kruppe and his Purity League are already an operational hazard and must not become even more so. To this end, you and your partner will help disrupt the League's organizational effectiveness. Attached is the detailed Job Number. Good luck.

A. N. du Remise
—Senior Info Coordinator, Extreme Operations Division

29

I cram the small, heavy bomb between a pair of commercial-size refrigerators. When it explodes, it'll probably eject the outermost fridge right through this butcher shop's front window. The man who runs the place is one of the Purity League's most active thugs and has nearly caught Betti a couple of times.

Brando comms, "Got that bubba in place?"

"Yeah; let's scram."

We return to the taxi outside and get in the backseat. Our driver takes us to our next target. The quiet streetlit buildings of downtown Calais float by our windows.

Until recently, the Purity League's provincial character relegated it to being a hazardous nuisance. But now they're receiving assignments and information directly from the Gestapo, which could make them much more dangerous.

After we left the party at Chateau de Cocove, Brando commed his boss with descriptions of the stakeouts at Garbo's house and my close encounter with Kruppe. That same night we received new orders.

ExOps is mounting a theaterwide Rock 'n Shock Job Number to see if we can terrorize these anti-Semitic pinheads back to their rat holes. We worked all week with local Circle of Zion people to set up our targets and timing. Tonight is the final stage where we bomb three Purity Leaguer–owned businesses here in Calais.

Marie found an antislavery activist named Josef to chauffeur us around in his taxi. The job has gone smoothly so far. After this assignment, the only thing on our calendar is snooping on Kruppe's meeting in Thiepval next week.

We stop in front of a tailor's storefront a few blocks from the butcher shop. The tailor is the bozo who's been watching Marie's house. He doesn't have much heavy equipment, but he does have a lot of flammable fabric. Instead of the high-explosive device we used at the butcher's shop, we plant a lava-spewing incendiary bomb in his storeroom. We're in and out in three minutes flat.

In the car, I say to Brando, "I think fire will be very 'in' this season."

"Oh, most definitely," he answers. "Nothing says 'fashion forward' like being wreathed in flames."

Josef drives us to our third and final target, a large department store in downtown Calais. It's also the Purity League's regional distribution center. Uniforms, provisions, even weapons are shepherded through this place by the store's ex-Nazi owner.

One of Marie's associates, an electrician named Bruno, was here earlier tonight to disable the security system. In fact, he's the person who originally installed it. Marie said she had to talk Bruno out of removing the equipment entirely. He wanted to save it from being destroyed along with the building. She had to illuminate for him how unbelievably suspicious that would look.

"Bruno is a good man," Marie told us, "but not the ripest tomato in the garden."

Josef the cabbie deposits us at the store and drives away. We'll meet him at a prearranged extraction point a couple of blocks from here. When Josef heard our plan for this place, he declared he didn't want to be anywhere near it while we're inside.

My partner and I sneak around behind the store. It'll take three bombs to ice this place, one for each floor. We've already decided to go from top to bottom. I kick the rear door until it flies off its hinges. Nobody lives in this retail neighborhood, but even if someone hears us, we'll be gone before the cops get here. Sometimes stealth is about being quiet, and sometimes it's about being fast. Tonight's stealth is the fast kind.

As we run up the stairs, I can't help enjoying how much better I feel than when we crossed the Channel two weeks ago. My combat wounds are healing well, and all the time I spent in bed has restored my nervous system's ability to use Enhances. That downtime also allowed Brando and me to grow closer.

We haven't made love yet, but I don't mind taking it slow with Brando. Trick was my first real boyfriend, so trying sex was, y' know . . . ka-pow! Now, though, I've done it, I like it, but I don't need to rush it. And when it's time, all I've gotta do is put that skimpy black dress on. Patrick couldn't wait to get home and show me how much he likes the way I look in that thing.

We arrive at the third floor and hotfoot it to the elevators. They're centrally located and run parallel to the ventilation, plumbing, and electrical systems. Wiping out this infrastructural spinal cord will completely disable the building. Even if the owner can salvage the structure, he'll still need months to repair the place. And he'll need even longer to explain why there are so many military-grade firearms mixed in with the beer steins and sausage stuffers.

I stand in front of the elevator, heave the doors open, and hold them while Brando adheres the first bomb inside the elevator shaft. While he works, a quiet scraping sound ripples up the elevator shaft. I listen closely, but I don't hear it again. Maybe sticking the bomb in place made a funny echo.

When my partner finishes, I let go of the doors and we run downstairs to the main office. The locked door graciously defers to my boot heel. I keep watch outside while Brando goes inside to wedge our next bomb wherever it'll do the most damage.

A tight click skips up the stairs. I know that sound—

someone's trying to be quiet while they cock their weapon.

"Darwin, I hear company downstairs."

He hurriedly finishes arming the bomb. "How many?"

I activate my infrared and peer through the floor.

Oh, my God. Where did all those fuckers come from?

I comm, "I have eyes on fourteen armed competitors."

My partner rejoins me in the hallway. "Are they SZ?"

"Negative. Their load-outs are all different. I think they're Purity League militia."

Our teachers at Camp A-Go-Go drilled many things into us. One of them was the importance of not freezing in a situation like this. "Act!" they would bellow. "Even a bad decision is better than no decision!"

I comm to Brando, "Roof?"

"Yes."

We charge back upstairs and keep going. I bash a service door open, and we step through to the top of the building. The stars glimmer above us, and the only sound aside from our heavy breathing is the dull hum of traffic on the A16 a half mile away.

The rules of engagement for this Job Number don't exactly cover this situation. These toads are regular civilians. Granted, they're packing, but the German press and public might view them and their untimely deaths differently than if they were Gestapo or SZ. This is a challenge. It'll take much longer to *not* kill these shit-kickers than it would to straight-up grease the lot of them.

Brando and I hide behind a commercial air-conditioning unit. The thing is four feet tall and ten feet square, so it should provide solid cover. I boot up Li'l Bertha and aim her at the doorway. She detects and labels the string of red figures zigzagging up the stairs from below. I set her for .22-caliber standard bullets, take a deep breath, and dose some Kalmers.

The first dickwit through the door swivels from side to side, searching for us. My infrared picks his weapon out in bright blue against the shimmering red of his body. I wait until his automatic pistol is in profile, then fire a round through its bolt chamber, blowing the gun out of the guy's fingers. He yelps and presses his empty gun hand against his chest.

A second militiaman runs from the stairway and aims directly at me. This presents me with such a small target that I can't count on disabling his weapon. Li'l Bertha switches to .45-caliber standard slugs and puts the brownshirt on his ass with a bullet through his right shoulder.

Meanwhile, Brando crawls to the roof's rear edge and pulls his rappelling line out of his X-bag. He uncoils the synthetic rope and secures it through a piece of stone railing in the building's facade.

He comms, "Ready when you are."

"You go first. I'll fend them off while you make your descent."

My partner climbs over the stone railing and disappears from view. I'm about to follow him when three more brown-shirted goons pour onto the roof and fan out. The competitor in the middle fires on my position to keep me suppressed while the other two move to my flanks.

I slide to my left. Flanker number one is sneaking along the air conditioner's side toward the back corner, where I wait. His next step brings him into glomming range. I rush around the corner, wrench his weapon out of his grasp, and bash its shoulder stock into his schnoz. Then I pick the dude up and heave him—bloody nose and all—over the big metal cooling unit. He plows into flanker number two, knocking the other man to the ground.

The remaining jughead ducks out of sight, and I sense this is my chance to bug out of here. I turn to the rappelling line—

—but it's gone! The loop of rope around the railing now ends at a truncated stub.

"Darwin, our rope's been cut!"

"No kidding. I was still ten feet off the ground," he comms. "Must have been a shot from one of the militiamen."

I grab the flying flanker's weapon, a vintage MP-41, and return to the backside of my bulletproof air conditioner. "What the hell should I do?"

"Can you jump down?"

"It's forty feet, Darwin. That'd wreck my knees for sure."

Four more militiamen storm onto the roof, and five still wait on the stairs, but with my partner in the clear there's a new option available to me.

"Darwin, how about I bull-rush right through these shitheads and exit from the ground floor?"

"Go for it."

I make sure the submachine gun is ready, then spring onto the AC unit and spray bullets all the fuck over the place. My startled opponents dive for cover, and my feet hightail it off the roof at top speed.

I fly into the stairway and crash into the row of men waiting to come out. The impact knocks them down like a line of dominoes. My boots leave tread marks on their heads as I literally run over my competition to get out of this goddamn department store. I scramble downstairs, third floor, second floor, first floor, and barge through the front doors.

The street is jammed with vehicles. Cars and trucks have been carelessly parked at every angle. One even rests on the sidewalk. Brando huddles behind a Volkswagen parked across the road. I jump over the VW's roof and land next to him.

He says, "Looks like the Circle has a leak."

"Yeah, but what a bunch of fuckchops these patsies are," I say. "All they had to do was wait for us to come out." The beer-swilling idiots didn't even post anyone to cover the exits.

We watch the store through the windows of our four-wheeled hiding place. Cop sirens wail in the distance as militiamen straggle out of the store. Most of them wear brown military-style uniforms. We only count twelve of them. They mill around, hollering at each other. Nobody seems to be in charge.

Brando asks, "Can you see if there's anyone left inside?"

"No; it's too far for my vision Mods."

The sirens are louder. "Well, forget it," Brando says. "We're outta here." He pulls his remote detonator out of his X-bag, takes one more peek across the street, and presses the button.

The entire neighborhood lights up like it's high noon, except high noon is happening inside the department store as it flies apart at the seams. The ground shakes under my feet, and the Volkswagen we're hiding behind skids sideways at us. My partner and I squeeze ourselves against each other. The blast topples the Purity Losers like a rack of bowling pins. Moments later they and their vehicles are pelted by a rattling rain of building chunks, broken glass, and shredded merchandise. The building lists to one side like it was hit by an earthquake.

I brush small pieces of stone and glass out of my hair. "Holy Toledo! I can't believe we were gonna put a third bomb in there."

"Actually, I planted the third one at the base of the wall where I landed." Brando shrugs as we stand up. "I figured, 'What the heck?'"

We make a break for it while the militiamen are still struggling to their feet. Brando looks back and focuses on something behind me. His eyes open wide, and he draws in breath to call out. I spin around and draw Li'l Bertha. One of the brownshirts has already pointed his weapon at me. Before Li'l Bertha can lock on to him, a bright rose blossoms on the gunman's forehead and he falls to the pavement. A rifle's report cracks through the air.

"Shit, Scarlet. Don't kill them!"

"I didn't! That—"

A second militiaman swings his gun in my direction,

then violently whirls face-first to the blacktop. The sound of another shot reverberates through the streets.

Brando shouts, "Scarlet!"

"It's not me! There's another shooter."

I backpedal away from the burning store. Every militiaman who aims at us gets a long-distance lobotomy. I count five shots and five hits. Then the rest of the losers wise up and play possum. The sniper fire stops. I try to see where it came from, but there's too much dust and smoke. The delay between the impacts and the bangs tells me the sniper is about a half mile away.

The sirens are very loud now. We run toward our pickup point with Josef.

I comm, "Five kills, all from about eight hundred yards. If I didn't know better, I'd swear that was an ExOps sniper."

"I *do* know better," Brando replies. "There aren't any other agents within thirty miles of here."

We swing around a corner, bolt down an alley, and charge into a small street where Josef's idling taxi waits for us. I open the rear door, and we dive inside. Josef floors it.

Brando comms, "My Info Coordinator confirms we're the only assets in the area."

"So who the fuck was that? The Sniper of Christmas Past?"

"My guess is it's someone from the Circle of Zion."

I say, "Somehow 'the Sniper of Hanukkah Past' doesn't have the same ring to it."

CORE   MIS-ANGEL-3727

Translated from *Der Pure*, March 2, 1981

Jewish terrorists attack Greater Germany!

Early this morning, a series of bombings rocked Greater Germany and confirmed the fears so often espoused in this very publication: the Jews have declared war on decency and freedom! Once again, our kind-hearted humanism has been repaid with hatred and violence.

More than fifty stores and offices were destroyed in last night's raids, all across the Reich. The attacks' tightly coordinated nature reveals that our Jewish problem is worse than ever, for the Jew has clearly enlisted a new ally: the bloodthirsty mobster and notorious genetic mongrel President Henry Jackson of the United States.

How long will we hardworking and honest Aryan citizens of Greater Germany submit to the whips of the CIA and their Jewish overlords? The Purity League demands these death-dealing fanatics be harshly punished! Our readers are urged to write to their government representative and call for swift reprisals against the menace lurking within our peace-loving borders!

30

*I fly over Paris, arms outstretched. Warm wind washes
around me and whips down my shirt between my breasts.
I bank left to circle the Eiffel Tower. I flap my arms to
gain some altitude and come in for a nice soft landing on
the tower's observation deck.*

*A hawk circles lazily above, then dives straight at
me. I reach for my gun, but it's not with me. Even if it
were, I couldn't wield it because I've been transformed
into a mouse.*

*The hawk's black claws glint in the sun as the ruthless
hunter stabs its knifelike talons into my little gray body.
The bird's stone-hard beak opens and screeches—*

"Scarlet!"

I open my eyes, grab Li'l Bertha from under my pillow, and leap out of bed. Someone gasps and falls backward away from me. I hit the floor in a firing stance,
ready to riddle my would-be murderer into Swiss cheese.

Marie sprawls on the rug, her hand over her chest. I'm
in her little office, on the third floor of her house. My
body is slick with sweat under my T-shirt and panties
despite the cool air. Patrick scurries in to see what's
going on.

"Scarlet, please forgive me," Marie exclaims. "I didn't
mean to scare you."

If this weren't so embarrassing, I'd laugh at the irony
of her apologizing to me when I'm the reason she's on
her butt. Patrick helps Marie up while I deactivate Li'l
Bertha and sit on the edge of the bed. My nostrils flare

from breathing so hard. I release some Kalmers to help me deal with a normal, everyday situation that doesn't require fighting like a cornered animal.

Marie puts herself in her desk chair. "I've never seen anyone wake up like that."

The bed gently creaks as Patrick settles next to me, "It's her Enhances. I usually use my commphone to wake her. The smell of brewing coffee works pretty well, too."

"Coffee, of course," Marie says. "Yes, obviously she needs extra stimulation." She watches me for a few moments. "I'm very sorry to have frightened you, dear."

"Don't worry about it, Marie." I don't mention how my explosive wake-up act has been the last thing some people ever saw. "Are you okay?"

"I'm fine." Marie waves her hand. "Next time I'll rouse your partner first. That way he can be the one on his backside." We all laugh. Marie's smile fades as she leans forward. "But there is something I need to talk to you two about." She wrings her hands. "My sister Betti is missing."

Marie's sister is an active part of the Floating Railroad. When Betti carries out an operation, she always phones Marie to let her sister know she returned home safely. Marie never received that phone call last night, and there's been no answer at Betti's house all morning.

This situation illustrates a downside of decentralized organizations like the Circle of Zion. Last night's bombings prompted the German authorities to declare a three-day curfew. Those involved with the Floating Railroad had no idea this was coming. Activists like Betti are now stranded wherever they happened to be when the lockdown kicked in.

Marie paces around the room. "My press credentials will get us past the checkpoints, so leaving Calais will not be a problem. I have to file a report on the bombings, anyway. What I'm worried about is entering Brussels with a vehicle full of Stars. The guards will be on high alert, and if they do a search . . ." She leaves her thought unfinished.

"How does Betti normally move these people around?" Brando asks.

"She uses one of the trucks from our family's business." Marie tells us Betti left her home in Brussels last night to retrieve a small group of escaped slaves from a farm out in the Belgian countryside. She normally brings the runaways—or "Stars"—to her office, where she hides them in a storage room. Then she arranges the next leg of their journey out of Europe. This time, though, Betti was snagged by the crackdown. The longer she's gone, the harder it becomes to explain what she was doing.

"She can't just go home without the runaways?"

"She could, but every day a Star spends on the run dramatically increases the danger."

"What do you think?" I comm to Brando.

He doesn't answer, but I can tell he heard me. He holds up one finger and gently nods his head.

"Is he all right?" Marie whispers to me.

I point at my head and say, "He's talking to HQ."

Marie waits. I tune in to Brando's comm-call in time to hear his Info Coordinator say, ". . . CIA has confirmed Garbo and her sister are VIAs. You and your partner should undertake all reasonable measures to ensure their continued contributions to our information stream."

Well, well. Very important assets. Marie and Betti are hot shit back in Langley.

Brando says to Marie, "We'll definitely help. The question is how. Shooting up a checkpoint isn't exactly within our rules of engagement."

"What if it's manned by SZ?" I ask.

"No," Marie interjects. "I go through checkpoints almost every day, and they're always manned by regular police."

"Even during a time like this?"

"Especially during a time like this," Marie answers. "The Staatszeiger will be fully occupied investigating the bombings. But the police will be on edge. We must assume they will search a large truck."

Brando takes off his glasses and polishes them with the tail of his shirt. He *hmms* to himself. He has an idea.

"Smoke," he says. "You're right. The cops will search us, so we won't even try to pass through normally. We'll smoke 'em out and then dash through." Brando runs the plan past his boss, who approves it on the spot. I admire my partner's braininess until it dawns on me that we don't have any smoke grenades.

When I point this out, it becomes clear to me Brando has lost his mind. He puts his glasses on, turns to our hostess, and asks, "Marie, can I use some of your Ping-Pong balls?"

CORE   MIS-DATA-DAVID-519

Floating Railroad, Midnight Railroad

An escaped slave in Greater Germany has three choices, all of them dangerous: sneak into the Soviet Union, cross the Atlantic, or remain in Europe and join the Circle of Zion. Trying to pass as a free citizen is not an option because all slaves are clearly marked with a facial tattoo, typically a Star of David around one of their eyes.

Approximately half of all German citizens openly oppose slavery. Some of these people have established an underground network of like-minded activists who conspire to escort fugitive slaves out of the Reich. In Eastern Europe the collected efforts are referred to as the Midnight Railroad, while in Western Europe they are called the Floating Railroad.

For runaway slaves and the citizens who help them, both routes are long and perilous. The penalty for helping or hiding a slave is a heavy jail sentence. Anyone convicted of coordinating a group that aids in the escape of a slave is sentenced to death by decapitation.

31

We ride in Marie's bright orange Volkswagen Beetle. The spluttering little car bravely maintains a speed of 120 kph, or about 75 mph. The Belgian countryside rolls by as the sun sets behind us. Vast brown and green fields stretch to the horizon and nuzzle against the skirts of the absurdly tall cloud formations they have in this part of the world.

I tug my thoughts away from the passing landscape. "Marie, any word from Victor?"

"He's been . . . delayed, somewhere north," she says vaguely, "but he should return soon."

Brando leans forward from the backseat. "Does he need help? I could find out if we have anyone in his area."

"He'll be fine." Marie smiles to herself as though the idea of Victor Eisenberg needing help is amusing. "He was very unhappy about being captured in London. I think it's *die Teutsch* who will need help."

I comm to Brando, "Has ExOps heard anything about Victor?"

"Nothing definite. Holland is rumbling to a full-scale rebellion, but that's not the only place north of here."

We're quiet for a few minutes, then Brando asks, "Marie, why are reporters permitted such freedom of movement during the curfew?"

"The authorities find out more from us than they do from their military news sources."

No wonder our cover is working so well. Marie's press pass, the fake IDs for me and my partner, and a very official-looking heap of professional audio/video equipment have allowed us to breeze through the check-points outside large towns like Dunkirk, Brugge, and Ghent. Brando and I pretend to nap or fiddle with the cameras while Marie does all the talking. Our spur-of-the-moment road trip has been blessedly uneventful.

Except for that pest on the motorcycle.

I spotted him thirty minutes ago. He *could* be coincidentally going to Brussels—it's a big city, after all—but there's something about the way he's remaining the same distance behind us. Plus, who the hell rides their motorcycle in March? I commed to Brando about him, and my partner agreed the guy is definitely somebody.

Marie has been chattering away about . . . actually, I lost track a few minutes ago. She realizes we aren't listening and asks, "What are you two staring at?"

"We're being followed," Brando answers.

She says, "The motorcyclist in the black helmet?" Garbo can multitask with the best of them.

"Yes. He's been following us for a while."

"Well, that won't do at all," Marie says. "We're almost there." She downshifts from fourth to second, and her car pitches us all forward. She floors the gas for a moment, then takes her foot off the accelerator. Her little Volkswagen bucks like a bronco. Marie furiously runs the shifter all over the tree: third, fourth, second, back to fourth. Her savage shifting would roast the transmission right out of most cars, but the Orange-mobile takes it in stride. All this insane abuse fires a series of loud backfires from the tailpipes.

I comm, "She's pretending her car is stalling!"

"Yah, no kidding." My partner literally has his hands full holding the hopping electronic gear in place. "I think I'm gonna puke."

Honking cars flow around us as the heaving Orange-mobile slows to a pathetic 50 kph. Marie clicks on the hazard lights while she hyperextends her car's gearbox. There's no way that motorcyclist can stay back there without making it obvious he's following us. He moves to the far left lane and roars past. I snap a series of images of him with my retinal cameras.

Even through his full-face helmet I can tell he's young, maybe even younger than me. He's on a BMW R80G/S with a custom bag attached to the front fairing.

Hmm, you could pack a nice rifle in that bag.

"Was that him?" Marie calls over her self-inflicted wild revving rodeo.

"Yes!" I shout.

We pass a sign reading BRUSSELS: 10 KM and another that says ASSE, TERNAT, HERFELINGEN.

She shifts into third and, blessedly, leaves it there. "Good. This is our exit." Marie swerves onto the exit ramp. I grab the Jesus strap while Brando's flock of cases and cables shoves him off his seat and buries him on the floor.

The exit ramp leads to the N285, a smaller road that arrows through several farming villages. As we cruise by compact, weathered farmhouses, I reach into the backseat to extricate my partner from the heap of equipment.

"Thanks," he groans. "Hey, Garbo, where'd you learn to drive like that?"

"My first CIA case officer," Marie chirps. "We were followed while he was training me, and he used that technique to make it impossible for the person to remain behind us."

"Remind me to send the CIA a thank-you card," Brando grumbles.

Marie swings us onto a dirt road that leads to the hilariously unpronounceable town of Borchtlombeek. The little road morphs into a rough track that leads to a sprawling white farmhouse set on a low hill.

Our car jounces through some spectacular potholes. I press my hands against the ceiling to hold myself down. Brando hangs on to the back of my seat and leaves the shifting gadget pile on the floor. Marie parks between the white farmhouse and a black barn. The cloud of dust created by our entrance floats past us and leaves a thin layer of grit on the car.

A large delivery truck rests in the barn's shadow. The truck's side has OPEKTA emblazoned over an illustrated crowd of jam jars and sausages.

What the heck does Betti's company make again?

We clamber out of the VW. I take a moment to stretch my muscles while Marie rushes into the house. A moment later she's talking with another woman. Both of their voices gabble away in something like German, except a lot of the words are different. They speak so fast that I miss most of it, but I do catch one thing.

I comm, "Isn't Marie's sister named Betti?"

"Yeah."

"Then why did she call her Margot?"

Brando comms, "I don't know, I heard that, too. They seem to have special names for each other."

We walk into the farmhouse. Once we're inside, the sisters go back to their normal names. We take their slip of the tongue and file it away.

Marie introduces us. "Betti, these are two new friends of mine. They're here to help. This young lady is Scarlet, and her partner is Darwin."

Betti smiles and shakes our hands. "Pleased to meet you. Thank you so much for escorting my sister all the way out here."

The Van Daan sisters bear a strong resemblance to each other, but Betti is taller, wears glasses, and has a quieter presence than her energetic younger sibling. Betti introduces us to the farm's grizzled owner, who nods and shyly mumbles something in German.

Betti leads us out into the evening gloom and walks to the barn. Her wards are hidden in the hayloft. Betti calls out to them, and they descend a thick wooden ladder. I'm about to ask where their belongings are when I realize what a stupid question that would be. *They're slaves.* They have nothing except one another.

There are four of them: two women, an adolescent

boy, and a girl who's still a toddler. Each of their left eyes is surrounded by a Star of David tattoo.

One woman carries the girl in her arms, and the other woman tries to hold the boy's hand, but he keeps pulling his fingers out of her grasp. These people are ashen, skinny, and bedraggled, but the steel in the women's eyes and the firm set of their jaws convey their determination.

We help the runaways into the back of the truck and shut the big door with a rattling bang. Betti climbs into the driver's seat, and Marie, Brando, and I return to Marie's car. I swear her Beetle is so bright, it glows in the dark. Our two-vehicle convoy drives to the highway and heads for Brussels.

There's no sign of motorcycle boy, but that only means I don't see him.

32

The way Betti smuggles runaways in her company truck is a good example of hiding in plain sight. Opekta is a busy company, and its trucks make frequent deliveries in and around Brussels. The police see the jam-and-sausage trucks so often that normally they barely notice—much less search—one of them. Today, though, even the familiar Opekta truck will be stopped.

When we're less than a mile from Brussels, our mini-motorcade pulls into a small rest area. There's a parking lot, a low cement building with restroom signs that read DAMEN and HERREN, and a carpet of half-dead grass that stretches to a thick stand of woods.

I step out of Marie's Orangemobile and mosey around behind the concrete structure. *Nothin' to see here, folks. Pay no attention to the sexy vixen with the pocketful of homemade smoke bombs.* Once I'm in the woods, I break into a full run. After a few minutes I arrive at the highway's off-ramp for one of Brussels' quieter neighborhoods. Seventy or eighty yards up the exit, a brightly lit checkpoint forces all exiting traffic to stop and be inspected.

I crouch down in some undergrowth and watch four policemen in body armor and riot helmets thoroughly check each vehicle before they allow it through. One cop examines everyone's paperwork while another inspects every car and truck. The last two keep watch from raised platforms on either side of the road, their MP-50 submachine guns ready.

"Darwin, I'm in position."

"Roger, Scarlet. We're leaving now."

I reach into my cargo pockets and fish out the three smoke grenades my partner made last night. Externally, these doodads are simply soda cans with fuses sticking out the tops. I thought Brando was kidding when he asked Marie for Ping-Pong balls, but it turns out if you mince them up and burn them, they produce a whopping amount of smoke.

My initial contribution to their construction was rapidly ingesting the cans' original contents. Brando took the empties and melted a candle into each one for weight. After the wax cooled, he added the shredded remains of a half dozen Ping-Pong balls and a bullet's worth of gunpowder. Meanwhile I made fuses by smearing pieces of string with model cement. A dab of wax affixed my fuses through each can's opening and formed a nice firm seal. Even the fussiest of anarchists would proudly foment revolution with these tidy little buggers.

A long sedan pulls into the checkpoint as Darwin comms, "Scarlet, we're almost in sight of the target."

"Roger that, Darwin."

I take out my lighter, ignite the fuse on one of Brando's contraptions, wind up like Tom Seaver, and whip it at Paperwork Cop. The can hits the guard in his butt and thumps to the ground. Herr Paperwork shouts in surprise, then the billowing white Ping-Fog swallows him whole.

My second fastball hits Vehicle Cop in the leg. Before he can kick the hissing hazard away, he starts coughing and choking from the fumes spewing out of the first grenade. Moments later, he's engulfed in the second grenade's swirling discharge. The two Smoka-Colas are already generating their maximum concealment—the sedan has practically vanished—so I tuck Smokey number three back in my pocket.

The pair of platform sentries are above the thickest smoke, and we can't take any chances. I draw Li'l Bertha and spray short bursts of .12-caliber pellets at the metal supports and railings of the two scaffolds.

Both men flop to their stomachs. I charge through the smoke, spring to the nearest platform, and furiously pistol-whip the first guy until he stops moving.

By the time I turn to deal with the last remaining sentry, he's already got the drop on me. His trigger finger tightens, then he suddenly reels, stunned, as the front of his helmet is loudly inflicted with a bright, clanging dent. The piercing sound of a rifle shot immediately follows.

I quickly look around. Nobody's in sight. Whoever placed that nonlethal strike did it from so far away that I can't even see him. I climb onto the railing and launch myself across the street. The instant my feet touch the other platform, I coldcock the faltering policeman into next week.

"Darwin!" I comm. "All clear. Make your run!"

"Roger that, Scarlet. Here we come."

Marie's bright orange car careens off the highway exit, closely tailgated by Betti in her truck. Brando rides next to Marie in her Orangemobile and holds his infrared scope to his eye. His mouth moves while he directs Marie through the smoked-out intersection. She hunches over the steering wheel as she avoids the stopped car and the guards crawling around in my Ping-Pong pea soup.

Both vehicles whoosh through the checkpoint and into the city. Now the sisters will drive to Betti's office, where Brando and Marie will spend a night or two to let things cool down.

The rest of our plan calls for me to acquire transportation and get back to Calais. I'll lay low at Marie's house until she and my partner return. But first, it's time to locate that sniper. While help is always appreciated, I don't dig some mystery guest crashing my Job Number.

Who is it? If it were someone from ExOps, we'd have been informed. If it were an opponent, I'd be dead. I bend down and examine the silvery dent on the unconscious guard's helmet. The indentation's shape indicates the shot came from the highway, but between here and there is nothing but open terrain. There's nowhere to hide except . . .

Except for a dense patch of tall brush in the triangular island between the highway's on- and off-ramps. It has excellent cover and a built-in highway-shaped escape route. That's the place.

I holster Li'l Bertha and jump off the platform. Mr. Sharpshooter can obviously see me, so I don't bother hiding my intentions. I point myself at the stand of bushes and blast off. My flickering legs whisk me to my objective in nothing flat.

A young man materializes in front of the leafy concealment with his hands out. I ram him at full speed, and we fly into the bushes. I ride him like a surfboard until we skid to a stop. On the ground is a scoped rifle, resting on its case. Next to that is a small BMW motorcycle with a black helmet hooked on the seat.

I seize the front of the dude's jacket and snarl, "Who the fuck are you, buddy?" *Wow, his face is awfully familiar.*

Instead of speaking, my human carpet waves his hands around. After a moment I realize he's using sign language.

Switch off your commphone, he signs.

"What?" I say. "Why?"

He has to spell out his next message one letter at a time: F-r-e-d-e-r-i-c-k-s.

I cautiously take my hands off his coat and sign, *What about him?*

He sent me to kill you.

Now I recognize this kid's face. I've seen it in my scrapbooks, in my parents' wedding album, and on the Memorial Wall at ExOps. Every night, when I shut my eyes, I see this face.

It's my father's face.

33

"Falcon," the young man gasps around my right hand, which is clamped on his throat. "I'm called Falcon."

Even his voice sounds like my dad. That's all I have to go on right now because I suddenly can't see anything.

An image of Trick coalesces from the blackness. "You're hysterical," he says.

Somehow I find a snappy comeback. "If you think this is funny, wait'll you see the dancing panda bears."

"No, I mean you're emotionally hysterical. That's why you've lost your sight."

"Will it come back?"

"Take a deep breath . . . that's it . . . try to relax until—"

Click! I can see again. Trick vanishes. I blink away the ghosts and resume strangling this teenage version of my dad.

I deactivate my commmphone, just in case, so nobody but the two of us can hear me demand, "Why do you look like my father? What the hell *are* you?"

He begins turning blue. I relax my grip slightly. Li'l Bertha hovers an inch from his face, so any false moves will result in a splattery cloud of deconstructive dentistry.

"Fredericks raised me," he pants.

"That's impossible! I'd know if my father had given RUACH permission to clone him."

"Not RUACH." His voice croaks around my choke hold. "I'm from ARI."

"You can't be. ARI was shut down—" I hesitate. "Unless . . ."

The punk nods his head a little but doesn't say anything.

"No . . ." I whisper, "unless Fredericks kept it going as a—"

"Skunk project, yes."

I let go of his throat but keep my gun aimed at his jabber hole. I fish around his left side and remove a pistol from his holster. His stomach and chest heave under me while he gulps in a few breaths.

"How old are you?" I demand.

"Seventeen," he says.

"How do I know you're not a German plant?"

"This morning I shot five Purity Leaguers for you."

"So what?"

"Can I get up?"

I have *no* idea what to do with this guy. Normally I'd ice him, but he *has* helped me—twice in one day. This kid had two golden opportunities to shoot me dead, and he didn't.

If he'd been speed-grown in Carbon's Gen-2, he'd appear a little older and act a lot younger. So let's say he really is seventeen years old. I suppose Carbon could have acquired cell samples from my bad-ass father seventeen or more years ago and produced Falcon in Gen-1. But the Germans have plenty of their own bad-asses for that sort of thing.

My dad is in Carbon's Gen-3 for what he can offer mentally, not physically. If Falcon were—through an incredible fucking miracle—a Gen-3 clone of my father, the kid wouldn't merely look and sound like him, he'd *be* him. And trust me, Falcon isn't him. There's no way in hell Dad's bombastic Greek parents created the personality I see before me. No one from that family would *ever* be so composed while being assaulted like this.

I climb off the kid. Li'l Bertha remains ready, but in a

less menacing way. "Okay, Falcon, what's your deal? What do you want?"

He slowly stands up. He's dressed in blue jeans, short black boots, and a black leather jacket over a dark gray hooded sweatshirt. "Maybe I should tell you on the way."

"Way where?"

"Anywhere but here. We can take my motorcycle." Falcon nods his chin toward the checkpoint. A police car has arrived, and my smoke-bomb victims are on their feet.

"Fine." I holster Li'l Bertha. "But you ride bitch."

We saddle up, and I steer us onto the highway. I crank the throttle over, and his bike whisks us away. I keep our speed reasonable so I can ask Falcon again who he is and where he came from. His story chills me even more than the winter air we're riding through.

Falcon is a product of the supposedly defunct Asexual Reproduction Initiative. I already knew this program was closed because they used genetic material from an off-limits minor. What's news to me is the cell sample that grew Falcon was stolen from ExOps's medical offices—two years after ARI was canceled.

This explains where ARI's old equipment went. All that kaboodle was going to be transferred to the new American cloning program, Reproduction Using Asexual Cloning Heuristics, to continue cloning research. However, the moral and legal realities of cloned humans were so convoluted that Congress simply gave up and limited RUACH's charter to shepherding ARI's offspring through their childhoods. The Asexual Reproduction Initiative was packed up—lock, stock, and barrel—then stuffed in a government warehouse under the desert outside Phoenix.

During the probe of ExOps's notorious moles, the Office of Security investigators traced some of their activity to that warehouse. All the ARI gear was missing, but who knows how long it had been gone? Now, hav-

ing met Falcon, I'd say Fredericks swiped it within a
year or two of ARI's demise. Plenty of time to establish
his own personal cloning program.

Fredericks, as the Front Desk of ExOps's German Section, had full access to his agents' medical profiles and
lab samples, including Dad's. What on earth Fredericks
thought he was doing is beyond me. For now it's all I
can do to wrap my head around a universe that includes
this young version of my father.

I turn off the A10 and onto the A18. I accelerate to
200 kph to see what Falcon does. His arm around my
waist tightens, but he keeps his cool and doesn't say
anything. The freezing wind makes my eyes water, so I
slow down again. When I ask Falcon about Jakob Fredericks, he lets out a sharp breath.

"He's got stacks of incriminating files about everybody in Washington. They're all scared to death of him.
The man is absolutely batty, but nobody has the guts to
bring him down."

"Has he always been crazy?" I ask.

"I don't know, maybe. He's been a bastard all my life,
but he gets more unhinged every year. He raves about
you a lot."

Great.

Talking on a motorcycle is a bit of a chore, so we
stay quiet. Avoiding the checkpoints requires a series of
creative detours. We cut down dark alleys, zigzag across
parking lots, and sneak through people's backyards.
Once we even putt-putt through the lobby of a blocklong office building, waving at the flabbergasted guards
like it was *Candid Camera*.

I still don't know if this kid is telling the truth or if
he's playing me. It's probably best to keep him away
from Marie's place. Unless, of course, he already knows
about it.

"How much do you know about where I'm staying?"

"You and Darwin have been crashing at Marie Van

Daan's house in Calais while you heal from wounds you suffered in London."

Fuck. If Falcon knows all this intel, he probably got it from Fredericks. "Was that you watching Marie's house the other night?"

"No, that was an amateur, using his own car. The dope even left his real plates on it."

Falcon takes his surveillance seriously. He even spies on the people who spy on the people he's spying on.

We wheel onto Marie's street. I switch off the headlight, goose the engine, and then switch that off, too. We silently coast down the road and into Marie's driveway. I drag my feet to stop the motorcycle so the brake light doesn't come on. We hop off the bike. I walk it into the garage, leaving the door open since that's how Marie left it. I unclip Falcon's rifle case, tuck it under my arm, then lead the way into the unlit kitchen.

Nobody's home. Marie is still in Brussels, and her husband is away on business. We leave the lights off, and since Falcon doesn't bump into anything, I assume he has the same vision Mods as me. I pitch his rifle up on top of the kitchen cabinets, then grab two bottles of Beck's from the fridge while my brain tries to figure out what to do.

Falcon cracks open his beer. He's about to take a swig when he stops short. His eyes flit to one side, at the doorway to the living room. The kid silently puts his drink on the kitchen table, and—forgetting that I've disarmed him—reaches into his empty holster.

I whip out Li'l Bertha and jab her at Falcon's face. The young sniper freezes and holds his hands out with his fingers splayed. Then he very deliberately inclines his head toward the living room.

Dammit, did this punk set me up?

My system has absorbed a heavy dose of Madrenaline, so it'll be nothing to ventilate him if he tries anything.

But then, why would he tell me where they are?

I wave my sidearm toward the other room. *Move it. You first.*

Falcon slowly walks into the living room. I layer infrared over my night vision and follow him. A hot red blob hides behind the sofa. A long blue shape overlaps the red blob and clearly outlines an automatic weapon.

I shout, "Hey, Peek-a-Boo! You've got one fucking second to put your hands up or I'll—"

"Scarlet?" The red figure lays the blue weapon on the floor. "Don't shoot; it's Victor. My gun's down. I'm coming out." He slowly rises. I shut off my vision Mods and flip on a light switch. We all cringe in the glaring brightness.

"Vic, it *is* you! Where have you been?"

"It's a long story." Victor climbs from behind the sofa.

"Why didn't you comm that you were here?" I go to shake hands and only then realize I'm still holding my fucking beer.

Victor smoothly lifts the bottle out of my grasp, winks at me, and takes a gurgling chug. "Ah-h-h, thanks." He wipes his mouth on his sleeve. "I'd have called ahead, but I found out the hard way that comm-sets aren't waterproof." He extends his hand toward Falcon. "Hello. I'm Victor Eisenberg."

The kid, who clearly recognizes the famous underground leader, recovers his wits enough to take his hand. "Uhh, hi. I'm Falcon."

"Hmm," Victor says quietly, "another American. Very interesting." He turns to me. "You look much better, Scarlet. How are your injuries?" While I answer him, he retrieves his weapon, an MP-52-S with a very nice scope, from behind the couch.

We settle into the kitchen. I tell Victor what's been happening around Calais. He almost dies laughing when he hears how I knocked out Kruppe with a wine bottle. He makes me repeat the part about the meeting at Thiepval, which Patrick already told me is a French town with a gigundous war memorial. While Victor ponders that, I tell him about the bombs we set off last night. He says he saw the wrecked department store on his way through downtown Calais earlier today. I finish with our rescue mission to Belgium.

"So, Falcon," Victor asks, "you're new to the team?"

"Falcon was there, Vic, but he isn't ExOps."

A car's headlights swing through the kitchen windows. The vehicle pulls into Marie's driveway. I draw my sidearm, and all three of us crouch down low.

Now what? Did Fredericks send these people, too?

I hand signal to Falcon: *You wait here.*

He frowns and holds his fingers out like a gun.

I shake my head, "No way." Then I whisper to Victor, "Can you cover me in case I need to fall back?"

Victor nods and gently cocks his weapon.

The driver pulls into the garage, shuts off the car's engine, and douses the headlights. I dive into the garage, roll across the cement floor, and take cover below the vehicle's hood. Doors open on both sides of the car. The interior dome light casts a dim glow.

A woman's voice asks, "Where did that motorcycle come from?"

Wait a minute. The car is bright orange. Li'l Bertha's targeting screen fills with the tired-looking face of my partner. It's Brando and Marie.

"Darwin, what the fuck are you doing here?"

Both of them nearly jump out of their skins. Marie exclaims something in that weird language she speaks. Brando's training allows him to resist saying anything, but he still instinctively hides behind his car door before he recognizes my voice.

"Scarlet? Damn, you scared the crap out of me! What are you doing here?"

"I'm *supposed* to be here, dummy."

"I mean, why are you lurking in the—" My partner spots Falcon in the doorway and switches in midsentence. "Who in blazes are *you*?"

Falcon taps his ear and doesn't answer. I get Brando's

attention and sign to him, *Deactivate your commphone. Comm-code cracked.*

Brando's eyes flare open. Being compromised like this is potentially catastrophic, but his more immediate concern is to find out who the new kid is.

"Okay, it's off," Brando declares. "What the hell is going on?"

34

I introduce Falcon to everybody and give Brando a recap of my evening. It sounds like a child telling her parent about a stray cat. *This clone followed me home; can we keep him? He's housebroken, plus he's a terrific shot!*

My partner is very quiet. Anything to do with Fredericks is suspect. Falcon seems like he genuinely wants to escape the man's clutches, but for all we know this kid has been secretly equipped with remote-controlled surveillance gear or a tracker or a bomb or something.

Hmm, tracker.

"Falcon," I ask, "do you have a No-Jack installed?"

"Yes, but it doesn't work with my commmphone off-line."

Brando continues glaring at Falcon but remains silent.

Marie clears her throat. "I think I'll go inside and let you people sort this out." She switches on the garage's overhead light, walks into her house, and closes the kitchen door. Then she screams.

I run inside. Marie leans on the sink with her hand over her chest. "I'm all right," she says breathlessly. "Victor surprised me, that's all."

Victor earnestly apologizes to Marie for scaring her so badly.

Jeez, what a night.

Falcon and Brando follow me in from the garage.

"Hey," my partner exclaims, "Victor's back." He raises an eyebrow at me, "Anything *else* I should know?"

"Yeah. There's a well-dressed rabbit stuck in the chimney who says he's late for tea."

"Wiseass." Brando crosses the room and gives Victor one of those manly half-hug handshakes. "How are ya, Victor?"

"I'm well, Darwin." Victor puts a brotherly arm around Marie. "Have you been taking good care of Garbo?"

Brando sits at the kitchen table and grabs Falcon's bottle of Beck's. "More like the other way around. She's been awesome."

We all look at Marie. The attention makes her cheeks flush. "For goodness' sakes, stop staring." She bustles over to one of the cabinets. "It's been quite an evening. How about I make us something to eat? Victor, can you reach that pan for me?"

While the very important asset and the charismatic rebel leader set about cooking a late dinner, I pull up a chair next to my partner, who swigs beer and studies Falcon.

"Wow, Scarlet, I can't believe how much this kid resembles your dad."

I hit Brando's upper arm with my watch. "No shit, Sherlock!"

He winces and rubs his shoulder. Then he asks Falcon, "Hey, can you hack our commmphones so we can use them locally without Fredericks tracking us?"

Falcon shrugs. "Yeah, no problem."

"Okay, great." Brando mulls this over for a few moments. "Falcon, would you excuse us? I need to talk to Scarlet."

"Sure thing. I'll take a look outside." Falcon flips his dark hood over his head and goes out to the garage. His silhouetted figure strolls down the driveway.

Marie and Victor chat at the sink while they rinse vegetables. The water splishes and gurgles noisily down the drain.

Patrick leads me into the living room, pulls me close, and lightly presses his lips against my ear. "Falcon could be from anywhere," he whispers. "I don't like this at all."

"Me neither, but he *did* help us out. And I think he really wants to escape from Fredericks's skunko cloning program. Can't say I blame him. What should we do?"

"Normally I'd check in with HQ for direction, but if our comms are being intercepted, we have to stay offline and figure this out ourselves. I have *no* idea what the kid will do if we tell him to beat it. If he's telling the truth, he'll be on his own and really vulnerable. If he's lying, then he'll keep following us."

"Or," I whisper, "we could punch his ticket and bury him in a bog."

My partner considers this, then shakes his head. "Let's keep him with us—I mean, he's already proved useful—but don't tell him anything he doesn't already know." Patrick sighs. "Now that we've met Falcon, I'd say it was Fredericks who betrayed us in London. Which means we have to leave Calais tonight."

I nod in agreement. "Why did you come back from Brussels so soon?"

"You didn't answer my comms, and I was worried sick." He takes one of my hands into his. "I thought something had happened to you."

I turn Patrick's face toward me and kiss him. His tongue flicks against mine and fires twin bolts of electricity down the length of my body. The bolts ricochet off the carpet and shimmy up my legs until they meet at the tops of my thighs. I moan and have to push away before I commit international perversion right there in Marie's parlor.

I take a second to recover while we stare into each other's eyes. Then I squeeze his hand. "We'd better go. Let's bring Falcon inside and tell Marie and Victor we're leaving."

While we pack our stuff, Falcon repairs Victor's comm-set and reprograms our commphones to operate on a private network so no one else can hear us. I've been on the ExOps grid for years, and the moment I'm disconnected, it's like the whole world goes quiet.

It wasn't until then that I asked my partner what made him think the kid could do this for us. Brando gave me a two-word answer: "Your dad." He meant Falcon has inherited Dad's technical aptitude and probably other things, too. I hope the poor kid didn't pick up my father's love of drinking himself insensible.

Meanwhile, Marie goes into cooking overdrive. She won't hear of us leaving empty-handed, and her experience with the Circle has taught her how to make very portable food that will keep without being refrigerated.

The three of us gather in her kitchen and pile our backpacks on the table. Victor walks in from the garage and adds his field pack and ammo satchel to our luggage heap.

"Uhh, Victor, sir," Brando says, "we're kind of on the lam. It might not be a great idea to come with us."

"Hah!" Victor's voice booms. "Hunted? Cut off? On the run?" He spreads his arms out. "Welcome to my world." His bright smile sweeps away much of the anxiety filling the room. "Besides, the Circle needs your help."

I glance over at Brando to see what he thinks. He shrugs and says, "Sure, why not? You know the region, and it fits our overall mission. Plus, it's probably the last thing Fredericks will expect."

We pack Marie's field rations into our bags. Then she hugs us all good-bye, even Falcon, who she just met. Marie gives me and Brando an extra hug each. "Good-bye, young ones. Thank you so much for your help today."

"Thank *you*, Garbo. We owe our lives to you."

"Pah, it was nothing. You are easy guests, and having you here made me feel safer than I have in years." She pokes Victor in his chest. "Do not let anything happen to them, Herr Eisenberg."

He beams. "I think they will see to it nothing happens to *me*, Frau Van Daan."

We say another round of good-byes in the garage. Marie tries to convince us to take her car. We politely say no thank you.

She presses us. "How do you plan to travel?"

Considering Marie is a CIA stringer and an underground slave smuggler, she can still be preciously innocent sometimes.

"Marie," I answer, "we're Americans. If we need anything, we'll just steal it."

This cracks her up. She's still laughing as she walks inside.

The four of us slink away from her brightly lit house and fade into the night. At the end of Marie's street we turn toward the train station a few blocks away. Our first task is to get out of the area.

A few minutes later we enter the train station's parking lot, which is full of free cars.

"All right, boys." I rub my hands together. "Mamma wants leather seats."

CORE   MIS-ANGEL-3922

ANGEL SIT-REP: IRELAND. 22 February 1981

Entire island aflame with rebellion. German resources strained beyond capacity. Local underground has high morale and many new recruits, most of whom have begun work to maintain an orderly transition to home rule.

—Pericles, IO/Jade, L5 Interceptor

35

The ground swirls, my ears ring, and my stomach barely hangs on to the lunch I stole earlier today. The concussion is so intense that my entire body feels like it's been flattened in a vise. The sky rains shredded concrete, burning paper, powdered glass, twisted metal, and splintered wood. It looks mighty loud.

At Camp A-Go-Go, they taught me that 90 feet from a deafening blast is 210 feet too close. They didn't go into why it's too close, or if they did, I wasn't paying attention. Either way, I find out now because I lose my hearing, my sense of up and down, and my ability to form coherent sentences or even single words.

"Scarlet, you all right?" I can't tell if it's Brando or Falcon.

"Yeh, shuzz kug thuff." *Fuck, I can't even comm straight right now.*

"What?"

"Ee'm oka!" *Oh, forget it.*

Our ROAR Tour has entered the Somme, made famous during the Great War for the unprecedented scale and savagery of the battles that happened here. Sixty years later, the region's farmers still find dud artillery shells buried where the trenches used to be. Lord only knows what lies buried even deeper. Our action today is a dust speck compared to those sprawling campaigns, but it's gotta be the noisiest dust speck ever.

The debris falling around me used to be the Wehrmacht supply center for Belgium and northern France. Last night, one of Victor's Circle of Zion contacts advised him that if this facility suffered a devastating explosion, it would . . . well, actually he had me at "explosion," so I stopped listening.

The smoke clears a bit, revealing the pancaked army warehouse. The ground has stopped clobbering me, but I'm still too dizzy to walk. I crawl on all fours until a pair of hands helps me up. It's Brando. He drags me away from the blazing wreckage. Falcon arrives, and the two of them wrap my arms over their shoulders.

This job began nine hours ago when we paid a visit to a liquor store owned by another one of Victor's underground connections. The guy had three beer kegs full of fertilizer-based explosive waiting for us in his back room. Brando estimated that if these suckers went off together, the resulting crater could be a bathtub for the Statue of Liberty.

We gingerly loaded the kegs into the trunk of our Mercedes, then went shoplifting for breakfast. We've developed a few routines to defeat the security at grocery stores. My favorite is when Victor distracts the employees with his impressive stockpile of jingoistic wisecracks.

Ever hear the one about the Austrian who married his rooster?

We spent the rest of the day staking out this supply depot, waiting for the shifts to change. As soon as the day crew was gone, Victor started the car, rolled up to the front gate, and savaged the young guard with a terrifying hurricane of Teutonic attitude.

"Open up!" Victor barked at the guard.

The sentry was nonplussed. "Your identification, please."

"WHAT?" Vic screamed. "Why, you insignificant worm! I'll have your balls on a pike! Open this fucking gate!"

"Sir, I . . . uhh . . ."

Twenty years as a Wehrmacht officer has made Colonel Eisenberg a grand master of intimidation. "Listen, you walking stack of pig intestines, I'm delivering three kegs of Bavaria's finest for *your* commanding officer's birthday celebration. Every second *your* stupidity makes him wait will be another fistful of SHIT he shoves down *your* throat! OPEN THE GATE, YOU PISS-BLOODED MANURE-FOR-BRAINS WHORE SPAWN!"

There's no tirade like a German tirade.

The petrified soldier threw the gate open. Victor drove into the depot with absolute disregard for the posted traffic patterns, and his truly obnoxious parking job blocked three loading bays. The moment he was out of the car, he began storming around, terrifying the night crew. Meanwhile, the boys and I carefully humped the three kegs down to the basement.

Then Victor, Brando, and Falcon got in the car and roared out the front gate. I stayed hidden among the crates and barrels until Brando commed that they were clear. Then I sparked up the leftover smoke grenade from Brussels and threw it into a ventilation shaft. By the time white fumes started drifting out the other vents, I could already hear soldiers asking one another if they smelled something burning.

Now.

I pulled the fire alarm and hollered, *"FEUER!"* FIRE!

Other voices echoed my shout, and the entire shift ran for the exits. When all I could hear was the alarm, I beat feet out a side door. This was when I underestimated the minimum safe distance from our keg bombs, which is why Brando and Falcon are still lugging me across a field.

We make it to where Victor waits in our misappropriated Mercedes. My partner deposits me in the backseat, then scoots in next to me. F-Bird gets in front. Victor sticks the car in gear and puts the pedal to the metal. The acceleration is the last straw for my poor stomach.

Here it comes!

I open the window just in time to puke all over the

outside of our gigantic luxury motorcar. I flop back inside. My skin shimmers with stinging sweat.

Brando takes my hand. "I don't suppose it would help if you ate something?"

"Guh." My tongue tastes like flat orange soda, stomach acid, and half-digested cheese pretzels. "No." At least my hearing has returned.

Ahh, the glamour of a career in espionage.

Victor studies me in his rearview mirror. "You don't look well, Scarlet."

"All part of the act." I take a slow breath. "Vicberg, that was a great performance."

He smiles. "*Danke, fraulein.* It was my pleasure."

I lean toward my partner. "How'd we do?"

"Well," Brando says with a shrug, "half the building flew away, and the rest collapsed like a house of cards. I'm not sure how many of the contents were destroyed, but I'd say we achieved our objective."

Falcon nods and quietly says, "That was outrageously rad."

The kid looks and sounds like Dad, and he inherited my father's chops with weapons and technology, but he has his own way of expressing himself. Plus, he's *so* much younger than I ever remember my dad. These aspects have made it easier for me to accept him as our new teammate. Maybe my pre-cloning-era mind has decided Falcon is a long-lost cousin from Dad's side of the family and left it at that.

He has our family sense of humor, for sure. I came up with an acronym for Really Outrageous and Radical to tease Falcon about saying "outrageous" and "rad" so much. He loved it and christened Victor's series of missions the ROAR Tour.

Our tour's goal runs parallel with the objectives of Operation ANGEL, namely, to foster an environment of chaos and confusion within the Reich. Victor's long-term intention is to spread the slave rebellion across as much territory as possible. His immediate objective is to give the Circle of Zion a head start on the Krauts. To this end we've been tactically speed-blasting our way south from Calais.

Brando asks, "Victor, what do you think? Should we go to Saint-Quentin or Amiens next?"

"Whichever is closer."

"Saint-Quentin it is." Brando still holds my hand. "Think you can hold down some food?"

"Maybe. Lemme try one of Marie's eternity biscuits." Supposedly these thick, crackerlike biscuits never go stale. My partner rummages in our burgled cooler. Victor peeks in the rearview mirror again, but not at me. He's checking out whatever's behind us.

"Scheisse, Polizei!"

The rest of us spin in our seats. There's a single police car following us with its lights flashing.

Victor looks at the speedometer. "Dammit, I'm over the speed limit."

Brando and Falcon trade places, clambering past each other like kids on a jungle gym. Falcon and I open our windows and face backward.

I comm, "Darwin, what do you think? Should we take them out or let them pull us over?"

"If a close encounter goes wrong, we'll have to kill them. You'd better put on those bandanas and shoot out their tires."

Falcon and I each pull striped bandanas out of our hip pockets, tie them over our faces like Western banditos, and draw our pistols.

"Ready?" Falcon comms to me.

"Ready. I'll hit the front passenger side."

"Roger. I'll take out the driver's side."

We both lean out our windows and take aim. The cop car has pulled in close, so this shot will be easy. I dump a .45-caliber slug into the passenger-side front tire. Nothing happens. I fire again. The tire's center tread splits wide open, and the steel wheel clanks onto the road. Falcon's shots snap open the driver's-side tire, and the entire front end of the police cruiser drops to the pavement in a howling cloud of sparks.

Time for a quick exit and a new car. We've compared notes and figured out I'm the group's best getaway driver. I've got the most biorobotic upgrades and have spent so much time at the track that I could be a traffic cone.

I climb up front and sit on Victor's lap, and then he eases out from under me. Brando gives Victor his seat and transfers himself to the back with Falcon, who has left his bandana on in case he needs to provide cover fire. I floor the accelerator and leave it there. We flash down the freeway so fast that we could probably outrun a small airplane.

Brando spots a service station at the next exit. Our car's brake pads cook down to nothing as I sling us off the highway and into the station. It's five-thirty in the evening, and the garage is closed. The parking area is filled with vehicles in for repairs. I park our Mercedes behind the low building, and we hunt around for our next ride. Victor swaps the Mercedes's license plates with another car. Then he casually walks toward the road to keep watch.

"This Opel looks okay," Brando comms.

Bah, Opel. We can do better than that. That's when I see the gorgeous black Audi sedan with a sunroof and alloy wheels. There isn't any visible damage. Maybe it's just in for a tune-up. I try the door. It's open.

"Fellas, over here!" I get inside and hunt for the keys. Sun visor? Floor mat? No dice. I reach under the dash to rip out the ignition wires as the boys dump our bags into the Audi. I hot-wire the starter, and the engine growls to life. Brando jumps in front with me while Victor and Falcon pile in back.

I ratchet my seat all the way forward, adjust the mirrors, and pilot us out of the lot. Brando directs me to the A26, and our ROAR Tour is off to bring our crime spree—uh, I mean the Rising—to Saint-Quentin.

ANGEL SIT-REP: HOLLAND. 1 March 1981

The news from England has inspired local Circle of Zion cells to launch a sabotage campaign. Train yard bombed in Amsterdam, airplane hangar burned in Rotterdam. A good start.

—King, L16 Vindicator

36

Except for running low on ammo for Li'l Bertha, our biggest supply problem is we're out of cash. This doesn't matter for meals or cars since we don't pay for them anyway. Hotel rooms and gasoline, however, are more of a challenge. Bank robbery is way-y-y outside our mission parameters, and without direction from ExOps we don't know where most of our safe houses are.

On our first night out of Calais, we broke into an unoccupied motel room. It was comfortable, but we were so worried someone would barge in on us that we all slept like crap. We might as well have spent the night in the car.

Except it's too cold to sleep in a car in March, as we found out the next night. Victor has a lot of experience as a guerrilla, but he and his gang never stayed in cities. All of it was spent camped out in the woods, with occasional raids into towns for supplies. But the underground contacts Victor needs right now are in the more developed areas, and he never knows when they'll be available. So we make like big-city hobos and sleep where we can.

The morning after our second restless night, during an all-star breakfast of stolen bratwurst and Cokes, I proposed an idea: "Let's spend the night inside a store we're gonna rip off anyway. We'll bust in after they close and scram before they open."

My three stiff and grumpy colleagues agreed it was worth a shot. That night we slept in the small warehouse at the back of a grocery store. This was better, but supermarkets open early and we barely made it out before the morning shift came in to make doughnuts and chop up dead animals.

Last night we finally found a much better place: a gun shop. The building had a beefy security system, but anything less than Fort Knox is cake for us. We parked the Audi behind the store, and three minutes later we were inside.

It was like spending the night in Willie Wonka's chocolate factory. Falcon found himself a well-maintained Luger, and Victor lifted a nice pair of Walther PPK pistols. I was tempted by one of those blocky Mauser C96s, but then I'd lose all the targeting abilities of my dad's LB-505.

Li'l Bertha can use regular bullets when necessary, although I sense she feels like it's beneath her. Her gyroscopes shuddered a little when I manually locked her bore setting to fit the same 9×19-mm Parabellums used in Victor's and Falcon's new toys.

We packed up as many boxes of ammo as we could carry and racked out for the night. The store's sign said they didn't open until 10:30 A.M., which sounded great to me. I really needed the extra sleep.

The Gestapo, on the other hand, never seems to sleep at all. The pricks based here in Saint-Quentin push people around all day and drink booze all night. If they receive intel about escaped slaves or any other subversive activity, they pull a predawn raid.

Today will be different.

Victor met with a couple of his Circle contacts and learned there's trouble on the Floating Railroad. A group of runaways have been betrayed to the Gestapo. Victor didn't say how it happened, but my guess is it was a nosy neighbor in the Purity League.

Here we face another disadvantage of working with an aggressively decentralized organization like the Circle of Zion. Vic's contacts don't know where the fugitives are hidden. Only those directly involved in a smuggling operation know where the Stars are kept. Except tonight, someone else knows.

The Gestapo knows.

Brando and Victor worked out our game plan for this morning. We'll use the Gestapo's knowledge against them by tailing them to their raid. Then we'll fit them all for wooden overcoats.

We're parked across the street from Gestapo HQ, huddled in our car. Victor wants us to switch vehicles every couple of days, so tonight's job will be our last in this car, which I'm sure the poor thing is glad about.

The Audi looks like it's been inhabited by wild animals. The once-pristine floor and dashboard are now buried in food wrappers, magazines, newspapers, coffee cups, and soda bottles. Except for last night at the gun shop, we've basically lived in this car since we stole it outside Arras.

Brando, in the driver's seat, nods his chin toward the building across the street. "Here they come."

Eight Gestapo hooligans clomp out of HQ and file into a pair of cars and a heavy box truck parked next to the building. Three men per car and two in the truck. The headlights stab through the early-morning murk, their snarling engines stomp all over the peaceful late-winter silence, and the convoy moves out.

Victor leans forward from the backseat and says, "Let's go." Brando starts the Audi and pulls into the street.

I turn to Falcon, who's sitting in back with Victor, and whisper, "Ready to be outrageous?"

F-Bird smiles. "Don't forget radical."

We met this kid less than a week ago, and it already feels like we've worked together for months. He and I recheck our pistols and SoftArmor as Brando remains a block or so behind the convoy.

Victor slips his matching Walthers out of his coat pockets and places them on his lap. He activates his comm-set and transmits, "Once we know where these

Geschlechtsriesen are going, we must kill them immediately." Victor isn't ExOps, but he's a natural leader, and these are his missions. Moreover, it's impossible not to follow somebody who growls the German word for "limpdicks" the way he does.

Saint-Quentin is large enough to have streetlights, but they're all concentrated in the compact town center. Within a few minutes we're out in the countryside, and the black sky wraps around us like a shroud. My partner switches off the headlights, and I help him put on his starlight scope. The device fits into a band that wraps around Brando's head, so his hands are free for perfectly sensible things like driving at night with no lights on.

Twenty-five minutes later the Gestapo convoy cruises into the town of Péronne. They pull onto a quiet street lined with small houses. The cars slow down and stop, and the truck parks behind them.

Brando juices the accelerator and rolls down the windows. Victor, sitting behind him, hikes himself onto the rear windowsill so he's positioned to fire over the roof. We skid past the truck and screech to a halt next to the two cars.

Victor's raucous fusillade catches the Gestapo agents still in their seats. Falcon and I open fire at point-blank range, and between the three of us we grind our six competitors into guacamole. I cram a new magazine into Li'l Bertha and get out of the car. Lights come on in a few houses. I stand next to the lead Gestapo vehicle, which has been transformed into a gruesome death cart by our 9-mm hurricane. Two of the three occupants have been blown out of their seats. Glass shards sparkle in the dim glow from the houses. Blood has splashed all over the interior, and a handful of teeth are sprinkled across the dashboard. The hoolies look plenty dead, but I fire a slug into each of their heads to make sure.

Falcon sanitizes the second car while Victor runs toward the truck behind us. His job is to neutralize the driver, but the Gestapo son of a bitch has impressive reflexes. The driver shifts into reverse and floors it. The goon in the passenger seat sticks a pistol out his window and takes a few poorly aimed shots at us. The truck accelerates backward until the motor whines like a jet engine. The driver slings his big vehicle around so it faces back the way we came, jams it into first gear, and spits gravel at us as he speeds away. We try to shoot out the truck's tires, but our bullets are blocked by the folded steel loading gate mounted on the vehicle's tail.

I jump in the Audi. "Darwin, catch those fuckers!" Then I comm, "Victor, we'll be right back." Brando cranks the steering wheel over and stomps on the gas. The rear tires burn a capital C into the pavement, and we take off after the Gestapo truck.

We quickly catch up to the truck. My partner moves up on the rumbling vehicle's left side. The Gestapo driver swerves into our lane and tries to push us off the road. Brando hits the brakes and moves directly behind the hefty roller.

"I guess they saw us coming," he calls out.

Time for plan B.

"Get us closer." I hoist myself out the passenger-side window and crawl onto the car's hood. Brando pulls forward and tailgates so closely that we move into the pocket of dead air directly behind the truck. I fling myself onto the truck's back side. My feet find the top edge of the folded lift gate, and my right hand clutches onto one of the heavy door hinges. The wind whirls around the truck's flanks and presses me against the metal doors. Brando moves the Audi to one side so he won't run me over if I fall.

I kick at the door latch, but it's blocked by the gate. I dance my toes around until they hit the button that activates the lift. I ride down on the unfolding gate. A yellow-and-black sticker tells me not to do any of this shit while the truck is in motion. I'm gonna bet that sticker was not intended as in-flight reading.

The loading gate now sticks straight out like a porch.

I unlatch one of the rear doors and swing inside. Twin benches line the side walls, and twin rows of ring bolts line the floor. This is basically a supersized paddy wagon.

A small window into the front cabin slides open and extrudes the business end of a sawed-off shotgun. The weapon belches fire and kicks itself back through the window. I dive under the blast, but my right foot seethes like it's been bitten by a red-hot wasp.

I draw Li'l Bertha and shoot a row of holes through the metal divider between the cab and the rear area. Her first bullet doesn't seem to hit anything. Shots number two and three result in high-pitched screams. The fourth and fifth shots miss, but shots six through eight all produce somewhat lower-pitched cries of anguish. I swing to where the high-pitched noise came from and fire a tight circle of bullets. The screaming stops.

The truck swerves. I hear a loud crunch, and the ride becomes exceptionally violent. I bounce around like a piece of popcorn until we slam into a solidly anchored obstacle. My body bashes into the bullet-pocked divider and—

I wake up with a throbbing headache. Outside it's very quiet except for a low groaning from somewhere. I crawl out past the truck's twisted lift gate and drop to the ground.

The instant I land, a scalding shock lances through my right leg. I yell and put all my weight on my other foot. While I wait for my neuroinjector's Overkaine to kick in, I take a moment to get oriented.

We've collided with a stone wall set forty feet from the road. The truck is trashed. Its cargo box is bent like a used burger container, liquid drips from the undercarriage in three places, and two of the wheels have fallen off. I limp around to the driver's side to check the Gestapo thugs. One of them is mashed under the passenger-side dashboard, his head at an impossible angle to the rest of him.

Está muerto, Jim.

The driver's-side windshield has been blown out like a glass fountain. I walk to the truck's front. Herr Stunt Driver sprawls on the ground, covered in blood. His eyelids twitch and his nostrils flare as he breathes. I draw my F-S knife, slit his throat, and gouge a Star of David into his face. My vision flickers on and off a few times like a strobe light. The black flashes make me so dizzy that I almost pass out again.

From the truck's far side, a car horn blares and startles me out of my swoon. I shamble around the mangled vehicle. My foot stings, my head pounds, and I ache everywhere, but that all evaporates when I see the crushed Audi. It's a disaster. Most dramatically the truck's rear axle has ripped through the car's roof, broken the steering wheel, and mashed into the horn button.

Patrick!

I bound to the passenger-side door and peer inside. My partner is slumped on his side, and his eyes are closed.

"Patrick! Can you hear me?"

His eyes flutter. "Alix? What . . . happened?"

"Hang on; lemme get you out." The door is bent and won't open. I rip it off its hinges. The Audi's roof settles even further, and the seats begin to crumple under the pressure. I reach inside, extract Brando from the jumbled, honking mess, and ease him to the ground.

"Where are you hurt?"

He inhales slowly. "I'm okay," he says. "Just . . . had the wind knocked out of me."

"Patrick, that can't be right. Stay still."

I fetch his X-bag from the Audi, sling it over my shoulder, and bend down to examine my partner. His limbs are straight, and he's not bleeding. His breathing is strained, but his pulse is steady and his pupils aren't dilated.

"Heaven help me, you really do seem fine."

"Yeah, but I think we need another car."

The Audi's axles are broken, the windows are dust, and the roof is trying to limbo under the floor covers.

"Uh-huh, we definitely need another car," I say. "Can you walk?"

"Gimme a sec." He gingerly moves his arms and legs back and forth. Then he turns his head toward the street. "Do you hear that?"

A vehicle approaches. Its lights are off, so all I see is a dark gray smudge that slows down and stops at the roadside. I take cover behind the Audi and aim Li'l Bertha at the sound.

"Scarlet, hold your fire. It's me."

"Falcon! Can you help me with Pat—uhh, with Darwin?"

"Sure thing." The car door opens, and his footsteps thump across the dirt toward us.

"Holy shit!" Falcon exclaims. "What happened?"

"I'll tell you later. Help me get him outta here."

"No, no," Brando says. "I can walk." My partner heaves himself upright, tips over, and falls to the ground with an *oof*!

"All right, forget it," he grumbles. "Help her get me outta here."

Falcon and I each take one of his arms and lift him to his feet. The three of us scramboozle away from the wrecks.

"Where's Victor?" I ask.

Falcon says, "He said he'd catch up with us after he found the assholes who tipped off the Gestapo."

Brando drawls, "Glad I'm not *those* assholes."

We make it to the car and carefully deposit my woozy partner into the backseat. I scootch in next to him while Falcon gets behind the wheel and starts the engine. My hand skims something slippery as I pull the door shut. I examine my fingers. They're wet and smell like blood.

"Shit, who's bleeding?"

Falcon steers the car toward Saint-Quentin. "Don't worry. It's from the Gestapo creeps we wasted."

I scan the vehicle's interior. Riddled upholstery. Smashed windows. Teeth.

"Ah," I say. "We're in *that* car."

"Yeah," F-Bird says. "We'd better find something else before it gets light out."

Brando puts his head on my shoulder. "I vote for something armor-plated."

CORE   MIS-ANGEL-4399

ANGEL SIT-REP: SPAIN. 2 March 1981

The situation here in Spain is growing unstable, especially in Andalusia. German reinforcements from Madrid are sufficient to control the local outbreak, but now the north is unprotected. Expect further news tomorrow.

—Ghost, L12 Infiltrator

The titanic British monument at Thiepval was built on the Great War's bloodiest battlefield, where almost 20,000 British soldiers were killed in a single day and over a million men died in a matter of months. At first I thought this monument was a mausoleum for the dead from those battles, but Patrick told me that many bodies would fill the Empire State Building.

Even so, this heap of bricks is stupendous. It juts from the surrounding gardens of white crosses and rises high above the houses in the nearby town of Thiepval. Names of dead soldiers swarm over practically every surface, including the many supporting pillars. One of these pillars is specified by the last three characters of Kruppe's directions:

7 March 1800. Thiepval, 11A.

I lurk off to one side of the monument and watch pillar 11A, which stands under the central arch. My partners are positioned around the vicinity to form a surveillance box that monitors the monument, the graveyards, and the parking lot. This is a great place for meetings because treacherously skulking is indistinguishable from pensively brooding. This also makes it a great spot for spying on meetings.

After this morning's predawn game of whack-a-jerk, us three youngsters laid low until Victor rejoined us. He took us to a partisan doctor he knows in the area, who patched up my foot and Brando's cuts and bruises. Then we committed one act of grand theft BMW, shoplifted the shit out of another grocery store, and spent the rest of our day resting up for Kruppe's meeting tonight.

Brando, out in the parking lot, comms, "Kruppe has pulled in." A few moments later he continues, "Falcon, he's headed your way."

Falcon replies from the opposite side of the monument, "Understood."

"Victor, any competition out there?"

Victor replies from the park's far end, "Negative."

It's very quiet here, befitting the somber nature of a colossal monument to a lost generation, so when I hear laughter, it catches my ear. Two boys, grade-schoolers, chase each other up and down the main aisle between the fields of tombstones. Their parents are nowhere to be seen, so one of the park's visitors takes it upon himself to sternly shush the kids into submission. The boys quiet down.

Falcon comms, "I don't see him yet, Darwin."

I return my attention to—

Damn!

—two men in front of my column! One is tall, and the other is short and very thin. They brush past each other, but their eyes don't meet. The tall one jams his hands into the pockets of his long wool coat and stalks in my direction. It's Kruppe. I turn away and study the list of names on the column in front of me. Kruppe passes directly behind me. I recognize his aftershave from Calais.

"Darwin," I comm, "they've made their exchange. Kruppe is walking to the parking lot."

"Roger that. Scarlet, you and Victor follow his contact. Falcon, come to the car. We'll take Kruppe."

"Roger that."

Kruppe's message bearer is a greasy-looking runt in a leather jacket. He slinks to the other side of pillar 11A. I cross under the main arch and follow Greasy's steps around the column. I casually move my head from side to side as though I'm appreciating the architectural dignity of—

He's not there.

"Where the fuck is he?"

"You lost him?" Brando comms.

"Victor, do you see a skinny white male, dark hair, black leather jacket?"

"No, Scarlet."

Christ almighty, did I hallucinate him?

"Darwin, do you have eyes on Kruppe?"

"Yes. He returned to his car. Falcon and I are following him in the Bimmer." My partner pauses, then switches to our private channel, "Alix, you okay?"

"Brando, I swear I saw this fucker!"

"I believe you, but . . ."

Victor speed-moseys up to me. His face is shadowed beneath his coat's hood.

I ask, "Vic, you really didn't see him?"

Victor shakes his head. He looks like he wants to hit my nose with a rolled-up newspaper.

"Well, then where the fuck . . ."

Hang on. Kruppe's real, and he definitely saw this greaseball. The little butthead *can't* have actually vanished. Wherever he is, he's still close.

I face the rear of pillar 11A and fire up my vision Mods. My infrared scores right away. One of the engraved panels has a glowing handprint on it. My millimeter-wave scanner shows me a hollow space behind the panel. The top of a curved flight of stairs peeks from the floor inside.

"Darwin, there's a secret passage inside this column!"

Brando comms, "You've *got* to be kidding."

"I'm looking right at it."

Victor listens to us through his comm-set, but he can't see what my vision Mods let me see. His expression has shifted from "You're incompetent" to "You're insane." But when I press one of the carved names and the panel swings open, he's flat-out stupefied.

Welcome to ExOps, Vicberg!

I dart inside and swoop down the spiral metal staircase. Dim red lights illuminate my feet. At the bottom, more red lights shine along the floor of a long, straight tunnel cut through packed earth. Soft footsteps recede up the corridor. My neuroinjector stokes me and I race after Kruppe's courier.

The greaseball hears me coming, but by the time he reacts, it's too late. I spear him like a bull goring a matador. We tumble past thirty feet of red lights before he pushes me off him. When he scrambles to his feet, I collar him in a headlock. High-pitched gurgles rattle from his throat as I arch my back, lifting him until his shoes are off the ground. Then I fall backward and bludgeon Mr. Greasy into the ground head-first. His limbs collapse into a pile of spaghetti.

Victor rushes up the passageway, takes in me and my vanquished competitor, and sighs. "Americans." He bends down to untangle Greasy's arms and legs.

"I know, right? Great pile driver, huh?"

Victor raises one of his eyebrows sardonically.

"Darwin, can you hear me?" I comm. No answer. We're too far underground.

Victor slaps Greasy's face to wake him up. Our captive mumbles something slurred and incoherent. Victor grabs the numskull by his armpits and heaves him into a sitting position against the wall. By the time I've finished going through his pockets, Mr. Greasy is conscious enough for Victor to lay into him.

"What mission did you give Herr Kruppe?" he demands.

Our captive rubs the top of his head and growls in guttural German. I catch the word *"mutterfinken."* *Motherfucker.*

Victor stands back from our captive and says, "Scarlet, do something terrible to him."

I catch hold of Greaseball's arm. The fingers of my replaced right hand wrap around his skinny forearm and crush it until the bones break. Much screaming ensues.

"Well?" Victor shouts.

Our slimy yardbird is a lot tougher than he looks. He spits on Victor's shoe.

"Again, Scarlet. But much worse."

I grab Greasy's arm again and forcibly rotate it in its socket. Ninety degrees gives me a satisfying snap, and 180 degrees produces a nasty, moist-sounding crackle. At 270 degrees his ligaments and tendons tear apart and emit a loud, definitive pop.

The nitwit shrieks louder this time. Victor smacks his face. "Talk or she rips it off!"

I comm, "You really want me to do that?"

Victor shrugs, "He's Gestapo."

"Ah," I reply.

But Gestapo or not, Mr. Greasy's pain threshold is somewhere below having his arm nearly wrenched off, and he passes out again.

"Damn," I say. "Sorry, Victor."

"Do not worry. He will wake." Victor runs his hand through his salt-and-pepper hair. He surveys our subterranean setting and grunts, "Interesting."

"What?"

"This tunnel is from World War I."

Vicberg's army time included a bunch of military history classes, so he knows a lot about the trench warfare that stretched across France from 1914 to 1918. He tells me one of the tactics employed by both sides was to mine under the enemy's trench system, cram in a heap of dynamite, and blast the enemy to smitherooskies. Because of the war's ebb and flow, sometimes the project would be abandoned, which Victor guesses was the case here. After the war some of these excavations became part of underground smuggling routes.

The tunnel has been well maintained, presumably by the Gestapo, so rat-faced shitbirds like Mr. Greasy can sneak around without anyone seeing him.

"Scarlet, *bzzt* did *bzzt-bzzt* guys go?" It's Brando. His signal is weak, but I still catch the stress in his voice.

"Darwin, we're down under the monument."

"What? I *bzzt* barely *bzzt-bzzt*."

"HANG ON! I'll come up!" I run to the stairs and return to the ground level. My hand finds the switch that opens the panel.

I peek outside. Brando and Falcon are right in front of me, but they're facing the other way.

"BOO!"

The boys both jump a foot. Falcon spins toward me with his hand on his pistol. Brando leans forward with his hand on his knees.

"Crap!" my partner gasps.

Falcon grins and laughs. Naturally it reminds me of my father's laugh, and a frightsicle courses down my throat.

"That was outrageous." Falcon jovially bumps my shoulder as he enters the secret chamber. He walks down the stairs. His voice echoes from below, "Man, this place is rad."

I pull Brando inside the column and close the panel behind him. "Gotcha good, didn't I?"

"Yeah, yeah. Real good."

As we descend the stairs, I ask, "What happened to Kruppe?"

"He drove to Thiepval's town hall, showed his ID, and went in past the gate. It's like a fortress: armed guards, barriers, spotlights, the works. There was no way Falcon and I could infiltrate the place without more prep, so we came back." He wraps his fingers into mine when we reach the bottom of the stairs. We hold hands until we rejoin Victor and Mr. Greasy, who have been joined by Falcon.

The Gestapo courier has woken up again. He tries to scoot away from me as I approach. Victor says, "Scarlet, give him a scare."

I latch on to Mr. Greasy's uninjured arm.

"No!" he bawls. "Please, no!"

"Then talk, Herr Ludwig," Victor intones.

I guess this sucker has a name. But he still doesn't

want to spill the beans. I say out loud, "Anybody want a wing?"

"No!" Herr Ludwig shouts. Tears stream from his eyes.

Victor whacks Ludwig's face. "TELL ME!"

"I . . . I dare not. They will, they . . ." Herr Ludwig descends into unintelligible blubbering.

Victor plants his hands on his hips and sticks out his chin. "Scarlet, I want you to—"

"Wait." It's Brando. "Let's use this." From his X-bag he produces a pair of needles, each connected to a heavy little box by long coiled wires.

I say to Falcon, "You better back up, F-Bird. This gets real messy."

Herr Ludwig's face has turned white as a sheet. He's so scared of those infamous needles, I swear the jagoff has stopped moving at a molecular level.

"Seems like our messenger here knows about the Thackery Procedure," I comm.

Herr Ludwig's attention is riveted on Brando's hands, and the crying blaggard finally tells us what we want to know. "Reims!" he peals. "Kruppe is going to Reims!"

"Why Reims?"

Our captive's eyes are locked on the needles. Brando wiggles them back and forth and repeats Victor's question. "Why-y-y Reims?"

"La Jeune." Herr Ludwig chokes out. His eyes roll from side to side. We're losing him again. "Michel La Jeune. In Reims." He passes out and slumps into his jacket.

"Michel!" Victor exclaims, looking at his watch. "And Kruppe has the lead on us. Hurry, my friends. We must go."

Brando stuffs the Thackery needles in his X-bag as we tear-ass toward the exit. "Victor, who's Michel?"

"Michel La Jeune is a very good, well-connected man who runs an important safe house in Reims. He *must* be protected."

We scurry up the stairs, pour out of the secret panel, and gallop to our car. My foot is starting to sting again, and Brando notices me limping. He opens the car's front passenger door and says, "Falcon, how about you show us what you can do behind the wheel?"

The kid grins broadly and hops in the driver's seat while Victor and I climb in behind him. F-Bird cranks the ignition, floors the gas, and lays a pair of black stripes across the parking lot. We hang on tight while Falcon races out of town.

"Well," Victor yells over the car's wailing engine, "we know he can do that!"

38

"This can't be the place," I say from the rear seat of our BMW. I lean across Victor's lap to see out his window. Falcon hunches behind the wheel, and Brando sits next to him.

"This is where La Jeune is based," Victor says, glancing at his watch. Navigating around all the German checkpoints made this drive take much longer than he'd hoped.

"Dang." Falcon nods. "Who'd ever search for the Resistance here?"

We're in front of the monstrously tall and outrageously decorative towers of Reims's Cathedral of Notre-Dame. The facade contains so many statues and stone carvings that it could be a thirty-story wedding cake. We've been using this thing as a landmark since we were on the highway, but I never thought it was our destination.

Falcon drives down a side street and pulls into the private lot of a small office building. One of the best things about riding around in stolen cars is not caring where we park. *Go ahead and tow it, fuckos. It's not ours anyway!*

My partner pivots around in his seat so he can see me. "How's your foot?"

"Sucks." My right foot is swollen from the buckshot pedicure I got in Saint-Quentin.

Brando says, "Maybe you should stay here."

"No way." I open my door. "We've never met this so-and-so, and I might have to shoot him for ya."

Brando gives me a look and follows me out of the car.

Victor fills us in as we cross the plaza in front of the Cake. "I know La Jeune from Holland. He was in the Dutch Underground during the war. He is effective at what he does, although I think he has become too vocal in his opposition to the Reich's policies."

This is a good one coming from a man who's about as discreet as a rockslide. My partner drily says, "Victor, isn't that like poop holding its nose at shit?" Incredibly, this is a real German saying.

"Ha." Victor smiles. "Perhaps it is, but we each have our roles. Mine is to be the voice of the Resistance. This defines the range of what I am capable of contributing. Monsieur La Jeune could contribute much more if he stayed—how do you Americans say?—below the radar."

We finish crossing the plaza and approach the Cake. The front doors are so tall, even the Jolly Green Giant wouldn't bump his head. A sign lists the cathedral's hours and mass times. It opened only a few minutes ago, with today's first service fifty-five minutes from now.

We enter the dimmed interior and take a moment to let our eyes adjust. Sunlight filters through the extravagant stained glass windows and melts across the polished floor and soaring stone pillars like Technicolor butter. A few people sit or kneel in the pews, deep in contemplation. Our footsteps echo down the massive central nave. The sound seems to resonate forever.

We go to the visitors' desk and ask for Michel La Jeune. The ancient old woman behind the counter goggles at us through thick-lensed glasses. "More of you?" She points her bony finger at a small door beside the first chapel on the left and cackles, "Michel must be having quite a party."

Oh, crap.

Brando quickly leads us toward the chapel. The door abruptly swings open. Four tense men parade out of the narrow stairway beyond and shoulder past without looking at us. They're neatly dressed in button-down shirts and sport coats, but the first thug is a bit of a slob.

His coat is rumpled, and his tie has a goopy food stain on it. When the fourth man walks past me, I turn my head away. He's Johannes Kruppe.

I comm on our team channel, "Darwin, do you recognize that white-haired bastard?"

Victor isn't wearing his comm-set, but he sees our expressions. He discreetly holds his palm out to us, then points at himself.

Kruppe separates from the other three men and heads for the cathedral's front door. Without another word, Vic follows him. The rest of us exchange glances.

Spontaneously, my partner and I both whisper, "Okay, bye, Victor!"

Falcon snickers at the two of us parroting each other. We watch the remaining three palookas as they walk up the center aisle toward the main altar.

Brando comms, "Scarlet, you'd better follow them. Falcon, come with me."

Falcon and I simultaneously answer, "Roger that," and smile. Spending a week in a car together has all of us talking like Huey, Louie, and Dewey, where we start and finish one another's sentences.

Brando and Falcon plunge through the small door next to the chapel. I clasp my hands behind my back and try to look unthreatening as I tag along after the sport coats. They've reached the hugely ornate altar, where the middle aisle crosses the side transepts. One of the sport coats is a real geezer; he could have kids older than me. The other young dude, the one with no food on him, is built like a pile of brick shithouses.

The trio struts onto the central riser. Geezer slithers behind the altar and bends down, out of sight. Shithouse and Slobbo keep watch. I pretend to study the ceiling's intricate stonework while my feet edge closer to their position.

Brando comms, "Scarlet, do you have eyes on those men?"

"Affirmative, Darwin."

"Well, keep your distance. Michel La Jeune has been shot through the head and had one of his arms torn off."

Jesus. I gently backpedal up the aisle, gazing at the massive rose window over the entrance. I'm only a few yards away from Slobbo when something on his person emits a sinister metallic click.

Madrenaline whips into my blood, Li'l Bertha skips into my hand, and the floor drops away from my feet. Slobbo fires the first shot, but he's aimed too low. His bullet streaks under me. My pistol spits a slug at his face. He shifts laterally and nearly slips out of the way. Instead of hitting him in the center of his nose, where Li'l Bertha was pointed, her shot smashes into the edge of Slobbo's eye socket. The bullet takes a weird bounce and comes out his cheek while his face collapses in a bloody cloud of bone fragments.

I land on the altar's platform, close to Shithouse, who bum-rushes me. I barely have time to sidestep his lunge. I dose more Madrenaline as he charges by. I try to whack him in the back of his head, but he spins around, blocks my punch, and takes a big swing at me.

Fuck! Why am I so slow?

I juke away from Shithouse's haymaker and sweep a roundhouse kick at his legs. He leaps over my attack and counters with a front snap kick at my chest. I roll backward, get to my feet, and shoot at my competitor's stomach.

Wait. I'm not slow.

Shithouse dodges Li'l Bertha's shot before it's left her barrel.

They're incredibly fast.

"Darwin! These fuckers are Levels!"

"Can you evade them?"

"Negative! I'm too close. Falcon, get up here!"

"On my way, Scarlet."

Geezer joins the party and fills the air with bullets while I fend off a flurry of martial-arts attacks from his

younger colleague. The noise is spectacular. Gunshots in
this space sound like cannon fire and nearly drown out
the screaming civilians.

"Scarlet," Victor comms, "what's going on?" He's put
on his comm-set. "Should I return?"

My defensive gymnastics trick Geezer into shooting
Shithouse in the shoulder, but the tall drink of lumber is
so cranked up that he doesn't even flinch.

"Stay out of here, Vicberg," I comm. "These assholes
are too—"

Shithouse's fists and Geezer's bullets overwhelm my
situational awareness, and I trip backward off the riser
and topple to the floor. Shithouse tries to stomp me with
his size fourteen critter crushers. I roll out of the way
like a hot dog on a skillet.

Another gun opens fire. It's Falcon, from the back of
the church. Shithouse ducks under the kid's first volley.
The distraction lets me stagger my opponent with a karate chop to his ankle. My hand balls into a fist to smash
this blockhead's kneecap into cookie dough.

Shithouse exhales sharply. I look up. There's a hole in
his left temple. He sways like a ship's mast in a storm.
Something rips through his neck, then most of his nose
vanishes, and finally a hunk of his lower jaw breaks off
and clatters to the platform.

"Got him!" It's Falcon. The kid's aim is fucking incredible.

By the time my towering competitor timbers to the
floor, the structural integrity of his skull has been so severely compromised that his head shatters like a vase in
a rubber bag. A pool of gray and red liquid splooshes
out.

Geezer has seen enough. He hurdles his dead colleagues and sprints past me toward the cathedral's exit.

I get to my feet. "Brando, Falcon! The last one is coming your way!"

"Roger that. We have the exit blocked."

Our adversary's speed and agility defy his years. He

evades a shot from Falcon and changes direction so abruptly that it's like he's on rails. The fleeing agent streaks through a doorway into the south tower, where he mounts a flight of stone stairs. I charge after him, with Falcon right behind me.

We vault up the steps. I'm only a few paces behind Geezer, but the stairway's spiral is so tight that I can't shoot him. Our footsteps' racket is joined by the gasps of our heavy breathing. I flash back to my Eiffel Tower chase last year. There's no way this pig has a parachute, too.

Geezer's footsteps stop echoing. I pop into the bright European sunshine as my opponent launches himself over a railing toward the cathedral's other tower. He flies across the gap between the spires, grabs a hunk of decorative stonework, and sticks to the tower like a fly. Then he swings himself around the corner onto the structure's east face. I can barely see the crazy old shit-bird through all the carved festoonery as he jungle-gyms down to the cathedral's main roof.

Falcon runs past me and swoops after our competitor. The kid purposely lets himself plummet a little ways before he grabs a carved stone handhold. He wants to cut the enemy agent off, but Geezer has a big head start.

"F-Bird, keep on him and I'll cover this side."

Falcon speedily crab-crawls down the tower's ornamented facade. There's no time for me to make a normal descent. I climb over the rail and drop straight down, inches from the face of the tower. My hands grab and release swirly stone elements to help slow my fall. Before hitting the roof, I latch onto a sneering gargoyle and rip the thing out of its mount.

I land hard on all fours. My right foot throbs like it's being stabbed with red-hot needles as I dive away from the crumbling stonework.

"Darwin," I comm, "our target has descended the north tower to the main roof."

"Roger, Scarlet. I'm already in the car."

"Great; stay close. We're gonna need a fast pickup."

"Understood."

I comm, "Hey, Vic, any sign of your old school chum?"

Victor replies, "Negative, Scarlet. I broke off when the shooting started. Kruppe can wait."

"All right; whatever you say, Vicberg." Then, "Falcon, where'd our target go?"

"He's across the roof from you, running toward the back of the building."

I dose a bunch of yummy chemicals and scamper down my side of the roof. "Is he ahead of me?"

"Affirmative," Falcon comms. "He's already at the far end, above one of the flying buttresses."

"Copy that. I'll cover him here. Can you take position out front?"

"On my way."

I make it to the transept. My feet tap-dance their way around all the corners and bring me to the Cake's semi-circular rear section. Flying buttresses splay out like a fan.

Victor comms, "The target is on the ground outside the northernmost chapel."

"Roger that, Vic." I charge past the buttresses until I'm over the last chapel. "F-Bird, where are you?"

"Out front, coming to cover the north side."

Meanwhile I'm stuck up here. I'm about to repeat my falling-leaf routine when I notice a thick black power cable. The heavily insulated wire links the cathedral to a telephone pole down in the street.

I run at the cable and leap off the roof. My metal-and-plastic right hand wraps around the wire, and I soar down it like a zip line. Before hitting the telephone pole, I let go, fall to the pavement, bounce across the road, and bash into a parked car.

Ow! My bruises are getting bruises, but at least my foot has gone numb. I comm, "I'm on the ground. Anybody have eyes on the runner?"

"I see him," Falcon answers. "North side, running toward the front of the church."

Man, it'll be a pisser if we wind up right back where we started after all this dogging around. I hobble across the street and finally catch sight of Geezer. He's halfway to the front, but Falcon has a bead on him. F-Bird's shots ring out. I add Li'l Bertha's firepower to the mix.

We both aim low. Now that we have Geezer in a pincer, we'll try to take him alive. The man's legs collapse under him as our bullets crash through his shins and ankles. He rises to his knees and draws his pistol. *These people never give up!* I take aim for a kill shot, but my target doesn't aim at Falcon or me. He points his weapon at his own head.

"He's gonna off himself!"

A figure flies out from behind a parked car and pounces on our injured enemy. It's Victor! He tries to disarm the suicidal German. Eisenberg may be a great fighter, but he's way out of his league. Geezer grabs Victor's neck and slams him to the ground like a plush toy.

I crank a ton of Madrenaline, hurtle up behind Geezer, and plow into him so hard that we pitch over Victor and spill onto the sidewalk. The exceptionally durable German agent lands on his face and finally stops moving. A thin trickle of blood leaks out of his ear.

Meanwhile my battered body sprawls on the sidewalk and rides out a nasty bout of emotional recoil. My head spins like a cat in a dishwasher while my hands and feet bang out a fast dance beat on the brick sidewalk. I inhale large gulps of air but forget to exhale. One of my eyelids begins to flicker. I hold it still and try to push myself off the ground.

Our Bimmer flies up the street and screeches to a stop. Brando jumps out. He DOSEs Geezer with knockout juice, and then he and Falcon dump the droopy result in the trunk. I tell my neuroinjector to throw me some Kalmers as Victor helps me struggle to my feet.

Owl-eyed civilians on their way to church crouch for

cover. The women have their hands over their mouths and their men's arms around their shoulders. I nod and give them a shaky thumbs-up as Victor drags me to the car. The neighborhood is deathly quiet.

Brando and Falcon jump into the front seat while Victor and I flop out in back. My partner revs the engine, and we speed away from the scene of today's shocking gun battle in broad daylight.

"You know what?" I say. "If church were always that exciting, I might go more often."

CORE   MIS-ANGEL-4414

ANGEL SIT-REP: PROVINCE OF IRAQ. 3 March 1981
   The local German governor declared martial law last night to forestall anticipated unrest today. Regional Circle of Zion leadership ordered central army barracks burned anyway to maximize German retaliation. Massive public outcry predicted. Iraq should be in flames by next week.

—Copernicus, IO / Raven, L7 Interceptor

39

SAME DAY, THREE HOURS LATER, 2:58 P.M. CET
OUTSIDE REIMS, PROVINCE OF FRANCE, GG

Patrick shuts the trunk. "That should keep him out for a while."

The problem with captured Levels is figuring out what to do with them. Geezer has such powerful Mods and Enhances that we don't dare let him out of the trunk. Hell, we can't even let him wake up. Patrick has to DOSE him every hour to make sure the fucker stays unconscious.

I pull out a stolen pack of Marlboros and tap a coffin nail into my hand. It slips through my trembling fingers and spins to the ground. The next one gets crushed flat. Deep breath. I jiggle a third cigarette loose and draw it out of the pack with my lips. I lean on the car to make my lighter stop shaking long enough for me to spark up.

I'm not stupid. I know what's happening to me and that I'll have to 'fess up about it back home. The hallucinations are bad enough, but now my after-action emotional recoil is so pronounced that it's a challenge just to light a cigarette.

If Cyrus saw me like this, he'd bench me for sure. Cleo would probably threaten to disown me unless I retired. Patrick promised he'll convince the doctors to keep me in the field, but he still had me back up my Day Loop. He wants the Med-Techs to review my vitals along with the external events that caused them. This'll help the Meddies retune my neuroinjector to match my field experiences, which in turn may help suppress my zonkadelic mental wipeouts.

We're quiet. Patrick dolefully watches me smoke but

doesn't say anything. He sits on the trunk, crosses his arms over his chest, and looks at the sky.

After a minute he says, "So. Nice day, huh?"

My eyes shoot daggers at him for trying to cheer me up. And yet—despite our chaos casserole in Reims, my imminent demotion to mall cop, and the crazed one-man wrecking crew stuffed in our trunk—I start laughing.

Nice day, huh?

The more I think about it, the more it makes me laugh. I smile at him and twirl his fingers into mine as we take in our surroundings together.

This is champagne country, so every square inch of soil is meticulously cultivated. We're parked well off the main road on a tiny cart path in the middle of an endless field of grapevines. The ride here was surprisingly easy. Our blunderfuck in Reims was so sudden and the setting so appallingly sacrilegious that we got away scot-free. Not many civic authorities anticipate firefights in their churches.

Patrick bandaged the worst of Geezer's wounds and patched up my dents and dings. Victor is stretched across the car's backseat. He nearly got his neck broken outside the Cake. We all advised Vic not to move around too much, and the man didn't argue.

Falcon is perched on top of the BMW, keeping watch. He slowly pans his gaze across the striped green vine-yards and gently hums to himself. F-Bird's profile is strikingly similar to Dad's, of course, but his manner is so relaxed and mellow compared to my father's per-petual intensity that the resemblance is more like some incredible coincidence than the unnatural freak-out it ought to be.

Maybe if Falcon were the same age as my Dad, it would be as weird as it was, well . . . actually, when I think about it, like it *is*, with Patrick. Trick has been dead for less than six months. I still have dreams about him.

Then I wake up, and he's been reincarnated right here. Sort of. But not really.

God, this could drive me nuts. Comic books make it seem like sets of clones all think and act exactly the same way. Running around with Patrick and Falcon has taught me clones are definitely individuals. It's like close siblings who have a lot in common but retain a separate sense of self. Maybe if someone raised a group of clones in identical environments for identical lengths of time they'd all come out exactly the same, but what do I know about biology?

While Falcon and I chased Geezer all over the Cake, Patrick ran to see what the sport coats were doing at the altar. He found a false panel in the altar's base. Inside was a small notebook filled with names and addresses. Patrick thinks it's the recently deceased Michel La Jeune's little black book of underground contacts and safe houses. This means we can sleep somewhere that isn't—at best—the floor of a gun shop. It's also a chilling reminder of how easily the Circle can be compromised.

I lean against the car, nod my head toward the trunk, and hold my hands down so only my partner can see me sign, *What should we do with our new luggage?*

Patrick signs, *I'd love to give him to the Circle, but I doubt they can safely hold a Level.* He tips his head from side to side, considering different possibilities. *I don't know. This competitor is no use unconscious, and he's incredibly dangerous awake.*

I finish my smoke and stub it out on the car's bumper. *Want me to whack him?*

My partner shakes his head. *No. He must have some good intel, but we can't interrogate him out here in the open.*

Think we could turn him?

I doubt it. He was ready to kill himself to avoid being captured.

We mull in silence for a minute. Then Patrick rubs his

chin and cocks his head to one side. *You know what? I'll bet Jacques could handle this guy at his place in Paris.*

The Paris safe house is one of ExOps's busiest and most important European locations. The place is strictly off-limits to non-ExOps agents, especially agents deployed by a raving lunatic.

I sneak a peek at Falcon. He's still scouting the area. *Do we trust Falcon enough?*

Yeah, I think so, Patrick signs. *Here are our options. One: all of us go to Paris. Two: we kill Trunk Man and don't go to Paris. Three: we bring Trunky to Paris and kill Falcon.*

Well, there's no way I'm gonna kill Falcon. I could care less about the schmunk in the trunk except that he represents a lot of potential intel about the Purity League and the German response to the Jewish Rising. Of these three options, the first one is most challenging, breaks the most rules, and—if successful—will have the biggest positive impact on our mission.

I extend my index finger.

Patrick nods. *Paris it is.* He hops off the trunk, stretches his arms, and calls out, "Hey, Falcon, ready for the best food of your life?"

CORE   MIS-ANGEL-4576

ANGEL SIT-REP: FRANCE. 9 March 1981

A notably destructive quartet of anti-German saboteurs tore through northern France this weekend. Based on their tactics and effectiveness, I could swear they were ExOps, but I was unable to establish comm-contact. I last saw them driving toward Paris.

Luna, L6 Infiltrator

40

NEXT DAY, ELEVEN HOURS LATER, MONDAY, MARCH 9,
2:02 A.M. CET
PARIS, PROVINCE OF FRANCE, GG

My left hand clutches Li'l Bertha in my coat pocket. My right hand pounds on the apartment door again. Despite the cool air in here, a trickle of sweat runs between my shoulder blades. I'm about to give up when footsteps approach the door and three separate deadbolts clack into their housings. My pistol is ready to shoot whoever opens the door if it isn't—

"Jacques!" I say. *"Ça va?" How are ya?*

The French spymaster blinks his eyes and blurts, "Holy shit!" although it sounds more like "Olly sheet." He pokes his head into the hall, looks around, then beckons me inside.

Jacques leads me into his small kitchen. He doesn't switch on a light, so we talk quietly and quickly in the filtered glow from the streetlights outside. He asks, "What are you doing here?"

"My partner and I have a package for you."

Jacques stares at me.

"What?" I say. "What's the matter?"

"When I asked what are you doing *here,* I didn't mean here in my house. I meant what are you still doing in Europe? Haven't you heard?"

Now it's my turn to stare at him. "Huh?"

His brows rise like he just remembered something. "Mademoiselle Scarlet, before I forget, I am so much sorry to hear about Solomon."

It's perfectly natural for Jacques to mention Trick's death. After all, this is the first time we've seen each other since it happened. But it's the last thing I expected him to say, and I'm so tired and stressed I burst into tears.

"Oh! *Je suis vraiment désolé*. I am so sorry, Scarlet. I did not mean to upset you."

The tension of transporting our captured time bomb has my nerves as taut as a guitar string, plus I haven't slept in two days. I choke out a couple of wet sobs. "It's okay, I'll be okay. Can . . ." I will myself to stop crying. "Can I bring my partners in here?"

"Of course! How rude of me. They must be frozen, waiting outside."

Well, no, Jacko. Actually they're hiding down the hall ready to help me fold, spindle, and murdilate anyone who gets in our way—including you, if necessary.

I comm, "Guys, come on in," as I dry my cheeks on the sleeves of my coat. The boys schlep a large, heavy body bag into the apartment. It's too dark in here for them to notice how damp my eyes are.

It's not too dark for Jacques to recognize Victor. "M'sieur Eisenberg! Good to see you again."

"Hello, Jacques." They briefly embrace. "*Ça va?*"

Jacques shrugs and gives a lopsided smile. He's accepted that part of his job description includes receiving a gaggle of surprise guests in the dead of night. What isn't part of Jacques's routine, however, is to receive visitors from beyond the grave. When Brando walks in, Jacques is rendered speechless. Almost.

"*Non* . . ." Jacques sputters. "*C'est impossible!* M'sieur Solomon?"

Brando's eyes narrow, and his jaw tightens. He's had to meet a lot of his late brother's contacts, and their initial reaction is never easy on him.

"*Bonjour,* M'sieur Jacques. It's good to meet you. I'm Darwin." He takes Jacques's hand and shakes it. "This is Falcon, and this—" He drops the body-shaped package on the floor. "—is a live German Level."

Jacques forgets his shock at meeting Trick's doppelgänger and steps away from the body bag like it's radioactive. "Mother of God, why have you brought zat here?"

Brando and Victor bring our French buddy up to speed while Falcon and I move to the windows to watch out for competitors. I keep one eye on Jacques. We have no idea if he's been turned by Fredericks or what. Having already been smoked out of two places on this trip, we're done with the whole trust thing.

Rather than meet Jacques at the safe house he runs here in Paris, Brando thought it would be appropriately unpredictable to come to his residence. Less people, less chances for leaks. We'd rather stay off the grid—things have gone fine since we went offline—but we need help, and we've worked with Jacques before. Once my partner finishes giving our host the *Reader's Digest* version of our recent adventures, it's Jacques's turn to fill us in on current events, many of which have been triggered by our ROAR Tour.

The Rising has flourished into a full-blown revolt. Slaves have risen against their masters and escaped in droves. Berlin has declared martial law throughout the Reich to curb the violent three-way clashes between abolitionists, proslavery militias, and the government forces caught in the middle. Farms and factories have ceased production, and most civilian offices are closed.

The rebellion is so out of control that the German chancellor reached out to the United States for help. The President countered with a most unexpected offer: release the Jewish slaves and send them to America.

Jacques slaps his forehead. "Can you imagine? Shipping ten million people across ze Atlantic? It would take twenty years!"

I comm to Brando, "I'm not sure if Jacko here understands how much stuff we have in the States. Would this really take that long?"

"No," Brando comms. "We could do this with . . ." *whirr-whirr* ". . . three hundred cargo vessels in ten months."

Brando then asks Jacques, "What did the chancellor say?"

The Frenchman leans against his kitchen counter. "Ze chancellor has not replied yet, which tells me he is considering it."

It seems that Washington's controversial proposal caught Berlin by surprise. The controversy centers around Greater Germany's attitude toward Jewish people. The Reich's liberal left wants to allow the Jews to return to German society, while the conservative right wants them back working on the farms and in the factories. The far right wants them all dead, and the Christian moderates are so conflicted that they have no fucking idea what they want. The chancellor has to deal with the fact that many citizens of Europe and the Middle East are as vehemently anti-Semitic as they were when Corporal Adolf's Maximum-Butthole Circus was running things.

The stunning depth of the Nazis' racism was unknown in the States until 1956, when American intelligence agents uncovered the Wannsee Documents. Those papers, written in January 1942, showed the Nazis were planning to murder every single Jewish person in the world. Hitler's timely assassination derailed this terrifying plot, although the Reich's Jewish population still got utterly shafted.

We silently mull this for a moment. Then I ask, "Jacques, what did you mean when you asked what we were doing in Europe?"

"Ah, yes! I was distracted by zis, uh, gift you've brought me." Jacques unhappily regards the bag o' vipers on his floor, then says, "You've all been recalled. Well, almost all. Some Infiltrators stay, but all other Level classes were ordered to return to America four days ago."

Brando groans and flops into a chair.

I say to Jacques, "Recalled?"

"Yes, mademoiselle. The Rising has taken on a life of its own, thanks to you and your colleagues. But Washington feels negotiations for a cease-fire will not be made easier with your continued, uhh, shall we say . . . disruptive presence here in Europe."

Victor follows my partner's lead and finds himself a chair. Falcon and I prop ourselves against the kitchen table. Brando takes out a small cloth and polishes his glasses.

"We'd better go tonight, then." My partner sighs. "So much for getting a decent meal."

Jacques crosses the room and crouches in front of a small cabinet. "Well, not so fast, my young friends." He stands up with a bottle of Scotch and a handful of small glasses. "As I said, some of your Infiltrators are still here, and I know one who will be *very* glad to see you."

41

I slap the blabscreen's side. "Mom, can you hear me?" I'm in the vault at Jacques's safe house near Saint-Sulpice, trying to talk to Cleo, but the satellite feed is borked out. "Jacques, it isn't working!"

Me and my road buddies crashed all day at Jacques's apartment. I slept until 5 P.M., when our host came home and asked for my help with food shopping. Once we were outside, Jacques said he'd received permission for me, if I wanted, to make a brief video call to my mother. I grabbed his hand and ran to his office.

So far the only thing working is the call timer, which is counting down from ninety seconds. Jacques says a call that short is very difficult to trace.

Cleo's voice crackles through the speakers, "Alix? Are you there?"

Finally the sound and image snap into sync, and there's the red-haired top of my mother's head. Mom is crouched down in front of her screen, frantically fiddling with the controls. She looks up to see if it's worked. Her face is ashen.

"Oh! There you are! Alix, can you see me?"

"Yes! Hi!"

Our first comments overlap: "Alixandra, you're so thin!" "Mom, you look exhausted!" We each stop, then simultaneously say, "You go first." Then we both giggle and cover our mouths with our hands.

Cleo's eyes are getting moist, so I take the lead. "I'm fine, Mom. Don't worry. The House said he's going to fatten us up while we're here."

Mom tries to maintain her composure. Her pink lips

press together like a pair of battling butterflies. She stammers, "Well, make sure you . . . that you . . ." Finally she breaks down. "Honey," she chokes, "I've been so . . . I've missed you . . ."

This Job Number hasn't left me with much time to think about home. But now, talking to my mother, I miss her so much that I start crying along with her.

"I miss you too, Mom." I press my palm on the blab-screen. She does the same on her end, and I swear her hand touches mine right through the glass.

I wipe my nose on the sleeve of my shirt. Only my mother can generate the expression I see when she catches me being so uncouth. Cleo is about to correct me, then stops herself and laughs through her tears. I sniff in sharply, shrug, and smile at her.

The call timer is down to fifteen seconds. The vault door glides open. Jacques leans in and whispers, "Keep talking. I'll zay we had technical trouble."

I nod and turn back to the screen. Cleo is drying her eyes with a tissue to keep her makeup from running. She places her hand on the screen again.

"Mom, are *you* all right? You really do look tired."

"We've been so worried, sweetheart."

"Are you sleeping?"

"Well," she says, glancing away, "no. Not for a few days." Her eyes return to mine. "But neither is Cyrus. Every morning I ask if he's heard from you." She starts to cry again. "Alix, when your comm-signal disappeared, the Info Department thought you'd been captured. But Cyrus and I know how much you're like your father, and when you didn't come home with all the other Levels, we thought . . ."

She thought I was dead.

"Oh, my God! Mom, I'm so sorry. I couldn't call. But I never would have wanted you to—" Now I choke up. "I *couldn't* call, Mom. I'm sorry."

"It's all right, angel. I know you couldn't." Mom

wipes her eyes with her handkerchief. "You're safe; that's what matters."

I choose not to remind her I'm in enemy territory during a plague of violence. Cleo knows my current situation is classified, so we catch our breath and briefly chat about small things. The Redskins have hired a new head coach, and she had to fix the porch light after the paperboy broke it one morning with an especially vigorous throw. It's trivial stuff, but I don't care. I've never missed her voice as much as I do now.

Jacques apologetically leans into the room again and gently draws his finger across his throat.

"Mom, I've gotta go."

"Okay, sweetheart." She takes a deep breath. "I love you, and be careful."

"I will. I love you, too."

We stare into each other's eyes.

She's brave and goes first. "Bye, angel."

"See you soon, Mom."

The blabscreen disconnects. The call timer indicates we talked for three minutes and ten seconds.

Jacques opens the vault door again. He lets me blow my nose once more before he asks, "Okay, Mademoiselle Scarlet?"

I nod.

"*C'est bon.*" He pats my shoulder a couple of times. Then he says, "Time for *la boulangerie discrete*. Will you accept this critical mission?"

"All right, Jacko." I dry my eyes with my hand. "Let's see this secret bakery."

Back in D.C., Cleo and I—like the citizens of any civilized society—shop at a zillion-aisle mungamarket with abundant quantities of every product on earth. Here in France, the natives gather their food from a series of tiny, crowded shops that each sell one kind of item. Butcher, baker, other stuff maker.

Jacques knows all the shopkeepers, to whom he bitches about his hometown soccer team and from whom he receives street-level intel about everyone's favorite foreign occupier, *die Teutsch*.

As we shop, it becomes clear why Jacques had me accompany him.

"Scarlet, can you hold zis bag while I pick out some wine?"

The bag is added to the seven I'm already carrying. "You know, Jacques, if you'd said I was going to be your damned pack mule, I would have told you—"

"To shut off ze blabscreen ninety seconds earlier, when I was supposed to?" he interjects.

I clench my jaw and frown at him. "Fine, whatever. But no more jibber-jabbering. Buy your stuff and let's go home. My arms are falling off."

Later that evening, Patrick, Falcon, Victor, and I sit in Jacques's kitchen and consume a humongous home-cooked dinner. It is easily the greatest meal in the history of eating. I gobble so much food, I barely feel the bottle of wine I suck down.

"Jacques," Patrick asks, "when are we meeting with Grey?"

Our host answers from the stove. "Tomorrow morning. He'll meet you here."

I swallow a mouthful of Jacques's roasted chicken, then ask Victor, "You gonna come with us, Vicberg?"

The lean-faced old soldier wipes his chin with a napkin and quietly stifles a belch. "Sadly, no. I have some urgent business to attend to in Italy." Victor lifts his wineglass and says to me, "But fate would not keep a beautiful fighter like you from my side for long, Scarlet. I am sure we will meet again." He winks at me and adds, "*Mein Füchslein*." *My little fox*.

Falcon and Patrick both stop chewing and gawk at me with amused glints in their eyes. The wine has all our faces a little flushed, so I look down at my lap and hope nobody notices as I blush like a schoolgirl.

Jacques noisily scolds Victor for flirting with his agents, then the Frenchman circles the kitchen table and dispenses heaps of desserts. As he piles cookies and petit-fours onto my plate, I lean back and hold my hugely full tummy.

"Ugh, no, Jacques," I groan. "I can't eat any more."

"You must! My poor dead grandmother taught me how to make these when I was a boy. If you do not eat zem, she will rise from her tomb and haunt you forever."

I reluctantly lean toward my overloaded plate. "Do you Frenchies eat like this all the time?"

He shrugs. *"Mais oui!" Of course!*

"Then why aren't you all a bunch of blubbery hulks?"

"Zat." Jacques points to his ancient tanklike bicycle ensconced next to the front door of his apartment. The two-wheeled relic could have survived the Battle of Verdun.

I cock my head to one side. "You French are thin because you all love prehistoric modes of transport?"

"No, we *exercise*! Unlike you flabby Americans. Sit around, do nothing." He pauses to take in all of our tightly ripped and fat-free bodies, then adds, "Present company excluded, of course."

I stuff a cookie into my mouth. Crumbs fly back out as I yell, "Ha! *Mais oui.*"

CORE   MIS-BB-RECOVER-001

TO: Grey, L13 Infiltrator
FROM: Front Desk, German Section, Extreme
Operations Division
SUBJECT: Carbon Snatch Job

Attached you will find intel acquired last month from the Tower of London. Of particular interest is the Carbon installation in Carentan, France. The attachment indicates this secret facility is part of the German Veterans Medical Center, which is located next to the town's church.

You are requested and required to investigate this installation, specifically the roster of Originals, and report on what you find. If they have who we think they do, you are preapproved to employ any means necessary to extract him.

—Cyrus El-Sarim

TO: Front Desk, German Section, ExOps
FROM: Grey, L13 Infiltrator
SUBJECT: RE: Carbon Snatch Job

Sir,

As requested, I have reconnoitered the German Veterans Medical Center in Carentan. I confirmed the existence of an entirely separate group of medical personnel and also noted the constant presence of an SZ security detail. These troops are well equipped with weapons and armored vehicles from the Staatszeiger barracks in Saint-Lô. I infiltrated the restricted research area and acquired documentation confirming the presence of our man.

While inside I discerned that the Carbon installation exists entirely under the hospital and the neighboring church. In fact, the Carbon labs and offices were expanded into what were once the church's medieval catacombs. The old entrance from the church's undercroft is covered by a wall in the staff's break room. This led me to examine the church next door, which I found has no security presence.

I submit that a team could enter the church's cellar, break through the wall into the Carbon facility, and extricate our target before the security forces in the hospital can react. Per your directions, I have already begun to assemble the necessary assets to accomplish this mission. Please advise if you have further direction.

—Grey

42

TWO DAYS LATER, WEDNESDAY, MARCH 11,
10:30 A.M. CET
OUTSIDE CAEN, PROVINCE OF FRANCE, GG

"Outrajuff!" Falcon blurts through a mouthful of baguette. "Loof a'all tha cowfs!"

"Gah!" yawps Grey. "Falcon, you just spit food on me!" He makes a face and brushes bits of half-chewed bread off his shirt. "Take it easy, okay?"

Our young sniper swallows his apple-sized bite of bread. "I've never seen so many cows all at once."

Grey grumbles, "You'd think you'd never eaten bread before, either." The Infiltrator looks out the car's windows at the passing scenery. "Welcome to Normandy, kid. Cows, cheese, and the biggest damn hedges you'll ever lay your eyes on."

Speaking of big, our latest car—a bargelike white Cadillac—is immense, even for Greater Germany. Motor vehicles in the U.S. are efficient little things because fuel is so expensive. The Reich controls half the Middle East, so their gas is cheap and their cars are enormous.

Brando sits up front with me, navigating while I drive. The bench seat is so wide that I can't even reach him. Grey and Falcon sprawl in the rear cavern. The Caddy's size, weight, and color inspired me to nickname it Saint Peter's Heavenly Barge.

We had a good couple of days in Paris despite all the rioting in the streets. Staying at Jacques's place gave us a chance to catch our collective breath. Our French host hooked us up with bread, beds, a couple of new gadgets, and, most important, ammunition. I press my right arm against Li'l Bertha as she hums to herself in her holster. She's happy to be full of genuine Lion Ballistics Multi

Caliber ammo instead of that peasant fixed-caliber crap I've been stuffing in her for the last few weeks.

The day before we appeared on Jacques's doorstep, Grey was ordered to recruit a team for a special Job Number. Since ExOps had withdrawn all their Interceptors and Vindicators, he asked Jacques to find some local people. When Jacques told him about his unexpected American house guests, Grey was delighted.

"Well," he told Jacques, "Scarlet will be motivated, that's for sure."

Grey has been nosing around one of Carbon's nine cloning labs. It's in a small town called Carentan in Normandy. The Carbon techs there are cloning a former ExOps agent. That agent is the baddest-ass Level 20 Liberator in the world.

His name is Philip Nico.

Yeah, I'm pretty friggin' motivated.

Grey reported to ExOps that Brando and I needed a new encryption code for our commphones. Once the new code was installed, Falcon reconnected us to the ExOps network. Cyrus hosted a conference-comm to brief us.

The massive heap of Carbon intel we swagged from the Tower of London triggered a flood of revelations and developments. The Information Department used it to trace my father's location, and it allowed the Med-Techs to prepare a three-part life-support strategy for him. The first part is a hand-carried ventilator kit so Dad won't suffocate if we have trouble extracting him from his Original tank. The second part is a medevac helicopter to spirit him out of Carentan. Part three will be flying him home in an A-3 Skywarrior converted from electronic surveillance to ambulance duty.

When I asked Grey where these aircraft will come from, he said, "The Squids."

As a show of support to Greater Germany, the U.S. Navy has stationed a task force off of Europe. One of these ships is the aircraft carrier *Indefatigable*. When we call for it, the *Indy* will dispatch a helicopter with an ExOps Medical-Technical team and a portable life-support system. After they return to the *Indefatigable,* the Med-Techs will tuck Dad into the modified A-3 for his flight back to the States.

All we need to do is bust him out of the lab in Carentan. Normally, a foursome of modified and enhanced field agents like us would make short work of this job. These aren't normal days, though. The Rising has every German in uniform watching, harassing, and too often shooting anyone who even remotely seems like a trouble-maker. Our forged papers from Garbo have held up so far, but the amount of scrutiny they're being subjected to keeps increasing. It's only a matter of time before one of these checkpoint-watching, stick-up-his-ass ding-dongs asks too many questions and I have to blow his cocka-mamie head off.

Brando keeps an eye on the road signs. "Okay, we've passed Bayeux. We should be clear for a while now." He looks around. "Anybody feel like a game of chess?"

Grey opens his window and says, "Yeah, man. I'll play you." He lights a cigarette.

"Hey, Grey," I say to his reflection in the rearview mirror. "Got one for your driver?"

"Sure thing, Red." He passes me a cigarette. I stick it between my lips and turn my head to one side so Grey can light it for me.

"Thanks." I open my window.

Falcon and Brando switch places. My partner takes out a little magnetic chess set Pericles gave him back in England. He and Grey whip through a game in less than three minutes.

"Nice." Grey nods. "You like the Russian players, eh?"

Brando resets his pieces. "And the Chinese. Everybody studies the Europeans and the South Americans, but fewer people follow Asian players."

The two whiz kids begin another game. Falcon quietly

sits next to me. He swivels his head around like he wants to see every single thing we pass.

"Hey, F-Bird." I blow smoke out the window. "What are you gonna do when we get home?"

He takes a minute to answer. "Not sure. I'd rather die than go back to the lab." He turns to me. "Maybe I can work for ExOps."

I glance over at him. Now that he's fatigued and road-weary, he looks a lot more like my dad. His skin is smoother and his teeth are a lot better, but Falcon's eyes have acquired the same silent intensity Dad's eyes had.

Do. The same that Dad's eyes *do.*

"Yeah, we'll vouch for ya," I say around my cigarette. "You're the best shot I've ever seen."

"Thanks. Do you think ExOps will have a problem with my . . . resemblance to your father?"

"Hell, no." I take one last drag and toss the butt out the window. "They'll think you're manna from heaven."

Falcon shuts his eyes and doesn't say anything. Then, softly, "Scarlet, I've been meaning to . . . to ask you something since we met in Brussels." He stares at his hands. "Do *you* have a problem with my resemblance to your dad?"

This question has already cost me a few nights' sleep. The fact that Falcon is a clone of my father should weird me out as much as Brando used to, but for some reason it doesn't.

"Not really. I mean, it's not like you asked for it." I roll up my window. "It might be strange when you're older, but for now it feels kind of like you're my brother."

Falcon's reaction surprises the shit out of me. His features quiver, and his skin flushes red. He spins his face away, but before he does, a teardrop flows down his cheek and drips onto his collar.

I keep an eye on the road, but after a moment I sneak another peek at Falcon. He holds his head in one of his hands.

I comm just to him, "Hey . . . Falcon, what's wrong?" I reach over with my right hand and put it on his arm.

He takes my hand in his and squeezes it. He quickly checks that the two boy geniuses are still engrossed in their chess game, then turns his tear-streaked face to me and comms, "Thanks, Scarlet. I don't know if someone like you . . . can have any idea how much that means to me."

"Someone like me how?"

"Like that you have parents, and grew up in a house, and had holidays." He lets go of my hand and wipes his face on his sleeve. "That you don't care I'm a . . . fucking lab rat, copy of someone else . . ." The young version of my father takes a deep breath and whispers. "That you don't care I'm a clone."

"You're right, Falcon. I don't care about that."

CORE   MIS-ANGEL-5203

ANGEL SIT-REP: BERLIN. 10 March 1981
   Countrywide slave revolt and sympathy strikes have thrown country into absolute chaos. Our work here is done.

—Tiger, L17 Infiltrator

43

Carentan is cute. Not that I want to move here, but of all the towns with top-secret mad-scientist laboratories, this one isn't so bad. Gotta give the Krauts credit. Hiding one of the nine Carbon cloning labs in this sleepy little burg is like hiding a 100-karat diamond in a bread box.

We're parked across the street from the German Veterans Medical Center, which squats next to the town's main church, the Notre-Dame de Carentan. Grey silently smokes a cigarette and watches everyone entering or leaving the modern, brightly lit hospital. Most of them are civilians visiting patients.

Then there are the husky Staatszeiger apes. A pair of them are always posted at the entrance, and two more patrol the hospital's perimeter. We saw a twelve-man squad enter the building. A few minutes later two of them walked out and drove away in an officially marked Staatszeiger car.

I say to Grey, "There isn't much competition. Why don't we just F.U.C.K. 'em up?"

Grey taps the ash off his cigarette. "We need to keep the con after we're done."

I frown in confusion.

He elaborates, "We don't want Fritz to know ExOps pulled this job. The plan is to make it look like it was the Circle of Zion. So, to do it like the Circle would, we'll sneak in through the church to avoid the hospital guards, snatch Big Bertha, and make a discreet getaway." He pauses. "Unless you feel like killing every potential witness in that hospital." He gives me a steady stare. I say nothing. "Right." He turns back to the car's window. "We do it the sneaky way."

Notre-Dame de Carentan is much smaller than Notre-Dame de Reims, but it's still cluttered with statues, stained glass, and carved stone knickknacks. It's like a really fancy cupcake except for the tall, spearlike central tower that stabs a hole into the night sky.

I tried to use Li'l Bertha to comm my dad. I'd hoped being so close would put me in range again, but it hasn't worked. Patrick quietly keeps an eye on me when I hold my pistol next to my head.

The decision about when to begin a mission falls to the senior Level in charge. In this case, that's Grey. He exhales smoke through his nose and says, "I think it's time to get this show on the road."

I start the car, drive up the street past the fancy little church, and park in front of a small shop. Grey stubs out his cigarette, opens his door, and leads us out of the Barge. When I stand up, my head spins like a weather vane. I hang on to the door and have my neuroinjector give me a swish of uppers. I sway after my team and pat down my toys. Stabby—check. Shooty—check. Boomy—check.

Falcon holds his sniper's rifle flat against his side. I say to him, "This is gonna be close quarters. Sure you need that cannon?"

"Like the man says," Falcon says with a smirk, "don't leave home without it."

I smile and poke my elbow into his arm as the four of us stalk down the street. We approach the Cupcake's foreboding unlit side entrance. I try the heavy wooden door. It's locked. Brando pulls out his lock-breaker kit. Falcon and I keep watch while Grey shines a penlight on the lock for my partner. Except for the hospital's hustle and bustle, the neighborhood is quiet.

Brando's efforts bring about a declarative clunk. "Got it," he whispers.

Grey shoves the door open and enters first. He comms to us, "All clear."

The rest of us slip inside. The church's dark walls and stone floor seem to suck the warmth right out of me. I tighten my jacket around me and—

Alix?

It's him! I hold Li'l Bertha beside my head.

"Daddy? We're here!"

Alix, I . . .

"What? Dad, what's the matter?"

No answer. A dancing crowd of spots appears before my eyes, and my dizziness returns.

"Hang on, Daddy; we'll get you out of here." The floor shifts from left to right so dramatically that I feel motion-sick.

Brando, still watching me, remains silent. Grey and Falcon have walked to the shadowy rear of the church. I hold my partner's arm, and we follow them down a gloomy flight of stairs. A thick metal door yields to Brando's lock-picking prowess, and we're in. The atmosphere in the Cupcake's cellar—or "undercroft," as Grey calls it—is thick with the zesty smell of fresh mouse turds, damp earth, moldy stonework, and ancient corpses interred in the walls.

"Not spooky," whispers Falcon. "Nope. Not at all."

We follow Grey in the glow from his small flashlight. He leads us into a low hallway. Even I have to stoop to pass through. We quietly assemble at the end of the corridor and all hunker down on one knee. I'm grateful for the chance to steady myself.

Grey comms, "Okay, this is the walled-over passage to the lab." He reviews the next phase. Grey and Falcon will rush to secure the entrance. Brando and I will find the Originals. Then we'll do the extraction.

My partner reaches into his X-bag and takes out his millimeter-wave radar sensor. He begins to pass it across the wall, searching for the old doorway.

As he works, a surge of nausea grips my stomach.

Sweat breaks out on my forehead, and my hands spasm like worms on a hook. The floor turns into a frozen lake and—

I plunge through the ice, and my skates drag me down to the bottom. I push off the mud and punch the shimmering roof, but the thick water clutches my hands like a thornbush. I try to swim to the hole, but I'm all turned around and can't find it. Bubbles rush past my nose. I'm not cold anymore. Something heavy crashes in on top of me and—

—hands prop me against a decrepit, dusty crate. All three of my companions bend down to look at me.

My mouth feels like the floor of a coal mine. I clutch my head to keep it from splitting apart. *"Urgh,"* I groan, "this hurts worse than a hangover." Something drips off my sleeve.

Brando fusses around me. "Hang on, hang on. Let me clean you up."

"Scarlet," Grey hisses, "you need to stay quiet."

I pull in a slow breath. This helps clear my head, but now I'm aware of something else. "Ugh! What's that smell?"

Brando whispers, "Alix, you threw up, and then you fainted. Stick your arm out. I'll clean off your jacket."

Sweet Jesus! I blacked out in the middle of a mission. Grey silently holds his penlight and watches my partner clean puke off my jacket sleeve. "Darwin," he slowly asks, "what's the matter with her?"

Brando finishes his nursemaid duty. "She'll be fine. It's only a nervous reaction." He helps me sit a little more upright. I nod that I'm okay, and my partner returns to examining the wall with his radar gadget.

Grey squats down in front of me. "You all right, Red?"

"Yeah." I goose some Overkaine to suppress my headache. "I'm sorry, Grey. That won't happen again."

"It shouldn't have happened at all."

"Yes, sir."

"Has it happened before?"

"Not like that, sir."

Grey sternly asks, "How *has* it happened before?"

Oops.

"Sir," Brando interjects, "I've found the doorway."

Grey's expression softens a little. "Scarlet, just stay cool, okay? We'll get him out."

"Yes, sir." I rub my sweaty palms on my pants. "Thank you."

Grey points at Brando's X-bag. "Okay, Darwin, let's try the Super Momma we got from Jacques."

CORE   TECH-SPRMAMA-003

Sonically Powered Retrogressive-Method Anti-Material Array (SPRMAMA)

This handheld device generates a pair of short-range, high-intensity, high-frequency self-balancing sonic waves that can be employed against a variety of surfaces to cause anything from mild damage to complete structural disintegration.

Although SPRMAMA is nearly silent on its own, when this system is used against a wall, floor, or ceiling, the demolished elements are likely to create significant aural disturbance.

Prototypes have been adapted into the casings of cordless drills. A few teams involved in Operation ANGEL have deployed with these preproduction units. Operatives will field test SPRMAMA at their first opportunity.

44

Brando presses the Super Momma against the wall and activates the sonic wave. My headache resurrects itself like a howling harpy, and I clap my hands to my temples. "Agh, fuck!" I glance up and see Grey and Falcon are doing the same thing. "Darwin," I grunt, "hurry up! That thing is turning my head into mush!"

My partner presses the Super Momma against the wall and "draws" a door-sized rectangle. Severed pieces of wood, chunks of plaster, and piles of stone filler crumble to the floor. Dust-filtered fluorescent light spills through Brando's sonic-boom doorway, and he finally shuts the frickin' thing off.

"Wow," he exclaims over the settling debris. "Talk about instant hole!"

My headache recedes almost as quickly as it started, but I still make sure to voice my low opinion of this new hoozie from the Technical Department.

"Next time let's just use a fucking chain saw."

Brando guesses that our vision Mods may have resonated with the frequency from the Super Momma, since my partner wasn't affected and he's the only one of us with plain old eyeballs.

We pick our way through the carpet of rubble and enter the Carbon lab. A layer of plaster dust is settling over a neat grid of tables and chairs. A refrigerator hums in the corner next to a counter and kitchen sink.

Falcon and Grey run to cover the lab's front door. Brando and I scamper toward the center of the facility. My partner sticks close in case I have another lunch-spewing panic attack. We hustle into a white hallway of offices and cubicles.

A pair of dull thuds echo down the linoleum-floored corridor.

"You got 'im?" Grey's comm-voice snaps.

"Yes, sir. He's down," Falcon replies.

The two of them have taken the entrance. Brando and I run past the offices and skid to a stop at a row of small laboratories. The doors are all secured with pass-code locks. At first we take the time to carefully disable them, but that's way too slow. I start kicking the doors in. This speeds things up significantly, but we haven't found any Originals.

We aren't finding anyone, actually.

"Hey," I say. "Where the fuck is everybody?"

Brando says, "I've been wondering the same thing. The scientists we pinched in London said these labs are staffed around the clock."

We enter an open foyer with a circle of long, low planter boxes arranged like Old West wagons defending themselves against an Indian attack. The plants are fake, but they still take the edge off the decor-by-Sparta feel of the place. It's also the only area with any decent signage. We spin around and read the signs.

"There!" Brando says. He takes off past a placard that reads PRIMÄR ENTWICKLUNGSLABOR. Primary Laboratory. I catch up to him, and we push open a pair of frosted-glass doors.

We're in a wide, rounded room like the lab in the Tower of London, except there's nobody home. The middle of the floor is dominated by a massive metal sarcophagus with thick cables and tubes coiled around it. Most of this techno-spaghetti runs across the floor to a series of shower-stall-size cylindrical tanks lined up against the walls. Each tank contains a person, a clone presumably, viewable through a glass window. The clones are all male, but they don't look like each other. Their features remind me of some of the thugs I fought in Zurich last year.

Brando moves toward a raised platform slathered in computer gear. I run to the Original container with my stomach in knots and peer into the window.

It's him! It's really him! I hug Li'l Bertha to my cheek. "Daddy, can you hear me?"

Yes!

"I'm here, in the room with you! We've come to take you home."

I . . . knew you'd come for me, Hot-Shot.

His skin is sallow and his lips are dry and colorless. His eyes are closed.

"Can you open your eyes?"

No, I can't . . . move anything.

Maybe it's because I haven't seen him in nine years, but I almost don't recognize him. It's weird how lifeless he is in there. He was always in motion, even when he slept. When I used to find him passed out on the couch down in his workshop, I'd curl up with him and study his face. The muscles in his jaw would twitch while he dreamed.

He's in a padded metal envelope, like the woman in the White Tower back in London. A breathing mask covers his mouth and nose, and a metal helmet hides his hair. The helmet sprouts a small galaxy of fine wires leading to a silver panel with blinking lights mounted to the inside wall of the chamber.

"Darwin," I comm, "do we take that helmet off his head?"

"Only after we've disconnected the wires," he comms. "But we need to detach them in the correct sequence."

"How can I help?"

"Have your father tell you what he's experiencing as I switch his IV from pancuronium to neostigmine and atropine."

"What?"

"I need to activate his musculature. Then we can take

him off the ventilator and move him much more easily. Disconnecting all the Carbon crap will take some guesswork, and it'll help if I know what it feels like."

I look at my dad. One of his eyelids pulses irregularly, and his comm-voice strains with great effort.

Oh, my God! Honey, they must have found our comm-connection.

"Dad, don't worry. In a few minutes you won't need it anymore."

No, listen, they've set . . . it's a . . .

"Scarlet," Brando says. "You ready?"

"Shh! He's trying to say something."

. . . trap.

My pounding heart nearly stops. A loud bang ricochets down the hall, instantly followed by a rapid exchange of gunfire.

"Falcon!" It's Grey. "Back up; lemme get 'em!"

Falcon comms, "Watch it! On your left!"

The firefight out front goes from zero to bullet blizzard in nothing flat. The floor starts to vibrate. Pieces of electronic gear scattered on a stainless-steel workbench totter over the edge and crash to the floor.

"Shit!" Brando yells. "Okay, change of plans. We'll disconnect him from Carbon first, then run him out of here on our portable ventilator."

"What should I tell my dad?"

"Well, normally this is done under anesthesia. It'll feel like hell when he comes off the lab's ventilator."

I swallow a lump in my throat. "Dad, we're going to unhook you from the lab. We'll need to know what you feel so we do this in the right order."

Understood.

"Then we'll switch you to our portable ventilator. My Info Operator tells me that part will be extremely unpleasant for you."

Let's get it over with, then.

I nod to Brando. He begins typing on the keyboard in front of him.

Hot-Shot?

"Yes?"

I love you very much, honey.

I promised myself I wouldn't cry, but twin streams of tears course down my cheeks. I close my eyes and gently cradle Li'l Bertha to my face.

"I love you, too, Daddy."

The teardrops run down my neck as I holster my pistol. Then I heave the sarcophagus's lid open and disengage the row of latches that hold the metal envelope shut. When I open the envelope, I nearly faint again.

My father has wasted away to almost nothing. All of his ribs show through his thin white shirt. His white cotton pants droop around thighs and calves as skinny as curtain rods. His powerful arms have withered to twigs with nearly skeletal hands sprouting from the ends like the claws of a monster.

Only my partner's steady direction keeps me focused. Brando has me start with the monitor pads and sensors, the stuff that reads data. I rip them off my dad's shrunken body. My eyesight has lost all color. Brando's instructions come so fast that I need more Madrenaline to keep my hands moving quickly enough. Then it's time for the helmet.

"Dad, you all right?"

Peachy.

"Darwin, he's good so far."

"Anybody have a free hand down there?" Falcon comms in. "It's gettin' a little radical up here." His call is almost drowned out by the metallic bark of a machine gun.

"Negative, Falcon," Brando replies. "We need another minute or so."

My vision has lost its midrange shades. Things are either white or black. I'm also sweating like crazy. Moisture sizzles down the sides of my body and soaks into my pants and underwear. My knees falter. I lean against the sarcophagus.

On close inspection, the helmet's wire nodes all have little numbers next to them, like network addresses. The numbers appear as thin black characters against a glare-white background. Brando starts at the low end.

"Try 192.1," he comms.

I find the correct node and pull the wire out.

"Dad? How's that?"

Nothing, then he begins to violently batter against his restraints.

I plug the wire back in.

Li'l Bertha transmits white noise instead of his comm-voice. While his depleted body continues writhing, my sight shifts to dark burgundy and white. Then he lies still.

Alix, that wasn't . . . correct.

"Daddy, I'm sorry! Are you all right?"

It hurt, but . . . keep trying.

I stare at my partner. His snow-white face is wet with perspiration, and his red eyes are jammed wide open. "Christ," he whispers. "Okay, let's try the other direction. Pull 192.255."

I find the node ending in 255 and yank out the wire.

"Dad?"

Much better.

I spend the next minute ripping wires out in descending order until I'm back to the node ending with a 1.

"Scarlet, hang on," comms Brando. "That's the wire that'll disconnect him from the ventilator."

Grey comms the two of us. "Shake a leg down there, people. The competition brought a lot of goodies to-night." To underscore his point, a piece of the ceiling cracks loose and smashes a rack of glass vials into skittering shards.

Brando runs across the room and takes our portable ventilator out of his X-bag. It's the size of a hardbound book. The front is covered with knobs and switches, topped by a small screen that lights up when my partner turns it on. From the device's side hangs a cluster of clear plastic tubes that converge at a round plastic something or other.

Brando leans over the sarcophagus and freezes when he sees my dad. "God almighty."

Grey comms, "Scarlet, Darwin, we've lost the entrance and are falling back. You need to get moving right now!"

The gunfire marches closer. A shot bangs down the hall and puts a hole in the lab's door, shattering the frosted glass. Brando reaches in to my father.

He calls out over the din from the hallway, "Now, Scarlet! Pull that last one."

I pull out 192.1 and stand back. My partner extracts the sarcophagus's breathing tube from my father. Dad begins to convulse again. Falcon and Grey bolt past the door as a stream of bullets explodes into the floor behind them, scattering chipped linoleum in every direction. Brando guides the ventilator's business end down my father's throat and presses the clear plastic mask over his mouth and nose.

Five black-shirted Staatszeiger soldiers charge past the lab and continue down the hall. My vision has gone from burgundy on white to burgundy on black, like a negative print from a slasher movie. I'm sweating so heavily that I can shake water out of my hair like a wet dog.

Another group of SZ men tromp down the hall, but these jerkoffs catch sight of me and Brando. Their black silhouettes raise their dark red weapons.

So much Madrenaline pours into me that pearls of white sweat fling off my black hand as I whip out my sidearm and stab her into air between me and these malignorant shit-for-nothing motherfuckers.

Li'l Bertha ejaculates her entire ammo pack all at once. Her squadron of black bullets slams into the meat bags and ignites a multicolor fireworks display that explodes out of the riddled bodies and sprays itself all over the wall.

That's my girl!

"Fuckin' outrageous!" It's Falcon. "Scarlet, was that you?"

I stalk into the hall on hooves of blazing coals. The mangled soldiers sprawl like smashed mannequins, but they're still alive. Li'l Bertha begs for more ammo. My hand rams a pack up inside her. She howls and pulverizes the screaming troopers into Meat-Whiz.

"Scarlet!"

Black water pours into my eyes, and I go blind. The bawls of the dying troopers and their gushing blood fade away until I can't hear or feel anything.

"Scarlet?"

Mom, Dad, and I sit in a circle. We all wear flowing white robes and leather sandals. My robe smells like damp earth and ancient bones. Mom glares at Dad. "I told you this would happen to her."

Dad pours his drink on the floor in the middle of our circle. It burns a hole through the carpet and floorboards. A long tentacle snaps out from the abyss, grabs my dad, and drags him down below. My mom cries out and plunges in after him. Sickening snaps and wails of agony erupt from the depths as their bodies are chewed and crushed. I scream and scream and scream until someone pulls me out of the room—

—through Brando's instant door and into the undercroft. My jacket is dripping with blood.

"Hey, you're awake!" Brando kneels down to check on me. "You all right?"

My breath hiccups in shallow gasps, but I see in full color again. My hearing has returned, too. Brando helps me up.

"Jeez," he says, "you look terrible."

"Gosh—*hic*—thanks."

Falcon and Grey, who have already passed through the undercroft, lug something up the stairs to the church. It's a blue plastic body bag.

"Patrick! My dad, is he—"

"He's alive, Alix." Patrick holds my hand. "The bag is the best way to keep him protected. Plus, it stabilizes his IV feed."

"How is he breathing through the bag?"

Brando squints at me like, *duh.* "I left the bag unzipped over his face."

"Oh. Of course, sorry."

"The ventilator will work for an hour, but your dad's really sick, Scarlet. I think he's going into shock."

"How long will he last without a Med-Tech?"

"Fifteen minutes, maybe less."

"Is he awake?"

"No, as soon as he was stable, I gave him a DOSE."

We race up the steps and return to the dusky church interior. Falcon and Grey set their burden down behind the altar. Grey checks my father and his bag to make sure everything is in place. Falcon, his rifle slung across his back, runs to the church's north windows.

Brando says, "I've induced the process that'll start your dad's breathing, but in his weakened condition I'm not sure how long it'll take."

Grey walks toward us as he comms, "Linebacker to Coach. We're ready to get in the game, but we have lousy field position."

"Roger that, Linebacker. Stand by for Playbook." Coach, our Navy mission coordinator, must be a big football fan. All the codes he sent make us sound like fucking Howard Cosell. "Lousy field position" means we're still in Carentan. Ideally, we would have transported my father out of town—good field position—to maintain our sneakiness quotient. But my dad's poor condition means we have to cut some corners.

Outside, a diesel engine roars to life, followed by an ominous mechanical rumble. Shouted orders ring from the dark streets around the church.

Falcon backs away from the window. "GUYS! Watch out—"

A storm of gunfire hammers through the windows.

Breaking glass and zinging bullets fill the air and chop
into the walls, benches, tapestries, and statues. They
also arrow through the negative spaces we each leave
behind as we hit the floor like cats falling off a table.

Grey comms, "Scarlet, Falcon, return fire! Darwin, on
me!" Grey propels himself across the floor in a fast in-
fantryman's crawl. Brando follows close behind.

I dose Madrenaline until my toes tingle and then roll
toward Falcon's position. I clench my eyes shut against
the flying splinters and chips of stone until I bump
into the wall. Falcon's fist clutches his sidearm, and his
eyes are as big as baseballs.

I call to him, "Get a spud ready," as I prep one of
the pineapple grenades Jacques gave us. Falcon fishes
around in his jacket pocket and produces a German
potato masher. He primes it and chucks it through the
nearest window as I toss my pineapple outside.

A man's voice squeals something before it's drowned
out by one of the grenades going off. A second later, the
other one explodes. I stick my pistol out the window.
Li'l Bertha's infrared shows me we're surrounded by
competitors, so I authorize her to automatically shoot
everyone. My gun knows she only receives full fire control when I'm really in the shit, so she loads up her craziest ammo without even asking.

Her whirling gyroscopes snap my hand from target to
target. The best part about .50-caliber Explosive bullets
is that every hit is a kill shot. Three SZ dummies disappear in shrieking clouds of meat chunklets. Then three
more. Body parts sail across the pitiless sky like glow-in-
the-dark slabs of beef.

Falcon is so stunned by what happens to these hosers
that he can only stare at Li'l Bertha with his trap half
open.

"C'mon, F-Bird." I replace my pistol's ammo pack.
"Pass the Lord, praise the ammo, and let's check the
south side."

Brando is behind the altar, huddled over my father.

He's comming with our Navy pals, but the gunfire is so loud that I can't hear what they're saying. Grey joins me at the southern windows.

Falcon, Grey tells us, using field signals to communicate, *I want you and your rifle in the spire.*

F-Bird nods and dashes up the stairs of the central tower. Grey and I tuck ourselves behind a heavy pillar between a pair of blown-out windows. Heavy incoming suppression fire keeps us tightly pressed into our cover.

A shadow moves behind Grey. Two black leather boots thump onto the floor. An SZ trooper has jumped through the window to flush us out! I point and fire Li'l Bertha at the intruder as Grey jabs his pistol past my head and looses a short burst at another attacker behind me. We both wince as the reports from our pistols pummel each other's eardrums. The two soldiers crumble to the glass-strewn floor.

"Okay, I'm on station," comms Falcon. "They seem to be hanging back—oh, wait. I see."

"What?"

I can almost hear Falcon gulp. "They've brought a tank."

Shit. *That's* what the deep rumbling sound has been.

"Darwin," I comm, "where's that duster?"

Brando answers, "Playbook can't land until we take out that armor."

"F-Bird, watch the tank and tell me if this does anything." Staying low, I stick Li'l Bertha out the window. Her optics feed into my Eyes-Up display so I can aim her at the metal menace outside. I bang a few Explosive 50s at the thing.

I zip my pistol back inside as the panzer's machine gunner responds with a rattling shower of bullets that pound into the windowsill above my head. Bits of broken stonework rip hot slashes across my scalp.

"Did that do anything?" I comm.

"Not really," Falcon replies. "You made some scrapes in the paint and shot out one of the lights."

Grey's brow creases as he considers our next move. A bug-eyed girl dressed in a petite SZ uniform appears next to him. She holds her chin in her hand like the statue of that thinking guy. She pretends to be nodding along with Grey's thought process. Then she snaps her fingers and disappears. A splinter of ice claws at my heart.

Grey gives me a hard look. "Scarlet, stay with me, okay?" He can tell I zoned out just now. "I have an idea, but I need your help."

"Yes, sir."

"You sure you're operational?"

"I'm fine, sir."

Grey switches to the team channel. "Falcon, cover us. We're going after that armor. Darwin, stay with Big Bertha. Scarlet, follow me." Grey leaps out the window. Then he activates his cloaking Mods and disappears.

"Grey, I can't see you. Where are you going?"

"Meet me under the panzer!"

I freshen my Madrenaline and bounce outside. Despite our desperate situation, I can't help laughing about the crazy shit we Levels say to each other.

45

I race outside after Grey, rush at the tank, and slide under it like I'm stealing second base. Grey is already there. He rubs his hands around the bottom of the vehicle until he finds what he's searching for.

"Here! Red, rip this panel off."

Of course! It's the escape hatch. Grey needs my help because part of what makes him so fast is that he isn't weighed down with strength Mods. I feel around the metal door's edge. The fingers on my synthetic right hand act as a wedge and pry one side open an inch. I stuff all my fingers into the gap and wrench the hatch door off its mount. Dim blue light glows from inside the armored menace.

"Nice!" Grey calls. "Back inside with you. I'll be right there."

I crawl out from under the panzer and crouch behind it. Screams resound from inside the heavy vehicle. I wait for a moment to make sure my fellow Level is okay. Falcon's rifle bullets zing around us and keep the SZ infantry under cover. The access hatch on top of the tank flips open. Grey jumps out.

He sees me, hollers, "RUN!" and charges toward the Cupcake.

It's gonna blow! I sprint after him. Grey dives through a blown-out window and lands inside on his feet. I'm in midflight through the same window when the SZ tank goes up like a steel geyser. The blast wave throws me off balance, and instead of landing next to Grey, I plow into him. We clatter to the floor in a heap.

"Grey, how about a little fucking *warning* next time?"

"How about you *do* what I fucking *tell* you to?"

My partner interrupts us. "Sir, the helicopter?"

Grey glares at me as he comms, "Falcon! How we looking, kid?"

Falcon answers, "The tank is toast, and we've killed or disabled the infantry. But there are three military trucks coming from the next town over. I think it's now or never for that dust-off."

"Roger that." He switches channels. "Linebacker to Playbook. LZ is clear, and subject is ready for extraction."

A man's voice with a southern twang responds, "Roger that, Linebacker. Playbook on approach, following your comm-signal."

I dash to Brando's hiding place behind the altar. My partner has a nasty head injury. A streak of blood courses from his scalp, around his ear, and down his neck, where it soaks into his collar. When I notice it, he shakes me off.

"Later," he says.

The two of us hoist Dad onto our shoulders and carry him toward the side exit. Brando is limping. Grey joins us and holds the door open. A loud bang resounds from the stairs down to the undercroft.

"Heh," grunts Brando. "Got 'em."

"That was a mine?"

"Yeah. I set it in case anyone tried to sneak in through the cellar."

We lurch outside while Grey covers us. An unmarked black helicopter floats over the rooftops and quickly swoops toward the street in front of the Cupcake.

"Shit!" Falcon comms from above. "I see a soldier— no, two—with a rocket launcher!"

"Where?"

He doesn't answer. The three of us all look up as Falcon takes a running jump and flings himself off the church spire. The kid has lost his fucking mind! He sails over the spinning helicopter blades toward the far side of the street. F-Bird keeps his rifle's stock pressed into his shoulder and unloads six shots so fast that it sounds like an automatic weapon.

"Falcon!" I scream.

He soars out of our line of sight, but the pilots see the whole thing, and since their comms are open, we hear their reactions.

"Rocket launcher! Two Krauts with—"

"Oh, my God, where'd that guy—"

"Wait, they're down."

"—come from?"

They both yell, *"Oh!"*

"Did he—"

"Holy shit!"

"—go through the roof of that house?"

We look at each other, astounded. My mouth goes dry. "Grey," I rasp, "you wanna go get him? Darwin and I can take care of this."

The color has drained out of Grey's face. "Y-yeah. Okay, I'll be right back." He ducks under the descending chopper and runs to the house Falcon crashed into.

The helicopter finally touches down. Smoke from our firefight swirls through its rotor wash. Brando and I lug our precious bundle forward as the chopper's big side door slides open. Three Med-Techs reach out and guide their patient inside the evac. The helicopter's interior is crammed with medical equipment, pressurized bottles, and electrical gear. There's so much stuff in there, I'm surprised the Med-Techs fit.

The Meddies gently deposit my dad on a low gurney mounted to the floor and zip open his blue body bag. Two of them hurriedly flip switches, twist valves, and connect tubes while the third Med-Tech slams the helicopter's door shut. My partner hustles to the front and gives a thumbs-up sign. The pilots gun the engine and lift off. Their downdraft dumps my butt on the pavement.

Big Bertha rises into the starry Norman night.

I sit on the cobblestones, struggling to breathe around the end of the last nine years of my life. All my sweat has evaporated, and I'm desperately thirsty. Brando bustles over and helps me up. I wrap my arms around him and press my face against his chest. His jacket muffles my gasping sobs.

"You did it, Alix." Patrick strokes my hair. "You saved him."

Mommy?

Yes, angel?

"C'mon, Scarlet. We've gotta go."

When is Daddy coming home?

My partner guides me to the car.

Soon, baby. Soon.

46

Saint Peter's Heavenly Barge whispers through the early dawn gloom. The car's lights are off, but my night vision reveals the deserted, neglected little road and the close-passing French countryside. I slouch behind the wheel. Dried blood in my hair crunches against the headrest. Earlier, Brando wrapped an entire roll of bandaging around my head to protect my lacerated scalp. I don't even remember what hit me. Eventually the first-aid turban stopped soaking up Alix juice, so I took it off. But physical injuries are the least of my problems.

I'm a fucking mess. My hallucinations and shaking hands are pretty bad, but I can handle those with my neuroinjector. However, even *I* don't think it's a good idea to pull missions if I'm passing out in the middle of them.

Grey is required to report my fainting spells, but both he and Brando assured me that after dumping a jillion bucks into my development, the last thing ExOps wants to do is park my butt in some human resources hellhole. Of course, before any of this becomes relevant, we have to get home.

"Are we there yet?" I grumble, even though I'm the one driving.

"Not long now," Brando responds from the seat next to me. My partner wears a bandage on the side of his head and has gingerly propped his injured left leg on the dashboard to keep it from swelling. He took a nasty hit when a statue's severed arm flew across the church and landed on his calf.

I glance at Grey in the rearview mirror. "How's F-Bird?"

"He's asleep, finally." Grey yawns. "I think his leg was keeping him awake."

I tilt my head from side to side to stretch my neck. "Lucky little fucker."

The kid's stunt, which we've already dubbed the Outrageous Flight of the Falcon, eliminated two moving targets from what can only be described as a treacherously unstable firing position. *Jumping over a helicopter. My God!* It was the most incredible combat sniping move any of us have ever seen.

It also left a Falcon-size hole in the ceiling of someone's unoccupied bedroom. The residents had all retreated to the cellar to hide from our ear-splitting firefight. F-Bird's body crashed onto their bed and cracked the frame in half. He doesn't have as deep a Madrenaline reservoir as I do, but he was hopped up enough to survive his rough landing with only a broken leg and a dense patchwork of bruises. He's so black and blue that he reminds me of one of those circus freaks with a million tattoos all over them.

But, he isn't dead, which is the important thing. As he flew across the night sky, I was struck by how much I like having him as a sort of brother. While we carried Falcon to the Barge, I told him he was crazy.

Between shallow, painful breaths Falcon murmured, "I couldn't let them kill Big Bertha."

"F-Bird, you idiot, you could have been killed yourself!"

"Yeah, uh-huh." He grimaced. "Look who's talking."

"That's different. He's *my* father."

As we loaded him into the car's backseat, Falcon grasped my hand and said, "He's my father, too, Scarlet."

A window flew open in my mind. Through it, I could see Falcon hasn't had much of a life. Labs, training, tests, and blessedly unsuccessful brainwashing. The thing that stuck out most to me was a single word: *lonely*.

"Yeah," I said. "He is, Falcon."

We dragged ourselves into the Cadillac and lit out. After escaping from the area, we hunkered down for the night in a large pasture. The Barge spent the evening indignantly hidden under a fat haystack. Early this morning we received our exit orders: get to Cherbourg, get on a boat, and get out of Europe.

Those orders were soon updated with a big piece of news. The chancellor accepted the President's offer. For the sake of restoring order as soon as possible, he immediately initiated the Reich's expulsion of its Jewish population. The far right's response began that same hour.

Elements of the Purity League and other proslavery groups attacked the Reichstag in Berlin. They also assaulted the trains and buses bringing the former slaves to the ports. They've even raided some of the transport ships.

One of those ships has been besieged by a large company of proslavery militiamen in Cherbourg, where we're going anyway. Our updated orders instructed us to assist the captain and crew and to protect the Jewish passengers.

I asked Brando why the German authorities didn't fight the militia themselves.

"Us," he answered. "We've given the Fritzes more than they can cope with. It's the Wild West out here."

Now we're a few minutes away from Cherbourg. The sky is brightening, so I switch off my night vision. Out of curiosity, I turn on my infrared and—hey—whaddaya know?

"Smoke! Over there." I indicate a column of heat rising from the far side of town. "Is that where the docks are?"

Grey leans forward. "Yeah, that's them, all right."

He watches for a moment. "Wow, they're really going at it."

I shift my head so I can see Falcon in the rearview. His eyes are closed. "Should we roust F-Bird?"

"It's okay, I'm awake," Falcon says. "Are we there yet?"

"Almost," Brando says. He points out the windshield. "What's that?"

Directly ahead is a large heap of hay bales and old furniture. Militiamen stand behind and around the heap. It's a roadblock made out of whatever odds and ends these putzes could lay their hands on. I press the gas pedal to the floor and put my seat belt on. My companions follow suit, then Grey and Falcon draw their pistols. I open the windows so we won't be shredded if they break.

The buttheads on the roadblock don't realize how fast we're moving until it's too late. The Caddy's four thousand pounds of Detroit thunder bashes through their pathetic pile of bedknobs and broomsticks like an all-state quarterback gliding through a sorority. My luckless victims all wear brown shirts, black armbands, and expressions of anguish and terror as I crush them under my pounding radials. The Barge accepts this abusive driving so gracefully that I wonder if the engineers at Cadillac actually had the foresight to consider how their vehicles would perform while ramming a mountain of junk.

We blast into the city, trailing anarchy in our wake. Several cars packed with gun-toting scumbags chase after us. Falcon and Grey take off their seat belts, turn around, and begin to exchange small-arms fire with our brown-shirted pursuers. Meanwhile, Brando guides me through town to the docks.

"Left forty," he comms to me. "It's a one-way street."

I power slide the Barge into the first left and nearly smash head-on into a truck. I swerve to the sidewalk and miraculously avoid the truck, a telephone pole, a baby carriage, the baby's mother, and two nuns. I have to slow down to do this, and now the pursuit cars are right on our ass.

"Why's that truck goin' the wrong fuckin' way?"

"He's not," Brando comms. "*We* are. I told you it was a one-way street."

"Darwin!" My feet fly across the pedals, and my hands swirl the steering wheel left and right. "I thought you meant one-way *our* way!"

My partner skips this argument. "Right fifty. It's a two-way street."

I slalom the Barge off the sidewalk and onto the road in time to gun a tire-smoking turn to our right. I lean on the horn and do my best New York City cabbie impression: "*Move it*, fuckòs! C'mon, shit-for-brains, *outta the way!*"

Falcon and Grey hang on tight in the backseat as we induce maximum traffic turbulence. I pass on the right, I pass on the left, I roar into the oncoming lane, I swerve onto the sidewalk again. Mailboxes, park benches, and small trees all meet their doom on the hungry grille of my deathmobile. So much garbage jams itself into our Caddy's air intake that its monster V-8 begins to overheat.

"Darwin, the Barge can't take much more of this. How far?"

"Right seventy, just before that scrap yard. Then it's a straight shot into the port area."

"Hang on, boys!" I keep the accelerator on the floor and stomp the parking brake long enough to slap the rear wheels into a skidtacular smoke show. Grey is shoved across the rear seat and squishes Falcon against his door. Brando holds on to the dash with both hands while the Barge's hypertaxed suspension gives me this one last, sweet turn before finally crapping out. My Jackie Stewart maneuver completely bungholes the fuckfaces following us, and they all crash into the scrap yard's front office.

We power through the port's main gate at a hundred miles per hour. The rattle and hum of a good-sized fire-fight jaggers through the car's windows. The action is centered around a very large cargo ship with *Longstreet* painted on its stern. Men on the ship exchange fire with brown-shirted jackanapes on the ground.

I plow the Barge into the proslavery militia. Their brown uniforms and black armbands are instantly slathered with the liquefied remains of their occupants. My car's tires are so coated with blood and guts that I lose control of the vehicle. The Caddy's irresistible form finally meets the immovable function of a gigantic dock crane. The engine compartment crumples up like a thousand-pound accordion, and the entire rear end comes off the ground. Brando is momentarily suspended in midair by his seat belt, I brace my arms against the steering wheel, and both guys in the rear are scrunched against our seat backs. We land with a shuddering *whonk*.

Saint Peter's Heavenly Barge is dead. The gunfire has stopped. Only the seagulls' shrill cries cut the stillness. Then time whooshes forward, and a curtain of bullets clatters against the twisted trunk of our demolished Cadillac. We all crawl forward through the missing windshield and take cover in front of the mangled chrome grille.

Our training allows us to maintain some composure. Grey comms, "Checkdown, youngest to oldest."

Falcon gasps, "My leg is a mess. I need help moving."

I say, "I'm good," and lean out from cover to see who's coming. *What a shock! Baddies.*

Brando comms, "I'm no worse than before," as he moves to examine Falcon's leg.

Grey also leans out from cover for a moment, then continues, "Darwin, how's F-Bird's leg?"

"It's pretty bad, sir," Brando answers.

"Falcon, how's your Overkaine supply?"

"It'll take care of the pain, sir, but I can't walk."

Grey peeks over the wrecked Caddy again. "Darwin, see if you can help Falcon onto that ship. Scarlet and I will cover you." He looks at me. "Ready?"

I nod at Grey and brandish Li'l Bertha.

Grey and I leap from behind the car and lay down a storm of suppression fire. The approaching brownshirts dive for cover. Grey reloads and keeps firing. I reload and dump a couple of Explosives into the pavement near the shitheads' hiding place. We scurry away from our ruined vehicle and get ready to rush onto the *Longstreet*.

A breathtaking explosion rips into the schmucks in front of us. A second blast, then a third slashes into the proslavery slobs. The surviving thugs flee in panic. Up on the ship, a hulking apparition rains destruction on the brownshirts. The air around him ripples every time his gun goes off.

"Hey, Shortcake," Raj comms. "What's with the luxmobile? I took you for more of a sports car girl."

47

The *Longstreet*'s crewmen extend the gangway. Raj
meets us halfway and takes Falcon from the limping
Brando. Grey and I go up last to cover the group. We
spatter a few rounds into likely hiding places around the
docks and surrounding warehouses. When we're safely
aboard, the crew retracts the gangway. Raj helps Falcon
lie down on a stack of rough shipping blankets. Grey
rushes to the bridge to check in with the ship's captain.

"Raj!" I call out. "Weren't you recalled with the rest?"

He says, "I've been ordered to escort you people out
of Europe before you reduce the entire continent to rubble." He leans down closer to me. "Hey, I heard about
your dad. Nice job, Scarlet."

"Thanks, Rah-Rah."

Brando's hastily commed after-action report for that
mission consisted of the single phrase "Subject retrieved
from Carbon facility." Raj and I both know how seem-
ingly dry phrases like that can bury a lot of people. They
can also break roofs, beds, and legs.

"So," Raj says to Falcon, "you're the flying sniper."

F-Bird nods and winces as Brando adjusts his broken
leg. Raj watches my partner work and says to himself,
"Sounds like Fredericks named you well."

The deck is littered with expended bullet casings and
chips of painted metal from the shiny pockmarks in the
bulkheads. Two long bloodstains show where wounded
men were dragged inside. Several crew members armed
with shotguns or pistols crouch along the rail. They're
tough-looking *marineros*, but these sailors are prepared

for isolated raids by pirates, not a large assault by a paramilitary group. They watch us intently.

Grey returns from the bridge. "All right, I've met with Captain Demet, and here's the situation.

"On the landward side, we're dealing with a full company of Purity League militiamen. Out at the port's entrance are two sport fishing boats full of men, watching this ship. A few of those men are armed with rocket launchers. One good shot from them and the *Longstreet* is done for."

Brando asks, "Can we just take out the rocket launchers?"

Grey shakes his head. "Not good enough. This vessel isn't armored, so the passengers are in danger from the small arms, too."

Brando asks, "Has Captain Demet received any demands?"

"Yes," Grey answers. "They want the Jewish passengers."

"What'd the captain say?"

"Well, he's part Jewish, which he's successfully hidden. But an entire branch of his family was abducted into the slavery system." Grey pauses. "So he told the militia's commander to shove it."

I keep an eye on the docks. "Who's the militia's commander?"

Grey shifts his weight from one knee to the other. "His name is Kruppe."

Brando and I lower our heads. "Figures," we sigh.

Raj asks, "You've met him?"

"Yeah. A couple times."

Captain Demet's blunt reply led to the standoff we crashed into. If it weren't for Raj and his 50-mm grenade-spewing Bitchgun, the brownshirts could overwhelm the badly outnumbered crew. But the Purity Leaguers aren't professional soldiers. They're ass-faced weekend warriors who are used to beating on unarmed civilians, not riding the Afterlife Express from fighting a fully enhanced Vindicator like Raj.

Kruppe doesn't want to sink the *Longstreet* unless he really has to. For one thing, the ship is smack dab in the middle of the region's biggest commercial port. It won't go over well with the locals—anti-Semitic or not—if Cherbourg harbor gets fouled up with a shipful of diesel fuel and dead bodies. Plus, Kruppe still thinks of Jewish people as private property. To him it'd be like destroying livestock.

Once the Jewish emigration got under way, the battles between abolitionist and proslavery forces moved from the capitals to the ports. The contested points of departure include Amsterdam, Portsmouth, Antwerp, Le Havre, and here, Cherbourg.

The Purity League didn't have the clout for an action like this until Berlin lost control of the country. Then Kruppe and his loudmouths spurred the area's conservative factions into a self-righteous furor with a carefully selected crossbreed of recent events and ancient hatreds. Next ol' Kruppy positioned himself as Germany's last hope, concentrated his Purity League here, and used it to take over the city.

Eventually, Berlin will recover enough control to bounce these buffoons back under their rocks. But Captain Demet and the *Longstreet* can't wait. If Kruppe loses his grip on the city, he'll sink this ship, local opinion be damned.

Grey asks Raj, "How much ammo do you have for that cannon of yours?"

"I only have nine more rounds." One corner of his mouth turns up. "But . . . I'd say this qualifies as the special occasion I've been saving them for."

A bullet twangs off the ship's bulkhead a few feet from us. We all flinch. The brownshirts have recovered from Raj's explosive smack-down.

Grey selects a crewman and asks for the gangway to be extended again. "We need to eliminate the offensive capability of these militiamen." He draws his pistol with one hand and his knife with the other. "As senior Level, I authorize discretionary lethal force—" He sees the light that prances into my eyes and directs the rest of his sentence at me. "—as long as it helps get this ship safely out of the harbor." I stifle my beaming expression and join Raj, Brando, and Falcon in a chorus of "Yes, sirs."

"We'll take care of Kruppe and his boats last." Grey assigns himself, me, and Raj each a sector of buildings to clear out. He says to F-Bird, "Falcon, can you lay down some cover fire?"

The kid nods. "As long as someone props me on the railing, sir."

"Good lad." Grey's eyes go out of focus for a moment. The hair in his eyebrows fluffs out a little. *Weird!* I didn't know other Levels had that happen when they dosed Madrenaline. His voice becomes faster, thinner, and a little higher-pitched. "Okay, kids. Let's show 'em what happens when you fuck with ExOps." All of Grey's muscles twitch, and he leaves a hole in the air.

Raj's voice sounds funny, too. "Man, that trick of his is pretty cool." His skin is covered in goose bumps, and the hair on his arms is rippling. He slings his Bitchgun over his shoulders, grabs an MP-50 in each hand, and lumbers down the gangway.

I breathe in the brisk sea air, close my eyes, and tell my neuroinjector to Madrenalize me. I mix in some Kalmers to keep my teeth from chattering and a touch of Overkaine to numb the pain in my foot. Then I'm off.

"Go get 'em, Scarlet!" Brando comms as I fly down the ramp. I take a hard left toward my sector of the dockyard and switch on infrared.

A pair of warm blobs lurk behind a flatbed truck directly in front of me. I somersault over the truck's cab. My legs point skyward as I sail above the two militiamen. One of them sees my shadow and looks up. His stunned expression tracks me all the way through my midair flip. My feet thump to the ground directly behind him and his partner. My right fist uppercuts the first bubblehead in the jaw, blowing him off his feet, then I spin and roundhouse kick his buddy so hard that his forehead slams into the flatbed truck before his legs go out from under him. I quickly gather their weapons and fling them into the harbor.

Turning back to my objective, my infrared detects a man-shaped hot spot on top of a three-story office building that's set next to the water. The enemy takes a shot at me, which I dodge easily. Before my pistol can return fire, the gunman's head kicks back and his body falls away from the roof's edge.

"Nice shot, Falcon," Brando comms.

There's still someone hiding up there. I comm, "Darwin, I'll get the spotter."

"Roger that, Scarlet."

I enter the building and run upstairs to the roof's access door. It's open. I poke Li'l Bertha through the doorway and use her onboard optics to peek outside.

The dead shooter sprawls in a pool of blood. There's someone else here, sitting on the roof, but it's not who I expect. He's a fair-haired child, crying, maybe eight years old.

I walk into the open. "Darwin, there's a juvenile up here. I think we greased his father."

The boy stares at me with eyes like burning ebony.

Brando responds, "Do *not* terminate him, Scarlet."

"C'mon, Darwin, I know *that*. What should I do with him?"

"Take him downstairs and restrain him. That way—"

While Brando comms instructions, the boy wipes his tear-streaked face, gets up, and runs to the dead militiaman. The child reaches into one of the man's bulging coat pockets and takes out a potato masher grenade.

No, this can't be real.

He twists the fuse—

I must be imagining this.

—and charges straight at me.

I grab him by his coat and throw him off the roof. His little hand is still clutching the grenade when it explodes as he splashes into the harbor.

Oh, my God—

The detonation ricochets around the port. I know this nightmare is real when Brando comms, "Scarlet, what was that?"

—oh, my GOD!

"Hey, Scarlet! You all right?"

"Y-yeah . . . I'm . . . I'm f-fine." My lips quiver against my fingers. I'm light-headed, and my brain is trying to cast itself adrift. I slump to the roof and hide my face in my hands.

"Was that the juvenile?"

"Patrick, he . . . he had a grenade."

My partner pauses. Everything pauses. Then he comms, "Jesus."

"I'm sorry, Darwin. I . . . he . . ."

Grey breaks in, "Scarlet, stop it! It's not your fault he was brought into this."

"But—"

"He was so young," Grey interrupts me. "I know, but he was old enough to kill you. Stay focused on the job, Scarlet. We don't have much time."

"Yes, sir." I struggle to my feet and wobble downstairs—slowly, in case I need time to cry. But my eyes aren't wet. I see spots again, though. They dance around when I blink.

Trick appears next to me.

Alix, why didn't you take the grenade away from him and throw that instead?

I don't know, Trick. I . . .

Trick's brows extrude a pair of bug-eyed lenses. The shiny surfaces reflect a tortured field of fire and ash.

Trick, I don't want to see that.

He morphs into a girl about my height, dressed in black. Her lenses retract. Where her eyes should be is a blank expanse of skin. As she walks beside me, she softly sings, *I fell into a burnin' ring of fire. I went down, down, down, and the flames went higher.* Then she claps her hands and disappears. My body shudders all over as I rush downstairs and outside.

Next to the small office building is a blocklong warehouse. That's my next objective. Once I sterilize it, my sector will be clear.

Later.

I dose chemicals until the spots stop swirling in front of me.

Think about it later, Alix.

48

The cargo elevator slowly ascends to the dockside warehouse's fourth floor. I hide under a mound of packing blankets. Finally, the car gronks to a halt and the doors clatter open. German voices call to one another, but nobody joins me on the elevator.

I peek out from under my cover. *All clear.* I throw off the blankets and walk to the main floor. The high unfinished ceiling extends away from me in all directions. It's striped at regular intervals with long tubes of fluorescent lights. Rows and rows of shipping crates create temporary passageways and innumerable hiding places. It'll take me forever to physically explore every inch of this warren. I check out the ceiling again. *That's it.* I jump on top of a wall of boxes. Now the entire space is laid out in front of me.

A half dozen brown-shirted knuckle draggers have clustered near the windows overlooking the *Longstreet.* Gunshots and screams resound across the harbor. Grey and Raj are really bringin' the pain.

Behind the jerkazoids, huddled away from the action outside, is a group of kids. I double-check with infrared. *Yep, little heat sigs.*

It won't help the Rising retain popular support if I make these kids witness the untimely demises of their elders. I move across the stacks of cargo toward the wall of windows. When I reach the wall, I turn toward the men and speed up. My feet skip and skim across the containers until I'm right on top of the dirtbags looking out the windows.

My body sails into the group. I grab two heads and

bash them together. My hands wrench rifles away from two more men, and I spin like a semaphore, my arms out straight with the rifles extended. After two revolutions I've clubbed the remaining opponents to the floor.

I scoop up their firearms and carry them to an emergency exit on the far side of the cargo grotto. Through the door is a small metal catwalk with stairs leading down the outside of the building. I pitch each weapon over the small building next door and into the water beyond.

When I go back inside, one of the men, a late-twenties-looking guy, is trying to stand up. I grab him by his jacket and hoist him until his feet leave the floor.

"Your name!" I shout in German.

"W-Wilfried," he stammers.

"Wilfried," I repeat as I lug him over to the kids. "Get . . . those . . . children . . . *out of here!*" I throw Wilfried on the floor and scream, "*Mach schnell, mutterfinken!*" This sort of language may not be so great for young ears, but their asshole parents have probably exposed them to worse things than R-rated curse words.

Wilfried gathers the munchkins together and leads them to the emergency exit. The shorties all look at me with big saucer eyes as they're ushered out the door.

"Brando, be aware that I'm sending a group of kids down the fire escape."

"Roger that, Scarlet. I see them."

"I've disarmed their chaperone, so don't shoot him."

"Got it. We'll leave him alone unless he tries something."

I return to my entry point and pitter-patter down the metal stairs wrapped around the elevator shaft. As I descend to the third floor, I take in my next battleground, first looking for small heat signatures. No kids. Everyone I see skulking about is a full-grown adult.

The warehouse's third floor has permanent partitions dividing the floor into six sections. The closest zones are full of refrigerators and washing machines. The areas farthest away are lined with black fifty-five-gallon drums. In the middle are towers of brown cardboard boxes, smaller wooden crates, rows of plastic bottles, and a half dozen automatic-weapon-toting brownshirts. The men watch the line of kids descending the fire escape from above and look questions at one another.

Their answer comes from Li'l Bertha's hail of suppression fire. Her pellets splinter chunks out of crates, leave pinging dents in barrels, and break the windows overlooking the dock. The men drop behind the nearest divider while I rapidly advance at them. I jump over the low wall and put on an ass-kicking clinic. They've fallen into the amateur's trap of bunching together, which allows my pinwheeling arms and legs to hit them all at once. The *biffs* and *boffs* come so quickly, it sounds like a bunch of boxers working out on a side of beef.

My hands grab their guns and throw them in a corner, near the front windows. Nearby is a short stack of opaque blue plastic one-liter bottles with white caps. Hidden among the luridly illustrated stickers with melting fingers and all-capitals warnings like DANGER and ACHTUNG is a black-and-white label that reads "Salz-säure." My onboard English-German dictionary translates this as "hydrochloric acid."

Perfect.

I rip the cap off one of the bottles and empty the contents onto my pile of confiscated firearms. The clear liquid pours over the metal and splashes to the floor, where it condenses into a white cloud of evil-smelling gas. The repulsive odor makes me picture tin cans full of superconcentrated chlorine. My eyes, nose, and throat start to sting as the guns and floorboards begin smoking.

Wow.

I back away from the angrily fizzing mess and comm, "Darwin, I need to ask you a chemistry question."

He replies, "What'd you do?"

I tell him.

"Scarlet, get the fuck outta there and don't breathe any of that shit!"

"What about the Purity Losers?"

"Crap. Uhh, move them away from the spill, but make it quick."

I hold my breath and blink away burning tears. My hands hoist and shot put each of the six beefcakes far across the room. They ungently splonk into walls or bounce off wooden pallets full of stuff. Meaty cracks accompany their awkward landings.

Nobody said nonlethal meant non-limb-splitting.

I race back to the stairs, wiping salty dampness from my cheeks. As I rush down to the next floor, my eyesight slips into Weirdo-Vision again. My hands look orange, and Li'l Bertha is a charcoal silhouette against the bright yellow steps.

"Darwin," I comm, "something's wrong with my vision Mods."

"You're still functional?"

"Yeah," I reply with more confidence than I feel.

"Okay. Well, Grey and Raj have finished their sectors. Want help?"

"Sure; I still have two floors to clear out."

My infrared seeks out more little people but comes up blank again. It seems like they had all their brats on the top floor.

Wait, there's one kid. Ah, two. No . . . just one? Hang on.

Two of the five heat sigs in front of me switch from adult-size red blobs to child-size red blobs. Then they switch back again. Next, all five shrink to kiddy sigs before popping into grown-ups again.

"Darwin, I definitely need assistance. My vision Mods

are so screwed up, I can't distinguish adult hostiles from juveniles."

"Okay, Scarlet. Sit tight; help is on the way."

All this time I've spent being defective has given the militiamen plenty of time to see me and open fire. I duck behind a rack of long iron pipes and listen to the fog of lead whoosh past overhead. The gunsels adjust their aim, and the pipes absorb a clanging broadside of slugs.

Before I dived for cover, I saw that the second floor is dominated by a colossal pair of metalworking machines. They've each gotta weigh a couple of tons. I can't tell if they're installed here or waiting to be shipped out. They're a problem, though, because they're providing cover for this squad of militiamen.

"Cripes," I comm, "there's a lot of fucking jerks in here! What'd they do, bring every butthead in Greater Germany?"

"Scarlet." It's Grey. "Lay some Incendiaries near the competitors so Falcon can see them."

"Sir, I can't tell if they're adults or children."

"Raj and I are right outside, and I see five adult heat sigs. Light 'em up."

"Yes, sir. Falcon, you ready?"

"Affirmative, Scarlet."

I hold Li'l Bertha above my pile of pipes and return fire with a volley of small Incendiaries. Blaring orders resound from the other side of the warehouse, near the metalworking mills. The hyped-up voices are joined by deep rifle reports from the *Longstreet*. Two of the shouters turn into screamers as F-Bird scores a pair of hits through the windows. I stand up from cover and take aim, but the three remaining chowderheads have hidden behind the metalsmithing machines. They take turns blindly firing in my direction, trying to keep me suppressed.

The floor begins to pulsate in sync with a ballad of loud bangs and crashes from downstairs.

"Heads up, Scarlet." It's Brando. "Raj has entered the building and engaged the enemy."

Music to my ears.

All the racket down there must be the big man and his Bitchgun. "Darwin, tell him to shoot up, through his ceiling."

Brando comms, "Raj, did you hear that?"

Raj's comm-voice rumbles through the bedlam. "I hear you, Scarlet. Clear the area."

I crouch behind my cover and peer toward my competitors. A gigantic hole erupts in the floor from downstairs. Chunks of wood ricochet off every surface, and my incoming fire drops to bupkis.

"Raj," I comm, "shift your aim thirty-five feet toward the water!"

Another inverted crater punches through the deck. Raj's shots are so close to one of the giant-ass milling machines that the floor gives way beneath it. The monstrous device tips over and bashes a hole ten feet wide in the deck. The joists snap like matchsticks, and the floorboards sag like a hammock. The second machine loses its balance and follows the first one, expanding the instant atrium to a width of fifteen feet.

Two of my remaining opponents get sucked through the hole and cascade into Raj's merciless clutches. I aim Li'l Bertha at the remaining militiaman. Before I can fire, the man's head twitches and he falls over backward. A smoky shape resolves itself into the figure of Grey.

He holds his hands up and pretends to surrender to me, *"Nicht schiessen, fraulein."* He laughs and checks his fallen opponent's pulse. I walk over to the jagged hole in the floor. Raj stands in the heap of brown-shirted body parts he's created next to the two tipped-over shop machines.

Raj looks up. "You all right, Shortcake?"

"Yeah. Thanks for the help." I jump through the hole

and land next to Raj. "You guys made me feel like Catherine the Great."

"How'd we do that?"

"Well, you know—" I pretend to primp my hair. "—behind every successful woman is a devoted gang of homicidal maniacs."

49

"What are you talking about?" I gripe at Brando. "They're right there. Let's blast 'em!"

"With what?" Brando takes off his glasses and wipes them on his shirt. "This is a cargo vessel, not a warship."

We're all in *Longstreet*'s bridge, smokin' 'em if we got 'em. Sitting down for a bit has given my vision's oversaturation a chance to return to normal. I'm holding my eyes closed as Captain Demet tells Grey and Brando he can't risk moving his ship out of Cherbourg's harbor until Kruppe's proslavery militia on the two fishing craft has been eliminated.

I open my peepers. "Raj, can't you hit them with your Bitchgun?"

Raj leans on a desk in the corner. "Sure, if I had any ammunition for it, but my last shells brought down that warehouse floor."

I already know Falcon is out of ammo for his rifle, and even he's not good enough with a pistol to neutralize every person on two bobbing boats from a half mile away. If F-Bird actually hit someone out there, the rest of the assholes would motor in and sink us with a barrage of rockets.

"So . . . now what? We're stuck here?"

The entire ship's company has gathered outside. They volunteered for this voyage with the understanding that they'd be protected from proslavery scum like the Purity League. The government vastly underestimated the scale and severity of the far right's response, and Berlin's attempts to restore order have been comprehensively overwhelmed. I think *Longstreet*'s crew is worried we're going to abandon them here.

Grey squints through the front windows and rubs his stubbled chin. He hasn't had a chance to shave since we left Paris, and his beard grows in fast. He turns and quietly scrutinizes me, still brushing his scruffy facial hair with his fingertips. Then he smiles.

I spread my hands. "What?"

Finally, he says, "How fast can you swim?"

"Real fuckin' fast. Why—oh! Wait, you're not thinking to—"

"Swim out there, yes," Grey says. "You and me. We each attack one boat and eliminate Kruppe and his men before they can react."

Captain Demet, his crew, a contingent of former slaves, Raj, Brando, and Falcon—all of them—watch Grey and me. I never miss a chance to fuck people up, but this is crazy, even for us.

"Grey, our pistols will be so waterlogged, they won't—"

He holds up one hand and cuts me off again. "No guns." A nasty sneer slithers across his face while his eyes narrow down to slits. "Knives."

My heart thuds like a mallet. He's practically daring me, and Alixandra Janina Nico never, ever turns down a dare.

I lean toward Grey. "All right, tough guy. We'll do them with knives."

The two of us walk outside. Everybody follows. We're hidden from Kruppe's boats by the *Longstreet*'s bridge. I hand Li'l Bertha to Brando, who carefully accepts her with a solemn nod. Grey gives his small arsenal to Raj.

Grey and I both kick off our boots and socks. I unbuckle my belt and pull off my pants and then my coat, sweaters, and shirt. *Whoo! Chilly!* My nipples get as hard as pebbles in the winter air.

The sailors hoot and holler, their worries about imminent death washed away by the sight of female flesh.

I'm glad Marie has simple taste in skivvies. The black cotton underwear she bought for me has a bit of lace around the edges, but besides that I'm essentially wearing a plain bikini.

I buckle my knife holster around my upper thigh. The overstimulated crewmen loudly proclaim how much they like this sexy swashbuckler outfit. I shout at them in French, "Sorry, maternal parent fornicators. No American tail for your soft-as-cheese dicks!" Or something like that.

Grey has also shucked down to his underwear. He's pale, fit, and hairier than I would have thought. After he straps his knife around his waist, he turns to me, bares his teeth like a pirate, and snarls, "Eyyyy!"

I grit my teeth back at him. "Arrrr!"

We each take a long, deep breath, run across the deck, and dive overboard.

Holy fuck, this water is freezing!

I paddle after Grey to the ocean-facing side of the *Longstreet*, dose a bunch of Madrenaline, and shoot away from the ship like a torpedo. I add a measure of Overkaine to numb the pain from the cold.

"I'll go for the boat on the left," I comm to Grey.

"Yeah. I'll take the one on the right."

Our arms and legs churn the water and propel us toward our targets like a pair of biorobotic sharks. Grey can run faster than I can, but we're evenly matched as swimmers since here we work against liquid resistance instead of gravity.

With fifty yards to go, Grey comms, "Try to swim underwater the rest of the way to max the surprise." I switch to a backstroke and hyperventilate for a few seconds. Then I descend four or five feet under the surface. I raise my arms over my head so I'm shaped like a missile and kick furiously until I pass under the enemy vessel.

"In position," I comm.

"Me, too," Grey replies. "Give 'em hell, Scarlet."

I surface at the boat's stern. My last stroke launches me like a flying fish. I'm reaching for my fighting knife before my feet hit the deck.

Two brown-shirted men lounge on a pair of plastic chairs. One is a tall, chubby guy who holds a rocket launcher across his lap. The other guard is shorter and armed with a machine pistol. They're immobilized by the sight of a furious, nearly naked girl erupting from the briny deep like a merpsycho.

I yank my knife from its holster and charge them. Their eyes move from my tits, to my face, and then to the glittering blade in my left hand. The one thing they aren't looking at is my right fist, which crashes into their faces—one after the other—and smashes them out of their chairs.

First things first. The rocket launcher goes overboard, then the automatic pistol. I reach down and wrench the chubby guard off the deck by his coat. I herd him to the rail and shove him into the water. The shorter guard stands and puts up his dukes, like I'm going to box him.

Yeah.

I sweep my knife across his fists and gouge cuts into all his fingers. He recoils with his blood-spurting mitts against his chest. This presents me with so many options that I have trouble deciding how to finish this fool.

Finally I settle on a feint to his knee, then a crushing right uppercut to his chin. His colliding molars sound like a pair of bricks being slapped together. Down he goes.

Another KO for the Dazzling Dame from D.C.

I pick the unconscious guard off the deck and drape his warm, limp body against my icy skin. As I shuffle him forward, my bare feet smear thin streaks of blood across the deck, and my frozen teeth click like maracas.

A thin wail shimmers across the water, followed by a heavy sploosh. Grey is on his game. The morons on my boat are so distracted by watching his murderous rampage that I make it all the way into the wheelhouse before anyone sees me coming.

The thug nearest the door gets an agonizing trip to the disabled list when I shove my knife through the back of his knee. The remaining competitors spin around. There are four, and one of them is Johannes Kruppe. My sudden proximity and shocking appearance render them all speechless, but Johannes recovers quickly. The tall, white-haired rat-fuck swings himself through a small hatchway between the wheel and the navigator's station and disappears below.

There's no help for me out here, so my tolerance for back talk is much lower than it was on shore. When two of the brutes point Lugers at me, everyone in the room automatically qualifies for express checkout.

I hide behind my human shield and rush the nearest pistol-packing militiaman. Panicking, he fires his weapon and hits his unconscious colleague, which leaves me at liberty to jab my knife into his crotch.

And so it is revealed that for generating pure and unadulterated perturbation, pyrotechnics are nothing compared to shanking a man in the balls. The pinhead screams and drops his Luger so he can use both hands to protect what's left of his genitals. He bends down to see what's happened to him, and it's the most natural thing in the world for me to obliterate his central nervous system by stabbing him right in his fucking eye.

I bang too much gusto into the thrust, though, and my blade sticks in the dimbulb's eye socket. I hurl my human shield at the final three dummies, nab the Luger off the floor, and unload an entire clip into their screaming faces. The insides of their heads splatter all over the wheelhouse's windows, ceiling, and control panel. It looks like a raft to hell.

"Grey, my top deck is clear, but I have at least one more competitor down below."

"Be careful, Scarlet. I found a few militia still in their bunks over here. Some kids, too."

The small hatchway is propped open. A ladder leads down below. My infrared shows a warm square shape toward the boat's stern. That'll be the engine. Up front are two smaller blobs. Kruppe has company.

To retrieve my knife from Dead Crotch's face, I stand on his head and heave the blade out of his skull, like King Arthur freeing his magic sword from the stone. At that moment, my F-S fighting knife earns the name Deathcalibur.

I pitch myself through the hatchway. My feet thwap the lower deck. I'm in the main cabin and galley. I clutch Deathcalibur in my left hand and the Luger in my right. I move forward and push a thin door open. The small cabin is unlit, but I see two red-glowing figures cowering on a V-shaped bunk under the bow. It's a boy and a girl, eight or nine years old, like the kid at the dockyard who . . . Jesus, if they try the same suicide-grenadier move down here, we're all dead.

The girl's eyes flick to something moving—

—*behind me!*

I sling myself to one side. A man lunges into the space I've left behind and grunts. I crank around and jack my pistol into the face of—

"Johannes Kruppe," I sneer through my chattering teeth. I fire at his head. He dodges the shot and slaps the Luger out of my hand. I slash at him with Deathcalibur, which he also evades.

That's right; he's enhanced!

"Grey, I've got Kruppe, but—" The rest of my comm is interrupted as Kruppe seizes me and we violently wrestle all over the cabin.

"Hang on, Scarlet," Grey comms. "I'm on my way."

We rumble through the kitchenette. I can't find my Luger, so I throw anything that isn't nailed down: glasses, dishes, teakettle, whatever. Very little of it hits him, and he keeps grabbing more of me each time he chases me into a corner. I swing my knife at his hands and jump over his arms, but when I come down, long shards of broken glass stab into my bare feet.

"AHHGH!" I collapse to the deck. My neuroinjector hits me with Overkaine as Kruppe hoists me like a sack of potatoes.

The beefy fucker tries to crush me in a bear hug. I club my forehead into his nose. This draws blood but doesn't break his excruciating stranglehold. Kruppe squeezes me so hard that something inside my body snaps. My lungs strain for air, and my bloody bare feet kick at his knees. Finally, I switch my grip on Deathcalibur and jam the blade into Johannes's gut.

He shouts and lets go of me. One of his hands covers the wound in his midsection. I back away and kick at him as he tries to grab me with his free hand. He drives me against a bulkhead. I grab a metal folding chair and swing it at him. His upper body leans out of the way, but the chair solidly clocks his kneecap.

Kruppe's painful yell boomerangs around the cabin. He limps away from me, cursing a blue streak. His hand scrabbles a kitchen drawer open, and he hauls out an immense handgun.

This macho mental case had that the whole time?

He barely aims the beast before he starts blasting away. I jump across the cabin, slam into a small table covered with maps and papers, and stumble against the wall. I spin and draw my arm to throw my knife into Johannes's neck.

Then something brushes my ankle. I slash Deathcalibur at this unwelcome surprise.

The little girl appears in the doorway to the front cabin. *"Ach nein! Nicht mein kleines Pfefferchen!"* No! Not my little Pepper!

I freeze my swing and avoid stabbing the kids' small black dog by less than an inch. The mutt scurries up the ladder to the top deck. By the time I turn to Kruppe, he already has his nasty-looking pistol aimed at my chest. His chin and neck are streaked with blood from his nose, and more blood dribbles across the hand he holds over his knife wound.

"Scarlet," Grey comms. "I'm bringing the other boat over. Do you need help?"

"*Yes!* Omigod, Grey, hurry before—"

"How much time do you—"

"*NOW!*"

Johannes draws in breath to speak, and then the world slams upside down.

I spin like a cat in a dryer. Shit flies all over the place, and everyone on board screams, including me. Nothing is where it was a second ago. It isn't until I feel water gushing into the boat that I realize what happened.

If we were following proper ExOps comm-protocol, I'd transmit something with the words "situation report" and "competitor status." Instead I comm, "Grey, you crazy fuck!"

"Did it work?"

"Yeah, it worked."

What worked is that my maniacal teammate commandeered the other boat and rammed it into this one. My cracked-up craft lies on its side and sucks in water like a sponge. I have less than thirty seconds before this tub sinks into Cherbourg harbor. I slosh across the cabin to check on Kruppe. A grisly crater in his head stains the flickering water around his body a deep crimson.

Cause of death: killed by unhinged boat pilot.

It's time to abandon ship, but my hasty exit is interrupted by the two kids bawling in the front cabin. I holster Deathcalibur and limp to the bow. When I barge into their room, the kids cry even louder.

I'm quite an eyeful. Soaked, covered in blood, and flush with killing rage, I must be an ice-white portrait of frozen ferocity. But there's no time to dick around, and there's no way to calm these kids down right now.

I reach out and glom one head of blond hair in each fist. The kids shout and try to pull my hands off them as I drag them across the flooding room and into the main cabin. I push them up to what remains of the deck outside. Then I follow.

Grey has guided his scratched and dented boat beside my sinking mess. I hand the kids to him. Then I throw him the damned dog, which somehow survived the aquatic T-boning. Grey reaches down and helps me aboard his boat as Kruppe's demolished vessel gurgles into the sea. Brando will be psyched that we've re-created his favorite line from *The Godfather* by sending Kruppe to sleep with the fishes.

Speak of the devil, Brando comms in: "Grey, Scarlet, it appears things have settled down out there. Is it safe to move the *Longstreet*?"

"Affirmative," Grey answers. "Come on out." He then leans down to the frightened children and whispers something to them. They both vanish below the deck. Momentarily, their little hands hold up a bundle through the hatchway. It's a pair of blankets. Grey drapes one around himself and gives one to me.

I wrap the blanket around my quaking body and say, "That was a pretty radical move for an Infiltrator."

He grins. "Must be all the time I've spent with you outrageous Interceptors."

Across the water, the *Longstreet* eases away from the dockyard. In the water, a small group of six men and three children swim toward shore. It looks like Grey's side of things was about as lethal as my savage little fatality fest.

I plop into the navigator's seat and clutch the blanket to me. Blood drips from my feet, and my ribs burn like cattle brands. Pepper the dog has already tracked bright red paw prints all over the boat.

My attention is drawn to a big plastic cooler full of beers. I grab a couple, give one to Grey, then crack the other one open for myself and chug it down. I help myself to a second brewski, chug that one, too, and let out a long, loud, rib-searing belch during which I rumble, *"Ü-u-u-ber Alles!"*

CORE   MIS-ANGEL-6133

Heavily encrypted intercept, source unknown:
START TRANSMISSION : ACTIVATE TERMINA-
TION SEQUENCE : TRANSMISSION END

50

Next morning, Friday, March 13, 5:52 a.m. CVT
Longstreet, Atlantic Ocean

Dear Lord Most High, please make this horrible feeling go away and I'll never chuzzle eleven beers after prolonged immersion in winter-degree water again.

Hypothermia sucks ass! My bedsheets are drenched with sweat, the covers are tangled around my legs again, and I have to pee like crazy. Plus, it's dark and the room smells like cheese. If it weren't for my night vision, I'd never be able to see where I am: in one of the food larders on the cargo ship *Longstreet*, bound for America.

The ship's regular berths are already stuffed with crew and passengers, so Captain Demet had to put us up in this supply room. Brando, Falcon, Grey, and I have been confined to our cots while we recover from the injuries sustained over the last two days of our ROAR Tour.

F-Bird's leg has finally been set in a proper cast, but that isn't the only broken bone our team has suffered. That bear hug Kruppe gave me broke one of my ribs, so I'm wrapped up tight to keep everything in place. I've also got puffy gauze marshmallows on my feet. Brando has bandages on his head and has been using an ice compress to keep down the swelling on his badly bruised thigh.

Grey and I are being treated for the severe loss of body heat we suffered while fighting the brownshirts on their boats. My hypothermia is worse than his, supposedly because I celebrated so much more than everyone else.

I gingerly extract myself from the blanket knot and hobble out to the bathroom. On the way back to bed, I check on F-Bird. He's asleep, and his eyes move around under his eyelids as he dreams. His breathing is shallow, and his arms twitch. Looks like a bad one. I should know.

I climb into my cot, expecting to lie awake obsessing about my father and which circle of hell I'll go to for killing that boy. Instead, I fall asleep right away.

It's light out. I walk up to the deck of a ship. It's covered in grass and trees, like a small park floating in the middle of the Atlantic Ocean. A group of children play on a little merry-go-round, laughing and calling to one another. I walk over to them.

The kids all stop and stare at me. The smiles drop from their faces like butterflies sizzling off a bug zapper. They stand still, staring at the ground. A few of them begin to cry. One boy, the tallest, frowns at me.

Wait. He's not looking at me. He's looking past me.

I turn around and nearly jump out of my skin. A desolate, brooding figure looms behind me, reeking of despair and ringing of pain. The grim spirit wields a heavy scythe and wears a black hooded robe. It's the same height that I am.

I step away from the deathly apparition. My feet trip over something, and my backside lands on the grass near the frightened children. The nightmarish figure strides forward and throws off its hood.

Huh, I always thought Death was a guy.

Wait a minute. Her face seems familiar.

A thick black snake oozes out of her mouth and speaks in Trick's voice.

"Scarlet!" the snake rasps. "Look out!"

"Whuh!" My forehead is slick with sweat, but my swaddled feet are like size-seven ice cubes. I push the covers off me and hold my side while I lie panting in the dark. Gradually, I become aware that I'm not the only person awake in here.

Falcon sways on his feet, ten feet from me. His arms twitch even worse than when he was asleep. Wait, is he sleepwalking? What's he holding? My hand worms under my pillow for Li'l Bertha.

She's not there.

She is *always* there.

"F-Bird? Can you hear me?"

The poor kid jolts in his skin like he's about to come apart from the inside out. "S-Scarlet? I don't want to." He presses something against his stomach.

"Hey, relax, man." I slowly place my feet on the floor. "Don't want to what?"

He grunts, and a stream of spit dribbles down his chin. *What the fuck is wrong with him? How is he even standing in his cast?*

I comm on a private frequency, "Brando! Wake up!"

My partner has been awake for days, tending to his wounded comrades and filing reports about all the crazy shit we've done. I glance at his bunk across the room. He doesn't stir.

This time I comm at maximum urgency, "PATRICK! WAKE THE FUCK UP!"

His head comes off his pillow, but he's really disoriented. "Alixsh? Waz'sh?"

Falcon swivels to see who's talking. *Now!* Madrenaline belts into my system, and I fly off the bed like I've been shot out of a cannon. The sudden motion fires a white-hot flare across my ribs. I slap at F-Bird's hands and knock him over. A pair of objects clatter to the floor as I land on top of the kid with my hand at his throat.

"Falcon! What the fuck's the matter with you?" My free hand gropes for the things he dropped. One of them is his pistol.

The other is *my* pistol.

"What the *fuck* were you doing with Li'l Bertha?"

Falcon writhes under me. Brando finally rouses himself, instinctively grabs his X-bag, and dashes to my side. "Alix, what's going on?"

"I don't know. Something's wrong with Falcon!"

Everybody else wakes up. Raj and Grey run over and hold F-Bird's arms and legs so I can get off him. The kid's body thrashes against the floor like someone whacking the dust out of a rug.

"Is he epileptic?" Grey asks.

I sit down and gingerly press my hand against my ribs. "I don't know. Dad isn't."

Raj pins Falcon's wriggling wrists to the deck. "Dammit, he's gonna self-destruct."

Brando asks, "Alix, did he say anything?"

"He said, 'I don't want to.'"

"And he had your gun?"

"Yeah. Swiped her right out from under my pillow."

My partner dives into his X-bag and retrieves his DOSE. He holds it against F-Bird's arm. The results are immediate. Falcon goes limp and passes out. Saliva trickles across his cheek.

I say, "You know, every time you do that to somebody, I'm convinced they're dead."

"Well, no, he's not. But he'll be out for a while."

"What's wrong with him?"

Brando inhales, then puffs out his cheeks. "I think he's a Sleeper. Given who sent him here, I'd say he was about to kill you, Alix."

We gape at each other in shock. A Sleeper is an agent with a preprogrammed mission that lies dormant in the operative's mind until his handler sends an activation signal. Once it's initiated, almost nothing can sway a Sleeper from attempting to complete the assignment. The brainwashing is so severe that activated agents tend to eschew tactics or restraint. This leaves them with limited opportunities for a safe escape, which is why Sleepers rarely get second missions.

Raj recovers first. "Why would Fredericks activate him now?"

Grey rubs his beard. "A last resort, I guess. Maybe he thought Falcon could kill Scarlet and dump her body in the ocean. Make it seem like she'd fallen overboard."

Brando sits on his bunk and wipes his face. "Or maybe Fredericks lost his connection with Falcon until tonight. We went offline for a while after we hooked up with the kid in Calais."

Grey regards Falcon, who's still unconscious on the floor. "What about when he comes around?"

Brando says, "We'd better keep him sedated until we're home. The Med-Techs can flush the mission out of him."

"And then he'll be okay?" I ask.

"I hope so."

"What if he's not?"

"Then . . ." My partner stares down at the floor and whispers, "I don't know."

Neither Grey nor Raj can look me in the eye. I contemplate F-Bird's immobile form for a moment, then say a quick prayer:

Dear Father, please restore my crazy brother to full health by the power of your Holy Spirit, and may you, Lord, be glorified by how much he kicks ass. Amen.

CORE   INT-GG-4629

FROM THE DESK OF THE EXECUTIVE
INTELLIGENCE CHAIRMAN
DATE: April 17, 1981
SUBJECT: **Greater Germany**

Dear Mr. President,

Per your request, I submit herein a summary of the developing state of affairs in Europe. In brief, it is extremely dynamic.

The German government's abolishment of slavery has met fierce opposition from the political right and pro-slavery paramilitary groups like the Purity League. These groups are well funded by anti-Semitic institutions and may require aggressive neutralization. Nationalists from the former countries of France, Great Britain, Spain, Holland, and Italy, sensing an opportunity, have called upon their countrymen to liberate themselves from German rule.

Violent public conflicts have erupted across the German Empire. The fighting is especially pronounced in the "New Reich" states where slaves were most widely used. As we have discussed, slavery was restricted within Germany's prewar borders to minimize domestic unemployment.

We forecast that Greater Germany will soon be embroiled in a full-scale civil war. A significant percentage of her citizens—including many high-ranking Reich officials—feel that slavery is a moral blight. This sentiment is shared by the majority of Americans, who will expect our military to join the emerging antislavery coalition. I'm sure you share my sense of irony at helping a German force reconquer Europe after we supported Germany's enemies during the early 1940s.

Despite the ongoing turbulence, the mass migration of former slaves to Cuba progresses steadily. The U.S. Army has secured the goodwill of the native Cubans toward their new neighbors, the entire island swarms with American construction crews, and our media outlets tirelessly announce how this is the dawn of a golden age for Cuba and her people.

Obediently yours,
George H. W. Bush, XIC

51

The biggest advantage to sleeping in a chair is that it gives me a break from my nightmares. In truth, that's the *only* advantage to spending the night in this damn thing. Some evenings I just lie on the floor. It's not like I actually sleep, but most nights I let Mom have the couch.

We've maintained a vigil at my unconscious father's bedside since we got home. Mom flew down to Cuba in time to meet the *Longstreet* as it docked in Havana. I spotted her turquoise scarf from halfway across McAuliffe Harbor.

When I appeared at the top of the gangplank, she waved at me with both hands. Her happy smile faded as she watched me limp down the ramp. By the time she saw my bandages, my bruises, and the shadow in my eyes, she was positively distraught. Mothers know when their babies have been in over their heads.

Cleo held her arms out to me. "You did it, angel! Daddy's home."

My vision blurred as I staggered to the bottom of the walkway. *"Mom!"* I held her as tightly as my ribs could stand and cried out nearly two months of anxiety. She kissed my forehead and gently rocked me in her arms. "It's okay, honey. You're home. We're all okay." The rest of the disembarking passengers flowed around us like a stream washing around a fallen tree.

On the rare evenings when I actually doze off, the chair twists me into an aching pretzel. My mother, on the other hand, seems capable of snoozing anywhere. She tells me it's all the practice she's had.

I've been home for almost three months. My small

galaxy of injuries has healed, my Mods have been repaired, and my Enhances have been replenished. Raj and Grey are all fixed up, too, and they've both been assigned new missions.

Patrick and I see each other every day. We're officially an item, but I'm too distracted by my father's condition for anything super serious, which Patrick seems to understand. The two of us work together all week, and most Saturday nights we go to the movies. When I have my period, we go for ice cream afterward. When I don't have it, we fool around in the car and *then* we go for ice cream.

Most of our classes and briefings are about the wild situation in Greater Germany. The country is tearing itself apart over Jewish emancipation. All of us ExOps Levels are being prepped for missions on the Continent, and once the dope addicts on Capitol Hill figure out which side we're on, we'll ship out and kick butt. Should be fun.

Falcon survived the Med-Techs' procedure to extract the Sleeper mission Fredericks embedded in the kid's onboard software. The Meddies said it's an all-or-nothing operation and this time we got "all." Now ExOps needs to figure out what to do with its bonus Level.

Fredericks set the kid up to be a Malefactor, which is a Level who specializes in sniping. They're deployed on all types of jobs, but there's one particular mission these agents own outright. Covert-action agencies develop Malefactors and their long-range lethality because they're perfect for killing other Levels.

The ad-hoc program that raised Falcon left him deficient in some skills. He needs updated Mods, and his hand-to-hand skills are for shit. But his acrobatic ability is on a par with an Infiltrator's, and his technical skills are top-notch. Falcon would make a good Protector, but his fantastic marksmanship wouldn't see much action.

Cyrus sounded confident when he said he'd find something for the kid. "There are plenty of enemy Levels out there. I can think of a dozen Job Numbers right now that could use a good Malefactor."

F-Bird stops by my dad's room a couple of times a week, but he keeps the visits short. He can tell his resemblance to my father gives Cleo the heebie-jeebies. It's like meeting a friend's identical twin and feeling just a little nutso until one of them goes away. Falcon also doesn't stick around because he's received strict directions that he must leave the room if Dad comes out of his coma. The Med-Techs want to minimize their patient's emotional shock as much as they can.

The Meddies have done a great job so far. As soon as the Navy airlifted him home, the ExOps medical staff rushed Dad here to Bethesda. His years in a Gestapo jail and the time he spent immobilized in the Original tank had wrecked his body. Dad's muscles were atrophied, he'd lost way too much weight, and he'd become a smorgasbord of viruses and infections.

Keeping him alive was incredibly hairy, and nobody—including Cleo—would tell me the details. All she said was, "Alix, your father is here. That's what matters. Now we wait and see."

I cajoled Dr. Herodotus into telling me Dad had suffered a series of heart attacks and was in the ICU for over a week—a very long time to be at death's door. My mother was by his side for all this while I butchered my way out of Cherbourg and floated home in the *Longstreet*.

The Med-Techs transferred Dad from intensive care to this private room after he stabilized a bit. This doesn't mean his condition is any less critical, but it did mean Mom and I could set up camp. We're with Dad so much that the ExOps mail room delivers our paychecks here instead of to our house out in Arlington.

Mom could tell this was going to be a long wait, so she's done some things to make the room a little cozier. The sofa she's sleeping on is from the Med-Techs' lounge. "They all owe me favors anyway," she said.

Cleo also brought in a few table lamps from home so we don't have to sit under the fluorescent ceiling lights all the time. A throw rug helps soften the tiled floor. You'd hardly know it was a hospital room except for the side rails on Dad's bed and the heavy rack of medical gear mounted to the wall over his head.

I creak out of the chair, stretch my arms, and swing them in a flat circle to loosen my joints. A long yawn reminds me what terrible breath I have in the morning. Cleo is still asleep, so I ninja walk into the bathroom and close the door so she won't hear me brushing my teeth.

It's too early for hallucinations, so I avoid looking in the mirror. It's like being a vampire, except instead of not being able to see my reflection, I see myself and lots of other scary people, too. I told Dr. Herodotus about them in one of our daily therapy sessions. He didn't like hearing that my phantom playmates have become a full-time phenomenon.

Dr. H. also didn't like hearing about all my other symptoms. His face grew longer and longer as I told him how I suffer from dizziness, shaking, fainting, and majorly trippy vision malfunctions.

He filled page after page in his notebook and told me I'm suffering from practically every post-traumatic stress reaction on record. He said I have a lot of work ahead of me. "You'll have to park your attitude at the door, Alix. Not long ago your symptoms would have had you committed to an asylum."

My shoulders shiver as I try not to think about nuthouses and shock therapy and all that shit. I rinse out my mouth and pad into Dad's bedroom. Cleo has shifted position on the sofa, but she isn't awake yet. It's almost time for Dad's morning visit from the nurse, so I take advantage of the quiet. I go to his side and rest my head on his chest. His heartbeat gently thumps against my cheek.

When I've done this before, Dad's pulse has sounded

steady but weak. Today it sounds different, stronger, more like Patrick's heart sounds when we snuggle together. I close my eyes and think about how I used to fit on the couch with my father while he slept in his shop. I can almost feel the way his hands would stroke my hair as he slowly woke up.

Wait a minute. I *can* feel hands stroking my hair. I turn my head to say hi to Cleo, who must be standing next to me.

She's not standing next to me. She's still on the sofa.

I whip my head around to look at my father.

His eyes are open. They stare at me with the same intensity I've remembered for all these years. They're still a beautiful gray-blue with green flecks. The crow's-feet in the corners of my father's eyes crinkle a bit as he smiles at me.

The tube in his throat prevents him from speaking, so he comms, "My God, Alix. You look so much like your mother." Dad's eyes mist while he drinks me in. "You've grown so much, Hot-Shot, and you're so beautiful. I'm sorry I didn't . . . that I wasn't . . ." He tries to keep his composure and not cry in front of his little girl, but his brave expression crumbles like a snowman in spring rain.

I throw my arms around his shoulders and cradle his head next to mine.

"MOM, WAKE UP!" I shout as tears pour down my face. *"DADDY'S BACK!"*

ACKNOWLEDGMENTS

When I write the factual material for my books, I bring an enthusiast's foundation in history, but for everything else I start from square one. Filling in my yawning abysses of ignorance requires a lot of research and a great deal of help from many patient, intelligent people. As with *Blades of Winter*, I never would have finished *Hammer of Angels* without their priceless contributions.

My parents, George and Carol, set me up for all this by sending me to RISD and supporting me in my pursuit of a creative career. My sister Mary Rose generously introduced me to the basics of publishing and helped me avoid many newcomers' mistakes. My wife, Natalie, has enthusiastically read draft after draft and offered fantastic suggestions.

The final version of this book owes much to my talented, intelligent, and patient editor, Anne Groell, who coaxed better material out of me with every comment and question. The fact that I'm working with Anne is entirely due to the tireless efforts of my never-say-die literary agent, Tris Coburn.

I interrogated many friends about everything from gunshot wounds to psychology and ballistics to bombers. Please forgive me if I leave anyone out:

George S. Almasi, Andy MacInnis, Steven Sharp, Arthur V. Milano, Kirsten Schwaller-Sigrist, Diane O'Brien, Beth Kelley, Scott D. Packard, Len Freiberg III, Maureen Robinson, Christa Snyder, Lori Freiberg-Rapp, Paul

Muller, Jamin Naghmouchi, Claudia Wilcox-Powers, Gretchen Schwaller-Sharp, Peter Sigrist, Cathy Davis-Hayes, David Hayes, Carol DuBois, Emily Clark, and Lisa Cullity-Drennan.

A special thanks to the people who read *Blades of Winter* and/or the advance reader copies of *Hammer of Angels*. Your positive response has been fantastic.

I especially thank you, friendly reader, for joining me as I tell my stories. I invite you to http://www.facebook.com/GTAlmasi to follow my late-night writer's ravings.

—GTA